Best Wishes

Jerry & Paul

The Death Watch Beetle,
A Historical WWII Spy Thriller

David E. Huntley

By David E. Huntley

March 2019

Copyright

DEDICATION

This author survived the London blitz in WWII, and his French-born wife lived under Nazi occupation in France. As a result, we wish to dedicate this book to the Americans and Allies who landed on Normandy beaches in WWII and saved Europe from certain tyranny. A page, listing some of the current survivors of the Normandy Invasion and other European WWII Campaigns, can be found at the end of the book, as well as on the web site (http://deathwatchbeetle.net/WWIIVets.html) as a small token of our family's thanks.

DON'T LET THE GREATEST GENERATION OF THEIR TIME BECOME THE FORGOTTEN GENERATION OF OUR TIME!

READER'S NOTES

Readers can insert themselves in the story by visiting the places described. The streets, buildings, restaurants, pubs and cafes were all actual places in the '50's. Most remain today. The geographical, geological and historical aspects of the narrative in Europe and Africa, while fictionalized, are based on the authors' research or personal observation.

Reader's Prize (Prize was won in 2014)

The book contains a coded message as part of the story. The story will reveal how the communication is decoded.

There is another coded message in the book. The message comprises six words which are in the form of cipher text. These words are spread out and can be found at the END of random chapters. Readers are invited to try and decode the complete note using the previously described method within the main story. The KEY to decode this message is:

T F G L Z A B O Q U

Readers can send in their solutions by email at admin [at] deathwatchbeetle [dot] net Those who successfully decode the message in the opinion of the author, will be entered in a draw to select a single winner. The winner's name will be published on the author's web site http://deathwatchbeetle.net/index.html The deadline for entries is July 31, 2014. The Author's decision shall be final. one year from the date of the book's initial publication.

The Prize will be a family membership in Historic Royal Palaces* in the United Kingdom, with a private tour of Her Majesty's Tower of London and the Crown Jewels (Travel not included).(**Prize was won in 2014**)

*Historic Royal Palaces is an independent charity that looks after the Tower of London, Hampton Court Palace, the Banqueting House, Kensington Palace and Kew Palace. Although the palaces are owned by The Queen on behalf of the nation, it receives no funding from the Government or the Crown, so it depends on the support of its visitors, members, donors, volunteers and sponsors. Its aim is to help everyone explore the story of how monarchs and people have shaped society, in some of the greatest palaces ever built.

ACKNOWLEDGEMENTS

I would like to offer my sincere thanks to:

Alan Huntley for taking my idea for the front book cover design, and making it a reality using his skills with computer graphics and Photo-Shop©.

Dean Huntley my technical guru, for his invaluable suggestions on website improvements and marketing ideas.

Helen Matthews in England for her kind permission to use her photographic image of the High Wycombe Parish Church on my book cover.

My editor who took great pains and time to whip my tautological and grammatical errors into shape.

My three pre-publication reviewers who came up with such glowing praise of my work which has vindicated my own doubts as to, whether I could indeed, write a complex and thrilling plot. The people in question were:

Michael Baker, former CIA operations officer, President of Diligence, LLC, an international security company and a contributor to Fox News on security topics.

Dr Robert M. Hicks, Professor of History & Ethics Belhaven University/Orlando. Retired US Air Force Chaplain of 32 years, Reserve Officer Rank of Colonel, and published author of numerous books.

James L. Williams, Major General, US Marine Corps (retired). I was indeed honored to have General Williams write the Foreword to this book.

I am also grateful to USAF Maj. (Ret) Lucky Luckadoo a WWII pilot of the 100th Bomber unit in the Eighth Air Force. On several occasions Lucky has kindly allowed me to address the WWII veterans group known as Happy Warriors, which he leads at the Frontier of Flight Museum in Dallas Texas. As a result, I was able to meet a number of WWII veterans whose names are now recorded on these pages.

An additional thank you must go to Lt Col (Ret) Joe Turecky who flew C47 Troop Carriers in WWII. He arranged for me to attend the 2012 Veterans Day Luncheon in Dallas and was responsible for introducing me to other WWII veterans.

I would be remiss if I did not mention the Daughters of World War II Veterans Dallas Chapter. This organization does such a tremendous job of helping WWII veterans as well as keeping their memories alive.

A big thanks to my sister Pat, and brother Bob who, from our days together in the coal cellar of our house in Clapham, London, as the German bombs were falling all around us, have never to this day lost our closeness or our love for one another.

A huge thank you must go to my immediate family of Martine, Nicole, Alan, and Dean for their support and encouragement, and especially to my dear wife Sophie who had to endure the long hours of solitude while I labored on this tome. Sophie remembers her days in German-occupied France, as she and her family fled before the Panzers and infantry that roared across the countryside. Later on their return home, she recalls her school being taken over by the Nazis for use as their local headquarters. She too is supportive of this book's dedication to the Allies who sacrificed their lives to free France.

FOREWORD

"Here is an engaging novel of historical fiction, with rapidly developing plots and thrilling scenarios of espionage. David Huntley has accurately captured the times and tensions of global intelligence operations of post-World War II Eastern and Western Europe, the escalating concerns of the Allied Powers dealing with the rising Communist Bloc nation in the Soviet Union and Russia, the blooming Cold War, and the proliferation of the nuclear threat to the world. What I loved most about the story-line is that it places you in the middle of the action, as a participatory reader. In many cases, while reading David Huntley's work I relived much of my own personal adventures as a military veteran of war and post-war actions. Huntley is to be commended for having written a thought-provoking, suspenseful account of one of the most dynamic moments in history. As this novel takes you over several continents, through several adventures, with various individuals, you will undoubtedly come to appreciate the great critical thinking and rhetorical talents of David Huntley."

**James L. Williams, Major General, US Marine Corps
(retired)**

TABLE OF CONTENTS

PART THREE

PART FOUR

PART
ONE

Chapter 1

The Beginning

Prologue - The Mine Disaster

As he and Mandla ran headlong up the incline mine shaft, Donald's thoughts flashed through his head, *How had he got himself into this mess? For all the years the Toc Toc beetle had infested these ancient African mine shaft timbers, why were those timbers failing now?*

As the collapsing roof and walls began falling down inside the mine, the rumbling reverberated upward toward the two of them as they struggled to maintain their pace of retreat to the surface.

Was his life and that of Mandla his Zulu guide going to end here in South Africa, before he could make his report to the joint intelligence services about the incredible sight he had seen deep in this mine, and the person the world had been hunting for since the end of WWII? As the sweat poured off the two men in the oppressive humidity, fighting their way forward, as the onrushing vibrations and dust from below made them stagger involuntarily, the timbers began to crack and split around them. Suddenly, rocks burst from the walls and ceiling. A rock hit Donald, and as he began to fall, he saw and felt the dark arm of Mandla grabbing him as his eyes started closing into unconsciousness with a vision of Alicja reaching out to him through the mist of time, and his starting point in the verdant English countryside.

Donald Harvey in High Wycombe

Donald Harvey had grown up in High Wycombe, an industrial and market town nestled in a valley in the Chiltern Hills of Buckinghamshire, England. The summers always seemed to be endless with blue skies and picnics, or cricket on the Rye which was a large park or recreation area with well kept grass. The Rye was bounded on one side by the River Wye and the Dyke on the other. The Dyke was home to swans, ducks and other water birds and made an idyllic scene for the romantic couples who rented the row boats for slow meanderings along the water. The more energetic males would show off their prowess by rowing the fast racing skiffs to attempt to beat the unofficial record for the journey to the end of the Dyke, and back to the boathouse.

The footpath running along the opposite bank of the Dyke was the favorite promenade for many of the American servicemen based in the area who were dating local girls. Conveniently, for the more amorous couples, the forest was only a few feet off to the side of the footpath….

The winters here were another story, when the bitterly cold winds would come whistling down the valley from the north and cut through virtually any layer of clothing. That, together with the usual British rainfall would often make many days uncomfortable to be outside. The weather did not reduce attendance at local pubs, of which High Wycombe had abundance. The local cinemas were often packed and the Weekly Dance at Wycombe Town Hall was always a mass of competing bodies. Some men competing for attention over the latest men's fashion which was the Edwardian (Teddy Boy) look, or simply for anyone to show off in whatever way the individual thought appropriate The Weekly Dance was well represented by a 16- or 20-piece orchestra playing the latest hits. .

Donald tidied up his desk and looked over to Bill Richardson, the General Manager of Trandect Engineering Ltd and enquired, "It's Friday night. Are you going to the Coach & Horses tonight for a couple of spots?"

"Oh, I expect so," was the mumbled reply. Bill was a man of few words, but he was a legend in the aircraft industry and as GM of Trandect Engineering Ltd., he had guided the company through some tough times since the end of the war. He had helped the Managing Director and Owner, Colonel (Ret) Charles Blankenship, diversify the company's product line to include numerous areas of emerging technology in plastics,

3

electronics, aircraft instrument refurbishment, and complex prototype manufacturing. The company's main revenue stream came from the production of a "Brilliant Sea Marker" made from Yellow Fluorescein, and a "Shark Repellant" made from a black powder called Nigrosine. The two products were packaged and placed in all Air Force and Navy life vests in the event a pilot ditched in the sea.

"So what are you doing this week-end Don?" enquired Bill. "Don't forget I want another box of those Philly cigars and I'm still waiting for that bottle of Canadian VO you're supposed to be getting for me," he added.

Donald paused from his desk cleaning and replied, "I am going to the Odeon tonight with Alicja and tomorrow we are going to the Town Hall dance. I should be able to get the goods this weekend as I will be seeing my Yank friends from the base at the dance on Saturday."

"Okay, I'm looking forward to smoking another good Philly cigar. By the way, Don, don't forget, you have to visit the Farnborough Air Show next week to talk to Fairy Aviation and others."

"Yes, I know, I have everything scheduled and some samples have been molded already," said Donald confidently.

With that Donald and Bill departed from the building and went their separate ways. Bill to his ancient Morris 10, and Donald by foot to Frogmoor, a central part of High Wycombe where numerous buses fed the commuters to other areas and suburbs. Donald walked briskly toward Frogmoor which was about a quarter of a mile away from Trandect's plant. It was drizzling as he walked and like many employees of the company, he left a trail of yellow Fluorescein dye on the sidewalk. The stuff simply attached itself to anything and everything. If someone got on a bus and saw yellow stains on the floor, they knew a Trandect employee had traveled that route or was still on the bus. It was annoying and funny at the same time. Even the River Wye would become discolored by the brilliant yellow. The river would often be discolored on different days during the month when local paper mills would be producing colored blotting paper or other paper products.

Donald's New Lodgings

It never ceased to amaze Donald how on one day the river would be a brilliant green downstream from one of the paper mills, and the next day or two it would be crystal clear with small fish darting about, and ducks bobbing around with their bottoms in the air as they strained to reach some tasty morsel on the riverbed. He was thinking of this as he stepped aboard the red Thames Valley bus that would take him home to Micklefield where he had a rented room. Accommodation was hard to come by these days with the war only over less than ten years ago. He had been fortunate to have found this place after a friend rec-ommended him to the elderly widow, Mrs. Fenchurch, who owned the house and needed to supplement her income. Donald wanted to be independent of his parents and, at 26 with a good job and reasonable income, he had felt the need to break away on his own.

Jean and Alfred (Fred) Harvey were ready for Donald to leave home. The laundry and cooking responsibilities were becoming increasingly burdensome for Jean, and Fred was somewhat touchy about Donald coming home late on numerous occasions. As an old war horse, he felt a certain jealousy of his son's youth.

Mrs. Fenchurch had been impressed with Donald at their first meeting, and it helped that he had been very charming and considerate. Donald, at six feet two inches, with strong facial features, dark blue eyes, and light brown hair that he kept under control with the right amount of Brylcreme, was certainly an impressive young man. The fact that he used to practice the sport of Judo twice a week until a few years ago, still today gave him an appearance of easy movement and a confident air, unlike some of the shifty characters who had applied for the chance to rent the room before Donald had applied.

Mrs. Fenchurch had been widowed when her husband, a Lieu-tenant in the Guards Armored Division, had been killed at the Battle of Bourguébus Ridge in Normandy, July 1944, which was the largest tank battle the British Army had ever fought.

"How long do you wish to rent a room then, Mr. Harvey?" she enquired looking up at Donald who stood about two feet above her.

Donald said, "At this point, I think it would be at least a year before I would want to find a self contained flat, if that would be agree-able?"

Upon further discussion they had agreed on terms, the amount of rent per week, how much notice would be required for termination, an agreement of how the kitchen would be shared, and what utensils Donald was allowed to use. The room was large and comfortable, albeit slightly Victorian in décor, with a single bed, a sitting area with a large armchair, and side table. A couple of Windsor chairs took up a place alongside one wall, and a large fireplace with an antique mirror above it occupied the other side of the room.

The mantelpiece displayed a large chiming clock that Mrs. Fenchurch had said, "Will require you to wind up once a week." The fireplace contained a coal scuttle, which was empty at the time because the weather had not yet turned chilly. A large mahogany chest of drawers completed the complement of furniture in the room.

That encounter and agreement had taken place six months previously, and Donald was now comfortably installed in his new lodgings. As he rode the bus toward his destination, Donald thought fondly of the evening to come with his Polish girlfriend, Alicja Kozlowski, and their 7:00 p.m. date to meet at the Odeon.

Chapter 2

The Polish Émigré in England
& Hodgemoor Camp – Amersham

Alicja Preparing for a Date with Donald

Alicja Kozlowski looked at herself in the mirror as she prepared to

get ready for her date with Donald. She selected a dress that did not look too provocative but, at the same time, would make her look attractive. The reflection in the mirror displayed a young woman with a beautiful full figure and a face of exquisite fineness as if carved from the smoothest marble imaginable, and yet unlike marble, it glowed with a rose pink hue. Her lips were full and a ruby red that only youth can boast, as they had not yet sharpened to a tightness that age and hardships can bring upon an older person. Her shiny black hair had been shampooed, towel dried, and deftly curled with the heated curling iron.

As Alicja dressed herself, she thought fondly of Donald. He was the first non-Polish man who had impressed her in this English town. She had met him at the weekly dance in the Town Hall while with her two girlfriends from Hodgemoor Camp.

Alicja Reminiscing About How She Met Donald

It was Jalenka and Ola who had spotted Donald as he had walked by the crowded dance hall that night. They had nudged one another and laughed about how handsome he appeared with his smart grey suit which was similar in style to that which some of the American service-men were wearing. He was obviously quite different from some of his fellow Englishmen dressed up in their Teddy Boy outfits and who were strutting their stuff like proud cockerels in a barnyard.

A number of Americans were also interested in the girls, but the Polish ladies were reluctant to engage in any conversation with them because they knew their brothers and uncles were always getting into fights with the Yanks. The pubs would close and the fights would start, very often with the Irish and then the Poles entering the fray. The US Military Police would drive up in their jeeps and haul away the miscre-ant Yanks while the local constabulary would deal with the remaining crowd.

On this night, however, it was Donald who struck up the conver-sation and asked Alicja for the next dance. He had not even glanced at Ola or Jalenka, much to their chagrin, but had sought out Alicja. It was not that Ola and Jalenka were not pretty, but to Donald, Alicja simply stood out like an angel. When he took her in his arms on the dance floor, the electricity and the emotion they both felt was palpable. She resisted looking at him and held him at a distance to avoid the sensation she herself felt at that moment. Her strong Catholic upbringing was to ensure that she remain true to herself and to avoid any early passion. Alicja was unable to prevent herself looking up at him as he began ask-ing her about background, where she came from, where she lived, and who the girls were with her that evening. She responded, and he was again in awe of the beautiful face and her eyes that glowed with colors of the brightest blues and greens that were simply stunning. She explained she and her family had been victims of the invasion of Poland by the Russians, who had devised a pact with the Germans to split up the country.

"It's a long story, and not a happy one," she said with her little Pol-ish accent.

As the music ended, Donald guided her back to the girls waiting at the side of the dance floor, and Alicja introduced Donald to them.

Donald asked, "Where do you live in Wycombe?"

They all looked at each other, a little embarrassed at the question. One, they were not sure of Donald's motives and, secondly, they were not comfortable telling him they lived in a Resettlement Camp.

However, Alicja looked directly at Donald and said, "We live at Hodgemoor, the Polish resettlement camp."

"Oh, yes," replied Donald, "I'm aware of Hodgemoor. I often see some of the Polish chaps at the Corner Café. The owner John Mitchell is a friend of mine, and I help him out sometimes, especially at week-ends. His cook, Nobby Clark, is a real comedian, and he often chats with the Poles and makes them laugh, although I'm not sure if they understand his Cockney humor."

"What's Cockney humor?" asked Ola and Alicja, almost in unison. Donald tried to explain but was having some difficulty when the next dance began, and he hastily asked Alicja if she would join him, just before an American in uniform was about to approach her.

She took Donald's proffered hand, and he turned to the American and laughing said, "Hello, Cal, sorry you missed out this time. She's mine."

Cal grinned saying, "Hey, Don. How yer doin? I'll just ask this beautiful young lady here if she'll dance with me." With that, he turned to Ola, who blushing, was hesitant to accept the invitation from the American but felt she could not refuse a compliment like that. She looked apologetically at Jalenka as she slid onto the dance floor, but Jalenka just laughed good-naturedly.

The dance music was a slow waltz that allowed Donald and Alicja to be just that little closer to each other. Donald asked Alicja how long she had been in England, and she told him it had been about seven years. Alijica looked up at Donald and said, "I can tell you more some other time, but not tonight."

Donald was delighted that she was willing to see him again before he had even asked and told her he would look forward to that. The music ended, and the couple made their way back to the side of the hall. Cal walked Ola back to the group and thanked her politely for the dance, which caught Ola by surprise that this "horrible" American had been so nice. That was not the stereotype she had been taught to expect by her Polish relatives.

The crowd began chanting someone's name, "Tony, Tony, Tony," while pleading with the band leader.

Alicja asked Donald what was happening, and he pointed to an American sergeant in the crowd near the stage and remarked, "They're calling for Tony Carolla. He's a friend of mine who sings just like Dean Martin. In fact if you close your eyes and listen to this bloke, you cannot tell the difference. The trouble is that the band leader doesn't like having him up there because they have to improvise the music, and he takes away their own glory."

Well, the band leader gave in, and Tony was pushed up onto the stage. After he whispered to the band, they began the opening bars to "That's Amore." The crowd went wild but drew silent as he began to sing. The pure tone of his voice rang through the hall as the audience listened in rapt attention. Donald put his arm around Alicja who moved closer to him, and as their bodies touched, it created a warm, emotional feeling in both of them, while they listened to Tony's smooth, crooning voice.

A Recent Date at the Odeon Cinema

It was this memory of their first meeting that made Alicja smile as she got ready for tonight's date with Donald. They had met again and gone for walks on the Rye and taken a rowboat on the Dyke. She had not spoken very much about her background. Tonight, she felt comfortable in the fact that she trusted him, and would open herself up about her life in Poland.

She had arranged to meet Donald at the Odeon Cinema on Castle Street at 7:00 p.m. in time for the main feature, "On The Waterfront," with Marlon Brando. Alicja kissed her mother and told her she was off to see Donald.

"You have told us what a nice young man he is, but I worry because he's not Polish and your father is upset about it, too."

Her mother looked anxiously at Alicja but also with a little smile that lit up her prematurely-aged countenance. Her face showed the lines of hardship and deprivation from years of war and persecution. At the same time, these invisible scars of military conflict could not eliminate the inherent angelic face that once belonged to a beautiful woman, and whose genes had now been passed to her daughter.

She kissed and embraced Alicja telling her, "Baw si dobrze, ale uwa aj" (Enjoy yourself, but be careful).

"I will, Mother," replied Alicja as she slipped out the door. The bus from Amersham drove down Amersham Hill into High Wycombe, stopping at every bus stop, making Alicja anxious about arriving late. She got off at Castle Street and made her way toward the Odeon Cinema. Donald was waiting for her outside, and they embraced. He would have kissed her then, but she did not feel it was appropriate to behave that way in public, and she kissed him warmly on the cheek.

They joined the queue to buy tickets, and he made sure he was able to obtain two back row seats. They found their way inside, sat down and chatted a little about their respective days. Then it was time to stand for the national anthem, "God Save The Queen." A Pathé Newsreel followed, showing the arrival of the Royal Yacht returning to London after the Queen's Commonwealth Tour and Prime Minister Winston Churchill waiting at the pier to greet the Royal Party.

A supporting film followed, which neither Alicja nor Donald followed to any great extent as they cuddled together, and Donald was able to entice Alicja to more than one lingering kiss. At the interval they sat up in a respectable fashion and chatted some more. The lights dimmed again, and the Marlon Brando movie began. The movie had Alicja holding on to Donald during some of the tensest moments, especially during the fight scene at the climax of the film when she had to look away from Brando's bloody face.

As they walked away from the Odeon, she remarked, "I just could not stand that violence. I'm sorry."

"Alicja," he said, "I didn't know it would be so rough, and I'm sorry. Let's go to the Corner Café and have some tea or coffee."

"I'm ready for that," she replied, and they walked together down Castle Street, through the Parish Church Yard and onto the High Street.

Corner Cafe

Donald and Alicja arrived at the Corner Cafe, stepped inside and chose a table close to the window overlooking the little stream that flowed by the building.

They sat down and Donald asked, "So what would you like, a cup of tea or some coffee?"

"I think I'll have tea," she replied smiling.

"Would you like something to eat? We could have a nice mixed grill if you're hungry," he suggested.

Alicja thought for a moment, and said she would just have a fried egg and chips (fries). Donald moved off to the counter to place the order.

The place was crowded as Donald navigated through the tables to the counter and addressed John Mitchell, the owner, "Hi, John. The place is humming tonight."

"Yeah, it really is, Don. We could have used your help tonight, but I see you have more important things to do," said John smiling.

"Well, I don't get to see Alicja as often as I would like, with my schedule at Trandect and then helping you out," replied Donald. "Let's see, I'll have one egg and chips, a mixed grill, and two teas."

John yelled the order to the kitchen, and followed up with, "And it's for our Donald."

With that, Nobby Clark, the cook, popped his head around the corner and said in his inimitable Cockney accent, grinning from ear to ear, "Blimey, Don, you're not eating that lot by yerself are yer?"

"Don't be daft, Nobby. I'm with Alicja tonight who you've met before."

"Oh, right, mate!" said Nobby. "I'll bring yer grub right out me'-self." And with that, he returned to the kitchen. Donald took out his wallet, paid John the bill and walked back to Alicja.

Donald noticed the tables filled with US Air Force personnel, locals, as well as one table with around five Polish emigres, one of whom he identified as Karol Zaluski. Karol was Alijca's uncle.

Donald sat down and mentioned he had just seen Zaluski, and Alicja said, "I thought that was him on the corner table, but with all the smoke in this place, it was difficult to tell," she said with a smile. "There's a rumor at the camp that Russian agents are following him, but I think that's a fantasy."

Donald looked up at her in surprise. "What is the story of the Polish people here in Wycombe or Amersham"? he asked.

"Well, as you know Germany invaded Poland in 1939 on the pretext that Polish troops had been attacking Germans across the border and burning houses. Nobody really believed those lies, and we all knew the Germans did it themselves."

"You mean it was staged, or made to look like the Polish did it?" asked Donald, as Alicja looked puzzled by the word "staged."

"Yes, of course, that is what I believe from my family and what we learned much later from official sources," replied Alicja.

She went on, "Of course the occupation was bad enough, but worse was to come when the Russians, as part of an agreement with Germany, annexed part of Poland. Then in the winter of 1940, the Russian NKVD barged into our house and ordered us out. Some of us were beaten, and one who was really cruel also beat me."

Tears came to her eyes as she remembered the time. "We were allowed to pack a small amount of possessions before moving outside in the freezing weather. We were driven to the railway station near the Ukraine border where we were crammed into cattle wagons. We spent several weeks traveling through the countryside before finishing well into Siberia. My family and all the other families became slave laborers, and many, many people starved to death in those camps."

Donald looked at Alicja, reaching out to hold her hand he said, "Dear Alicja, I'm so sorry. I never knew exactly why you people ended up in the English Polish Resettlement Camps except that we know you could not return to Poland after the war because of the Iron Curtain. So what happened then? How long were you in Siberia?"

Before she could reply, Nobby Clark arrived with their food. "Who's 'avin the mixed grill then?" he asked. Donald put up his hand, and Nobby placed the egg and chips plate in front of Alicja. "There yer are duck!" he said, and then gave Donald his mixed grill.

Alicja exclaimed, "But I'm not having duck and, anyway, this is what I ordered, egg and chips."

Both Nobby and Donald laughed out loud. Donald explained, "That's a typical Cockney expression — duck, love, and 'darlin' for a woman, and 'mate' for a man."

Alicja giggled, "Oh, that's funny. We have some expressions in Polish, but not that funny."

Nobby grinned and said, "All right you two lovebirds. Get on with yer grub an enjoy yerselves."

"Thanks, Nobby," Donald called out as the cook dashed back to the kitchen.

"You were about to tell me how long you were in Siberia," reminded Donald.

"Well," Alicja said, "We spent nearly two years in that nightmare, and then, Germany attacked Russia. The Russians subsequently released the Polish people in their camps under an 'amnesty.' My father, together with many other Polish males, volunteered and joined the British Forces under Genera Władysła Anders of the Polish Free Army to fight the Germans. We as a family were separated from my father at this time. We became part of a mass exodus from Europe and were provided with safe passage through Persia or Iran, Pakistan, and India, where we joined a ship that took us to Durban, South Africa. From there we finally were settled in Southern Rhodesia, in a town near Bulawayo. The British had set up refugee camps for us, but it was not until 1948 that my father, Dymtry Kozlowski, who had no idea where we were, managed to track us down through the Red Cross. We were finally transported home by ship through Cape Town and joined my father at Hodgemoor Resettlement camp where he was assigned."

Alicja sighed, "That's a short idea of our story, and it carries a heavy load of hardship. I did like our stay in Southern Rhodesia, and I thought it was a lovely part of the world with wonderful people. It will be a place I will never forget."

Donald squeezed Alijca's hand as she looked wistfully into the past, but she quickly smiled back at him.

"My people love it here in England, but it's not our homeland. Our country is now part of the Soviet Socialist Republics, and we just don't know if we shall ever see a free Poland again."

Donald looked softly at Alicja and said, "You have certainly touched me this evening, I had no real idea of the severe hardships the Polish people had suffered. However, I'm sure that Western powers will prevail and Poland will be free in the long run."

"My father fought in many of the major battles, including the Italian campaign and Monte Cassino," remarked Alicja. "I am told that that there are still patriots in Poland operating underground cells of espionage in attempts to undermine the Soviets and their puppets."

"Well, let's cheer up and let me take you home," said Donald. "The last bus to Amersham leaves soon, so let's get ourselves to the bus stop."

The Polish group at the corner table looked up as they stood to leave, and Karol Zaluski remarked to his fellow Poles, "My beautiful niece seems to have found a handsome Englishman. I hope he protects her as well as a Polish man would."

Chapter 3

The Yanks Are Back!

The 7th Air Division of the US Eighth Air Force

Major James Wallace sat in his office at the Dawes Hill Base in High Wycombe overlooking the Abbey Girls School further down the hill, and he was pondering the history of his predecessors on this base. The school had been requisitioned by the British government at the beginning of the war, and which subsequently became HQ for the United States Eighth Army Air Force Bomber Command, code named "Pinetree," from 1943 to 1947. British kids would ask the Yanks, "Got any gum, chum?" and knowing the Brits were on strict rationing and often hungry, they would often respond to the youngsters with a stick of gum or some other candy. The Bomber Command guys in Wycombe were pretty popular with the local girls, too, and many of them married and returned to the USA with their English brides.

Although he had been stateside at that time, James was thinking of the guys who had been assigned to this very base during the war. Looking out of his office window at the grey wintry landscape with the trees bare of leaves and dampness in the air, he thought back to six months previously when, as a Captain, he had been summoned to a meeting by Colonel Albert Delong at Rapid City Air Force Base in South Dakota.

James arrived at Colonel Delong's office and greeted Lieutenant Bill Travis, the Colonel's Adjutant. "Hi, Bill, the Boss wanted me to see him at 1500, is he in?"

"He sure is Jimmy, I'll tell him you're here." With that Travis got up and entered the Boss's office and announced James' arrival, "Captain Wallace is here, sir."

A booming voice replied, "Show him in."

As James entered the large office, Colonel Delong stood up from his desk and put out his huge hand to shake, which James took gingerly. The handshake was firm but not overbearing like some people who try to crush another person's hand in an effort to demonstrate some kind of dominance. Although the Colonel was a giant of a man, his reputation as a great leader and one of the best B-17 bomber pilots of WWII was also renowned. He gestured to James to take a seat and sat down opposite him on his own leather armchair.

"Captain Wallace", the Colonel began, "You have moved up in rank very quickly, and I'm very impressed that you made Captain much earlier than most." As James smiled and nodded in appreciation, the Colonel continued, "We have admired the part you played in the building of Strategic Air Command's new Command and Control System. As you well know, this system is designed to be employed world-wide."

"Yes, Sir. I'm well aware of the importance of the system and its future implications on a global scale," commented James, "especially in terms of the Cold War."

Colonel Delong leaned forward, "Captain, I would like to recommend you for a new assignment overseas, a very significant assignment." He looked intently at James who waited for the Colonel to continue. "This assignment will have a two- fold and possibly a three-fold responsibility. The first and most important duty will be to set up a Command and Control Center in England which will link all Strategic Air Command communications worldwide with our main post here at Rapid City Air Force Base, South Dakota, and secondly to provide weather information to our units throughout Europe."

"That sounds pretty interesting sir. What is the other responsibility and when am I expected to be re-assigned?"

Colonel Delong looked even more intensely at James and went on, "The Weather Center at the Command Post will in addition to its normal function – it will be a cover for spying on the Soviet Union. This will require the deployment of high altitude helium balloons carrying our best camera equipment. The Soviet territories are vast, and we need to know what they are doing, what advances they making with their weapons manufacturing, missiles, infrastructure, etc. You are ideally suited to this assignment because of your background in Intelligence at Randolph Air Base in San Antonio, and your subsequent experience in managing the construction of the Command Control Center here at Rapid City."

The Colonel paused. "We will also want you to leave for England in about a month from now, and you will need to be briefed on further details from various Section Heads. Do you have any questions so far?"

"Will I be able to select my support team?" asked James.

"To some extent," ventured Delong, "However, it will depend on availability, and this will be decided by the Section Heads. Obviously, this mission is classified and will be code named, 'LANCER CONTROL.' Based on the initial success of 'LANCER CONTROL,' I can tell you that there will be a corresponding effort to be conducted in Turkey, code named, 'GENETRIX,' in a year or two. Based on what I have told you so far, is this a mission you would want to take on?"

"It sounds like it could be a challenging role, and it would certainly provide high visibility," replied James. "You say 'so far.' Is there something else I need to know, sir?"

Colonel Delong again looked very closely at James trying to see what reactions there might be to this discussion and gauging his responses.

"Captain, as I mentioned earlier, the mission I have described is classified as Top Secret and, while you already have clearance, everyone else involved with this mission will have to be vetted and undergo background checks. Now separately there is another duty that will need your attention. This is not an entirely clearcut mission, and it depends on numerous outside influences and intelligence. However, it is of such national importance it is classified as Above Top Secret. So there will be very few people that will be involved in this matter."

James stared at DeLong and wondered just where this was heading.

"Am I to be briefed on this aspect of the mission before I decide to accept?"

The Colonel replied, "As you already have Top Secret clearance, I can give you a briefing right here and now. Before I do that however, I want you to know that because of the nature of this mission and the level of seniority of the officers in the USAF you will be reporting to, and also the seniority of personnel in foreign military and intelligence services you will be liaising with, you are to be promoted to the rank of Major, should you accept the role. With that said, let me proceed…."

Chapter 4

The Added Mission

The Briefing Continued

Major Wallace recalled the next part of his briefing with Colonel Delong as one that left an indelible impression on him.

"James, as I said a moment ago, this part of your mission is classified as Above Top Secret (ATS). One of the main aims of the American forces in Europe has been to hunt down and capture Nazi war criminals and bring them to trial. Of no less an order of magnitude is to conduct such investigations and capture Nazis who have precise knowledge and know-how of secret weapon technologies that the Germans had been working on in the last days of the war."

"Yes, sir," replied James. "I am aware of the V2 rocket people and others who have come over to us."

"It appears," went on the Colonel, "that Himmler himself turned the SS into a massive secret technology/engineering development program, much to the chagrin of Albert Speer. There is one person, in particular, whom the US has been interested in, and his name is Hans Kammler. He was born in 1902 in Stettin, Germany (but since the Yalta Conference it became Szczecin, Poland). He was named Hans (Heinz) Frederich Karl Kammler. He was an engineer and originally worked for the Air Ministry before joining the Nazi SS. After making a name for himself in one of the main branches of the Black Shirts, he was appointed head of 'Development Tasks,' which included some special construction projects. These projects were concentration and extermination camps, as well as the destruction of the Warsaw ghetto, which is just one reason we want to bring this man to justice.

"Additionally," continued Delong, "we understand from intelligence sources he was put in charge of creating secret underground facilities that included certain advanced kinds of weapons. He had an equivalent title of Lieutenant General. Kammler had been put in charge of the V2 rocket program and met regularly with Major Wernher von Braun and a Major Walter Dornberger. As you are aware von Braun came over to our side after the war?"

James nodded and added, "Part of the project code named 'Paper-Clip'?"

"Yes," said the Colonel, "As well as the Alsos program, which is still classified There were a number of these individuals who had specialized expertise critical to our future military programs. The Russians had also spirited away some top specialists together with their complete laboratories to the Soviet Union, and were responsible for their eventual successful atomic bomb program. Fortunately for us, many of the German top scientists and facilities were in the French Control Zone in West Germany, which enabled the US forces to gain the advantage of German technology, especially in the area of rocket engineering development."

Colonel Delong continued, "We understand that Kammler had been supervising a stunning and unbelievable technology so far advanced as to be science fiction. We do know that the Nazis were spending a great deal of time and energy on aspects of quantum physics. There was some ideological reason for this, in as much that the quantum theory could not relate directly to Einstein's Theory of Relativity, and Einstein being a Jew, it made the study of quantum physics a natural and obvious choice of Nazi science."

"From my perspective," said James, "as a graduate in electrical engineering, the quantum particle did not make sense. It is said that a particle can travel faster than the speed of light and appear to be in two places at the same time!"

"Well, our man Kammler was reputed to be working on this super weapon at the war's end," said the Colonel, "together with a large number of scientists, engineers and slave laborers in an area close to the Czech polish border. General Patton and his Third Army were dashing into Czechoslovakia in an attempt to secure Kammler's secret weapons facility. Now, according to all records, we were unable to secure or complete that mission because Kammler and his technology, know-how, documentation, and records had disappeared. We do know from records that Speer, the Armaments Minister, had said that Kammler told him good-bye in early April 1945. Von Braun had also spoken to Kammler in April and was informed, 'I am going to disappear for an indefinite amount of time'."

"I understand that General Patton died in an accident in December that year. Did he not secretly capture Kammler and shouldn't that report be in the records, even if classified?" asked James.

"We have no record of Kammler at all, and we do not believe the Russians have him either, and I will now disclose to you the latest intelligence that we have," said Colonel Delong.

"In Poland today there is an underground spy movement that maintains contact with UK Intelligence through their old Free Polish Army veterans in the UK. They think they have something of importance relevant to the search for Kammler."

The Colonel looked over to James, and went on, "When the OSS was dissolved in 1945 and the Central Intelligence Agency was formed, certain files pertaining to Nazi super weapons were passed on, but there is no mention in those files about Hans Kammler or about a specific technology under his command. Most people believed the US under General Patton had succeeded in transferring Kammler to the United States in 1945, but, apparently that did not happen. At least, that is the information I am receiving in my orders."

Delong continued, "Others believe that Russia secured his services, but friends in Poland think the Russians are still looking for Kammler, and are closely watching for dissident Poles who may have information."

"What is the weapon everyone is so interested to learn about?" asked James. "Did we not secure documents and prototypes during the push into Czechoslovakia, even if we were unable to capture Kammler himself?"

Delong shook his head, "To answer the second part of your question, from what we had gathered from the interrogation of Speer, Kammler had set up some kind of Evacuation Commando Team that would enable him to leave rapidly from the US Forces, the Russian Forces, or somewhere else. As to the type of weapon or technology involved, we have some nebulous second- hand accounts that it was a type of device that emitted radiation when activated. We are not sure if this was a kind of centrifuge for uranium enrichment, which would not make this an exceptional device, or if it was something much more exotic. Because the Nazis were deeply involved in quantum experiments, it has been speculated that they were trying to build something with extremely powerful force fields."

"Do we know how big this thing was?" asked James.

Delong replied, "The sketchy information we have was that it was an approximately 9 to 10 feet high dome-shaped device. It also supposedly killed a number of scientists or engineers during its testing. It's these Polish cells that have provided the Brits with some recent intelligence. The Brits say that their underground sources in Poland have discovered there was an ex-slave laborer who survived assassination at the Wenceslaus Mine in Selesia, which was the location of the Kammler facility."

"James, are you ready to take this on, or should I say, these assignments in England?"

"I'm certainly intrigued and especially honored to be offered the opportunity to head up the Lancer Control project, which is within my realm of expertise. I am not so sure about the intelligence project and whether my past experience in this field is sufficient to handle it."

Delong looked directly at James and remarked, "If I did not have every confidence in your ability to handle the responsibility, I would not have invited you here today. Also, you will have major support from the CIA, if and when necessary."

"Well," James interjected, "That is exactly the question I have. Why isn't the CIA running this Kammler operation in joint operations with the British?"

DeLong went on, "It has been considered at the highest levels, that your position in running the Communication and Command Control System in the UK and using that role as a cover for the spy camera balloon function for the Soviet Union would, in fact, be a double cover for investigating any evidence that may arise on the Kammler issue." The Colonel added, "In any event James, the CIA will have a support team in place in the UK, as and when needed. Can I count on acceptance of this assignment?"

Now, six months later, James recalled his acceptance of the commission and Colonel Delong pinning the gold oak leaf insignia of the rank of Major to his lapel. He also thought back to how Delores, his wife, was very excited on hearing about the UK assignment. Sadly, under oath of secrecy, he had been unable to tell her his true mission other than that he was second in command of the USAAF Base at Dawes Hill in the town of High Wycombe, 20 miles northwest of London.

There was a knock on the door. Major Wallace, slowly chewing on his gum, growled, "Come in."

Chapter 5

The Mysterious Note

Sideline Business

Donald sat listening to the radio, which was playing the top hit, "Rock Around The Clock," by Bill Haley and the Comets, when there was a knock on the door. Donald rose and opened it to find Mrs. Fenchurch smiling and holding out a note.

"There was phone call, and I took the message for you," she said. "It was a Mr Jennings, and he had an American accent, but he was very nice. I wrote down his telephone number, and he wants you to call him back after you return from work."

"Well, thank you, Mrs. Fenchurch," responded Donald. "I will give him a ring shortly. May I use the phone and put it on my rent bill?"

"Yes, of course," replied Mrs. Fenchurch as she retreated back to her living room.

Donald smiled and walked over to the radiogram and switched it off. Cal Jennings had probably got his cigars and whiskey he had ordered. He left the room and made is way to the hall where the telephone was on the small Victorian table that had intricately turned legs. Donald guessed the legs had been made by one of High Wycombe's legendary 'bodgers' who had helped turn the town's plentiful supply of beechwood into a major furniture manufacturing center.

He picked up the phone and dialed the number on the note. Cal Jenning's smooth baritone voce answered, and Donald asked, "It's Donald here, do you have the goods ready for me Cal?"

"I sure do, pal. Where shall we meet?"

Donald suggested they meet at the bus stop at the top of Marlow Hill near the Dawes Hill Base to avoid Cal having to carry, what would be after all, contraband. Cal agreed, and they arranged to meet the next evening at 9:00 p.m.

The next evening Donald alighted from the bus as arranged and, after waiting for a few minutes, Cal came sauntering down the street at precisely 9:00 p.m. He handed Donald two bottles of Canadian V.O. from inside his leather jacket together with two boxes of Phillies No. 1 Cigars.

Donald counted out the money and handed it over to Cal who grinned and said, "Well, a little black market from the Air Force PX doesn't hurt anybody, and we all make a couple of bucks, right?"

"Yes, a couple, Cal, but it also keeps me in well with the boss at work," smiled Donald. As he spoke, he looked up at Cal and, startled, he exclaimed, "What the hell is that?"

As Cal turned to look, a bright white object rose up in the air above the trees and hovered for a brief moment before accelerating higher into the sky. They watched it for a little longer before it shot rapidly out of sight through the cloud cover.

Cal turned back to Donald and shrugged casually saying, "That was strange."

Donald felt Cal was too casual, and said, "That came up out of your base, so surely you must know what's going on there."

Cal looked at Donald carefully and said, "Look, you know and I know that all military bases have a number of functions which are not necessarily public knowledge. Our base in High Wycombe is no different, and it's obvious that, as part of Strategic Air Command, this base acts as a Command and Control center with a weather reporting function. So that was probably just one of our weather balloons taking off to analyze the atmospheric conditions."

"Well, that makes sense," offered Donald, although still somewhat shaken seeing such a strange object.

Cal thought to himself, *Shit, how the fucking hell did that thing take off at this time of night? We have these missions scheduled at around 1:00 a.m. to 2:00 a.m. in the mornings.*

He grinned again and said, "Hey, Don, how about getting me a date with Ola? I think she liked me at the dance the other night."

Donald smiled and said, "Let me see what I can do. I am off to Farnborough Air Show this week, and I will be seeing Alicja at the weekend and will ask her about Ola."

"Thanks pal," replied Cal. "I need to get back to the base. I'm on duty later tonight." He turned and strode off up the hill toward the base.

Preparing for Farnborough Airshow

"Morning, Bill, how was your weekend?" asked Donald, as he walked into the office at Trandect.

Bill Richardson's face creased into a smile as he saw Donald and immediately asked, "I hope that parcel you're carrying is my passage to some luxurious minutes of heightened well being?"

"Yes, of course. How could I forget?" the younger man replied as he handed the package to Bill.

Bill opened up the parcel to reveal the Canadian V.O. and Phillies No. 1 cigars. His face lit up as he savored the thought of future nights with an after-supper whiskey and soda together with a fine cigar. Bill was not a heavy drinker, but he did indulge in constant cigarette smoking, which gave him a sometimes bronchial disposition.

"So how much did we agree on then for this little lot?" inquired Bill.

Donald said, "The whisky is twelve pounds, and cigars will cost you seven pounds, so a total of 19 pounds." Bill handed over a twenty pound note and told Donald to keep the change for the trouble. Donald thought. *Well, that's nice. I already have a profit of six pounds, so an extra pound is welcome.*

Bill looked up and said, "Here comes Chalky. I think he will want to talk about the Fairy Aviation job."

Chalky walked up to Bill and Donald and remarked, "Good morning, gentleman. I need to get some directions from you chaps, but especially from Donald regarding these prototype instrument covers."

Colonel Blankenship, the company owner and Managing Director, had secured a contract with Fairy Aviation for Trandect to supply initial prototypes of some cockpit instrument covers using a new kind of plastic. Donald's responsibility was to get these produced within the time-frame specified. These prototypes were to be used in the secret aircraft, the Fairy Delta, which was a new delta wing plane for the Royal Air Force. The material for these covers was to be made using polystyrene, also known as "organic glass," which was a new thermoplastic

24

and very lightweight. This material was invented by Germany during the war but was now being produced by Britain's Imperial Chemical Industries. In fact, a Dr. Joseph Pringle from ICI had visited Trandect to observe the very first product to be injection-molded in polystyrene. There were specific techniques in using this material for the way the molds were designed and the manner in which it was processed through the injection molding machine.

Chalky wanted to know how many cavities would be required in the production mold. Donald told him not to be concerned with that issue because Fairy only wanted prototypes at the moment. He didn't want to disclose that there were only two planes to be built right now, and the British Government would only order more once the plane had been proven in tests.

Bill and Donald made their way to Colonel Blankenship's office for a meeting where they would discuss their upcoming trip to the Farnborough Air Show later in the week. The Colonel welcomed them both and gestured to the chairs around his massive oak desk. In fact, everything about the Colonel was massive and impressive, including his white, curling, bristling mustache that overflowed his upper lip.

He began by saying, "I know you will be going to meet with the Fairy Aviation company to discuss our project for the new Delta plane, but I also have plans for you to meet a couple of chaps with De Haviland. As you know the Comet 2 has been re-built and is ready to fly commercially again very soon."

Bill spoke up, "Have you managed to get us some business there, Colonel? That would certainly give us a boost for our aero division and for Donald here."

The Colonel looked over to Donald and said, "Don, I believe we can get their injection molding business because they have seen the work we've done for the Fairy Aviation Gannett aircraft, as well as the work we have done with the Vickers Viscount plane."

"I'm pretty confident we can hold our own there, Sir," offered Donald. "Who are we to meet at De Haviland?"

"I have everything established on who you will meet, times, and other details. Your itinerary is being typed up now by Jill," replied the Colonel.

Bill said, "I assume I will be discussing with my counterpart anything to do with design, materials, etc., and Donald will be discussing manufacturing issues with their project manager?"

"Yes, and I will handle all the contractual issues at the appropriate time," replied Colonel Blankenship. "By the way," he went on, "Any of you chaps see strange lights last night over toward Marlow? My neighbor and I've heard from others about a weird-looking white shape shooting into the sky last night."

Bill said, "I didn't go outside last night."

Donald just looked blank and shook his head. He didn't want to say where he was last night or that he thought there was something odd about Cal Jennings' expression. Somehow, the weather balloon story just didn't sound right.

"Well, ever since that Roswell incident in America, people are seeing UFOs all over the place, so I assume we will get our share of crazy reports," remarked Bill.

After some more time discussing aspects of the company's avionic instrument business the meeting was drawing to an end with the Colonel remarking that the whole world of aviation will be at Farnborough except of course the Soviet Bloc.

"But," the Colonel added, "The Russians or their surrogates will be snooping around anyway."

With that the meeting ended.

Wycombe Anglican Parish Church

Donald was ambling through the Wycombe Street Market after having an after work beer with Bill Richardson at the Falcon pub close to the Guild Hall. He had time to kill before the next bus would come for Micklefield. Feeling a little peckish after the beer, he walked across the High Street, which was also the A40 and main road to Oxford.

Donald walked over to the Cornmarket Building and to the ladies selling winkles and cockles, and after some Cockney banter from them; he bought a small china dish of mixed little delicacies for a shilling. He dropped some vinegar into the dish and with the pin supplied, he deftly inserted it into the shell of the winkle, pulled out the tiny morsel, dipped it in the vinegar and into his mouth. The tangy but juicy *fruit de mer* tasted fresh and delicious. He polished off the rest, returned the empty shells and dish to the stall owner who promptly disposed of the waste into the rubbish bin and the dish into the large enamel bowel of water for later washing.

Donald still felt somewhat hungry and was not sure what he was going to eat when he would arrive home. He had a look around and strolled over to Bill Tucker's fruit stall. Everyone knew Billy; he been bringing his stall to the Wycombe Market for over 20 years. The Wycombe Market in the High Street had been a tradition going back to the Middle Ages.

"You've got some lovely looking apples, Billy. I bet they cost an arm and leg," Donald taunted.

"Nah," growled Billy through a cloud of cigarette smoke, "I'm givin' em away today like I'm Father Xmas, mate. Wot d'yer fink I am then? You fink I comes dahn 'ere from the Smoke to give stuff away? They are a bob a pound just for you."

Donald laughed as he knew the Smoke was the nickname everyone, and especially the Cockneys, called London, as it was badly polluted with smog from chimneys, trains, and industry. Efforts had begun to clear it up due to the number of deaths attributed to bronchial problems in the population.

Donald said, "All right, Billy, don't get your knickers in a knot. I'll take a couple of apples, but I don't need a whole pound."

"Gor blimey, the poor git can't even afford a pound of apples. Wot they payin yer up at that factry, Don? they payin yer in packets of that yeller powder you spreads all over town? I even take that bloody yeller dye back 'ome to the Smoke. That'll be sixpence for those two apples, mate."

Donald laughed again, handed over sixpence, and said "cheerio" to Billy and walked through the market place toward the Parish Church. Looking up, he noticed the massive sign that had been placed on the face of the church. It was in the image of a very large thermometer, and it was depicting a target of 30,000 Pounds. The amount was to be raised to help combat a deadly infestation of Death Watch Beetle. This was a pest that bores into old oak beams or other hardwoods, and is difficult to detect until after many years when the beams can disintegrate.

Donald still had a little time to pass before his bus was due at the Frogmoor terminal, so he slipped into the side door of the church, while taking a bite out of one of Billy's apples. As he entered, his eyes had to adjust from the outdoor light that was a fading evening grey but, nonetheless, much brighter than the murky darkness of the church interior. He could clearly see the altar and sacraments just to his right and the rows of pews stretching further away to his left toward the massive front door of the church. This was a very old church, having been originally consecrated by St. Wulstan, Bishop of Worcester, in 1087. It had been extended and renovated over the centuries, but many of the original timbers and roof beams remained. It was these that were the main cause for concern over the Death Watch Beetle.

Donald remained in the shadows near the side door as he looked up at the roof beams, straining to see evidence of infestation. It was too dark to make out signs of the damaging insect, but an occasional "tock, tock" could be heard in the echoing silence of the building. Although Donald was not aware of it at the time, the little noise he was hearing would have a gut-searing and fearful impact on his life in the not too distant future.

He came across a plaque fastened to one wall close to the side door where he had entered. In the semi-darkness, he read the inscription:

> The original cruciform church was consecrated by St Wulstan, Bishop of Worcester, in 1087. In 1275, major extension and rebuilding took place, and the shape and size of the pre-sent building stems largely from this work. In the mid-fifteenth century, the roof was removed, the pillars remodeled, and the clerestory windows added, and in 1521, the building of the tower was started. This now houses the peal of 13 bells, which are rung for all main services, and on special occasions. The Lady Chapel (of the Guild of St Mary) was originally built in 1273 and rebuilt between 1500 and 1510.

Suddenly, a different rustle or disturbance startled him, and looking toward the main door, he noticed in the dim light a figure of a man standing in the back row of pews. He was holding what appeared to be a book which he put down in front of him and quickly left the church.

Donald thought the man looked like Karol Zaluski, Alijca's uncle, and was acting somewhat strangely. He knew from his conversations with Alicja that most, if not all Polish people were Catholic and would not be frequenting the Wycombe Anglican Parish Church.

He took another bite of his apple and strolled up the aisle toward the big door. Stopping at the last row of pews, he hesitated and then decided to step to the place he thought Mr Zaluski had stood. Looking down at the spot he noticed a red hymn book, which was strangely out of place as all the others in the row were blue! Reaching down he lifted the book and saw a piece of paper sticking out from the pages. Thinking it was marking a particular hymn, he saw it was on number

39, "All Things Bright & Beautiful."

He was about to replace the paper marker when the apple that he had been holding in his mouth while manipulating the hymn book generated a little extra apple juice which he was unable to control. The juice dripped from his mouth and dropped on to the paper. He quickly sucked on the apple, brushed the paper with his hand, and was about to close the book when a couple of letters appeared on the paper: *M Z.*

Although curious about the letters, his main concern was that he did not want the stained paper to mess the page in the hymn book. He quickly grabbed the paper and roughly folded it into his jacket pocket. Unfortunately in his haste, the paper tore and was now almost in two pieces. Replacing the hymn book, Donald turned and headed for the door, biting and chewing on his delicious apple.

As he left, he almost bumped into a large man in a dark coat.

"Oops! Sorry about that," exclaimed Donald.

"Eet is notink," declared the man in a very deep foreign accent, staring intently at him before rapidly moving off.

The intensity of the man's eyes made Donald's skin crawl for a minute, but he shook it off and thought nothing more of it. After all, Wycombe was full of foreigners.

It was now almost dark as he headed over to Frogmoor to catch his bus to Micklefield. There was a queue already forming at the Palace Cinema to see a popular film, "The Caine Mutiny," starring Humphrey Bogart. The double decker Thames Valley Bus drove up, and Donald jumped aboard and settled down for the twenty-minute trip home. His main thought on the way was his business meetings the next day at Farnborough Air Show.

Z   W   K   L   S   E   T   H

The Note Markings

As Donald walked in the door of his residence, he was greeted by Mrs. Fenchurch. "Did you see the 'Bucks Free Press' today?" she asked.

The local paper was widely read throughout the County of Buckinghamshire, and although Alesbury was the county seat and administrative authority, High Wycombe was probably considered the more important industrial center.

"No, I haven't read any papers today. What have you learned?" asked Donald.

"Well, people are reporting a UFO over that American base yesterday. Even a local policeman reported in his official duty report last night. Now, you know a lot of these Yanks. You need to find out what they are doing up there." Mrs. Fenchurch looked up at Donald expectantly.

Donald smiled, saying, "I'm sure there's a rational explanation. And it may not have anything to do with the Yanks." Donald thought, *I'm certainly going to ask Cal a few more questions about that, but if it's secret, he's not telling me about it, that's for sure.*

"Are you cooking supper tonight, Donald?" asked Mrs. Fenchurch.

"No," replied Donald, "I'm having a tin of soup, an apple, and off to bed for an early night."

With that he turned and entered his room, saying goodnight to his landlady.

He took off his jacket, placed it on a coat hanger, and was about to hang it up when he noticed the paper he had stuffed into the pocket was protruding a little. He took it out and unfolded it on his chest of drawers. The smaller torn piece finally came loose, and Donald gazed at the larger piece with the two letters exposed. Wondering if the apple juice had caused the letters to appear, he grabbed another apple, dashed into the kitchen, rinsed and dried it (just like his mother had always berated him to), sped back to his room, and bit into the ripened fruit.

He allowed the apple juice to drip from his mouth onto one of Mrs. Fenchurch's heavy crystal ornamental dishes where he usually kept his keys and loose change. Dipping his finger into the copious juice, Donald spread some next to the exposed letters and very quickly more letters appeared. After spreading the apple juice over the whole piece of paper, he exposed a total of forty nine letters and three numerals. As the jumbled letters were in groups, it became obvious this was some kind of coded message. The groups read: *M Z X A R H G L F 123 R G L M L D M J Q Y R X O D P H M N U N A U A X Q L Y W I H O Z A J I D H N U L* .

The paper was, by now, quite damp, limp, and smeared with a little pulp from the apple. Donald set the paper aside and thought about the significance of his discovery.

Was this a kid's prank of an experiment in invisible writing and then forgetting he'd left it in his hymn book in the pew? After all, the title of the hymn was certainly one used frequently for children's Sunday school. However, Donald thought it was a little longer than a school prankster would have patience for.

Or could this have been what Mr. Zaluski had left there, and why he had appeared agitated when he had hastily vacated the church in the waning hour of daylight?

These were thoughts crossing his mind as he contemplated the note in front of him, but he was leaning more to the kid's attempt at invisible writing because the letters had no meaning or pattern to them. Donald pondered to himself; *I wonder who told the tyke how to make invisible ink? I know I tried it myself at school with lemon juice and toilet paper!*

He glanced up and, noticing the other smaller torn piece of paper, Donald thought he had better test that piece, as well. He was almost out of apple juice by this time, and he had only bought two apples with his frugal purchase. The first one had already been fully eaten, and the second one was virtually chewed out of juice. There was some liquid remaining in the crystal dish but it was drying up fast.

Donald quickly smeared some of the pulpy mess over the paper, and with a little rubbing was unable to create any images. Donald felt it was time to prepare his thoughts for the next day's business meetings. He opened a drawer of his chest of drawers and was about to select a clean shirt to lay out on a chair for tomorrow, when he thought he had better wash the sticky juice from his hands. Leaving drawer open, he crossed the room and opened the door to go to the kitchen, which caused a draft of air to blow both pieces of the note off the furniture. The larger piece with the letters fell on the floor, but the smaller piece fell directly into Donald's shirt drawer where it nestled against the side.

Donald returned and, selecting his shirt, closed the drawer. It was then he noticed the piece of note on the floor. He picked it up and carefully folded it and placed it gently in his wallet. He looked for the other piece of paper and not seeing it anywhere, made no real effort to look under the furniture, as it did not appear important.

He wondered to himself whether he should ask Alicja about her uncle's strange visit to the Wycombe Parish Church. He felt this may not be a prudent enquiry and decided he would not ask her unless he knew more about Zaluski's motives or intentions.

Donald prepared his soup and sat down to listen to the news on the radio. The Cold War was in full swing, and the Soviets were clamping down even tighter on East Germany after the popular uprising the previous year in 1953. There was news the United States had just launched the first nuclear powered submarine, USS Nautilus, The BBC turned their attention to some local stories on the homefront, and Donald switched it off and got ready for bed.

Chapter 6

New Business and the Note Explained

Aviation Business

At Farnborough, Donald walked through the static display of some of the latest aircraft in the world, noting the new Comet jetliner MkII. He could also hear a huge bang as Martin Baker demonstrated their latest ejection seat. He found his way to Fairy Aviation's office to discuss his company's unique capability in plastics and present the prototype instrument covers for the cockpit of their new delta wing aircraft.

The British Government had ordered the funding for two of these special aircraft with its unique delta wing, and a special 10 degree tilting snoot nose. In the following eighteen months, Peter Twiss, the Fairy Aviation test pilot, would go on to break the world speed record. This new record at 1820kph (1132mph) had been a significant achievement considering the old record had only been set the previous year by an American F100 Super Sabre, and had been so much slower.

Donald concluded his meeting satisfactorily and strode over to DeHaviland Aircraft Company to meet with its Product Development Manager, Harry Barnard. Walking past the new Comet with its completely hidden jet engine cowlings, the plane looked the most aerodynamic and graceful aircraft on the tarmac. He went inside the DeHaviland offices and introduced himself. Harry Barnard greeted Donald with a firm handshake. With a shirt pocket full of pens and a small vernier caliper, he led him back to his office.

After ordering tea for Donald and himself from the secretary, Harry said, "Colonel Blankenship gave us a report on what you were doing for the Vickers Viscount aircraft, and we liked the very low failure rates you were generating on the nylon electrical terminals."

"Yes, we believe we have a methodology in our mold design, coupled with a specially designed injection molding process that enables us to embed a large number of terminals to a block of nylon," replied Donald.

"Well," continued Harry, "we would like you to look over these drawings and tell me if you think this electrical terminal for the Comet II would be feasible. It's designed to reduce weight while maintaining strength and electrical viability."

Harry led Donald to the table showing him the blueprint of the model. After some discussion about the number of metal inserts that would be needed and the specific dimensions, Donald felt he had sufficient information to take back with him for a discussion with his Tool Room Manager, Chalky White.

Leaving DeHaviland, he strolled around the Comet II on display, along with a large crowd that had gathered. As he looked around the sleek aircraft, his eye caught someone in the crowd and his hair stood up on the back of his neck. A man had quickly turned away just as Donald glanced at him, and he could have sworn it was the same person he had bumped into outside the church. The stranger had quickly dispersed into the crowd on the other side of the plane and then vanished.

Maybe I'm just imagining things, but this bloke definitely puts the wind up me, he thought to himself.

Harold Sloan Looks at the Note

On returning home, Donald decided to see an old friend, Harold Sloan, who was a neighbor to his parents. Harold was an artisan cabinet maker who could make any kind of furniture using a variety of materials, from local beechwood, to the more exotic woods like mahogany. Donald also looked up to him as he was older and had been in the military during the war.

Donald had begun to feel uneasy about the note in his wallet and wondered if Zaluski and the stranger were connected in some way. Although Donald had spent his two years of compulsory national service in the Royal Air Force, mainly in a technical capacity, he knew

Harold had been in British military intelligence during the war and thought he should show him the note.

Harold said, "Hello, Donald, me old mate. What have you been up to, then?"

"Oh, usual stuff with work, although I did have a nice couple of meetings over at the Farnborough Air Show which should please the boss, I think," replied Donald. Donald went on, "How about you, did you get Lady Conworth's job you told me about?"

Harold grimaced, "No, afraid not. Too expensive, she says. She's such a bloody tightwad. Got bags of money and yet wouldn't part with a farthing if she thought she could get something for nothing. I could've made her a lovely set of Windsor chairs. I don't know where she will go now, because there are few of us bodgers left who have the skills or craftsmanship to make really fine hand-made furniture."

"Ah, well," laughed Donald, "You still have your bees so you can sell honey for a living." Donald had always been amazed at Harold's skill with his beekeeping. Harold had also shown Donald, how in cold weather, to pick up a bee, cup it in his hands and gently blow in warm air. He would watch the bee crawl out of his cupped hands, sit on his thumb and then take off to find its hive.

Harold said, "Talking of honey bees, why don't we have spot of honey mead?"

"Good idea, I just love the stuff you make," replied Donald.

"I don't make it, the bees do. I just ferment it till it tastes like good booze," the older man said.

As they sat in the garden outside Harold's workshop sipping nature's alcoholic nectar and watching the fading light of day, Donald began to feel warm and comfortable. He felt that he should ask Harold his opinion about the note.

"Harold weren't you in the Army during the war and in some kind of intelligence you told me a while ago?"

Harold looked up from his small glass, poured another golden shot from the bottle and offered some to Donald who nodded in acceptance.

"Yes, I was indeed, and, coincidently, I was posted to Hughenden Manor. So it wasn't far from home. I was in the Photographic Reconnaissance Unit evaluating aerial photos taken over enemy positions. Why do you ask?"

"I didn't know Hughenden Manor had been taken over by the RAF during the war," said Donald.

The large Manor and Estate just outside High Wycombe had been the original residence of Britain's Prime Minister, Benjamin Disraeli, who had purchased it in 1848.

"Anyway," continued Donald, "I am wondering what you may think of this." He opened his wallet, gently pulled out the note, and handed it to Harold.

The big rough hands of the cabinet maker unfolded the paper and began looking intently at it with a furrowed brow. "What is this Don, have you got me on a quiz of some kind?" he asked. "Where did this come from and how did you get it?"

Donald explained how he originally thought it was a place marker for the hymn book, and again, he omitted the part that Zaluski played in the process. He just wasn't sure just where this might lead and the less he said the better, especially because Zaluski was Alijca's uncle. However, he was extremely interested to find out all he could.

"What do you think Harold, is this a kid just practicing his chemistry experiments or something a little more complicated?"

"Don, I have to say it could be either. It could possibly be what's termed a 'dead letter drop,' but I don't think it's a highly professional method of nefarious communication, if that's what you're inferring. You were able to revive the lettering using apple juice. Well, in France during the war, many messages came from the Resistance using a primitive but effective technique of cigarette paper, lemon juice, vinegar, etc. In many cases, or in fact most cases, they would use what is called a "one-time pad" to encrypt the message and someone on the other end using the same key from a duplicate pad, would decrypt the message. Each party would destroy that pad so that it could not be used again, or be detected by an enemy."

"Tell you what, Don, there had been two cryptoanalysts seconded to Hughenden Manor from Bletchley Park, our deciphering HQ. I am still in touch with those chaps in civvy street, and I can ask one of them what they think of it, if you like," offered Harold.

"What do you think Harold?" asked Donald. "I don't want to appear an idiot."

Harold responded, "There's no harm in taking a look and, anyway, it'll keep my chap's hand in for when the next war comes along."

Donald laughed, "The next war will be annihilation by atomic bombs."

"Okay. Let's make a copy and give it to my friend, Roger Hewitt-Benning, for his analysis. Who knows, this may be the doodling of a bored or drunk parishioner?"

Harold got to work and copied Donald's messy and mangled original as follows....

MZXARHGLF 123 RGLMLD MJQYRXOD P HMNUNAUAXQ LYWIHOZ AJ IDHNUL

"Right then," remarked Harold, "I'll get this to my mate, Roger, and we'll see what he comes up with."

Donald and Harold had another tot of honey mead and parted company for the evening.

Major Wallace and GENETRIX

Major Wallace began the long climb back upstairs from the underground bunker that had been WWII's Eighth Army Air Force Bomber Command from 1944 to 1947, which was code named "Pinetree." He thought to himself the big job it had been to get this place operational again for the 7th Air Division of SAC and to turn this into a state of the art Communications and Control Center for all of Strategic Air Command units and airfields around the world. The code name for this operation was "Lancer Control." They were also in direct and immediate telephone link with Rapid City, South Dakota, stateside. The base had a Weather Reporting function for all of SAC operations and Atmospheric Balloons were being used to generate accurate weather maps and forecasts. However, this base and other bases around Europe and in Turkey were using high altitude balloons with special cameras for spying on the Soviet Union, Eastern Europe, and China. This task was code named GENETRIX. For the High Wycombe base, their weather forecasting function was a perfect cover for GENETRIX.

The bunker was built on three floors underground and was camouflaged above ground by various buildings and facilities, some of which were fake. The town of High Wycombe was situated in a valley between the Chiltern Hills in Buckinghamshire. The geology of the Chiltern Hills was chalk and, thus, the underground bunker that comprised the sensitive and secret facilities was immune from attack and suffered little or no water seepage or flooding.

However, due to a prolonged absence of any military units at the base, it had been under a significant amount of water when the 7th Air Division had reoccupied the place, but that had been quickly rectified.

Just at this moment, as the Major was passing the massive information boards which were on special rails at the 2nd level, his concern was the balloon escape the other night, and he wanted to find out from Master Sergeant Cal Jennings what the hell happened! He had had to field calls all the following day about UFOs and, of course, his superiors were none too pleased about the publicity. They were gaining small but valuable intelligence on the Soviets with the balloons flying at around 50,000 to 70,000 feet.

He was able to convince all concerned, including the press and local authorities, that they were sending up atmospheric weather balloons to supply data for the Weather Command System for all of SAC throughout Europe. What he obviously didn't tell them was some of the flights were very high altitude balloons with sophisticated cameras that were drifting eastward over the Soviet Union and eventually being picked up over the Pacific by tail hooks on American C-119 aircraft. Major Wallace paused on his ascent at the 2nd level and entered Ops Room GH24. He looked up at the massive display board as it was being pushed into place on the tracks, and he watched Lieutenant Palmer supervising the positioning of recent data captured by the T-11 trimetogon A-type cameras and also the B-type cameras that gave a much wider view. They had originally been using the XT-6 camera, but they were prone to mechanical failures.

He was pleased to see that new data showed an ever increasing number of new railroad ties being laid down as the Soviets built their infrastructure into Siberia and toward the Balkan States. The new military installations and missile silos were clearly being mapped on 'GENETRIX' display boards as photo reconnaissance personnel analyzed the films.

"How's it going Lieutenant?" enquired Wallace.

"Not too bad sir," replied the officer. "But, we are not getting a good percentage of successful flights. I would say it's around 7% where we get a film recovered and brought back to 'Lancer Control' or it's sent to Lockbourne AFB Stateside. It's a real crap shoot, if you ask me."

"Yeh, Lieutenant. No one's asking you though, or me, so we just do what we have to do."

"Yes, sir," Palmer saluted.

Not all of the balloon flights were successful as Palmer had indicated, and some had drifted off course, or the Soviets had shot them down and captured the cameras. President Eisenhower was anxious to obtain information through the GENETRIX program until he could get the Top Secret U2 spy plane operational.

"Where's that Master Sergeant Jennings? I need to know how his crew let that fucking balloon off early the other night."

"Well, sir, he was off duty at the time and had gone off down Marlow Hill a little way to meet someone. His early crew had got the system ready for take off later that night. From my investigation, sir, someone in his crew had left the helium valve open from the supply tank, and it strained the anchor ropes and released."

Major Wallace shook his head in disbelief, and just said quietly, "Have the son of a bitch report to me at 0700 in the morning. I also want to know who he was meeting with, even if he was off duty."

"I already asked him, sir, and it was Don Harvey, the local English feller. He is pretty popular with the guys on the base. He said he was trying to get Don to introduce him to a Polish girl up in Amersham."

Major Wallace fumed, "While he's trying to get laid, our mission is being jeopardized by his unsupervised crew. I'll have him on the carpet in the morning! Good-night!"

With that, Wallace continued his ascent and emerged into the fresh night air. He finished off some paperwork before jumping into his car and drove off the base to head home to his rented house in Beaconsfield, just north of High Wycombe.

Dolores Wallace had just finished the ironing when James walked in.

"Those Russkies keeping you late again?" she joked, but with a slight edge to it as she had once again kept the dinner in the oven to warm.

"Sorry honey, usual personnel issues and the odd technical problem."

"Hey, that goes with the job," she replied. She accepted his point because obviously everything was so secret there was no telling if or when he might go off on a mission someday without telling her its cause or duration.

Harold Shows the Note to Roger Hewitt-Benning

Harold Sloan had visited his friend, Roger Hewitt-Benning, who was living in retirement at Penn, a small village not far from High Wycombe. Roger had been one of two crypto-analysts stationed at Hughenden Manor during the war and had been seconded there from Bletchly Park.

Harold stepped off the bus and began a slow walk up the hill toward Roger's small cottage. It was a little chilly, and a faint mist of rain caused Harold to shiver.

38

I hope that's not a bad omen, he thought to himself.

He had been apprehensive about Donald's note and what it might mean. On the other hand, he could not imagine anything significant taking place in High Wycombe to warrant the attention of secret messages.

But, the Yanks are here, so maybe there's a connection there, he thought again.

Brushing all that from his mind, he arrived at Roger's door and knocked. After the sound of clumping footsteps the door opened, and Roger greeted Harold with an outstretched hand and a huge smile of welcome.

"Come on in and let me take your coat," he rasped in the bronchial fashion of a heavy smoker.

"How about a Scotch, Harold, to ward off that damp chill out there?" he asked.

Harold gladly accepted and asked for a dash of soda with it.

"Make yourself comfortable," Roger said as he busied himself with the drinks and Harold sought out the sofa with its deep cushions and high back. Roger's furnishings were neither skimpy nor extravagant, but were practical from a bachelor's standpoint. The carpet was an Indian hand-knotted Kazak but was becoming slightly threadbare in places. The end tassels were damaged in areas where they had been caught up in the vacuum cleaner. A wife would have prevented such damage occurring, but Roger had had no inclination toward a matrimonial state, and thus a little deterioration in his domestic domain could be expected.

Roger handed him his Ballantyne's Single Malt saying, "Here you are, Harold. Cheers!"

"Cheers," replied Harold, and he sipped the golden fluid, moving it around his mouth and relishing the distinctive and heady flavor of a top quality single malt Scotch.

"So you mentioned in your phone call about a mysterious note that your friend had picked up," Roger began. "Let's have a look at it see if we can make heads or tail of it."

Harold reached into pocket and removed the note from his wallet, handing it to Roger.

After studying the contents for a few minutes, Roger looked at Harold and remarked, "It does look like a one-time pad kind of message, but, if it is, it's not easy, if not impossible to guess the key that would unlock it. Although this method of communication is primitive for any kind of sophisticated espionage, it's still a pretty effective method for some people with limited tools."

"But do you think you could break this code?" asked Harold.

Roger thought some more before saying, "I would certainly like to give it a go, just to have something interesting to do instead of the Times crossword." He went on, "Harold, old chap, let me give you an example of what I'm up against." He tore a piece paper off of his notepad on the sideboard and scribbled the word N O T E P A D.

"Now, let's assume I want to send you this message in code, and let us assume you have a one-time pad and I have a one-time pad with an unused KEY. Let's assume the KEY is M J G O Z H L. Let's also assume that the value of letters is 0 for A, 1 for B all the way through 25 for Z."

TEXT	N	O	T	E	P	A	D
Now provide a numerical value	13	14	19	4	15	0	3
This is the KEY	M	J	G	O	Z	H	L
The numerical value of KEY	12	9	6	14	25	7	11
Add the KEY + NOTEPAD	25	23	25	18	**40**	7	14
Anything over 25 modify by diff of 26					14		
The result is the cipher TEXT	Z	X	Z	S	O	H	O
At destination enter numerical value	25	23	25	18	14	7	14
MINUS KEY value	-12	-9	-6	-14	-25	-7	-11
Add the two together	13	14	19	4	15 *	0	3

*If KEY negative value is greater than }
CIPHERTEXT take diff of KEY value} &
26 & ADD to CIPHERTEXT   }

The result is back to the Message Text N O T E P A D

"So Harold, as you can see from my little example it's very easy when you have the key. Of course anyone using such a pad will destroy the page from the pad, and the recipient will destroy their key also."

"Yes, that's impressive Roger," countered Harold, "but how the bloody hell are you going to find the right key to decrypt this message, if it is a message?"

"Well, it can be done Harold, but obviously it's not easy and it could take a long time. There are ways we can get around the problem. We have done it before during the war and, anyway, I have plenty of time on my hands," Roger said.

"How do you do it then?" asked Harold.

"Ah," exclaimed Roger, "That's an area I cannot get into with you. How about another wee dram?" Roger asked in his best imitation Scottish accent. Harold acquiesced and sat back in the sofa to enjoy the toast to Scotland's best.

Harold left Roger's cottage later in a warm frame of mind and body. They had agreed that Roger would need a few days to attempt what might be impossible. The rainy mist was beginning to penetrate Harold's contented feeling when he stepped up onto the bus that would take him home.

Roger Deciphers the Note

It was three days later when Roger telephoned Harold and told him had deciphered the Note. At least he thought it was as close to deciphered as he felt it could be, without knowing the real KEY. They arranged to meet at the Red Lion Hotel on the High Street in Wycombe, and Harold said he would bring Donald with him. They decided 7:00 p.m. would be a good time as Donald could get thereir on time even if he worked a little late that day.

Donald was excited when he heard the news and was ready the next day at the appointed time. He couldn't help feeling a little apprehensive, however, as he was not sure just where this might lead. He walked into the Red Lion Hotel and turned into the public bar. It was filled with patrons, gossiping, smoking and drinking their favorite beer, some playing darts, others dominos, but mostly huddled together in groups. It was noisy and full of cigarette smoke, but looking through the crowd he could make out Harold and his friend waving at him trying to get his attention. He made his way over to where they sat at a very small table.

Harold made the introductions and asked what Donald wanted to drink.

"I'll have a half a black and tan, thank you," he said.

Harold stood up and, leaning over the bar, placed the order and sat down again with half a pint of Bitter mixed with Pale Ale.

"So," Donald said as he lifted his beer, "Cheers, and what do we have tonight, then? Some news of the mysterious note, I hope."

"We do," replied Roger, and this is what I believe it says. However, it's completely foreign and a mixture of maybe some Slavic or eastern European language; I'm just not sure."

He laid the Note on the small table, carefully avoiding the beer drops.

Donald looked and looked, trying his best to make sense of it.

The deciphered Note read:

PETROWSKI 123 ULICA POMPOWAC SMIERC DZWON ODSZEDL DO LIDERA

Donald glanced at Roger and Harold and said, "Any idea what this means?"

"No idea", replied Roger, but obviously it must mean something to somebody."

"So how did you decipher something like this" asked Donald?

Roger gave a vague explanation and said Harold could give him a more detailed answer as he had no time right now.

"Deciphering without the original key is almost impossible, but my wartime experience gave me a little edge, so it's really an art or intuition than a science," explained Roger. "Meantime, here is the KEY that I believe gives us the right answer. I could be wrong, of course, but I'm pretty sure I am on the right track."

Roger placed another piece of paper on the table and on it was written:

X V E J D L O B

Donald picked up both pieces of paper, carefully folded them and placed them in his wallet. "Who's for another round?" he asked.

Harold said he would have another one but Roger declined, indicating he needed to be on his way. Roger shook hands and left the establishment, leaving Harold and Donald looking at each other quizzically.

"So what are you going to do with it now?" asked Harold.
"It looks to me like the Polish language, so I'll probably ask Alicja to translate it for me," replied Donald. He avoided mentioning Karol Zaluski, the Polish man who had deposited the message in the first place.

"I must say, it's getting a trifle weird isn't it," stated Harold. "I mean if this is something of importance, you may have to turn this over to the authorities, Donald."

Donald looked up sharply, "Well, we still don't know anything yet until I have it translated." Secretly Donald was concerned that if Zaluski was involved in some secret agent game, was it of benefit to us or our adversaries? Either way, he was even more apprehensive as the events were unfolding.

Donald and Harold finished their beers and arranged to meet again the following week before they left the bar at The Red Lion.

Chapter 7

The Intelligence Services

Roger Hewitt-Benning is intrigued

Roger had also suspected the note was in Polish and while at his club in London had had the transcript translated by a prior WWII linguist and scholar he knew at Kings College.

The note now read, "**Petrowksi 123 de la Pompe Death Bell departed leader to**"

Roger stepped up to the nondescript front door of the Special Forces Club in Knightsbridge in Herbert Crescent just behind Harrods department store, and was let in. As a member in good standing, he had full privileges as a WWII veteran of the military SIS. Founded by the Second World War Special Operations Executive (SOE) in 1946, the club became a second home for retired intelligence officers like Roger and others like him such as secret agents, veterans of the SAS, other special forces, as well as MI5, MI6 and CIA officers. Its motto 'Spirit Of Resistance' sprang from the war time exploits of its founders.

It was here that Roger could relax in comfort during his odd trips to London and meet up with some of the old boys. One of his pals, Richard Bates, was a current member of SIS, or MI6 as it is now known, and they now shared drinks in the club's library.

"Richard," began Roger, "I came across a strange incident last week which I thought I would share with you."

"Oh, really, old chap. What do you have that could be so strange in this decidedly weird world we're living in?" asked Richard, smiling with his pipe clenched firmly between his teeth and belching smoke like the Flying Scotsman train.

Roger then went on to describe how he had become involved with Donald Harvey and the mysterious note. On concluding his narrative, he handed a copy of the note to Richard who examined it with a mixture of curiosity and amusement.

He looked up and said to Roger, "It's certainly an interesting message, but whether it means anything to anyone is another matter. You say you had this translated from Polish?"

"Yes," Roger responded, "Interestingly, we do have a large number of Polish emigrés living in the High Wycombe area. Many of them were part of the Polish Free Army but were unable to return to Poland after the war because of the Iron Curtain that Russia brought down across Eastern Europe."

"I must say I have not heard anything official from any our Sections about contacts or missions relating to Poland," said Richard. "Nevertheless, I will make some enquiries among my colleagues and see if it spikes any interest."

"Very good", acknowledged Roger, "And I suppose if it does spike some interest, that will be the last I shall know of it, right?"

Richard laughed and with a big puff of smoke from his pipe filled with his Dunhill DeLuxe Navy Rolls tobacco replied, "Absolutely right, old chap."

After some further discussion of current events in Britain and elsewhere, they parted company and went their separate ways.

Russian Embassy - London

Second Secretary Dmitri Demidov had welcomed Yakov Malik, the new Russian Ambassador, and Mrs. Malik to London. They had settled in and were being given the usual round of invitations to various social functions, and the Ambassador had presented his credentials to Her Majesty Queen Elizabeth at St James's Palace.

Staff meetings had been held and responsibilities defined for each attache and assistant. Mr. Demidov then pulled aside the Military Attache, Leonid Tarasov, and asked him to come into his office.

"Has your man located the dead letter drop or the identity of the Polish agent for the Death Bell assignment?" he asked.

Tarasov replied tersely, "My agent 'Falcon' reports that, based on the intelligence from our mole in The Polish Underground State, the government in exile in London, an ex-Polish Free Army Officer now living in the city was to receive a coded message regarding the potential whereabouts of Herr Kammler."

Mr. Demidov then asked, "And has 'Falcon' made any further progress?"

"Yes, sir, he has, and was close to intercepting the message, but he suspects a local man accidentally acquired the note or letter as he was the only person in the vicinity of the drop at the time."

Demidov asked, "Can you identify this person and retrieve the note without any violation of laws, as we cannot afford a diplomatic incident with a newly credentialed Russian Ambassador in place?"

Mr. Tarasov responded assuredly that his operative Falcon had been able to identify a young man, Donald Harvey. He had seen him at the drop zone, but as a complete coincidence had spotted Harvey at the the Farnborough Air Show where Falcon had a product observation assignment from Tarasov. From there he was able to determine that Harvey was at the air show on business, conducting meetings with various aircraft companies. By feigning a business association with Harvey, he was able to convince the receptionist at DeHaviland that he had lost track of his associate in the crowd after he had left the meeting earlier.

The receptionist quite readily said, "Oh, Mr. Harvey left earlier and was going to look around the exhibits."

Mr. Tarasov went on to say, "Falcon was then able to trace Mr Harvey to his place of work and to his residence."

Mr. Demidov looked at Tarasov meaningfully, "The Polish agent who was to pass the note is a thorn in the side of our Polish comrades as well as a danger to the Soviet Socialist Republics. What is his name?"

"Karol Zaluski, sir," replied Mr. Tarasov.

"Have Falcon extract the verbal message from Zaluski but, in any event, eliminate him," ordered Secretary Demidov.

"But that would violate local laws," smiled Tarasov.

"Accidents aren't against any law are they?" growled Mr. Demidov without any humor.

"No, Comrade. It will be taken care of," concluded Mr. Tarasov.

MI6 Staff Meeting

Richard Bates, in his capacity as a staff member of MI6, was curious about the deciphered message that Roger had shown him and the name that stood out in that message was Petrowski. Somehow it seemed familiar, and he thought he would mention the name at this morning's staff meeting. Lowering his umbrella from the British curse of on and off rain, he ascended the steps to the front door of 54 Broadway in Westminster, the Headquarters of Britain's Secret Intelligence Service. At this post World War II period, it was restructuring itself from the various divisions of Wartime Military Intelligence to MI5 Security Service, MI6 Secret Intelligence Service, DIS Defense Intelligence Staff, together with some other agencies.

Richard walked into his office, greeting the office secretary with a cheery, "Good Morning, Holly. What's the Agenda for this morning?"

Holly answered, "Morning, Richard. Hope the weather clears up before we go home tonight. You have a Staff Meeting at 10:00 a.m., and I have the Europe files ready on your desk."

"Thank you, Holly. Any tea left in the pot? That British Railways stuff tasted like dishwater at the station this morning."

"I'll have a nice cuppa for you in a jiffy," she replied.

Richard entered the Conference Room promptly at 10:00 a.m. where four people had already seated themselves around the green baize table. Head of Section, Arthur Soames, came in and sat down at the head of the table. Everyone greeted each other and commiserated about the weather and the state of the football season, Queens Park Rangers and Arsenal in particular, which had lost their respective matches the previous weekend. Arthur called the meeting to order.

The group discussed the current counter-intelligence cases under way, the state of Communist Party membership in Britain, as well as the Daily Worker Communist Party Newspaper, although the latter was also under the purview of MI5 as a domestic issue. The Cold War cases of counter espionage were, however, at the forefront of the discussion, and important strategies were continuously being devised to meet the challenges of the new era.

As the meeting was drawing to a close, Arthur asked if there was any other business. Richard enquired if anyone had information about a Polish person named Petrowski, and he went on to explain in summary, the basis of his enquiry.

Bill Osbourne, an agent who had been a prominent member of the wartime team at MI4, the reconnaissance and aerial photographic division, spoke up, "That name rings a bell because there had been a file when I was dealing with recon photos of Nazi weapons sites, like Peenemunde in Germany and other suspected sites for advanced weapons research in Czecloslovakia and Poland. The file had come back to me a few months ago from another Section asking to verify a couple of items for the records Index and Archive. I happened to see the name Petrowski; at least I'm pretty sure that was the name. The reason it stuck out for me was that it was something recent, as the name had never been part of the file previously. I didn't take much notice, however, of the context. You will have to enquire with the Section Head, Colonel Blignaught."

Richard thanked Bill, "I appreciate your thoughts on that, Bill. It all sounds pretty interesting when a file actually comes to life, although we don't yet know if we have the right man."

Arthur said, "I will leave it up to you, Richard, to follow up and get back to me should it evolve into anything of value. I expect the Colonel will also advise me. With that, I shall close this meeting."

The group dispersed to their posts and offices.

Richard made his way to Colonel Blignaught's office and asked his secretary, Janet, if the Colonel had a few moments to spare. Richard explained his mission briefly, and she agreed to interrupt the Colonel's activity.

She came back saying, "He can see you for about 15 minutes if it's urgent, as he has a briefing to do over at the Ministry of Defense."

"Thanks, Janet. I'll be quick as this should not take long."

"Good morning, Colonel. I understand you have the responsibility of a Nazi weapons file that now features a Polish underground resistance person by the name of Petrowski."

The Colonel rose and gestured Richard to a chair. "Yes, it's a recent and an important addition, and we are supposed to be getting some important intelligence on this individual. What connection have you discovered about this person, Richard?"

Richard showed the Colonel the deciphered and translated note:

petrowski 123 rue de pompe death bell departed leader to

Studying the note, the Colonel expressed surprise and annoyance by indicating to Roger that a member of the Polish State Underground had said an encoded note would be left in a designated drop by one of their operatives from a friendly country, let's call that operative, 'A', or perhaps one living in England whom we can call, 'B.' The note would be retrieved by SIS, analyzed and passed on to a senior intelligence officer with the USAF at Communications Command at High Wycombe.

"This is a joint intelligence operation between the British and Americans," he said. "Don't ask me why the Yanks are using the US Air Force and not the new CIA people," he added.

Colonel Blignaught rang for Janet.

"Janet, call over to the Ministry and let them know I shall be a little late for our briefing. An important issue has suddenly arisen."

"Yes Colonel. Should I make a cup of tea for you both?"

"Yes, Janet. I think we are going to need one. What do you think, Richard?"

"I would love a cup right now," responded the other man.

"Richard, let me give you a significant briefing of what we have code named, The Kammler Death Bell."

The Colonel then described a German top secret weapons program in Poland that had been disbanded before the Russians had taken over the territory in 1945. General Patton had arrived in Berlin and then quickly moved his troops toward the suspected facility in Poland, but there is no official record of what happened on that mission. The Americans were hunting for the head of that weapons operation by the name of Hans Kammler, as well as Hans Frank, a German lawyer and prominent Nazi, who was appointed Governor-General of the Occupied Territories on 26 October 1941. Frank oversaw the segregation of Jews into ghettos in the larger cities, particularly Warsaw, and the use of Polish civilians as forced and compulsory labor in German war industries. He was caught by the Americans, tried at Nuremberg, and subsequently hanged.

The Colonel went on to say, "Some people thought Kammler was suspected of trying to do a deal with the Americans, but he could also have been captured by the Russians. But, he more likely escaped through the Nazi network, together with his super weapons secrets. Our SIS intelligence in Soviet- controlled Poland had received un-corroborated information that a slave laborer at the Kammler facility had survived a cleansing of personnel there (a massacre), and had since died under suspicious circumstances while in custody. Supposedly a Borys PETROWSKI, let's call him 'P'. *"That way, said the Colonel,* I won't make a mess of Polish proper pronunciation. 'P' had received information from a relative, Czeslaw CIEMINSKI, let's call him 'C', who had been working as a slave laborer for a highly secret German installation in Poland in the last days of the war. 'C' had observed preparations for the testing of a "super weapon," code named "Death Bell." Prior to the Russian advance into Poland and Czechoslovakia, the Germans had massacred everyone, including all key personnel, engineers, physicists, and laborers at the site. 'C' had been terribly wounded but played dead. He had in the subsequent confusion and clean up managed to crawl to a hiding place. Later, after the war according to a double agent acting as a mole we have in the UB Polish Ministry of Public Security, was able to verify that that agency knew about 'C' and verified he died under mysterious circumstances. His cause of death was never determined except to say it was from old "war wounds," but our mole was unable to confirm if the government agency had gained any valuable information from C. They also knew C had communicated to a member of the Polish Underground State, the resistance movement, but were unaware to whom. The Russian KGB was informed about 'C', and was known to be seriously following any trail for secret super weapons the Germans may have been developing. Polish Underground resistance sources said 'C' had subsequently died under mysterious circumstances in Poland, but, 'P' had fled Russian-occupied Poland and was now living somewhere in Europe. Neither the British nor Wallace knew if 'A' was the contact person for the church drop or if it were to be someone else. They believed it was unlikely it was 'A' because foreign travelers were still strictly controlled in this post-war period."

Colonel Blignaught concluded by saying, "Richard, it looks like your young man accidentally intercepted our message from Poland. So you can see we have a major problem here in more ways than one. What is his name?"

"Harvey sir. Donald Harvey."

Richard, who was used to some pretty involved and complex cases, said "This is quite staggering, Colonel. I never imagined for a moment I was walking into a case with so many unique implications. Who have you assigned this to, if I may ask?"

The Colonel replied, "I had Simpson on this, but as you have some local connection to the Wycombe area, I would like you to take this on, Richard, and I will have Simpson release the file to you. You will report to Soames, of course, but I will be fully engaged on this project."

"Now it's obvious we only have a portion of the message." The Colonel went on, "Does Harvey have additional messages or was it just one piece of paper? Did he see who put the note in the church or did he just happen to pick it up?"

"I really don't know, Colonel, but I will investigate this further."

"Richard, this case is obviously much more than chasing a Nazi war criminal, but that has to be the appearance of our major thrust of endeavor," said the Colonel. Now, I'll talk to Arthur Soames, but I'm sure he will agree we will need to interview Donald Harvey. We have to find more of that message and if he has it or not. However, we need to get some background on this chap, so I suggest you get Freddie Simpson to check him out and get a folio on him for our next joint meeting."

Richard agreed, "Yes, sir, I'll get on to it immediately."

The Colonel continued, "Our liaison at the US Air Force is a Major James Wallace with Strategic Air Command, Eighth Air Force, and 7th Air Division, based in High Wycombe. They have a global communications system developed there, plus a superior weather reporting and analysis function. I understand 'unofficially' they have something else going on which is validated by our Ministry Of Defense. Once we have determined our next step, we will arrange a meeting with Major Wallace."

PART
TWO

Chapter 8

The Reality Of Espionage!

Donald Gets a Translation

Alicja jumped off the Amersham bus in the High Wycombe

High Street and ran to Donald who was waiting patiently in Aldridge's shop doorway, trying to keep out of the bitter wind that was blowing that evening. They embraced passionately and kissed gently at first, but with increasing intensity as they both realized how each had been missed during a long week apart.

"How was the Air Show?" Alicja enquired after about the third lingering kiss and the tightening of Donald's embrace as he drew her closer to him. The question was more of a diversionary tactic than a genuine desire to know about airplanes. Donald was happy to respond with a rapid description of the Air Show and the people he had met. For him, too, it was a way of calming his rising desire to hold Alicja in a more romantic embrace.

"Why don't we go over to Frogmoor to the Tea Room above the Palace Cinema and sit there over some food? I've got a little job for you to do," Donald said.

"Oh, what kind of job, and do I get paid?" she laughed.

They walked briskly against the wind that came down the valley and through the town, cutting into their skin as they strode arm and in arm through the short path of the churchyard and around the corner toward Frogmoor.

They ran into the building, up the stairs to the Tea Room and found a table in the corner overlooking the street. They took off their coats and hung them on the coat stand near their table. Donald looked at Alicja, who was wearing a beautiful hand-made dress of light blue cotton trimmed with some traditional exquisite white Polish lace. Her full figure filled the dress and made him blush, thinking thoughts he should not have been.

He remarked, "Alicja, that dress makes you look stunning but then," he added, "you always look stunning."

"Well, thank you, Donald. You look handsome yourself tonight."

The waitress approached, and they ordered a couple of pies and chips with peas, together with a pot of tea.

"So what kind of job you have for me?" enquired Alicja smiling.

Donald produced the deciphered note and said, "I believe this may be Polish. Can you translate this?"

She looked at it and with a puzzled frown said, "Yes, I can, but it's an unfinished sentence. Is this all there is?"

"Yes," replied Donald.

"Well, what it says is, **Petrowksi 123 de la Pompe Death Bell departed leader to.**"

Donald took out his Biro and began writing the translation on a piece of paper he pulled from his pocket. He asked Alicja to repeat the sentence a couple of times to make sure he had it properly transcribed.

She continued to stare at the message before looking up and asked Donald, "What does this mean, Donald, and where did you get it? Is this something from the Air Show that you are trying to do some business with a Mr. Petrowski?"

She smiled at him coyly, "Or is this all a big secret, eh?"

He laughed, and caution told him that maybe he should go along with that premise, and replied, "Well, I don't think we would be doing any business with the Soviet block at Farnborough, but I will tell you more about it another day. Is that fair?"

She said, "Well, I cannot make you, so I will agree to that."

"How is your uncle Karol these days?" Donald enquired.

"I am actually a little concerned about him," replied Alicja. "He seems very worried, he is losing weight, and I don't know what kind of problem he is having. Why do you ask?"

"Oh. no reason. I just thought of him from when you and I were at the Corner Cafe that night."

They continued talking well into the evening before deciding to leave. Donald helped Alicja on with her coat, and they walked down the stairs into the nighttime air. The wind had died down and was chilly but not unpleasant as they waited for Alijca's bus to Amersham and to Hodgemoore Camp where the Polish exiles had made their home.

Donald and Alicja made plans for their next meeting, and Alicja wanted him to come and meet her parents at Hodgemoor, to which Donald agreed. He also asked her if her friend Ola would be interested in a date with Cal Jennings, the Yank she had danced with at the Town Hall. She said she would enquire.

With one long, lasting kiss and solid embrace when she could feel his firm body against hers, she pulled away to board the bus and, face flushed, she waved to him as she ran up the stairs of the double decker. He watched the bus draw away from the curb and waved to her as she looked out from the back window seat.

Donald's Intruder

Donald jumped off the bus at Micklefield and began making his way home. His thoughts were, of course, on the Note and its possible meaning, which he just could not fathom. As he got to the front door, he was overcome with an intuitive feeling of anxiety and, upon entering, he found Mrs. Fenchurch in a state of shock and white as a sheet.

"What's happened, Mrs. Fenchurch? Are you all right?"

"Oh, Donald!" she cried, "I came home from the greengrocers, and as I opened the door, a man rushed past me like lightning, jumped on a motor bike, and roared away."

"Are you okay, Mrs. Fenchurch? He didn't hurt you, did he?"

"No, he didn't touch me, but he ransacked your room, Donald."

"When did this happen?" Donald asked.

"No more than 15 to 20 minutes ago," Mrs. Fenchurch said.

Donald moved past Mrs. Fenchurch after assuring himself that she was all right, but a little shaken. He went through the open door to his room and looked at the mess left by the intruder. His clothing was strewn around, and the contents of his drawers were on the floor. Among his socks he spotted the torn piece of paper that had been part of the original note.

He thought, *Maybe this is the other part of the missing sentence. Lucky it must have dropped into the drawer unnoticed. I need to try again to retrieve the missing words if they are on here.*

He carefully folded the small piece of paper and tucked it into his wallet.

He repacked his chest of drawers and small wardrobe before tidying up the rest of the room. He noticed that his best 'Sunday' watch was still in its case on top of the bedside dresser. He turned and looked at the corner of the room, and his portable gramaphone was still there untouched. Donald felt the color drain from his face momentarily as he realized this was not an attempted burglary; someone had been searching for something they believed he had.

He quickly gathered himself together as Mrs. Fenchurch appeared in the doorway, "Can I help you tidy up Donald, and did that man steal anything of value?"

"Nothing Mrs. Fenchurch, and maybe because I don't have anything of value anyway," he replied. "Did you get a look at this man and could you describe him?" he asked her.

"I didn't get a really good look at him, but he looked a pretty frightening thug to me. He was tall and a big man and wearing a black overcoat or mac, and the one short glance I had of his face were his eyes. They were evil looking, and I cannot tell you their color or anything else about his face."

Donald was now even more anxious as thought he knew who this man might be, but wondering just what was he now involved in, and to whom he should report it. Mrs. Fenchurch's telephone began to ring and she went to answer it immediately.

Donald heard her speak briefly, and she came back saying, "It's for you Donald. It's your American friend, Cal Jennings."

Donald moved to the phone saying, "Hello, Donald here."

"Donald, could you come up to the base tomorrow?" Cal began. He sounded nervous, which was not like Cal.

"Oh,why, Cal? Have you got those cartons of Lucky Strike and Camels I asked for?"

"Well, yeh, but it's to do with something else. Major Wallace wants to talk with you."

"What?" exclaimed Donald, "The bloody base commander wants to talk with me? What the hell for, Cal? Am I in trouble for dealing with you and the PX store?"

He was speaking softly now so that he would be out of earshot of Mrs. Fenchurch as he didn't want any embarrassment.

Cal responded gently, "No, no, Don. He wants to describe the incident about the light in the sky the other night as he believes you may have raised it with the local press."

Donald was practically whispering now, although he need not have worried as Mrs. Fenchurch was busying herself in the kitchen.

"Cal, how the fucking hell would he know that I saw the damn light?"

Cal paused and said, "Because I told him, Don. He wanted to know where I had gone off duty that night and who I had seen, as that balloon had been my responsibility."

"So basically you need me to cover your backside, Cal, is that it?"

"Well, yeh, that's pretty much it. Will you come?"

"I can't get there til around 6:30 after work, if that's okay?"

Cal replied, "Okay, that's great. I'll tell the Old Man we're on for that time. Thanks pal."

"Thanks for nothing," said Donald and put the phone down.

He now thought about his current problem with the break-in. In fact upon reflection, he realized there had been no break-in. The thug had entered without breaking or forcing anything and must have a key of some sort.

Walking into the kitchen, he smiled at Mrs. Fenchurch and said, "Look, nothing was taken, nothing has been broken, and maybe you forgot to lock the door, so I don't think we need to get the police involved in this do you?"

He hated suggesting her memory was fading, but he felt he needed to get some advice about all this from Harry Sloan and maybe his cronies in London.

Mrs. Fenchurch agreed as she didn't want nosey neighbors looking on if the police came checking on the incident.

ZJTPQAUWEH

The Intelligence Plan

Major Wallace had received a secret cable with information from HQ that British Intelligence working on the Kammler case was supposed to have obtained a coded message via a local Polish emigré. The message had been inadvertently and, perhaps, innocently intercepted by a local man and deciphered by an ex-intelligence officer friend. The friend, realizing this was probably no prank or scribbling, had reported it to a colleague currently in the SIS in London.

Based on this information which was only partial, MI6 wanted a meeting with their US counterpart in the Kammler project to discuss strategy and to determine if there was a second part to the message that their local man may still have.   They named the local man as Donald Harvey, and it was this that got Major Wallace's attention in a hurry.

He quickly arranged a staff car to drive him to London. He was in civilian clothes, and he had the driver drop him off at Paddington Station. He walked into the station cafe near the platforms, getting away from the noise, the steam, and smoke coming from the train engines waiting to leave for their respective destinations. He ordered a coffee and, after the first taste, wondered how the Brits could drink the stuff. Whenever he was a guest at a Brit's house, they would always seem to fetch the Camp Coffee, which was a liquid mixture of coffee and chicory. Boiling water would be poured onto it in the cup and, if he didn't stop them, a helping of creamy milk would be added and stirred.

He sat there for a while and when the next train came steaming into the station, he got up and joined the large crowd as they jostled out of the building into the street where he jumped in a taxi.

"Where to, guv?" asked the driver.

"The Dickens Inn at St Katherine Docks," replied Wallace.

"Right, mate, you going to visit the Tower of London while you're here then, cos it's just rand the corner ya know?" piped up the Cockney driver.

"Well, I may if I have time," replied Wallace. "What makes you think I'm just visiting?"

"Oh, Gawd, blimey cock, you're not exactly a local yokel with an accent like that. You from New York or somefing, then?"

"Not too far," replied the officer, laughing at this cheerful taxi driver.

The taxi wound its way through central London passing some famous landmarks, and Wallace noticed areas where buildings had not yet been replaced and bombed out shells of others still remained in some places. The city was also grey and yellow with smog, and he was glad his base was situated in the country.

Leaving Westminster and driving past Trafalgar Square, Wallace imagined Churchill addressing the British people during the war. Passing Convent Garden on the Strand which was full of double decker buses rushing to points in and around London, he could see the pride and spirit of the ordinary people as they tried to rise above the remnants of war. Wallace simply marveled at the resilience and fortitude of the British and knew that the great sacrifices his own people had made on their behalf were something that would bind them forever. Or would it? He reflected to himself that history in the minds of those that made it, was like a vivid movie documentary, but as the generations pass; the movie images become scratched and grainy. Eventually, without specific efforts of dedicated people and institutions, the documentary is nothing more than a myth or legend, its veracity dependent upon those telling it. Worse still, leaders of nations for their own political reasons, can institute revisionist educational reforms that eviscerate the remainder of the documentary.

As Wallace watched the London scene pass by his taxi window, he pondered further about the future of Britain. Although most foodstuffs and goods were no longer rationed, it was only in July this year that meat and sugar were removed from rationing. The Conservative Party had gained power over the Labour Party in 1951, which had led to Winston Churchill being re-elected as Prime Minister. However, the Labour party had instituted such a massive socialist program of nationalization after the war that it would take generations to undo by successive governments. The health system was nationalized and, although doctors were now directed and paid by the government, bureaucracy and officialdom were hurting the efficiency of the system. British friends of the Wallace's were grumbling about crowded waiting rooms everywhere. Railways had been nationalized, along with road services for the transport of goods. The red lorries of the British Road Services were ubiquitous throughout the country. Entitlements of unemployment pay or 'the dole' as it was known, together with many other benefits legislated by the Labour party, enhanced the power of the union movement but also encouraged increased dissent in labor relations.

Wallace worried this trend toward increased government control of the economy in Britain and other parts of Europe could lead to problems in the future. After all, weren't the socialist programs of the Nazi Party in Germany the cause of eventual totalitarian rule in that country? As an American, he felt comfortable that he lived in a society governed by a Constitution that emphasized freedom and limited government that would ensure a peaceful and prosperous population to thrive. He did feel proud that the Marshall Plan to rebuild Europe was a magnanimous gesture on the part of the USA.

"There's the Tower of London on the left," the taxi driver called out, bringing Major Wallace out of his introspective thoughts.

"That's a really old edifice, isn't it?" remarked Wallace.

"If you mean it's an old buildin', mate, you're absolutely right," the driver said. "I mean the bloody Normans came over from France in 1066 and clobbered our King Harold, stuck him in the eye wiv an arrer and theys never left since. Then, when them Frenchys came here and saw a Roman Fort, they rebuilt the thing so theys could keep us Londoners under control."

"And did it work?" asked Wallace smiling.

"Na, I ain't speaking French am I?" he shot back quick as a flash. "Well, here you are mate, we've arrived."

Major Wallace paid him his fare plus a generous tip and thanked him.

The driver whistled and said, "Thanks, guvner, that'll help the missus get herself some stockings at Woolworth's and a pint of Guinness for me."

He drove off leaving Wallace at the Dickens Inn entrance.

He walked inside and was met immediately by Roger Bates who greeted him, "Hello, Major Wallace?"

"How do you know it was me? I guess you are Robert Bates, who I am supposed to meet?"

"Well, of course, Major. In our respective professions we make some form of preparation. I have a photo from the Ministry of Defense in Whitehall showing your command protocol for the Dawes Hill Air Force Base."

"Very good," replied the Major.

Bates led him to a private function room at the back of the inn, and as he entered a large man rose from his chair stretching out his hand in greeting.

Bates said, "This is Colonel Blignaught who is the Head of Section 6 at SIS."

"Pleased to meet you at last, Major, and my apologies for the cock up over the dead letter drop fiasco."

"Likewise Colonel, and I am anxious to learn where we stand right now."

The three of them settled down, and Richard Bates then gave Major Wallace a full briefing of how they eventually came into possession of the deciphered note, and why they were now concerned that another part of the note was missing. It was agreed that Petrowski could be tracked down to what appeared to be an address in Paris, France, but the missing part of the note may have critical implications.

Wallace had asked who was the local man who had discovered the note in High Wycombe, and he was told it was a Donald Harvey.

Wallace said in a shocked tone, "I'm not sure if we have a coincidence here, but I know who this man is. He is a friend of one of my men."

Bates spoke up saying, "I don't think you have anything to worry about there from a security aspect, as we've already checked him out. He holds a senior engineering management position with a company called Trandect Engineering Ltd. He handles some their sophisticated manufacturing in thermoplastics, as well as their aircraft instrument refurbishment division. He works with some of Britain's top aircraft defense contractors."

Colonel Blignaught then interjected, "Major, I would like to propose an unconventional way that we could run this project of finding Herr Kammler. First of all, we should treat it as a Nazi hunting project. After all, Kammler had some key responsibilities in the demolition of the Warsaw Ghetto in retaliation for the uprising there in 1943, plus all of his supervision of the various Jewish extermination camps before that period. Secondly, we should try to co-opt Mr. Harvey to act on behalf of British and American interests and use his position as a cover for our search of Kammler. We do not need to reveal to him our real cause of finding Kammler concerning the so-called 'Death Bell' or super weapon. That aspect would become apparent to him in due course anyway."

The Colonel paused, waiting for Major Wallace's reaction.

Major Wallace thought for a full two or three minutes before replying, "I will, of course, have to run this by our new CIA people who, after all, were the ones who wanted me as a top intelligence officer in the military to handle this project because of what could be technical, engineering, or even nuclear aspects to the outcome."

"In principle, I believe I have a good plan to co-opt your man Harvey."

Wallace then described how Harvey had been querying the early balloon lift off with one of Major Wallace's men and how UFO hysteria had then arisen in High Wycombe.

"Now you gentlemen are aware of our real functions with some of the 'weather balloons' in spying over the Soviet Union."

"Yes, of course, the Ministry of Defense has informed us of that," said the Colonel, "although Bates here was not aware of it til now." Richard looked surprised but did not make further enquiry into the subject.

Richard asked the Major, "So how will you be able to co-opt Harvey exactly?"

Wallace indicated that Donald Harvey had been engaged in some trivial black market activity with liquor and tobacco from the American PX on the base. He would have Master Sergeant Jennings invite Harvey to meet with Wallace to discuss the balloon incident. Wallace will shock Harvey by asking him about Petrowski. This fact alone should wake him up as to the situation he now finds himself in. He would soften him up a little further by mentioning the black marketing of USA goods and flouting Britain's Customs and Excise licensing laws.

Colonel Blignaught thought this would work, and we should also appeal to Harvey's loyalty to Queen and country. He should be told that he would be working for both the USA and the United Kingdom. The Colonel went on to say we could have him go to Paris on a mission for Trandect where he would be trying to negotiate contracts with NATO air forces at Supreme Headquarters Allied Powers Europe (SHAPE). This then would be his ideal cover for quietly finding Petrowski and obtaining further information. The balance of the original message was still a problem, however.

It was agreed this would be the first step in recruiting Donald Harvey, and a final plan would be devised at a later meeting.

Major Wallace had one further question for the SIS officers. "Who was the person who dropped the note, and why could he or she not be interrogated?" he asked.

"Ah," said the Colonel, "I'll let Richard here answer that one."

Richard then explained, "Our SIS agent in Poland has the connection to the Poland Underground State, the resistance movement in that country. It was one of their people who is resident in England who had been instructed to leave a message pre-encoded by a one-time pad at a designated dead letter drop off. The drop off had been the High Wycombe Church pre-arranged by our SIS agent in Poland. The local PU agent in Wycombe would have had no idea of the message content or have the key for decoding it. Of course we had the key, but, unfortunately, no message! Now we just need the lost piece of message. Because of the logistical difficulty, there had been no specific date or time of drop off; only a small range of days.

However, even from day one of that period, Harvey must have intercepted the message. One of our SIS people had been ready to retrieve it on any one of the specified days. Our SIS chap in Poland has been trying to get an identification of their chap who would have dropped the message, but they are now very apprehensive about releasing that information for fear of exposing him. They are worried about the Russian NKVD."

Richard concluded, "So you can see we have a lot invested in Donald Harvey."

"Yeh, I can see that absolutely," responded Wallace. "Let me see how we can pull this thing together, and we will coordinate our next meeting after I have spoken to Harvey."

They shook hands and left the Dickens Inn separately.

Donald Thinks About His Upcoming Meeting

Donald strolled into Trandect's front entrance and greeted Jill, "Good morning, Jill," he called out to her as he passed by on his way to his office.

She coughed, "Morning, Donald. Hope you had a good trip to Farnborough."

He responded, "It was interesting and hopefully we'll be able sign a couple of new contracts."

Bill Richardson came into Donald's office with a cheery, "Morning, Donald. I've been enjoying my cigars, although the Missus would prefer the smoke to be outside in the coal shed."

They both laughed at that.

Bill said, "When you've got some time today, I want you to look at this new Gyroscopic Direction Finder. We are going to be getting some of these from Sperry for overhaul and re-calibration."

Donald gave the instrument a cursory look and replied, "I'll see who we can allocate this to later, after I have looked over the Plastics Department this morning."

Bill said, "Oh, by the way, young Tommy Thompson in the instrument lab is asking if he can get a couple of cartons of Lucky Strike or Camel fags."

"Well, as a matter of fact I'm meeting my mate, the master sergeant, over at the base tonight, so I'll see what I can do," replied Donald.

The rest of the day went slowly for Donald as he was anxious about meeting the base commander and found it difficult to understand why he was being singled out for the enquiry. After all, it was virtually impossible for a non-Yank to get on that facility. The only time he had been on the base was when he had snuck in with a group of the guys when everyone was in civvies and the guard thought he was one of them flashing their passes.

He had been fascinated by the orderly appearance of the place and how it looked like some kind of village on the surface. He knew superficially, however, that there was a deep underground warren of floors and halls that defined the real purpose of the operations taking place there.

Donald was more interested in the camp's PX where all kinds of American goods were on sale — foodstuffs, clothing, tobacco, booze, etc. All unobtainable in England but with some cooperation here and there, he was able secure a small quantity of things that his customers craved. Donald sometimes wore a light colored wind-cheater jacket that Cal Jennings had bought for him, and so he often looked like a Yank in civvies himself.

The day ended uneventfully, and he bade goodnight to everyone and made off toward Marlow Hill and destiny.

Confronted With Reality

Donald walked briskly up Marlow Hill past the Abbey School for Girls. The Abbey had been the Headquarters of the US Eighth Army Air Force Bomber Command during the last war, coupled with the underground base to which he was now headed. The school had reverted back to being an elite educational establishment for the daughters of some of Britain's wealthiest families.

Reaching further up the hill, he turned left onto Dawes Hill Lane and made his way to the Main Gate of the US Eighth Air Force 7th Air Division. A single guard was on duty dressed in full uniform with the white belt and white helmet of a Military Policeman.

Donald thought to himself, *having seen these chaps on duty in town keeping the Yanks out of fights, sometimes arresting and chucking them into a jeep before sending them off to the brig, I wouldn't want to mess with these blokes.*

The sentry he approached was at least 6'4", had a massive chest and, if that wasn't enough, he carried an M1 carbine.

He did, however, greet Donald courteously, "Can I help you, sir?"

Donald nodded saying, "I have a meeting at 7:00 p.m. with Major Wallace."

The sentry stepped backwards into his box, scanned a large book and finding what he wanted stepped back toward Donald.

"Yes, sir, I need to call through to Master Sergeant Jennings to escort you to the Major's office."

With that he turned, picked up his intercom telephone, and rang through to Operations.

In a short while Cal Jennings appeared and greeted Donald with, "Hi, pal. You ready to meet the boss?"

"Not really," said Donald, "But I suppose it's unique being inside this place officially."

Donald followed alongside Cal as he briskly walked through the complex toward a low, well-lit building. They entered and were met by a non-com who told them to wait while he entered Major Wallace's office to announce them.

He came back out and said, "You can go in. He's ready for you."

Cal entered first and introduced Donald to Major Wallace.

"Nice to meet you, Mr. Harvey," drawled the Major while slowly chewing on his gum.

He continued eyeing Donald up and down while Donald was returning salutations, "I'm pleased to make your acquaintance although, I'm not sure I'm pleased to be here, sir."

Wallace thought, *ornery young devil, but courteous enough, though.*

"Please take a seat, Mr Harvey. Will you have some coffee or tea maybe? I don't have any Canadian V.O., I'm afraid, but then it's a little early in the evening for socializing."

Both Cal and Donald appeared a little startled by the Major's comment, and he was smiling rather benignly, but with a purposeful stare.

The Major turned to Cal and said, "Sergeant, you can leave Mr. Harvey and I to talk for a while, and I will have Lt. Bailey escort Mr Harvey to the gate when it's time to leave."

"Yes, sir, Major. I'll get back to the billet."

Cal glanced at Donald who had looked puzzled and slightly anxious since the Canadian booze reference, "See you later."

Donald nodded.

Major Wallace sat opposite and said, "Do you mind if I call you Donald?"

"Not at all," he replied. "I believe you wanted to discuss something about the light in the sky."

Wallace looked at Donald carefully and asked, "What is it you thought you saw that night. Donald?"

Donald said, "Frankly, sir, I haven't a clue what it was, but it most certainly was an odd sight for this part of the world. Cal had told me it was part of a weather reporting system using high altitude balloons."

Wallace agreed saying, "Cal was right, and we just want to make sure that the general public doesn't draw the wrong conclusions about our activity here. Your close relationship with this base can help dispel any rumors, right?"

Donald was wondering if he meant his close relationship with the PX store.

"Well, sir, I don't think I'm in any position to dispel rumors. I'm just an engineering manager and have nothing to do with newspapers or radio."

"Well, I guess so," drawled Wallace chewing slowly, "Plus I assume, too, that if people thought a sighting like that was a UFO, it would be a pretty good distraction away from our weather balloons?"

"But if people thought the Wycombe base was involved with UFOs, it would bring even more attention to it, would it not?" asked Donald.

The major replied, "You're right, of course, and I think we can move on from this subject," and without pausing for breath he quickly asked Donald, "What do you know about Petrowski?"

Donald nearly jumped out of his skin. He endeavored to compose himself before replying, "Uh, Petrowski?"

Major Wallace looked at him sternly and began to question him, "Look, Donald. I do not want to bring the local authorities here on this base to discuss your indiscretions regarding your black marketing efforts of American Air Force goods. However, there are some much more important things we need to discuss and for which I believe you have the answers to."

"Now," he went on, "Obviously you are not under any threat of arrest from me on this base, and you are free to leave at any moment you say so. However, just bear in mind my PX store would have to report to the Wycombe Customs and Excise Agents some activities that could incriminate you and also any accomplice you've had in the past."

"What is it you want from me?" asked Donald, who was now quite shaken by the turn of events.

"Look, Donald," said Wallace, "You have become involved, whether you like it or not, in something much bigger and more sinister than weather balloons. You have intercepted a message that carries some key information that our intelligence service is seeking. Also, there are other forces seeking this information, and this could become hazardous to your health. Donald, we need your cooperation, and you need our protection."

Donald immediately thought of the intruder at his lodgings, the person at the church, and also at Farnborough.

"Major Wallace," he asked nervously, "When you say 'we,' who are you referring to?"

"The British Secret Service, Donald," replied the Major.

"Oh my God, why did I ever pick up that note?" said Donald.

Wallace went on to describe how SIS had obtained the note indirectly through Roger Hewitt-Benning and had it translated into Polish. He told Donald that he needed to try and find the other part of the note that was missing. He said that they, the US and the British, had agreed they would try to recruit Donald for a mission to Paris to find Petrowski since Donald's job would be a perfect cover it.

"What job could I being doing in Paris?" asked Donald.

Wallace told him, "Look, the Brits know everything about you, your expertise in the aircraft industry, etc. We would have you set up to meet a number of foreign air force attaches of our Allies at the Supreme Headquarters of Allied Powers Europe."

"How will my boss at Trandect find how I get contacts at that level?" enquired Donald incredulously.

"Don't you worry about that. The Brit's SIS will handle that for you."

Donald was still hesitant. "What is so sinister about this affair and why pick on me for such an assignment?" he asked.

Major Wallace explained in as much detail as he could, the background to the mission of finding Herr Heinz Kammler. He described Kammler's role in the construction of the Nazi death camps, the destruction of the Warsaw ghetto, and his final role at the end of the war in special technology development. Wallace went on to discuss how the Russians would be anxious to capture Kammler for his knowledge, and the West would be happy to get him for the same reason.

"Wouldn't he be more of a target as a Nazi war criminal?" asked Donald.

"Well, of course," Wallace responded, "that would be hanging over his head in the form of a bargaining chip, wouldn't it?"

Donald thought, *How can anyone negotiate with a war criminal who was an accomplice to six million Jews being slaughtered, not to say countless numbers of innocent Poles who went to their deaths or were enslaved for the German war machine?*

"What kind of technology is he thought to have developed," asked Donald, "especially to turn a blind eye to this chap's blood-stained hands?"

"We don't know exactly, but from rumors and small clues it may be world shattering. We do know that their scientists were deep into quantum physics, and Kammler would have been fully in charge of any projects like that. We don't want him or his technology getting into anyone else's hands other than our own."

Major Wallace looked sternly at Donald and in a commanding voice said, "Donald, we don't know for sure what we are dealing with, but if it should be of really major significance, then better us to have it than our enemies, right?"

Donald proffered, "I suppose you're right in the sense that avenging the death of millions with the hanging of one man seems so futile in the overall scheme of your objective, Major."

"Chewing on his gum, the Major spoke softly but firmly and in deadly earnest, "If the mission were to simply catch a Nazi war criminal with murder on his hands, I for one would be happy to cast the rope around the bastard's neck myself, without hesitation. However, if that bastard has the means to elevate a nation's military superiority over everyone else, for the sake of the planet's survival, it had better be the United States of America who gets it."

He went on some more, "But, Donald. All we are asking you to do is to quietly track down Petrowski and find out what is meant by the 'Death Bell' and what is meant by the 'leader' in the Note. In any event, you may be able to negotiate a contract or two from some members of SHAPE."

"Can we count on you, Donald?"

"How can I refuse?" said Donald resignedly looking at Major Wallace. "What do you want me to do next?"

"I want you to shake my hand and, on that basis, I will arrange for you to meet your British counterparts who will complete a full background check and have you sworn in as an unpaid volunteer in Her Majesty's Secret Service. Of course, I don't need to tell you that you should not say anything to anyone about our discussion this evening. Obviously, we would not want to break your cover on the outside, so your acceptance of our little mission would enable you to continue your little marketing efforts with the PX. Legally, you would be considered a member of our counterparts in the British Secret Intelligence Service and, therefore, eligible to purchase goods to a certain limit. Your non-acceptance would make it difficult to withhold our reporting obligation."

Major Wallace put his hand out, and Donald, after a little hesitation, shook it.

Wallace smiled saying, "Don't worry. We'll look after you."

Don looked at him as he got up and said, "Well, Major, you had better, because someone is out to get what I have." He then went on to describe the incident at the church, at Farnborough and at his lodging. He also described who he thought was the courier for the message — Karol Zaluski, his girlfriend's uncle.

"This stranger is obviously a Russian agent who gets his orders from the Embassy in London," remarked Wallace. "They must have their own people in Poland trying to track down the information we now have. Donald, what concerns me is, if he bumped into you near the church the night you found the Note, he probably knows it was Zaluski who left it there. He may try to confront Zakuski although it's unlikely, as he must know that Zaluski is just the courier. That's why it was he who got into your lodging looking for the Note, thinking you wouldn't know what it was anyway."

"I assume you're right, Major. I just hope he does not try again," Donald said with a worried look on his face. "By the way, what about Cal Jennings? What do I say to him about tonight's conversation with the base commander, no less?"

The Major replied, "You just received a little chat about weather reporting systems and how they are used for the US Air Force Strategic Air Command and, in fact, some information is shared with your own Royal Air Force. I'll make sure he knows he can continue to provide PX service to you, within limits, and that you have reciprocity because of your Air Force reserve status."

"But I don't have such reciprocity," said Donald.

"I know," replied Wallace, "But Jennings doesn't know that!"

Wallace turned to Donald and said, "Okay, you ready to go?"

"I just have one more question. Who am I going to be reporting to or who will be directing me in this?"

"In your case it will be the British, however, because this is primarily a US initiative but in partnership with the British, I, as the lead US Intelligence Officer, will be following you closely. As I said before we collectively will be looking after you. I will be in touch with you once I arrange the meeting for you with British Intelligence."

Major Wallace opened his office door and told the non-com attendant to call Lieutenant Bailey to escort Donald to the front gate. A few minutes later Lieutenant Bailey came by and Donald shook hands again with Major Wallace and accompanied the Lieutenant to the main gate.

As Donald was walking briskly away, he suddenly stopped halfway back along the Dawes Hill Lane leading to Marlow Hill, and said to himself, *Oh, shit! I completely forgot about the second piece of paper belonging to the Note in my wallet.*

There was no point in going back to tell Wallace, so he decided he would just leave it until he would meet the British Intelligence chaps.

Chapter 9

The Price Of Espionage

The Watching 'Falcon'

The Falcon (aka Igor Martinovich) stepped off the train at Wycombe Station from Iver in Buckinghamshire where he was living, and walked along the platform to the tunnel allowing him to cross to the other platform for London-bound trains. Showing his train ticket to the attendant at the exit who clipped it as he passed through to the street, he made his way along Totteridge Road for a short way. He stopped at a point where he could look over the wall and peer down on the railway tracks below. He had followed this procedure a few times in recent days in order to view the shunting operations where goods trains were being assembled. He had noted the three-chain-coupling method used on British goods trains that caused them to clatter so much as the trucks banged against each other.

Falcon began thinking about how he had been assigned this mission by his Controller. As a long time member of the NKVD covert division in the Russian- dominated Ukraine, he had been posted to operate in Poland. He had successful post-World War II missions dealing with the current Polish Underground State or resistance movement in Warsaw. His wartime experience for Russia had been invaluable. When Russia annexed part of Poland under the Soviet-German Pact of 1939, he had been part of the NKVD contingent that rounded up Poles for forced transfer to Siberia, and thousands had been executed on the order of Stalin. An estimated 22,000 were massacred in the Russian forest at Katyn, and Falcon had helped spearhead the capture and transport of those prisoners.

Later, when the Germans invaded Russia, they took over all of Poland, and the large population of Polish Jews became victims of the Holocaust, and thousands of non-Jews were enslaved to work for the Germans. Ukrainian Nationalists living in Poland were encouraged by the Nazis to kill Jewish Poles, and thousands were massacred by them. Falcon was an undercover NKVD officer and helped participate in this murder. As a Ukrainian and Polish National, he worked for a transport company but had ingratiated himself with the Germans for inciting other Ukrainian Nationalists to do the Nazi's bidding. In this position he was able to feed strategic intelligence on German forces in Poland back to Russia for the time when the Soviets re-entered Poland later in the war. Falcon had received the Soviet Medal, "Partisan of the Patriotic War," which was awarded for "Participation in the resistance against the Nazi invaders behind enemy lines."

The code name 'Falcon' had been bestowed on him for his ability to patiently wait and observe his 'prey' from a distance or from a height before swooping in for the 'kill.' It was the same as he was doing now, waiting and observing the routines of trains shunting below him, watching the movements of the men who ran alongside the rail trucks with their shunter poles hooking the couplings on the moving trucks. He made note of the small shed-like building on the far side of the tracks where one of the workmen would take shelter for a cigarette. Just beyond the shed was the embankment where it descended toward a low fence over which lay the footpath leading to Station Road. Falcon made a mental note that often a single rail truck, and sometimes several, would be shunted by the engine and the shunter assistant would switch the lever to divert the trucks to another rail where additional trucks were standing. The shunted trucks would by their own momentum move slowly down the selected line without a shunter assistant running alongside, until they reached the stationary ones where they would come to a clanging crashing halt as they collided buffer to buffer and coupling to coupling. These would be coupled together later.

He was making this reconnaissance to familiarize himself with the topography and layout of the Wycombe Station, so that a night-time visit here to swoop down on his target would be free of unknowns. The target for this mission would be Karol Zaluski, ex-Polish Free Army, probable agent for PUS in the UK, and a British Railways shunter assistant who only worked the grave yard shift, 10:00 p.m. to 6:00 a.m.

F Z Y E

Karol Zaluski

Karol Zaluski had received word through his sources in Poland that a Russian agent had been infiltrated into the UK specifically to hunt down and find the contents of the Note Zaluski was to pass on. Zaluski had no idea of the Note's contents or its significance, other than it was of major importance to the USA and Britain. The Note had come to him via East Germany, then West Germany together with his drop instructions. He was simply a courier in the UK on behalf of the Polish State Underground Resistance Movement. Nevertheless, he was still sufficiently worried that an NKVD agent may be looking for him. Zaluski's informal contacts with other Polish re-settlement camps in the UK had been keeping an eye out for potential spies or impostors who might be living among them.

While having coffee with some fellow Poles at the Corner Cafe recently, one of them had said his brother at the Camp in Iver in Buckinghamshire had spotted a suspicious character. He said the man was supposed to be an ex-Polish Free Army fellow, but it was thought that he might be Ukrainian, due to the way he spoke Polish. He was fluent, but the hint of Ukrainian origin made his brother uneasy, especially as he spoke very little and had no family. The man had identity papers as Tomasz Bielski. He, like a number of the others in that camp, was a squatter with nowhere else to go.

Another worry he had now was that he had received word the note he left at the designated dead letter drop had been intercepted. He was still awaiting further instructions on how he should proceed.

Karol Zaluski had quietly made a name for himself back in Poland. Before coming to England, he had been in transition camps in Allied-controlled Europe. He had worked with some of the Holocaust investigators, and he had identified several of the Ukrainians who had been members of the Soviet Union's NKVD that had rounded up thousands of his fellow Poles, beaten him, his family and some of his extended family. He mentioned one man in particular who had viciously beaten his sister, brother-in-law, and their 11-year-old daughter. The man's name was Igor Martinovich, who he thought could not have been much older than 22 or 23 or so, but he had the hatred of an older man.

The investigators never found this individual and suspected he had either died in the war or had disappeared into the Soviet Union.

As Zaluski prepared for his night shift at the railway shunting yard, it was the thought of his niece, Alicja, that crossed his mind. He walked across the camp grounds to the Nissen hut where the

Kozlowski's lived. They had made a little garden with some colorful primroses, together with a tiny vegetable garden growing a few parsnips and carrots.

He knocked on the door which, Dymtri answered saying, "Witaj, Karol, co ci tu sprowadza, wejd " (Hello, Karol. What brings you here? Come on in.).

Karol stepped inside the neat and tidy home.

"I just wanted to bring to your attention that there's a new emigré in the Polish community, and he is living by himself in the Grover Park Camp site in Iver," announced Karol.

Dymtri replied, "Well, I don't think he will get to stay there for long because I heard the authorities down there have issued notices to residents that they are squatting illegally."

Karol said, "Yes, that's true, and it's been in force for quite a while, but they seem to be giving everyone time to find or apply for alternative accommodation."

"Anyway, Karol," responded Dymtri, "Why have you got so much interest in this guy? What's his name anyway?"

Karol said, "His name is Tomasz Bielski, and he is an ex-Free Army soldier. I was wondering, Dymtri, as you are president of the Veterans of the Polish Free Army, if you could make some enquiries as to the veracity of this individual? No one seems to know him and, based on my informant, they don't feel comfortable around him."

"Okay, Karol, I will put this on the agenda for our next meeting and see we can get him vouched for," Dymtri smiled.

Karol looked at him and said, "Just make sure you put it on the agenda above the football team selection process!"

Dymtri laughed but stopped when Karol looked seriously at him. Just then Alicja and her mother walked in with supper that they had prepared for the evening. They both greeted Karol, and Alicja kissed him saying, "Hello, Uncle Karol. Are you going to stay for supper?"

"Nie dzi mało siostrzenica," (Not tonight, Little Niece) he said, "I have to get ready for my shift this evening, but thank you anyway. By the way, how's that nice young man you're dating?"

Alicja blushed and said, "Oh, he's wonderful, Uncle Karol. I think I'm falling in love."

"Well, I'm sure your parents will be keeping up with that," he said with a rare smile.

Karol said goodbye and opened the door to step outside, turning for one more look at the Kozlowski family and strode off down the path.

"The Accident"

Karol Zaluski got on the Wycombe-bound double decker red Thames Valley bus, which was the last one for the night, took a seat near the entrance, and paid his fare to the conductor who gave him his ticket. He sat thinking of the hard night's work ahead and how his life had been one long roller coaster. Imprisoned in Siberia where he lost his wife to starvation, fighting in the war through North Africa and in Italy, and now fighting the Soviet's occupation of his homeland through subterfuge.

The bus stopped a couple of times to pick up one or two passengers, mostly young men, who probably had escorted their girlfriends home and were now making the return trip to their own destinations.

At last the bus reached the Amersham Road stop just before Castle Street near the railway station. Karol picked up his satchel containing lunch and thermos flask of hot tea and stepped down on the pavement. Polish men could often be identified because they would carry a leather satchel that would give them an appearance of important businessmen. Most people knew, however, that as in Karol Zaluski's case, it might carry nothing more than their lunch.

The air was brisk, and it was a cloudy night with poor visibility. He did not like these kinds of working conditions because even though the rail yards were well lit, visibility was much better on clear nights, especially if there was a moon and that made for much safer shunting when trying to couple rail trucks together.

He went through the station and to the end of the platform where he jumped down and made is way across the multiple tracks to the shunter's station to clock in. The one thing the boss liked about Karol was his on-time record. He was never late and had only been off sick once.

"Watcha mate," shouted Jimmy Hoskins, Karol's shunting partner that night, as he, too, clocked in.

"Hello, Jimmy. Hope we don't have too much on tonight," said Karol.

"I'll check with the foreman to see what's on the sheet for this shift," Jimmy replied. "There's a bloody lot'a coal trucks out there tonight."

Karol agreed and picked up his shunter's pole, which was 5'6" long with a tapered steel hook on the end, and marched off with Jimmy to look for the foreman, Tom Saunders, who was the night supervisor that week. They found him next to the shunting engine, talking to the driver and giving instructions for the night's work.

Tom Saunders greeted the two men and told them the schedule for the night, and then he moved off to the shunter's station. The shunt locomotive driver, Phil Green, said, "Okay, mate, who's gonna' take the first bunch? We gonna' take those six coal wagons over there and run 'em down to the Number 6 track to make up the train for Swindon. We've already got twenty-five out of fifty attached."

Karol said he would, while Jimmy ran the switch for the track. He quickly walked off down Track 6 to wait for the coal wagons to arrive. It was almost pitch black and very little light was reaching the area where he was to couple the incoming wagons to the stationary ones. For some intuitive reason, he felt he was being watched but, looking around, saw nothing. He shrugged it off as he saw the wagons approaching, and the noise of the steam engine with a shrill warning whistle from the locomotive made him pay attention to his job. As the lead wagon came into view and slowly rolled toward him, he moved his pole and caught the hook on the chain coupler and lifted it, then dropped it cleanly over the coupling of the stationary truck as they collided buffer to buffer with a huge clang and crash. He walked back along the track to see where his next load would be. Jimmy handled the next one on Track 3, which consisted of four wagons of cement to make up part of a mixed train.

Falcon had been carefully watching from a safe distance in total darkness near the embankment. He had come along Queens Road, then into Station Road and, without being seen, had jumped the fence and moved to his present position. He had watched Zaluski performing his shunting duties as he had on previous nights, *but tonight will be a different shunting function*, he said to himself in a grinning snarl.

The Falcon positioned himself in the darkest area of Track 8, which was the furthest away from the shunting station, and was the track already containing around thirty wagons of coal. He knew that the procedure with Track 8 was that the shunt engine would gently push about six wagons from the main line, where Jimmy would throw the switch to divert them to Track 8 allowing them to slowly roll under their own gravity about three hundred yards toward the stationary wagons. At this point Zaluski would be taking a quick break with his thermos flask in the small open shed just next to the end of Track 8. His job would be to wait for the incoming wagons and, as soon as they meet up with the stationary group, he would couple up the the two connecting wagons. This required a lot of skill if the incoming group was coming too fast, but Phil Green was one of the best shunter drivers and usually he had those trucks moving at just the right speed.

Falcon slipped quietly toward the shed as soon as he spied the engine in the far distance hooking up the wagons for Track 8. His eyes were now well accustomed to the night's darkness as he had been in position for a few hours. In the blackness he made out Zaluski with his thermos and the red glow of his cigarette.

As Falcon moved quietly to within just a few feet of him, he spoke softly, "Witaj Karol Załuski, wi c to, co jest litle zdrajc robisz dzi wieczorem?" (Hello Karol Zaluski, so what is the little traitor doing tonight?)

Zaluski spun around, dropping his thermos and cigarette, and cried out. "Kim jeste i czego chcesz?" (Who are you and what do you want?).

Almost instantly, Zaluski recognized Falcon and shouted. "Igor Martinovich, you bastard!"

Although Zaluski was momentarily stunned, his survival instincts from years of hardship suddenly kicked in, and as Falcon lunged at him he turned back to the shed and grabbed his shunter's pole. Just as Falcon grabbed him, Zaluski shoved him away with the pole. He then turned the pole and rammed the hook into Falcon's chest who roared in pain. With blood pouring from his wound, he was now like a dangerous animal, and all of his killer experience and instincts came to him in one mad feat of strength. In a split second he had pulled the pole away from Zaluski and threw it on the ground, and he placed Zaluski in a classic choke hold before he could move. He dragged Zaluski over to the stationary wagons and, looking up the line, he could just see the outline of the incoming wagons slowly rolling down toward them.

He began putting pressure on Zaluski's carotid artery, which caused the man to weaken and brought him close to passing out. Falcon moved him nearer to the wagon's buffers.

Zaluski, realizing what was happening, began struggling harder, but a further squeeze of his artery immobilized him.

"What was in the note you dropped?" asked Falcon.

"I don't know. It was blank paper," Zaluski sputtered.

"Who was supposed to pick it up?" Falcon growled.

"I don't ....know. I just was told to to to.....leave it there," gasped Zaluski faintly.

Falcon looked up to see that the incoming wagons were about a hundred feet away.

Falcon growled, "Who is Donald Harvey? Was he the pick up? He was at the church?"

Surprised and almost unconscious, Zaluski did not want to endanger his own niece, and he gurgled, straining to keep conscious, "I don't know him."

"What about the red hymn book? We know that's where it was supposed to be left?"

"That's where it was left," Zaluski gasped in relief, knowing Igor Martinovich had not got the note.

Falcon applied more pressure on Zaluski's neck, and he passed out. Keeping the hold for a few more seconds as the trucks came in, Falcon quickly pushed Zaluski over and in front of the buffers as they met with the stationary wagons.

The crashing noise of all the wagons together drowned the sound of the crushed body that lay between them with its bones, blood and flesh exposed. With adrenaline still at a high level, Falcon began moving away carefully. Like the skilled killer he was, he had taken care to move away at impact to avoid blood spatter, but he could not avoid his own blood seeping through his clothing. Now, as he made his way to the perimeter of the railyard and over the fence to Station Road, the pain in his chest began to take hold. He put his hand up to the wound. It felt warm and sticky.

Falcon knew he needed to get medical treatment as his shirt was now soaked in blood, and he would be the center of attention if he tried to get back to Grover Park tonight. To reach Wycombe Hospital, he would have to take a diversionary route to keep away from as many street lights as possible, so he turned and headed to the London Road. Although traffic was very light at this time of night, he waited in the shadows until he was sure it was all clear. He then crossed over and quickly made his way to the Rye which was, as always, in darkness.

Under this cover he made his way toward Abbey Way, then a short walk up Marlow Hill before arriving at the hospital. He was able to make it to the facility's main entrance before almost collapsing, but with the strength of a bear, the Falcon made it to the reception area where the night duty staff immediately took charge of him.

As two nurses began removing his jacket and shirt which were soaked in blood, the duty physician, Dr. Maurice Rose, began asking him about the cause of his wound.

Falcon had been trying to think of a plausible reason all the way to the hospital, and now he thought he had one.

"Well, Doctor," Falcon said in his Ukrainian/Polish accent. "I was on my way to the station when I realized I was late to catch the 12:30

a.m. London train, so I thought I would take a short cut. I jumped over the fence near Station Road. It was the section that has the cast iron railings with tall spikes on top. Unfortunately I slipped and so, here I am."

Doctor Rose looked sympathetic, but inwardly he was skeptical as the injury looked like a stab wound to him.

The doctor said, "Well, I thought you had been in a fight because we do frequently get the Polish, Americans, English, and the Irish laborers here getting into some pretty big scraps after clashing in the pubs. You don't have to make up a story to protect anyone. We don't report these incidents. So where was the fight?"

Falcon turned his piercing gaze at Dr. Rose and replied, "There was no fight, Doctor."

His menacing look and firm manner were enough for the doctor to change the subject.

"All right, Mr., ah, sorry, we don't have your name yet?"

"Tomasz Bielski", offered the Falcon, "Polish Free Army emigré."

"Do you have your National Health Service Card, Mr. Bielski?"

"It's in my wallet in my jacket. Your nurse can get it."

"Thank you," responded the doctor. "Now lay back while my staff dresses your wound, and I will give you a shot of penicillin as an anti-tetanus precaution."

The nurse retrieved the NHS card, which the doctor casually looked at, and asked his her to contact the man's doctor in Iver to let him know the situation of his patient. Under the Nationalized Health System, the patient was obliged to have a single responsible primary care doctor specified on the NHS card. Therefore, it was a little surprising when the she came back some time later to inform Dr. Rose that there was no doctor in Iver registered by the name given on the NHS card. In fact, the Dr. John Mullally was not registered anywhere in the system at all.

Dr. Rose brushed it off saying, "There must be some mix-up with government red tape, as usual, so we will treat Mr. Bielski as we're supposed to."

The Police Report

Jimmy Hoskins had been waiting for Karol to return from Track 8 and was getting impatient, as it was time for his break. He kept peering down the line into the blackness, but the Pole still had not appeared.

Phil Green looked out of his side window on the shunter engine and shouted for Jimmy, "What's happening? Where's Zaluski?"

"I don't know, Phil. I'll have to go down Number 8 and see if he's still drinking 'is bloody tea." With that, he strode off to investigate. He approached the small shed area but did not see Zaluski. He went a little further, suddenly stopped, and he went cold.

Zaluski's shunting pole lay on the ground.

Jimmy crept forward slowly calling, "Karol, you all right, mate?"

He was using his torch now to illuminate the area, and then as he looked between the next two wagons, the ghastly sight of Zaluski's lifeless, crushed form between the buffers came into view. The gory image and the smell of blood filled him with dread, and the scream that he was involuntarily making just died in his throat, and no sound came out.

At last he found his voice and began running back up the track, shouting at the top of his voice. He could be heard above the noise of the rail yard, the steam engine, and the workshop on nightshift. Tom Saunders, the foreman, came out of his office, and others gathered round as Jimmy came running up.

Tom said, "What's up, Jimmy? You look like you've seen a ghost."

"Yes, mate; it's the ghost of Zaluski. He's smashed to pulp down there on track number 8."

"Oh, my God!" cried the foreman, "He would have to have an accident on my bloody shift," but quickly changed his tone saying, "Well, I'm really sorry. Zaluski's a good man and great worker. I'll call 999 and get an ambulance here right away, but from what you say, Jimmy, he's a goner!"

"He's gone all right. There's nothing left of him," said Jimmy.

The ambulance crew came, and a policeman made a report of the scene and tried to assess how the accident happened. He established the position of the corpse and also that of the shunting pole a little further away. The policeman's description also noted that, in addition to a large volume of blood around the corpse and wagon, it appeared there was blood on the hook, as well as some smears on the handle just above the hook.

Tom Saunders said he would call on the Hodgemoor Camp in the morning and give his condolences to any family members Zaluski had.

F Z Y E

Alicja Is Informed of Uncle's Death

The policeman, Jarvis, and Tom Saunders knocked on the Kozlowski's door of their Nissen hut home. Mrs. Kozlowski answered it and was shocked to see a constable standing there.

Tom spoke first, "Mrs. Kozlowski, we are coming to you as we understand you are a relative of Karol Zaluski?"

"Yes," she replied, "Is there anything wrong? Is he in some kind of trouble?"

"May we come in for a moment, Madam?" asked the policeman.

"Yes, please come in. I am terrified of what you are going to tell me."

They moved inside, and PC Jarvis stepped forward saying, "Madam, it's my sad duty to inform you, as you are his next of kin here, that Mr. Zaluski suffered an accident at his place of work and has passed away. He was taken to the Wycombe General Hospital where he was pronounced dead at 3:00 a.m. this morning."

Mrs. Kozlowski went very white, but steadied herself. She had encountered death and suffering in Eastern Europe to such an extent that news of that kind, while still distressing, she refused to cry in public. Tears for her were now a private occasion when she would sob into her pillow at night, as memories of cruelty, starvation, and death in Poland, Ukraine, and Siberia haunted her

"I will have to get in touch with my husband and daughter straight away," she exclaimed.

PC Jarvis touched her arm gently and said, "Mrs. Kozlowski, Mr. Saunders and I will go ourselves to inform them so you don't need to go out of your way, all right?"

"Thank you, so much," she replied as they prepared to leave.

"Again, we offer you our sincere condolences, Mrs. Kozlowski."

She thanked them again as they left.

Later, a much shaken Alicja hugged her mother as they wondered how this accident could have happened. She had heard from other people who worked on the railways that the shunter's job was probably the most dangerous one at British Railways. She could not believe her favorite uncle could be dead from an accident. She thought to herself that maybe Uncle Karol had been worried recently and was possibly distracted. The policeman had said that Uncle Karol had been crushed between wagons being shunted.

She decided she needed to get in touch with Donald and tell him about the accident. It was getting late in the evening, so Alicja ran to a neighbor who had a telephone in their hut.

Donald was listening to the latest news on his radio when Mrs. Fenchurch knocked on his door.

"It's your lady friend Miss Kozlowski," she said. "She sounds quite upset."

Donald got up quickly and went to the phone. "Hello, darling, I didn't expect to hear from you this evening."

"Oh, Donald, my Uncle Karol is dead," she cried out.

Donald could hear her sobbing, and he became silent in shock.

"What do you mean he's dead? How did he die Alicja? I'm so sorry."

Alicja explained there had been an accident at work, and he had been crushed between two wagons during a shunting operation. After they conversed for a while and Donald tried to comfort her, he said he would get back with her the day after tomorrow because he had to make an important trip to London the next morning.

The Coroner's Report and Detective Warner

The next day after the dreadful "accident," the Buckinghamshire coroner submitted his standard report which indicated Mr. Zaluski's cause of death was by a train accident at the shunting yards of High Wycombe Station.

At this time the local Superintendent at the Wycombe Police Station, James Watkins, was looking over the reports from the preceding night shift. In PC Jarvis's report, he noticed that the shunting pole had been found more than fifteen feet away from the scene of the accident.

Well, he mused, *the pole could have been knocked or simply flown out of the man's hands. But then, how could there be blood on the end?*

Just to be sure, he ordered that the pole which had been secured as part of the British Railways Accident Investigation Team be tested for blood type identification and have it matched with the Coroner's findings on the accident victim's blood type.

In a few hours he was stunned to learn he now had a murder investigation on his hands. He called in Detective John Warner and explained his concern.

"John, take a look at Jarvis's report on a nasty accident last night at the shunting yards," he said, looking over his glasses.

Detective Warner quickly read through the report and said, "I suppose you have had a blood type test done on the pole hook, and the result is you have called me in?"

"Right on, John," replied the Superintendent. "I think there is a badly injured assailant out there who needs medical treatment. Can you get on this and open a murder file?"

"Yes, sir, I'll get cracking immediately and talk to Jarvis first."

With that said Detective Warner got up and left the office.

After obtaining a first-hand report from PC Jarvis, Detective Warner contacted the Wycombe Hospital and was informed that there had been several accident victims in the last two days. Warner jumped into his Austin 8 and drove immediately to the hospital and asked for the doctor who had been on duty the night of the Zaluski accident.

Dr. Rose had just come on duty for the evening, and, yes, he remembered a particular individual by the name of Tomacz Bielski, a Polish emigré with a strong foreign accent, whom he thought had a rather suspicious wound in his upper left chest area. Dr. Rose then mentioned that his NHS card had what appeared to be a fake doctor's name recorded on it. There was no one by that name in Iver or anywhere else in Buckinghamshire.

To Detective Warner this was a major red flag because foreigners at this time who had official residency status in England were still restricted by having to register with a local police station. He asked Dr. Rose if Mr. Bielski's blood type had been recorded.

"As a matter of fact," said Dr. Rose, "we did take the precaution of testing his blood, as we were concerned about the amount he may have lost. We can get the administrator to check the records for you. I have to tell you, Officer, I thought his wound appeared to be more representative of a stab wound than the accident Mr Bielski had described. Is he wanted for anything serious?" he added.

"Let's just say," replied Warner, "I cannot give you specific details, but your information has been very helpful, and it may lead to Mr. Bielski wearing a tight scarf at some point."

He smiled at Dr. Rose who nodded knowingly.

Warner got up and shook Dr. Rose's hand, "Would you have your administrator telephone the police station and leave the blood type information for my attention? I need to get to broaden my investigation. Thank you."

Detective Warner left the hospital and headed for the railway station to interview Zaluski's co-workers. He would also need to meet with his relatives at Hodgemoor Resettlement Camp in Amersham.

Chapter 10

The New British Secret Agent

Donald's First Intelligence Meeting

Donald headed to Westminster after arriving at Paddington Station in London, by jumping in a taxi and requesting the driver to take him to 54 Broadway near St. James Park.

The driver grinned at him, "So you one o' them spies then, mate?"

Donald laughed and quipped back to this cheeky Cockney, "If I told you, yes, I'd have to kill you."

The driver with a wry grin on his face responded, "Oh, Gawd! We gotta a bloody comedian on board. That joke's so old I nearly died fallin' out of me cradle for that one."

Donald laughed again. He just loved being back in London, even while great attempts were being made to clear up the soot and smog, the good nature of Londoners could not be smothered. Through thick and thin, through the Blitz, the bombed out shells of buildings, the industrial pollution, and the traffic jams, nothing seemed to shake the resolve or the humor of its residents.

He arrived at his destination, paid the driver, and thanked him with a decent tip, to which the driver said, "Thanks, mate. I 'ope this ain't fake money those blokes in there minted," before he drove off.

Donald looked across the street to the Broadway Buildings which was an imposing gray edifice of nine stories. Behind him was the St. James Park Underground Station.

He crossed the road and entered the building exactly on time. Richard Bates was waiting for him at the reception desk. The two shook hands warmly and Richard led the way to his office.

"Well, Mr. Harvey, please take a seat."

Richard's office was small, and most of the space was taken up with a huge oak desk that had multiple drawers of all kind and sizes. The desktop was inlaid with a dark red leather writing pad, more suited to Parker pens than Biro's.

Richard began the conversation by saying, "Well, as you know, after your conversation with Major Wallace, and following a detailed questionnaire from you, we have completed your background check to enable us to move forward. Everything looks quite satisfactory from the standpoint that we can maintain you in a compartmentalized role. In other words, you would be under the aegis of the Secret Service but would not be employed by us as a fully fledged agent."

Donald sat forward on his chair and said, "Yes, even now I find it difficult to comprehend how I, a civilian engineer, could be sitting here discussing my role in an intelligence operation."

Richard responded, "Donald, may I call you Donald?"

"Of course", Donald said as Richard continued.

"Obviously it takes a significant amount of training, and it requires a specific type of personality to be a successful counter intelligence agent." He hastily went on to say, "Of course, this is not to say you do not have those kinds of qualities, but there has been no fundamental training or analysis to find out."

"Yes, I understand completely," Donald assured him.

Richard continued further, "What we do know is that you had an exemplary record in the Royal Air Force, and as part of your National Service, you have no criminal record of even minor offenses, and that your work in the aircraft industry is highly regarded. Therefore, we are grateful that you are willing to work with us on this particular mission."

Donald thought to himself, *Yeh, right, you mean not being willing to be blackmailed over my little black market activity. Those American cigarettes and whiskey have turned out to be more costly than I expected!*

He then thought of Zaluski and poor Alicja grieving over the death of her uncle. So much suffering the Poles, the Jews, and others in Eastern Europe had endured. I need to at least put my best foot forward.

Donald addressed Richard, "Major Wallace has, no doubt, told you about Karol Zaluski and the concern about a possible lurking Russian agent?"

"Yes, he told me," replied Richard.

"Well," continued Donald, "he was killed the other night in a shunting accident, but I'm concerned that maybe it wasn't an accident.

Is there any way we can ensure a proper investigation is made in Wycombe?"

Richard got up and said, "I won't be a minute," and popped out.

He came back shortly after and told Donald, "I've got my Number Two, Freddie Simpson, on it straight away. He'll be in touch with the High Wycombe authorities and will make sure we know every detail of the accident and if it is, indeed, an accident. The NKVD or KGB, as they are known today, have some bizarre ways of eliminating people they don't want."

"Before we go further, Donald," Richard went on, "But while it sounds a little melodramatic, it is necessary for us to ask you to swear allegiance under oath even though you are not officially a paid agent of the British Secret Service or specifically of MI6, it is still required that you do so."

"Yes, of course," said Donald dutifully. He had heard of MI5 but never of MI6. Richard told him this was a relatively new designation named for counter- intelligence after the war.

Richard asked his secretary to come in and witness Donald take his oath of allegiance to Queen and country. Richard made it clear that he would not have free access to 54 Broadway MI6 headquarters, but all meetings from now on would be at external venues.

Donald asked if his allegiance was to Queen and country, then how he would be handled by Major Wallace. Richard explained that the mission was a joint venture initiated by the Americans and Major Wallace would be the primary controller for Donald. And then either Richard, or his Number Two, Freddie Simpson, would be a back up. Donald was thinking of the complications that could arise over this, but felt these people should know what they are doing.

Donald took out his wallet and placed the blank piece of paper on the desk in front of Richard.

"This, I believe, may contain the missing part of the note. I've had it all along in my sock drawer but never realized it. The intruder must have been looking for a complete note and never found it either, as it was just lying there among the mess he made of my belongings."

Richard exclaimed, "Ah, hah, that could be what we are looking for."

Donald said, "Well, I have not been able to get anything to show up using my apple juice trick, so it could be just a torn piece of paper."

Richard got up once more and told Donald to wait there.

"I want to give this to our lab, and they should know pretty quickly if a hidden communication is on here."

He quickly left the room.

He returned a little later and said, "That shouldn't take them too long so, in the meantime, let's continue."

Donald interrupted him with a question, "I understand I may be asked to conduct some business in Paris with S.H.A.P.E. and that, in itself, is supposed to be a cover for me to have time to look for this chap, Petrowski, but how do I justify expenses to my company for the extra time taken in this effort?"

"You will be given sufficient cash or traveller's cheques to cover any expenses," Richard explained, "We will have one of our embassy staff available to you in any emergency that may arise, monetary or otherwise. The Americans have also agreed that the American Embassy would be available."

Donald wondered what "otherwise" might mean but didn't press the issue.

Richard began detailing what Donald would be required to do in Paris.

"Firstly, you will need to locate Mr. Petrowski at the address on the Rue de la Pompe, according to the deciphered note. Depending on what if anything is on the second part of the note, you must ask him everything he knows about Herr Kammler and the Death Bell. How did he obtain his information and...."

A knock on his door interrupted Richard, who rose to answer it.

It was Freddie who announced, "Here's the result from the lab. There is, in fact, further writing in code."

The Note now read:

T J D I B F T S   P J W W V H S H L   K V X J O

Both Richard and Donald studied the inscription before Richard said, "Of course, I'll have to get this upstairs to the crypto people who have the key. Freddie, you'll have to check with them."

"No need," interjected Donald. "I have the copy that Roger Hewitt-Benning devised right here. I assume it will be the same." He then produced it from his wallet and displayed the Key:

X V E J D L O B

"Oh, good man," exclaimed Richard. "Do we know the method Roger used to break the Key?"

Donald said, "My friend, Harold Sloan, had spent an evening with Roger who had given him a lesson on deciphering using the 'modular addition' method and for this, in particular, he had used "Modulo 26." Harold had, in turn, instructed me on it, so I think I can get to it fairly quickly."

"Jolly good, Donald; let's see if we can crack this right way. If not, no worries, I can just get it done upstairs and our crypto chaps will have it done quickly if they have that Key. We will double-check it anyway."

Donald sat at Richard's desk, took a large notepad, and copied the **cipher text** onto a blank page in large letters:

The first word was	T	Second word is
		J D I B F T S
The numerical value	19	9 3 8 1 5 19 18
Minus the Key value	–23	–23–21 -4 –9 –3 -11–14
Result: if Negative Modify }	–4	–14-18 4 –8 2 8 4
by difference of 26 but if }		
Positive, use that number }	22	12 8 4 18 2 8 4
Value is now	**W**	**M I E S C I E**

Third word was	**P J W W V H S H L**
The numerical value	15 9 22 22 21 7 18 7 11
Minus the Key value	–23 –21 –4 –9 –3 –11–14 –1 –23
Result	–8 12 18 13 18 –4 4 6 12
Add 26 but if greater then}	
take difference of 26 }	18 14 18 13 18 22 4 6 14
Value is now	**S O S N O W E G O**

Fourth word was	**K V X J O**
The numerical value	10 21 23 9 14
Minus the Key value	23 21 4 9 3
Result	13 0 19 0 11
Add 26 but if greater then}	
take difference of 26 }	**N A T A L**

Message reads:

W MIESCIE SOSNOWEGO NATAL

Finally, the three men agreed that it appeared the message was now complete, and it looked like the Polish language in the first part. Richard told Freddie to get the copy upstairs to their linguists and have it translated.

Richard turned to Donald and said, "Now where were we?"

Donald replied, "You want me to quiz Petrowski on how he obtained the information about Kammler. What else is there to know?"

Richard looked at him saying, "That's where you will need to have a discussion with Major Wallace. He's the technical chap in this little venture and represents the United States, who has initiated it. Your background in the engineering field may prove useful if the mission is able to make any headway. By the way, while in Paris we may be able to fix you up with a meeting with a Jewish group of Nazi hunters. They may have some ideas on the Kammler case. However, any discussion with the Jewish group must be restricted to matters relating to Kammler's war crimes and nothing else, is that clear?"

"I understand," acknowledged Donald, "But what if they raise the question of his involvement with weapons or armaments of any kind?"

"You simply plead ignorance. You have been commissioned to conduct research on behalf of the War Crimes Commission Sub-Committee in England. I'll give you a reference name to use from the Committee later."

Donald again thought to himself, *I suppose a Nazi's crimes against humanity are somehow excised or sanitized if his knowhow or usefulness is of sufficient value to us.*

Donald and Richard went on to discuss some of the historical aspects of Kammler's background, including the Warsaw Ghetto, his design of extermination camps, and then his control of the Nazi weapons program. Richard explained how it was believed Kammler had wrested control away from Albert Speer, the armaments minister. Kammler was about three years older than Speer and supposedly his equal in architectural and engineering construction design.

"I think it's time for a little lunch, Donald, don't you?"

"I'm certainly getting a little peckish," replied Donald.

Richard suggested, "We can just pop over the road to The Old Star Pub, if you like. They have a pretty decent Ploughman's Lunch."

"Sounds perfect to me," agreed Donald.

During lunch Richard learned about Donald's involvement with his Polish girlfriend, Alicja. Donald explained how she had suspected that the Russians were targeting her uncle, and she thought it was the reason he had been depressed of late.

"I have never told her that I saw her uncle at the church when I discovered the note, or about the suspicious bloke I nearly bumped into just outside," said Donald sadly. "I'm not sure how I am going to handle this with poor Alicja."

"Donald," Richard broke in, "You cannot say too much. At this point officially, you only know that this was an accident."

"Yes, of course," replied Donald, hoping against hope that it was indeed an accident.

"Well," said Richard, "that lunch filled a hole. I think we had better get back to the office."

He pulled out his wallet and paid the barman the bill. Donald offered to pay his share, but Richard waved him off.

Richard grinned at him, "Now that you are a non-paid part-time member of Her Majesty's Secret Service," he whispered, "the least we can do is buy you a lunch."

Donald smiled and thanked him. He liked Richard who came across as a diligent civil servant but, at the same time, seemed a decent sort, and had a sense of humor. They walked back across the street to Richard's office and settled down for a further discussion.

There was a knock on the door, and Freddie came back in.

"I have some news on our enquiry with the police in High Wycombe. It appears that while it was thought to be an accident at first, the Zaluski case is now one of murder. It seems there was a struggle in which an assailant attacked Zaluski, who was able to retaliate briefly by stabbing his attacker with a shunting pole hook. The pole was found several feet away from the accident, and it had blood on the hook and handle. The blood has been identified with that of a man by the name of Tomasz Bielski who had visited the Wycombe Hospital for treatment that night on the pretense he had fallen on a railing."

Freddie paused to let his report sink in, and Donald had gone quite pale.

His thoughts had immediately swung to Alicja and what she must be thinking about her poor uncle. From an accident to murder, and he shuddered as he half knew that the man who had been tracking him was probably the killer.

Freddie continued, "This Bielksi had provided a false NHS card for his medical treatment in that the doctor's name on it was fake. The police have gone to his last known address in Iver in Buckinghamshire, but he has flown already. The name, Tomasz Bielski, was supposed to be a veteran of the Polish Free Army demobilized in England after the war. Efforts are being made to establish his whereabouts."

Richard spoke up at this point, "All right Freddie, thanks for the report. Good work. Now we can probably help the police and ourselves on this by getting our research people to check on Tomasz Bielski, as we are ostensibly the offshoot of Military Intelligence and will have records of all Allied forces that were under our command during the war."

"In the meantime, Donald, I will arrange a meeting for Major Wallace, you, and myself in a few days to discuss and finalize our plans to get you to Paris. We will have to meet at a neutral venue in London because we can't have Wallace walking into 54 Broadway, as we know everyone who comes and goes here is monitored by our foes."

Again, a knock at the door interrupted him, and he called out, "Come in."

Freddie entered once more and indicated he had the Polish translation of note number two. All three of the men looked at the translation which read:

W MIESCIE SOSNOWEGO NATAL
IN THE CITY OF NATAL PINE

Richard said, "It appears we have some kind of destination where the 'leader' was headed. We'll have our analysts work on this and come up with an answer before our next meeting, Donald."

"Right, I'll wait for you to notify me of the next get-together with Major Wallace," Donald responded.

Richard added, "This is the reason we need you to question Petrowski and get his story before anyone else lays hands on him."

They shook hands, and Donald walked across the street to the Underground Station. The trip using the Circle Line to Paddington Station gave him a little time to try and digest the day's discussions and their implications.

The Falcon Hides

Dmitri Demidov, Second Secretary, sat at his desk at the Russian Embassy wondering when he might be posted to a more pleasant climate. *It's bad enough coping with the Moscow winters, but England's summers were not much better,* he thought to himself. Not that it was cold, but it was so dreary and rainy all the time. *If this keeps up, I shall be growing web feet.* He was thinking of an assignment to Chile or, perhaps, Argentina when a knock on his door stirred him from his introspection, and he called out, "Come in."

Military Attache, Leonid Tarasov, walked in with a worried look on his face.

"Comrade," he began, "Our Falcon has been involved in an accident, sir."

"What do you mean, 'an accident'?" queried Demidov.

Tarasov relayed the story of the Zaluski incident and how Falcon was now holed up in a safe house until he could be spirited out of the country.

"I think his cover will be blown in a short amount of time, because the police will surely find that the real Bielski died in the war. He went missing in a battle in North Africa, but he had no next of kin so that made it fairly easy to duplicate his identity for our man, as no one was looking for him."

Demidov lit a cigarette and blew a long plume of smoke toward the ceiling.

After giving the matter some thought, he turned to his Attache, "Let's get him to East Berlin and tell him to lie low for a while. Get the Stasi to host him until we can rehabilitate him for the next stage of this little game. From everything Falcon has fed us so far, it appears this Englishman Harvey seems to be involved in the Polish Underground network. It could be because he has a Polish girlfriend or he is simply an unwitting witness or an accidental accomplice. I want you to get Natalia Volkov down here from Liverpool. This assignment is more important than the one she's on right now. What's her cover name in England?"

"It's Janet Rigby, sir. She was able to get that name from a deceased child's name in Yorkshire from about 50 years ago with no known living relatives. Plus, it's easy for her to pronounce. Natalia still has a little accent when speaking English."

"Good," said Demidov, "I want her to monitor Harvey and track his movements as much as possible to determine his involvement in the Polish affair. She is to make NO contact with Harvey and to avoid any embarrassments. I definitely do not want her trying to shack up with him or anything stupid like that, do you understand?"

"Yes, sir, but she is quite stunning, and he may take a liking to her if the circumstances take that kind of turn," said Tarsov.

"Well, Tarasov," growled the Secretary, "Just make sure that kind of turn is avoided. Falcon had a strong suspicion that this Harvey character must have picked up the note, right?"

"That is correct, Comrade Secretary," replied Tarasov, "He made that assumption because he had observed Zaluski leave the church. He also knew from our Polish intelligence that a dead letter drop was to take place, and they knew a red hymn book was the drop place. After bumping into Harvey, Falcon entered the church a few minutes later and was unable to locate the message."

Demidov's eyes narrowed when he suggested, "Perhaps the local priest got it, and maybe he is the real recipient. After all, we do not know everyone on Britain's Secret Service payroll, do we?"

"No, sir," said Tarasov smiling, "But we know a few, don't we?"

"Comrade Tarasov, I think we should get our Cultural Attache, Victor Abramovich, to undertake a trip to High Wycombe, and he could ensure that Natalia Kolkov, aka Janet Rigby, is making headway in our investigation of Mr. Harvey and any of his associates."

"But, sir, our diplomats are not allowed to travel more than 25 miles from Hyde Park Corner to anywhere outside London."

The Secretary replied, "As long as we give 48 hours notice and details of the purpose of travel to the destination is specified." The Secretary rummaged through his drawer and pulled out a document. "This," he said, "is a copy of the notice our Ambassador received from the British Foreign Office a couple of years ago in 1952 and is still valid."

Tarasov picked up the notice and it read:

"Following is summary of statement issued by the Foreign Office on 11th March, 1952:

Notes are herewith delivered on the 10th March to the Soviet Ambassador and the Roumanian and Bulgarian Ministers informing them that (with the exception of the Bulgarian Minister or Chargé d'Affaires), neither they nor the members of their staffs would in future be allowed to travel more than 25 miles from Hyde Park Corner without notifying the Foreign Office, or the appropriate Service Department 48 hours in advance. The same arrangement would apply to Soviet representatives not members of the Embassy, such as the staff of the Soviet Trade Delegation and Soviet commercial or news agencies in the United Kingdom.

The Bulgarian Minister or Chargé d'Affaires was exempted from this requirement since Her Majesty's Minister in Sofia was similarly exempted. Soviet officials would be allowed to travel to the Embassy's country house at Hawkhurst (Kent) by a regular route without notification. Members of the Hungarian Legation are already required, by a decision of the previous Government, to obtain permission for any journeys beyond 18 miles from London (the limit imposed on Her Majesty's Legation, Budapest).

The movement of British subjects and of foreigners generally has for a long time been severely restricted in the Soviet Union. As a result of restrictions imposed in September 1948, and increased in January of this year, virtually the whole of the Soviet Union east of a line running from Archangel to Astrakan is now inaccessible to members of Her Majesty's Embassy; and all the frontier and coastal districts (except Leningrad and Odessa) and the great majority of the main industrial towns are also forbidden. Members of Foreign Missions may only travel in those parts of the Soviet Union still in bounds by notifying in advance any journeys of more than 25 miles from Moscow. Even within this radius, large areas are prohibited.

A large area of Bulgaria, including all the frontier regions, has been out of bounds since December 1949. In order to travel in other parts of the country, members of foreign Missions must notify details of the journeys in advance to the Bulgarian authorities. The greater part of Roumania, including all the frontier regions, and virtually the whole of Transylvania, was prohibited to members of foreign Missions in May 1949.

Although members of foreign Missions are excluded from large parts of the Soviet Union, Roumania and Bulgaria, Her Majesty's Government does not propose at present to prohibit any parts of the United Kingdom to representatives of these countries."

Demidov told Tarasov, "I will arrange for Comrade Victor to conduct an historical research mission to Wycombe to study Benjamin Disraeli, his links to the Hell Fire Club he was famous for, and, of course, his illustrious career in British politics."

Tarasov grinned, "Very good, sir. That will be an excellent cover."

Tarasov continued by saying, "I will make arrangements for Falcon to get to Berlin in the next few days. We will have him spirited out as a deck hand on a freighter from Southhampton. There is a Liberian freighter, *Georgios*, that is heading to Japan, but will be stopping in Peenemunde to pick up freight.

"Very good, Comrade," responded Secretary Demidov. "I'm looking for a good lunch today with the Ambassador, Comrade Malik."

Falcon is Identified

Freddie Simpson sat down with Detective Warner in the office of the C.I.D. at the Wycombe Police Station. Freddie began the conversation, "Mr. Warner, the Secret Service notified you that I would be paying you a visit to discuss the Zaluski case, is that correct?"

"Yes, Mr. Simpson, I was told that you needed to come down from London to discuss this case, and I must say, it is intriguing this should have generated an interest from MI6, sir."

Freddie explained, "As you know, the United Kingdom keeps a close eye on all foreigners in this country, even those who have permanent residence such as Mr. Zaluski who must report to their nearest police station, to notify the authorities of any change of address. In particular, we keep a close eye, albeit not an oppressive one, on our residents who have originated from Eastern Europe, and as Mr. Zaluski was from Poland, he merited a certain level of attention from us."

"Yes, I see," replied Detective Warner. "The Cold War continues to require our vigilance in many areas, I suppose."

Freddie went on, "When we learned from our enquiry with your Superintendent Watkins that you had opened a murder docket on this case, and that a Mr. Bielski may be a suspect, it was necessary for us to become involved. The fact that he had a fraudulent NHS Card and was supposedly a veteran of the Polish Free Army, like Mr. Zaluski, really caught our attention."

Detective Warner nodded, and Freddie continued, "As a result of our own investigation, we can tell you in confidence that Tomasz Bielksi had been a soldier fighting for us against Germany, but he went missing in North Africa and is believed to have died. A direct hit by a 50 mm shell on a single foxhole leaves little to no trace of an occupant. He had no living relatives, all having died in the Russian internment camps in Siberia at the beginning the war as part of the annexation and division of Poland."

"So who was it that had taken his identity?" asked the shocked Warner.

"We believe it to be a Ukrainian agent working for the Russians by the name of Igor Martinovich," replied Freddie. "He is a particularly nasty character and goes by other names, as well. However, I am here today to let you know that we have a search under way to try and find him before he leaves the country. We need for you to maintain this case as an accident for a short time in order to draw him out of hiding. A hunt for him as a murder suspect would make him lie low. Superintendent Watkins has said he would leave the decision up to you, so can we count on you to maintain the status quo?"

"I expect that is entirely possible," Warner replied, "But for how long? After all, now that you have identified the suspect for us makes it all the more imperative that we act."

"Yes," said Freddie, "I understand your position, but with us having identified your suspect, we are the ones acting. Plus it's in the interests of national security," he added smiling benignly.

"How long can we prolong this?" asked Warner.

'We will try to get this wrapped up as soon as possible and allow you to make an announcement to the Bucks Free Press newspaper," responded Freddie.

Preparing for Paris

On his return from London, Donald had been busy in his office going over the prototypes for De Haviland, as well as reviewing the Operational Manual that Tommy Thompson had developed for over-hauling the Sperry Gyroscopic Direction Finders. It also reminded him that he was supposed to get Tommy some Lucky Strike cigarettes. He wasn't sure how this was going to work with Cal Jennings, but he would check with him later.

There was supposed to be a dance at the Town Hall that weekend, and he could pick up the cartons from Cal at that time. He was looking forward to seeing Alicja again, and he was invited to the funeral of her uncle on Friday. *I'm going to have to be so damn careful of what I can say to her now I'm a "British Secret Agent,* he thought to himself cynically.

Bill Richardson stepped into Donald's office, "Morning, Don. You seem to be fully engaged this morning. The boss wants us in his office at 11:30 before lunch."

"Oh," said Donald, "what does he want, do you know?"

"No idea," replied Bill. "I'm sure it will mean more work for one of us, though."

"Okay, Bill, I'll see you there; 11:30 sharp."

At 11:25 a.m. Donald rose to attend the meeting with the company owner and closed his office door. He walked along the corridor to Colonel Blankenship's office and greeted Jill Williamson, who had her perpetual cigarette in her nicotine stained fingers, and she responded to Donald with a bronchial, "Hello, Donald, how are you this morning?"

"I'm well, thanks. Is the boss ready?"

"Yes," she replied, "You can go on in. Where's Bill?"

As she spoke, Bill poked his head round the door and greeted the two of them.

Donald said, "We can go in now," and led the way.

The Colonel gestured to the men to take their seats. He began by offering congratulations to Donald for a well-executed mission to Farn-borough Air Show and bringing back some potential lucrative business. A discussion ensued over the some of the fiscal aspects of new raw materials for the Plastic Division and the need for a new draftsman assistant for the toolroom engineering shop. It was agreed the expand-ing business required someone to help prepare new drawings estab-lished for the new steel molds. The draftsman was hard pressed to get the drawing finished, and later to complete the changes when the tool-room decided the molds required modifications. The Colonel said he would arrange for Jill to place an advertisement in the paper.

"Now, Donald, I have a new assignment for you."

Donald and Bill looked at each other, wondering what was coming next. His following announcement shook Donald completely.

"I want you to go to Paris, Donald."

Donald thought quickly, *I must look pleasantly surprised, not totally shocked about the coincidence of the Colonel setting this up for him.*

"Paris?" he said incredulously, "What have you got in store for me there?" he asked.

"Well, I'm not sending you there to attend the bloody Follies Bergere, my friend. I want you to visit the Supreme Headquarters Allied Powers Europe, also known as SHAPE. There are fifteen member nations, and I have arranged with certain connections for you to meet with seven different Air Force Attaches representing seven different countries. This is an opportunity to determine if any of our business models or products can be incorporated into their respective aircraft, or that might be modified to suit. I know for a fact, the new prototype cockpit instrument covers you are producing for the Fairy Delta could be re-designed for a number of our Allied planes."

"That would certainly be an exciting challenge, Colonel," said Donald and wondered if the Colonel was also a compartmentalized secret agent by setting this up on behalf of Bates and Wallace. However, the Colonel simply went on with his discussion as if this was just another business opportunity gathered through his multiple connections and contacts.

"Have you got a passport, Donald?" enquired the Colonel.

"Yes, sir, I had to get mine a couple of years ago when I made a day trip to Boulogne," Donald confirmed.

Colonel Blankenship turned to Bill Richardson and asked him to draw up a job description for the assistant drafting position and give it to Jill.

As Bill and Donald were leaving the office, the Colonel called Donald back to tell him, "Look Donald, the Paris trip may take a little while to complete, but don't worry; just take whatever time is necessary to get the job done, or at least to fully explore potential leads."

He looked squarely at Donald who got the distinct impression there was an implication to his words that meant more than leads for Trandect.

"Yes, Colonel, I'll ensure we get maximum exposure."

The Colonel laughed and said, "I'm not sure what kind of exposure you mean, but just ensure you remain discreet. We don't want the competition following us, do we?"

"No sir, not at all. I'll be very careful about that," replied Donald, now clearly cognizant of the Colonel's meaning. He turned and left the office still shocked and surprised by what he now thought he knew about his boss.

The Falcon Escapes

Freddie dropped into Richard's office to provide an update on the Zaluski incident.

"We have Internal Affairs, Immigration and Customs all on the alert for Mr Martinovich," reported Freddie.

Richard put forth his opinion, "These ex-NKVD or current KGB blokes are really good at evading capture, so I'm not too optimistic of copping him, Freddie. By the way, have you made arrangements for young Mr Harvey to meet us again for his final briefing with Major Wallace and myself?"

Freddie replied, "I have the agenda, but I'm not sure we should use The Dickens Inn again for the venue. Would you agree to the Museum Tavern near the British Museum?"

"That's a splendid idea Freddie. You know we have an exclusive room there by arrangement with the owners."

In the meantime Falcon was preparing to leave his safe house in Portswood, a suburb of Southhampton. This was a one bedroom flat in a semi-detached home belonging to an absentee owner, George Watkins, who was a member of the British Communist Party. As an avid prior supporter of the "Hands Off Russia" movement, he had allowed his property to be used for advancing the cause of Socialism in England. If this meant hiding the odd spy from time to time, then so be it.

Falcon had dressed in the manner of a deck hand which could also be construed as a dockside worker. This dress included a strong pair of dungarees, a coarse cotton shirt with an open collar, and a rather threadbare brown jacket. He had been able to get a pair of second-hand steel-toed boots that were common among dock workers. He had a metal lunchbox and thermos flask.

He carefully tidied up the flat, making sure he left no evidence of his residency there. All previous clothing and personal items had been disposed of in the public rubbish bin. He opened the door and stepped outside. Making sure no one was around; he closed the door, locked it and pushed the key through the brass letter box opening in the door. The brass flap sprang firmly shut into place and there was now no going back as he would be unable to retrieve the key.

He quickly moved out into the street and headed for the bus stop 100 yards down the road. His upper chest wound was still painful and maybe getting infected, as he had been unable to change the dressing very often. He had timed his arrival at the stop to coincide with the transport company's timetable. They were running every fifteen minutes, but the wait seemed to take forever.

At last the double-decker came swooping down the street, and it was the correct one with its destination Western Docks, which would take him close to the berth of the Liberian freighter *Georgios* that Tarasov had told him would take him to East Germany. Falcon boarded the bus and, as was his habit, he sat down nearest the doorway of the vehicle, just in case he had to get off in a hurry. Always wary, always ready, Falcon was like a hyena - cautious, daring, but dangerous and powerful, if need be.

The conductor asked him, "Which gate, mate?"

Falcon looked startled for a second but quickly realized the man thought he was a dockworker. "Er, Millbrook Station Western Docks," he replied gruffly. He paid the conductor who reeled off a ticket from his machine and gave it to him. The conductor took a second look at Falcon but then moved on.

After a couple of stops, a uniformed man got on and moved to the front of the bus and requested to see passenger's tickets. Falcon began to feel uncomfortable as he was unaware that in England, it was common practice for ticket inspectors to ensure correct fares were being paid and conductors were not providing free rides to anyone.

As the inspector got closer, Falcon was able to see he was in fact simply checking each ticket for to verify the fare. He offered his ticket on demand and the inspector checked it and handed it back.

"So you're working Western Docks, then? What cargo are you offloading today, mate?"

Falcon replied in his thick accent, "I will know when I get there today."

The inspector looked at him in mock amazement, "Well, it's not exactly a state secret is it? I mean the Union Castle Line is either bringing in fruit or timber or may be a little wine. What else they goin' to bring from South Africa?"

"Maybe pineapples," suggested Falcon, trying to go along with the pretense of being a dockworker.

The inspector took another look at Falcon before getting off at the next stop. As the bus pulled away, leaving the inspector standing on the curb, he was still staring at Falcon through the bus window.

Finally after a few more stops, the bus arrived at Millbrook Station where Falcon descended to the pavement and began walking briskly to the dock gates. There were a number of workers walking toward the entrance to the docks passing by two policemen on duty. They seemed to be scrutinizing everyone as they went by, and Falcon was now nervous as he had no identity papers except the new East German Passport he had received from Comrade Tarasov. His new identity was Helmut Strossen. However, this was to be his cover behind the Iron Curtain and would be of no help now as he had no visa for entry to Britain.

The pain in his chest was not helping either. As he got closer to the gate, his heart rate increased which caused more throbbing pain in his wound. He moved closer to a group of dockworkers and tried to look as nonchalant as they were. Just as he was about to pass through the gate into the docks area, one of the policemen beckoned him over.

"Just a moment sir, is that your lunch there?" he said pointing to Falcon's lunch box. "You know we have to make a show of checking people now and again and you are the lucky one," he said, smiling at Falcon.

Falcon responded smiling as best he could, "Well, I have to eat something so I must bring the lunch." He opened the lunchbox and showed the sandwiches.

The policeman studied Falcon and said, "What accent have you got then?

Falcon thought quickly, "South Africa, that's why I'm working the Union Castle boats here."

It was then the policeman noticed a small bloodstain on the edge of the shirt just showing through Falcon's jacket.

"Are you injured, sir?" he said pointing to the stain.

"Oh, no, it's just a minor scratch, and I pulled the plaster off this morning and that made it bleed some more."

With that, the policeman told him to be careful and waved him on as he called over another worker for a random check.

Relieved, Falcon quickly made his way toward the dockside by walking along West Bay Drive, cutting through the sheds by Imperial Way and onto Herbert Walker Avenue. Reaching the dockside he could see the ship, "Cape Town Castle," and further along the dockside lay his escape vessel *Georgios*. It looked a somewhat scruffy ship, but he didn't care as he approached the gangplank and began the climb to the top.

He was met by a deckhand who spoke to him in German, "Sind Sie der neue Deck Hand Peenumunde? (Are you the new deckhand for Peenumunde?)

Falcon replied, "Ja, ich brauche, um den Kapitän zu treffen." (Yes, I need to meet the Captain.)

He followed the man to the Captain's cabin. The Captain rose to greet him.

"Glad you could make it. We're leaving in about two hours so come and have some coffee and I will get my bosun to show you a cabin."

Falcon thanked him and asked for some assistance with getting a dressing for his wound.

The Captain grinned, "I didn't know you were on active duty on the front lines."

Falcon smiled and said, "Just a little souvenir from England."

Back at the gate entrance, a new shift of policeman came on duty and showed the others a bulletin they brought with them which indicated they needed to be on lookout for a murder suspect and a national security threat. It described Falcon as a powerfully built Ukrainian or Polish National named Bielski, speaking English with a heavy accent, and with a possible wound in the upper chest area.

The policeman who had stopped Falcon now swore, "Shit, Tommy, I stopped this bastard on the way through here this morning. He's supposedly working on the Union Castle Line, and I think there are one or two of their ships docked today. You had better call up the Station and get support down here right away. I'll stay on if you like."

The call went out immediately, and law enforcement as well as immigration officers commenced swarming the Western Docks. The first contingent of officers arrived at the "Cape Town Castle" and began searching the ship from top to bottom. Another contingent searched the "Warwick Castle" berthed further down the docks.

In the meantime the Captain of the *Georgios* had noted the disturbance and called the First Mate to the bridge, "Prepare for departure. We're leaving an hour earlier. I've called for a pilot and he should be here in the next ten minutes."

"Yes, Sir," said the First Mate as moved quickly from the bridge to get his crew ready for sailing. The Captain left the bridge and descended to Falcon's cabin and without knocking, entered, much to Falcon's surprise.

"Herr Strossen," he said urgently. "There's a search being conducted on the Castle ships nearby. Were you suspected of being a docker there or one of the crew?"

Falcon said, "A policeman noticed my accent and asked where I was from and I told him South Africa because I knew the Western Docks here had Castle Line boats. He must have assumed I was headed there. They may have received an alert about my description."

"Right," the Captain barked, "Quickly now, because if they don't find you on those ships or nearby in the sheds, they may target this vessel as a possibility, especially knowing we're headed to East Germany. Follow me with your things."

He then led Falcon down into the depths of the ship to the engine room. Here they were getting ready by running up the big diesel engines and the noise was quite deafening.

The Captain showed him a very large green painted steel cabinet that was humming industriously.

The Captain said, "This is one of our main generators, but there is a small compartment here, look," and he opened a panel at one end of the generator where he told Falcon to get in. He had a crew member give him a folded tarpaulin for Falcon to sit on. There was just sufficient room for him to remain in a sitting position.

"You will need to remain there while we make our departure. You could be there for about one or two hours. You have your thermos from your lunch box. Just don't drink too much because you won't be able to pee for a while."

"I can handle that," said Falcon doggedly.

They closed the panel, and it was designed to look like the rest of the panelling on the generator with rivets and no door-like structures. The vibration and noise from the generator camouflaged any appearance of a hiding place that might be there.

The Captain returned to the bridge to find the official Port of Southampton pilot waiting to guide them out to sea through the Solent. The pilot rang down to the engine room and asked for an engine room check. Receiving the affirmation all checks had been made, he gave the signal to begin casting off the dockside ropes.

The *Georgios* began moving away from the dock with the pilot giving orders and directions. The vessel began the slow journey down the Southampton Solent toward the open sea.

As the search of the Castle Line ships came to an end without finding the fugitive, the Chief Constable and the Head of the local Immigration and Customs felt that they should have at least looked over the *Georgios*. They had obtained manifest records from the Port Office showing the *Georgios* was destined for Japan, but would be making stops in East Germany and South West Africa. Now that they knew the fugitive was of Eastern European origin, it was possible he had been smuggled, or had smuggled himself aboard.

Orders were given for the Coast Guard to overtake the ship to board and search her.

The *Georgios* was making good headway at around eight knots and was nearing Hamble on the port side when a Coast Guard cutter came up along their starboard side. The Coast Guard using a loudhailer called for the Captain to reduce speed to four knots and prepare for boarding.

A party of six officers boarded the vessel. The Chief showed his authority and credentials to the Captain and requested his cooperation in searching for a fugitive who was wanted for murder and espionage. The Captain raised his eyebrow momentarily at the accusation of murder, but offered no resistance or complaint about having the *Georgios* searched from top to bottom.

Every nook and cranny was thoroughly investigated while the crew looked on solemnly. The search eventually reached the engine room where even large toolboxes were opened. The generator cabinet where Falcon lay hiding and sweating remained secure. Although one or two officers had tapped on the walls, they appeared satisfied it was a solid piece of working machinery.

Another few minutes were spent in the bilges below decks to no avail. The six officers reassembled on the deck, and the Chief asked the Captain to sign a document absolving the Coast Guard from any damages or delays that might have occurred due to the search. This was purely a political procedure for handling incidents involving vessels among Cold War antagonists.

After they had left, the Captain of the *Georgios* asked the pilot to speed up in order to reach the open sea and regain time. Soon the yellow launch from the pilot's station in Gosport came out to meet the ship. The pilot handed over the ship to the Captain and disembarked.

The Captain set course to pass the Isle Of Wight and continue up the English Channel to the North Sea where they would make their way eventually around Denmark into the Baltic Sea and to Peenemunde to pick up cargo.

The Captain, having established his course, handed over to the First Officer and then proceeded to the lower decks and the engine room. He ordered one of the crew to remove the panel from the generator, and Falcon stiffly made his way out. He badly needed a shower and was slightly deaf from the noise of the turbine and his wound was beginning to become infected.

"Well, Herr Strossen. It looks like you got away with murder," announced the Captain.

"It was really just a serious accident," said Falcon stoically.

The Captain agreed, "Yes, of course. The important thing is we now have you well on the way to Germany."

"Thank you, Captain. I'm sure my superiors will be well pleased with your efforts today on my behalf."

The Captain looked happy with himself as he returned to the bridge.

Chapter 11

Planning for Paris

Russian Surveillance

Victor Abramovich left the Russian Embassy and drove through London to the A40 Road which would take him to High Wycombe. As he drove he continuously looked in his rear view mirror to see if he was being followed. This behavior was a natural instinct anyway as a Russian in a Western nation, but he felt it would be certain on a day when had received documentation giving him a British Ministry of Home Affairs authority to travel to the Wycombe area. His destination was thirty miles from Hyde Park Corner in London, and it necessitated applying for special dispensation on the basis he would be conducting a cultural study on the history of Benjamin Disraeli, a past British political icon.

He enjoyed the ride among the picturesque countryside as he motored through the small towns and villages on this main road. As he drove through Ealing, Denham, Gerards Cross, and Beaconsfield, the beauty and elegance of the towns did not fail to make an impression on him, compared to the bleakness and the characterless of the concrete towers of the residences in his own country. The poverty of the Russian peasants as they toiled on the collective farms in the name of the State just could not compare with these country villages where the people were going about their roles in life in relative comfort.

This is dangerous thinking and I should be proud of my nation's effort to bring the fruits of everyone's labor and endeavors to the collective advantage of all.

As Victor passed Loudwater on the outskirts of Wycombe he thought, *I must pull myself together. This is seditious thinking. Damn, I would be willing to die for Mother Russia, but why is the system not working? Is Capitalism really the answer as I see around me without a chaperone or cadre? Is this why Churchill got re-elected when nationalization just did not work in this country? Is this what he meant when he said,* "The inherent vice of capitalism is the unequal sharing of blessings; the inherent virtue of socialism is the equal sharing of miseries"? *The fact that, in my position, I am allowed to read Western newspapers is both a blessing of enlightenment, and a curse of treasonable thinking.*

Victor shut out the treasonous thoughts as he pulled into the parking area in front of the Red Lion Hotel in the center of High Wycombe. A red-coated porter came out from the front entrance to help him with his bags.

"Good day, sir. I'll bring these in for you, if you would like to register at the front desk."

"Thank you," replied Victor, and he stepped inside and found his way to the reception desk. He showed his diplomatic passport, signed the hotel register and was shown to his room.

Ironically, the room he had been assigned had windows directly over the balcony where Churchill had given a speech in his 1945 election bid after the war and which he lost to the socialist Labor Party. He was able to win again in 1951 after the electorate had had a taste of radical socialist policies.

After laying out his clothes and freshening up, Victor went downstairs to the dining room where enjoyed some of capitalism's finest cuisine. After dinner he retreated to the foyer where he was able to locate a public telephone.   He dialed the number for Janet Rigby (or real name Natalia Kolkov), who answered almost immediately.

"Hello, Janet," he began. "I have made the trip to Wycombe, and I am staying at the Red Lion. I would like to meet somewhere, and I suggest it could be at Hughenden Manor, as I am researching Disraeli for this trip and maybe you could help me."

She replied promptly, "Certainly, Victor. I shall look forward to it. Is tomorrow at 11:00 all right, at the Manor House?"

"That's perfect," he said and added softly. "It's been a long time since I have seen you, Janet. Til tomorrow, then. Goodbye."

He hung up and with a wistful look on his face he retraced his way upstairs to retire.

The next morning after a bit of a restless night with British Road Services lorries rumbling through the darkness in the High Street below his bedroom window, Victor went downstairs. The elegant dining room provided him a delightful English breakfast.

With a contented last sip of his morning tea, he got up and went to his car parked in the street. On the way out he purchased a newspaper, The Bucks Free Press, from the concierge's desk. Outside, the various stall owners were setting up their wares for the weekly market in the High Street. Another quaint tradition, Victor thought, but one that had been going on for a couple of centuries.

Victor got into his car and opened the newspaper. He turned the pages until he reached the classifieds and the employment section. He continued scanning the jobs until he found what he was looking for. In a separate display advertisement, Trandect Engineering Ltd was looking for a "Drafting Assistant" to work with the Senior Draftsman in the Engineering Tooling Department. Responsibilities include:

Maintaining the Blueprints Records Register
Conduct finishing details as specified by the Draftsman
Ensure Blueprints & Drawings versions are up to date
Prepare layouts and schematics from engineering design
Prepare information and specifications for mechanical detail shop assembly drawings, plus material and parts lists
Prepare illustrative materials for reproduction or publication
Perform engineering and statistical calculations

Victor carefully tore the advertisement from the newspaper, folded it up, and placed it in the top pocket of his jacket. He then started his car and drove off from the Red Lion, turning right at the Cornmarket Building as the road twisted around and past Burtons Men's Clothing, then through Frogmoor past the Repertory Theatre to Hughenden Avenue. After several miles he entered the main gate to Hughenden Manor and pulled into the gravel parking area.

Natalia came walking briskly toward him as he alighted from the car. She was wearing a conservative woolen suit in dark blue and a white blouse underneath. The blouse was not buttoned all the way to the collar which left a certain amount of cleavage exposed which was neither offensive nor demure. Victor however was not slow to notice and they embraced rather passionately, but briefly, to allay any suspicion of anything other than a professional relationship.

Victor spoke first addressing her with her cover name. "Hello, Janet, how are you?"

"Very well, Victor. You have some research you are doing here?"

Victor then explained his mission to study the Disraeli legacy and went on to tell Janet how Disraeli had bought Hughenden Manor as a fitting residence for a person of his stature.

Victor told Janet, "Today I want you to be an assistant that I have hired to help me with any translations as I look through the property and its archives. Then we shall have lunch in their tea room where I will give you your assignment for your stay in High Wycombe, all right?"

"Certainly Victor. I think I can handle that."

Together they moved toward the entrance to the Manor. They signed the visitors book, he as Victor Abramovich, Cultural Secretary Attache, Russian Embassy, and she as Janet Rigby, Translator Assistant.

Victor, accompanied by Janet, proceeded through various rooms open to the public. They admired the diamond-shaped plastered ceiling in the drawing room, the small desk or writing table of the favorite prime minister of Queen Victoria, and the leather bound volumes on the vast shelves in the beautiful library. As Victor pored over the archives, he tried to get a sense of the mind of this great British Statesman who had lived in this house from 1848 to 1881.

He studied the portrait of Mary Anne Disraeli hanging above the fireplace in the drawing room. She had been a beautiful and elegant woman, and the painting portrayed her with her bare bosom covered with a silk shawl in a manner almost of a Grecian Goddess-like stature. He looked at Janet who smiled artfully at him.

All the while Victor and Janet were studying the artifacts and archives on all three floors, they were totally unaware that deep down in the cellars of this great house the still-classified archives of military intelligence were stored. This was the photographic reconnaissance of German war-time targets made famous by the "Dam Busters" and others. Hughenden Manor at that time was code-named "Hillside."

It was getting late in the morning when Victor suggested they have some lunch in the tea room. After being seated and had been served tea and sandwiches, Victor slipped the newspaper advertisement across the table for Janet to review.

She studied it at length before looking up, saying, "Apart from doing this job, what is my mission in this company?"

Victor answered, "Janet, one of the managers there is a person by the name of Donald Harvey. The offices of the KGB think he has inadvertently or maybe intentionally intercepted an encoded message at a secret dead letter drop site. We know from our sources that the note had been intended for the British or American intelligence services.

Now, have they got their hands on this message, or does Mr. Harvey still have it? We have a strong suspicion that he may still be in possession of it, and he may even now be working for the American intelligence service. We know he has a very strong connection to the Wycombe US Air Force Base. On the other hand, it's possible he went to the police and they may have turned it over to Britain's Secret Service or have just ignored it."

Janet proposed a different scenario.

"What if he did pick it up? Why would he have kept it if it was just a piece of paper? Would it not have been been written in invisible ink?"

"Ah," Victor declared, "we had thought of that and, yes, the last report we had from our operative, who is now somewhat in-operative, was that his interrogation of the carrier yielded the information that the paper was blank. The one clue we have is we know Mr. Harvey paid a personal visit into the US Air Force Base at Dawes Hill here in Wycombe one evening and spent a considerable time there. He did not leave with cartons of cigarettes or other contraband, so how would he access such a highly secure base without knowledge of the base commander? Unfortunately, as I mentioned a moment ago, our operative has been incapacitated temporarily and we need your help to determine if Mr. Harvey is involved in this operation."

Janet looked at Victor, who appeared worried, "Victor, what is so important about this message? Why is so much attention being paid to this?"

Victor responded, "It's not necessary for you to know the full implications of the complete mission, but only to tell you that the KGB on the highest Soviet authority at the Kremlin has placed this mission as Code Red 3. In other words this project is critical to the Soviet Union, subordinate only to nuclear physics and protection of the Motherland."

"Will I receive any assistance on a secondary basis if and when this may be necessary?" asked Janet.

Victor answered, "Yes, if, for example, Harvey has to travel and we think there may be an element of suspicion he is involved in intelligence work, we will have one of our illegal residents stand by for surveillance duties for us. It was on the report of one of these was how we know he visited the Air Force Base."

"Good," said Janet. "I will make the application for the position at Trandect later this afternoon."

"Good," Victor reacted. "I think we could have dinner tomorrow evening, if you would like, and you could tell me about your interview, if you get one."

"Would that be wise, Victor? After all, our employer is not very tolerant of inter-departmental relationships."

"Well, Nata-, er Janet, it is not something you and I have made a habit of, is it?" he asked eyeing her with a meaningful glance that implied an existing guilt lay between them anyway.

She smiled mischievously saying, "I'm hungry already, even after this delightful lunch. Where will we meet?"

Victor was delighted and suggested that she have dinner in his hotel room to avoid being seen in public together in High Wycombe, with the risk of blowing her cover.

They strolled back to the parking area, briefly embraced and said good-bye until the following evening.

The New Drafting Assistant

Natalia Kolkov, a.k.a. Janet Rigby, walked into the reception area of Trandect Engineering Ltd and approached the reception desk. Janet was wearing the same woolen suit she wore when meeting Victor, but the white blouse underneath was buttoned to the top this time.

She addressed Jill Williamson smiling. "Good Morning. I saw your ad for a Drafting Assistant. I am interested in applying for the position."

Jill puffed on her cigarette, "The job requires previous experience with engineering drafting and dealing with control of blueprints. Have you had that kind of work background?"

"Yes, I have," she replied with complete confidence.

Jill said, "Please take a seat and I will get Mr. White to come and speak with you," and she picked up the intercom and dialed "Chalky" White. "Chalky, I have a young lady here interested in the drafting position. Can you come to the reception, please?"

Chalky came over to the reception office and walked in to meet Janet. He was immediately bowled over by her good looks, blonde hair, and stunning figure. He led her back to the Engineering Tool Room and laid a few blueprints out on the big table.

"Take a look at these," he said, "and tell me how would you determine if these drawings should be lying here and what would you do with them?"

"Well," she replied, "I would first look at the machines and find out what project was being worked. For instance that milling machine there is milling part of an injection mold so I would check if he has the right blueprint with the latest date from the blueprint register. Any others lying here would have to be filed away in the blueprint cabinet."

"Very good," said Chalky looking at her admiringly. "How did you know that was an injection mold?" he asked.

"I have worked in both compression molding and injection molding in a previous position," she lied confidently.

Chalky then quizzed her on some simple engineering questions that would apply to the job, which she answered hesitatingly but with reasonable accuracy.

Chalky said, "Let's go back to reception, and I'll have you wait there while I talk to Mr. Harvey, the Manufacturing Manager here, and see if he has time right now to speak with you."

"Thank you," she replied and followed him back to the reception area where she was invited to sit and wait.

Chalky knocked on Donald's office door and entered. "I have a very good prospect for the drafting job. I think she could do this job standing on her head."

"She?" asked Donald looking surprised.

"Yes," said Chalky smiling, "and very attractive, I might add."

"Oh, attractive, eh? Tell me is she wearing a skirt or slacks?"

"Er," stuttered Chalky, "A skirt. Why?"

"Because, Chalky, me old mate," replied Donald sarcastically, "we don't want an attractive young lady standing on her head in the bloody toolroom do we? So lower your male chauvinist instincts and send her in to see me, and if she is as good as you say, then we may hire her."

Chalky went off and came a few minutes later with Janet in tow. Donald swallowed hard when he saw her as she did indeed look stunning, and was hardly what he imagined a drafting assistant would look like. He dismissed Chalky and asked Janet to sit down. He had difficulty in diverting his gaze away from her legs as she lowered herself into the office chair. He went over the role she would have in the drafting position and asked her a number of questions similar to Chalky's discussion. She was able to answer most questions.

Donald then asked her where she went to school.

"In Yorkshire," she said, "Secondary Modern then a Technical School with emphasis on mechanics where I obtained my 'A' Levels."

Donald then enquired, "Are you Polish or Ukrainian, because you do have an accent?"

Janet was taken aback a little at first that he would be able to recognize those accents, but quickly recovered saying, "I came to England as a child from Yugoslavia. My parents are now dead. So maybe that's why you hear a little accent"

Donald laughed, "You certainly don't have a Yorkshire accent, Miss Rigby." He continued, "Anyway, I do like your background, and I think you could certainly do the job. When could you start?"

Janet responded straight away, "I can start immediately. Is there a weekly wage or fortnightly pay?"

Donald said, "The job pays seven pounds a week and it could rise to nine pounds within six months. If you agree, I would like you to start tomorrow morning starting at 8:30 a.m."

Janet replied that it would be wonderful and accepted the position.

Janet was happy that everything had gone so smoothly, and she was enthusiastic to learn more about her new boss. In the meantime she returned to the bed-sitter room she had rented and prepared for an evening with Victor.

At 7:00 p.m. she was ready and wearing a tight-fitting, light blue skirt, and a matching front-buttoned blouse with an open collar that was showing her ample bosom. She took a taxi to the Red Lion where she met Victor who whisked her briskly up to his room where a table had been laid out for dinner.

The table was set with wine glasses for both the entrée and dessert courses together with a fine table cloth and beautiful silverware. Janet surveyed the presentation and remarked, "It appears that the Kremlin is sparing no expense here."

"I think with the kind of work we do, Natalia," he said using her real name, "it becomes necessary to become part of the milieu from time to time. Otherwise we might come across to the local populace as Russian peasants without any class at all."

"I have ordered a delicious rack of lamb, and we have some Russian caviar that I brought with me on this trip just to set the mood."

"And what mood is that, Victor?" she smiled at him. He gently embraced her and they kissed passionately. She pushed him away gently with a mock admonishment. "I am hungry for that rack of lamb."

He poured two glasses of Bordeaux, and they toasted each other

"Budem zdorovy!," "Let's stay healthy!" Victor stated, "In our line of work, that's critical. Now tell me, Natalia, how did the job interview go?"

Before she could answer there was a knock on the door. It was room service with their dinner.

After everything was laid out and Victor had tipped the waiter, they sat down to eat. "You were about to tell me some news, Natalia."

"Yes," she replied, "you will be pleased to know I got the job at seven pounds a week which is not bad for a Russian spy." She laughed and took another sip of wine. "Mr. Harvey is quite handsome, you know." She grinned mischievously at Victor who pulled a face at her.

"Well, you need to find out if he has the message we want, the content of it, and if he is working with the Americans. If he is completely out of this picture, then we are at a dead end, and being at a dead end for the KGB is not a destination you want to be at, literally."

He offered her the caviar on a small cracker which she tasted and thought was of the highest quality.

"Yes, I understand, Victor. Comrade Demidov will not tolerate failure from either of us," Natalia offered, but with the emphasis on "either of us."

Victor changed the subject as he was not too happy with the implication that Natalia might compromise him in the event they failed their mission. In fact, she was the one who was supposed to *bring home the bacon*," as the locals say in their vernacular.

They started on the lamb and mint sauce with roast potatoes and young Brussels sprouts. Everything was cooked to perfection. Victor mentioned that he had been told the meat for tonight's dish was the finest Welsh lamb from a particular farm, and was supposed to be even better than New Zealand lamb.

With meat still on ration in England, the two Russians enjoying a gourmet feast was a contradiction of national character. At last, a small sampling of the decadent trifle pudding laced with sherry put the couple in a relaxed and comfortable mood.

They retired to the sofa to watch the news before the TV closed for the night. Victor put his arm around Natalia, and she responded by pressing her leg against his. He instinctively turned to her and they kissed while his hand moved gently toward the buttons on her blouse. She helped him remove the blouse and he pulled her up from the sofa, leading her to the bed while the television turned to snow as the the nightly transmission ended.

It was three o'clock in the morning when Victor called for a taxi to take Natalia back to her accommodation.

"I had better not be late for my new job, Victor."

"That would certainly be a black mark against you," he replied. He kissed her fondly goodbye and wished her good luck. He stood watching as the taxi drove off into the night.

Notice of Meeting Museum Tavern

Colonel Blankenship asked to see the new employee and spent a few minutes with Janet explaining the nature of the company's business. He was at the same time reviewing her credentials as presented by Donald. It was important to know a little more about her and he asked Jill to research her previous employment. With the amount of government work Trandect was engaged in, it was important to know one's employees background, particularly a previous foreign national.

Janet got to work in the drafting office under Chalky's direction and busied herself with the specifics of the job. She was a big hit with the toolmakers who thought she was a welcome addition to the firm.

Meanwhile, Donald had taken a telephone call from Alicja who told him that there had not been a funeral for her uncle because the coroner had not yet specified the cause of death. He told the family that he needed more time to ascertain exactly how he had died. The family was very puzzled by this as they were under the impression from the preliminary police report that he had suffered a serious accident with a train during a shunting operation.

Donald offered his deepest sympathies to Alicja and to her family. He was in no position to enlighten her as to the true nature of Zaluski's demise, and it troubled him greatly that it was a secret he would have to keep from her for the time being. Although she was reticent after he invited her to the weekly dance at Wycombe Town Hall on Saturday night, she eventually agreed that it would be good to take her mind off of her current burden of grief.

Donald asked her to bring Ola to meet with Cal Jennings and she said she would try, but it was up to Ola herself.

After he put down the phone, Chalky came in with the latest prototype for the Fairy Delta.

"It's looking good this new material. Pity this plane is experimental. It would be nice to have a decent production run of these things."

"It would," Donald replied, "but don't forget the government pays us handsomely for prototypes. After all an injection mold with one cavity to produce a single item is going to be very costly. How is your drafting assistant getting along?"

Chalky said, "Janet? She's doing well. She's already cleared up and filed quite a number of blueprints that were lying about. For others that are in valid use and up to date, she is in the process of registering the drawing numbers in the log and getting signatures for them."

"That's excellent, Chalky, but we need the obsolete drawings taken up to the front office for Jill to place in the Archives for any future Ministry audit."

Chalky responded, "I'll get on to it when I get back to the tool room."

"By the way," Donald looked at him, "I won't be in tomorrow. I have to be in London to talk to Imperial Chemical Industries about raw materials."

"All right, Don, I'll keep the wheels turning here."

He left Donald's office and returned to the toolroom.

Donald had received a telephone call from Richard that morning at home, advising him of the joint meeting that had been arranged. He was told he should make his way to the Museum Tavern opposite the British Museum in Bloomsbury, and Richard would meet him there at 11:00 a.m. Major Wallace would also attend, as well as Freddie Simpson.

Chalky got back to the tool room and began instructing Janet on how she should collect the obsolete or out of date blue prints. She should take them to the front office where Jill will show her how to place them in the archive.

Janet carried the drawings to the reception area and asked Jill how she should go about logging them in and placing them in the big cabinet in the archives room which was shielded by a large screen behind Jill's desk and to the left of Colonel Blankenship's office. Jill showed her the procedure and returned to her desk.

Donald entered the reception area and approached Jill who was puffing on her interminable cigarette sending out clouds of smoke like a Comanche warrior.

"Goodness, Jill, I'm glad you don't smoke Gauloise or we'd all die of congestion."

"Maybe you should get me some of those Yankee Camel fags you bring in for Bill Richardson," she replied with a hoarse laugh.

"I can do that if you got the money," he said.

"Listen, Jill, I'm off to London tomorrow to meet some people from ICI regarding the polystyrene pellets, and we're meeting in the morning not far from the British Museum. I know it's in Bloomsbury but what street's that on, as I'm trying to establish the nearest tube station?"

Jill began looking up her London map and Underground information. At this time, Janet had made a mental note of Donald's comments while continuing to write in the archive log her blueprint drawing numbers.

She listened closely as Jill finally said, "It's on Great Russell Street, and the nearest Underground would be Tottenham Court Road, leaving just a short walk if it's close to the Museum."

"That's good enough. Thanks, Jill," said Donald.

Janet took her time to complete her task after Donald had left the area, and she then returned to the toolroom with Jill commenting, "Goodness, girl, you were as quiet as mouse in there. I almost forgot you were back there."

Janet smiled and went on her way.

After work she went to the nearest public telephone and rang the Red Lion. She asked for Mr. Victor Abramovich and was put through to his room. The front desk attendant told Victor there was a Miss Rigby on the line and would he like to take the call?

He told the attendant to put her through. "Hello, Miss Rigby. How are you?"

"I'm very well, Victor, and I have some news for you."

He immediately became very attentive, "Please tell me something that will make me happy."

Janet was being careful saying, "My uncle will be visiting London tomorrow and may need help when getting off the Underground at Tottenham Court Road and making his way to the British Museum on Great Russell Street."

"That is good news," murmured Victor, "What time is he expected?"

"Not sure about that. You will just have to keep your eyes open during the morning."

"Thanks, Miss Rigby, I will make sure your uncle is well looked after. Goodnight."

With that, Victor made immediate arrangements to return to London that same night. He could not risk telephoning the Embassy to relay his information. He went to the foyer and reception desk. While he was standing there paying his bill and with the Porter waiting with his bags, Roger Hewitt-Benning strolled through the foyer on his way to the bar which he frequented on occasions. He glanced toward Victor and then took a second look before continuing.

Since Roger was friendly with a number of the staff including Bert, the barman, he felt comfortable asking Bert if he knew who the gentleman was standing at the reception. Bert leaned over the counter to get a better view through the open doorway.

"I dunno," he said, "but I've seen 'im a couple of times. Why do you ask?"

"Oh, just curious. I thought I recognized him from somewhere, that's all," replied Roger.

Bert half knew that Roger had been in some kind of secret service in the war, so he thought he might help him out here.

"Well, if you like Roger, me old mate, I can always find out from Denise at the front desk there, who this bloke is," offered Bert.

As he said this, the Cultural Attache walked quickly out of the hotel followed by the porter with his bags. Roger also got up and told Bert to guard his beer while he popped out for a moment. He was just in time to see Victor's car beginning to move off from the curb and made a mental note of the diplomatic license plate.

He returned to the bar, and Bert was now very curious as to Roger's movements.

"Bert, do me a favor, ask Denise to let you know who that chap was and how long was he staying here."

Bert put down the towel he was using to wipe a glass, lifted the counter top flap to release himself from the bar and quickly walked over to Denise to chat her up. He wasn't long before returning and customers in the bar were beginning to queue up for another round.

After he had served a few drinks, Bert returned to Roger and said, "He was a fancy foreign toff. His name is Victor Abramovich, Cultural Attache at the Russian Embassy, and he was here on a study mission."

Roger said, "Yeh, I bet he was. What was he studying, I wonder?"

Bert responded, "According to Denise he had been here to conduct research on local history and Benjamin Disraeli. He even visited Hughenden Manor."

"Really?" Roger sounded surprised. "It's hard to imagine the Soviet Union having an interest in a democratic icon of English history, that's for sure."

"Maybe he just wanted to get away to meet his girlfriend. Denise tells me he had a pretty sharp looking lass spend some time in his room with him having a private dinner."

Roger thought to himself, *Is the Disraeli thing a cover for getting himself laid, or is there something he was fishing for at Hughenden Manor? Everything we were doing over there is still classified and is completely sealed up in the cellars and basement. On the other hand, the local US Air Force Base would be of interest to the Soviets. There is complete security over that base and although there has been some talk of spooky lights and UFOs, he felt the place was just another strategic base.*

Roger stood up and thanked Bert, handing him a nice tip and said, "I may pop in for a quick one tomorrow."

He left the Red Lion and with the puzzle of why a Soviet Embassy official would visit High Wycombe on his mind, he resolved that tomorrow he would take a trip to Hughenden Manor to see what he could establish.

Getting to the Joint Briefing

Donald stepped off the train at Paddington Station and wended his way through the crowds toward the Undergound. He stopped at the Station cafe to grab a jam doughnut to help sustain him for awhile. He had not had time for breakfast this morning and was not sure how long the meeting would be. The cafe interior smelt strongly of tobacco smoke, together with the pervasive odor of overused cooking oil for the fish and chips. Donald quickly paid for his doughnut and left the cafe hurriedly to avoid having his clothes smell of British Railways culinary distinction.

Donald had been coached to some degree about taking a circuitous route to meeting places in an attempt to lose any potential followers. His lack of complete training in this regard, coupled with his relative inexperience, caused him to fail to see a man in a smart business suit carrying a coat and an umbrella following him from the station.

Comrade Tarasov had taken no chances that he would miss Mr. Harvey arriving in London. As soon as Victor had got back in town the previous night, he had reported to Secretary Demidov concerning Donald's impending visit. Tarasov immediately got in touch with two of their illegal residents who were skilled at surveillance. From Janet's intelligence, they knew he would probably make his way to his final unknown destination via Tottenham Court Road Underground Station. However, just in case and on the basis that he might use a different tube station, Tarasov felt it would be prudent to track him from the railway station. In this case there were two alternative trains from High Wycombe — one ending at Marylebone and the other in Paddington. Therefore, he had two people tracking Donald. He knew that their target could arrive at either station before taking the Underground. Tarasov positioned the man in the suit and umbrella at Paddington, and a lady dressed like a tourist with a camera was waiting at Marylebone. Both had been briefed on Donald's description and appearance, together with a grainy photo taken at a distance.

Tarasov had also positioned a spotter from the embassy staff at each station who would receive a pre-arranged signal from the successful "shadower" that the target had been found. In the case of Paddington, the "shadow" simply lifted his umbrella and placed the hooked handle over his arm. The spotter then went to a public telephone and called in to the embassy that the target was on his way from Paddington. The embassy then arranged for the other spotter who called in every 15 minutes to tell the lady shadow to travel to and position herself with her camera at the entrance to the British Musem.

As Donald descended the escalator to the Underground on his way to the Circle Line platform, the shadow kept a discreet distance behind with at least ten other people between him and Donald. There was a rush of air as the incoming train pulled into the station and doors opened allowing people to pour out onto the platform and hurry away. Donald joined the crowd that was boarding the middle of the carriage, and the shadow hopped on at the other door. The shadow made no attempt to look directly at Donald but was able to keep him in his peripheral vision at all times. The doors closed with a hiss of compressed air, and the trained moved smoothly into the tunnel heading for the next station.

With the train rocking gently back and forth as it picked up speed and with the loud clacking and whooshing sound of the typical London Underground rail train in his ears, Donald casually surveyed the scene, thinking about his upcoming meeting. He saw all the passengers in his compartment as the typical cosmopolitan genre of London: a couple of Jamaican immigrants seeking their future in England now that their country had gained its independence from the colonial master; the lady in the raincoat with her full shopping bag making her way home; the typical civil servant with his bowler hat and reading the Times newspaper so he would not need to make eye contact with any of the lower classes; and the man with his coat and umbrella hooked over his arm standing and holding onto the upright rail. The latter he thought strange, as there were a few empty seats quite close to the man. The train stopped at the Bayswater Station, disgorging and engorging the surging mass of humanity that is London.

The train continued its hypnotic rhythm of movement and sound until it began slowing down entering the Notting Hill Gate Station. Donald rose from his seat. The lady with the shopping bag was in front of him before he got to the door, and he waited for her to alight before stepping out onto the platform. The shadow also got out onto the platform from the other door and followed as he had in the previous manner, keeping a judicious distance between them.

Donald turned sharply to the left and entered the platform for the Central Line that was headed to Epping. His destination was Tottenham Court Road, and he studied the Underground map that was

enlarged on the wall behind him. Satisfied that he was on the right platform, he stood and waited for the next train to arrive. The shadow,
meanwhile, was well concealed from view by standing close to several
other commuters. In the interim, the shadow had now put on his dark
raincoat over his suit, but was still carrying his umbrella.

The train entered the station with its whooshing and brakes
squealing as it came to a stop. The doors hissed and slid open while the
train and the platform exchanged contents. Donald got on but was
obliged to stand, holding the overhead strap, as there were no available
seats. The doors slid closed again, and the train picked up speed on its
way to the Queensway station. The shadow had positioned himself
several feet away, also standing, but with his back to Donald.
However, he was facing the rear window of the carriage that looked
through into the next carriage. That window often reflects like a
mirror thus enabling the shadow to keep his vigil of Donald intact.

They passed Lancaster Gate, Marble Arch, Bond Street, and
Oxford Circus stations until they were approaching Tottenham Court
Road Station. Here, Donald squeezed past some passengers standing in
front of the door. The train stopped and Donald moved with those who
were exiting and finally was able to get out. The shadow, meanwhile,
had been waiting to make sure Donald was not doing an "out and in"
maneuver, before he, too, hopped out onto the platform as the doors
were closing.

The shadow knew in advance that Donald's destination was at the
British Museum or nearby, and so it was just a matter of which route he
would take to walk there.

Donald came up from the Underground to Oxford Street where
the cool air was at first refreshing, but soon became irritating from the
fumes of diesel- engined buses, taxis, and general traffic. He quickly
walked along Oxford Street and turned left into Bloomsbury and then
right onto Great Russell Street heading toward the British Museum on
the left. As he turned onto the Great Russell Street, he noticed the
shadow not far behind with other pedestrians. He thought the man
looked familiar but simply dismissed it. The shadow was no longer carrying his umbrella over his arm, but had it in his right hand swinging it
gently in time with his pace. This small change by itself was enough to
distract Donald's recent recognition of any similarity of perceived followers. The "shadow" crossed to the opposite side of the street to Donald, but kept pace with him.

Donald spotted the Museum Tavern opposite the Museum's main
entrance but before he entered, he turned and looked at the great edifice

across the street. Construction was in full swing where the Duveen Gallery that had housed the Elgin Marbles had been badly damaged by enemy bombing. The Marbles themselves had been safely hidden during the war deep in the Aldwych Tube Station. As Donald briefly admired the 44 columns of the Greek Revival facade closely resembling the temple of Athena Polias, he did not notice among the throng of tourists in the front of the building a lady with a camera taking pictures. She could be mistaken for being an American with the way she was dressed, together with her plimsolls or tennis shoes. Some of her shots were directed toward the Museum Tavern across the street where Donald was standing. At this point, his admiration for the Museum's architecture now sated, he turned and entered the tavern. His shadow, in the meantime, had turned and entered the Museum itself, his part of the mission completed.

The Joint Meeting Briefing

Donald entered the tavern to find the place crowded from front to back. He was just wondering how a meeting could be held in such a noisy and bustling place, when he felt a tap on his arm. Turning, he faced Freddie Simpson who was smiling, looking dapper in a blazer and wearing a cravat in place of a tie.

"Hello, Donald, glad you could make it," he said loudly over the hub hub. "We have a private room upstairs. I'll lead the way."

He proceeded to squeeze past the pub's patrons toward the back of the place and then to the end of the bar. One of the barmen nodded to Freddie and lifted the portion of the bar counter that provided access to the serving side. Freddie slipped through, followed by Donald, and then up a flight of heavily carpeted stairs that led to the landing. Freddie turned to the right and knocked on a heavy door which opened, and they both entered the room.

Major Wallace sprang up from a chair near the window with some papers in one hand, shaking Donald's hand with the other.

"Hi, Donald," he drawled slowly chewing his habitual piece of gum. "Nice to see you again, and you, of course, know Richard Bates here, right?"

Richard stepped forward, "Good to see you again, old chap."

Donald spoke, "I'm a little apprehensive, but at the same time I'm also pleased and honored to be entrusted with some secret activity of national importance."

"Well, yes, of course it is important, but we do not wish to overemphasize the significance of your role in it. You have a genuine commercial mission in Paris, and we are taking advantage of your civilian position, which minimizes the risk of exposing our task of finding Herr Kammler."

Richard gestured Donald toward a large, round, beautifully polished mahogany table and invited the others to join the two of them.

The room was big and furnished with heavy Victorian furniture, and the floor was thickly carpeted in a deep red color. The walls were covered in green wallpaper with an elegant floral design, and the whole room seemed soundproofed from the noisy din below. Two windows looked out onto Museum Street, and the window at the other end of the room faced the British Museum on Great Russell Street.

Richard began, "I think we should start off by saying that the killer of Zaluski seems to have got away. The police had tracked him down in Southhampton, but he may have escaped on a ship leaving that day. A thorough search failed to find him, although the logical choice of ship was this vessel heading to East Germany. Unless the authorities had made the vessel turn around and ordered it back to port, it would have required virtually stripping and dismantling machinery and equipment to find our man. Obviously, we could not do that under the political circumstance and without real evidence of him being aboard."

Freddie asked if he could now confirm to the Wycombe Police that a murder suspect had been sought, but not apprehended. Richard agreed that the coroner could state the cause of death was by homicide.

Donald asked, "Who was this thug?"

Freddie answered, "His pseudonym was Tomasz Bielski, a Polish Free Army chap who unfortunately went missing in action in North Africa, presumed killed. His real name was Igor Martinovich, a notorious killer originating from Ukraine. He has much blood on his hands, as well as assisting in the deportation of thousands of Poles to Siberia during the Russian annexation of a part of Poland in 1939."

"How were you able to identify him if he had a false identity established?" asked Donald.

Freddie continued, "Once we knew his National Health Insurance card had a fake doctor on it, we began checking the military records of the Polish Free Army under General Anders. We also checked the Home Office records because each foreign national in the United Kingdom must carry an identity card that has to be presented to a police station to record a person's current address. This would have a photo. The photograph at the Home Office did not match the photo of Mr. Bielski in the Polish Army!"

Richard picked up the explanation from there by stating, "We started looking at the records in military intelligence for anyone who resembled this man, and the connection was obvious when we came across the man we now know as Igor Martinovich, who was wanted for war crimes and aiding in the holocaust."

Major Wallace, who had been silent up to this point, broke in saying, "You can bet your ass that just because this son of a bitch got away, the Russians have not slacked off trying to get their hands on the lead that we have. They probably are still trying to find out if Don here is involved or not. They know that Don bumped into the Igor guy outside the church, which was soon after Zaluski left. Igor would have checked for the drop and, not finding it, was the reason he must have raided Don's place. He was also hanging around Farnborough, maybe on a separate spying mission, maybe not. I feel we need to keep a close protection on Don."

Donald glanced at the Major and mentally said, *Thanks for that!*

Donald spoke up now, "I have a delicate question to ask, and I am not sure how you will react. Being a sort of compartmentalized agent, I am not sure what my boundaries are in terms of sharing information."

Richard assured Donald, "Ask away, Donald. It's spontaneous actions without prior questions that are a problem for us. What's on your mind?"

Donald explained, "You will recall that when I received the deciphered note from my acquaintance, Roger Hewitt-Benning, it became apparent that it was in Polish or Russian. Following my curiosity, it was natural for me to ask my Polish girlfriend, Alicja, if it was written in Polish, and if it was, could she translate it, which of course is what she did. The fact that Roger got in touch with you people in the intelligence community was something out of my control. The question therefore becomes, how do I handle the matter of the note with Alicja?"

Richard had now filled his pipe and lit it in a cloud of smoke.

"Damn," said Wallace grinning good naturedly. "You could always get a job as a beekeeper. You would never get stung."

Everyone laughed at the American's quip.

Richard said, "Did Alicja ask you anything at all about the note, Donald, and how did you leave the subject?"

"I was being very cautious," said Donald, "because I had not mentioned her uncle, Karol Zaluski, so I more or less let her think it maybe had something to do with my work. However, when she discovers that her uncle has been murdered, she may begin to suspect Russian involvement. She had already told me she was worried about her uncle and some kind of Soviet influence or pressure on him."

Richard blew a stream of smoke toward the ceiling and invited suggestions, "Well, Freddie, Major Wallace, I have an opinion but would like to get your suggestions so that we can reach a consensus on Don's dilemma."

Wallace spoke first, "I think first of all we should NOT inform the Wycombe Police the identity of Zaluski's killer or that we know he was a Russian agent. It would create an unwanted and unnecessary diplomatic furor. They just need to know the suspect Bielski has escaped and is probably now out of the country."

Freddie added, "But the very fact we have a Polish name as the suspect will cause the Polish community itself to question the impact that one of their own is the culprit. They will try to find out who Bielski really is or was."

Richard now added his comment, "It does seem on the face of it, a tricky little conundrum. This could ostensibly become very difficult for Donald to handle if his lady friend becomes intensely curious about the coincidence of his Polish language note, and an unknown Polish emigré murdering her uncle. She is bound to ask questions."

Wallace interjected further, "She may not ask any questions, and so until she does, Don should not invite any enquiry by discussing the Zaluski incident at all."

Donald responded to that by saying, "I just need a contingency plan in the event Alicja brings up the question of the note again."

After further discussion, it was agreed that if Alicja raised the issue, Donald would give her the true facts of her uncle's demise at the hands of Igor Martinovich masquerading as Bielski. Donald "got this information from his friend, Roger Hewitt-Benning, who had contacts in the intelligence community." Donald knew nothing more about the note because he had handed it over to Roger for forwarding to MI6. He would be able to say to his lady friend that the Wycombe Police would only know about a Bielski, as a full disclosure would be diplomatically complicated. Donald would know nothing further than that!

The team agreed this was the best course of action for this situation, and they decided to move on to other matters on the agenda.

Richard tapped out his pipe in the oversize ashtray, much to the relief of Donald and Wallace. Freddie, in the meantime, had wandered off to the windows overlooking Great Russell Street straight across

124

from the Museum entrance. He had wanted to get a little relief from his boss's industrial strength chimney of a pipe. After looking across the street for a few moments, he turned to the others saying, "Take a look here for a moment."

The others got up and moved to the window.

"What do you see, Freddie?" asked Major Wallace.

Freddie pointed to the well-dressed woman with the plimsolls "looking" like an American tourist and holding a camera.

"She was there when Donald arrived, and she hasn't left since. She was working that camera at this pub before I went down to meet Donald. The fact she's still there and casually looking this way and not at the Museum tells me she is running surveillance for someone."

Richard responded, "Well, none of us are leaving the way we came in, so she's going to have a long wait. Hope she has a decent-size bladder because she will need it unless she has a back-up to relieve her. Forgive the pun! Let's get back to business."

The group returned to the table.

As they sat down, Wallace asked Donald, "Don, did you see her following you from the station or at any time?"

"No, Major. I saw a lot of people but none that I could positively say were following me."

"Just call me James," he said and then turning to Richard, "Richard, if we are going to use this young man in any kind of mission, whether it be covert, benign or outright overt, it's important you guys give him some basic training in evading surveillance. He was obviously followed today, and that lady across the street ain't no American tourist."

"Yes," said Richard, "I agree, and we'll make some arrangements for that. After all, if he is being followed now, it will continue in Paris, no doubt."

"That's not very reassuring," commented Donald while thinking, *This is like being in quicksand; the longer I stay in, the deeper I get!*

"You'll be okay," assured James.

Richard asked everyone to take a look at the Note which had been in two pieces, but were now placed together thus:

petrowksi 123 de la pompe death bell departed leader to
 in the city of natal pine

"Our moles in Poland have provided this lead concerning Kammler's current supposed whereabouts. We are expected to obtain more detail from a Mr. Petrowski, who had been part of the Polish State Underground movement recognized by the West. Donald is to make his way to Paris and locate our man at 123 Rue de la Pompe, which is in the 16th Arrondissement, and complete the following interview:

Donald should locate Petrowski and establish his status in France.

What is the name of the alleged Polish slave worker and what is the connection to Petrowski?

How did he survive the alleged massacre at the weapons site?

Where exactly was the site?

How did this connection observe or obtain the future plans of escape of Herr Kammler?

How accurate did the connection consider this information to be and why?

What is Petrowski's best understanding of the words "Death Bell" and its relationship to Kammler?

Have any Jewish organizations visited Petrowski? We want this question answered because the Jewish Nazi hunters are relentless and may have used their own intelligence groups or the MOSSAD to identify Petrowski for their own ends of getting Kammler

While we have our own ideas about the city of Natal Pine, we want Petrowski to give us his opinion based on his discussion with the connection.

Why did Petrowski flee Poland, and how did he obtain residency in France?

Richard asked James Wallace, "These are the main points that we have agreed should be asked of Petrowski, but I know you were thinking we need more. What did you have in mind?"

James thought for a moment and offered in his usual gum-chewing drawl, "It's essential that we try to find out if the 'connection,' as you call him, had any idea of the engineering, technology, or weapons experiments that were being conducted."

The question was added to the list.

"Donald, we're going to have you learn this list because you will not be able to take it with you to Paris."

Donald sat up, "Well, it's been a long time since I left school. I'm not sure I have that capability anymore."

"Practice makes perfect, old chap," interjected Richard.

"Now, Don" said James, "We're setting you up in a hotel close to the American Embassy. Obviously, we're not having you dropping by there or anything, but you will have an emergency number to call, if necessary. The hotel we have for you is the Hotel Cambon on the Rue Cambon just near the Place de la Concorde and not too far from our Embassy on Rue Gabrielle."

Richard asked James, "I understand you have some very good business connections laid on for Donald."

"Yeh, we've indirectly had our people at SHAPE feed some connections through to Trandect Ltd. on the basis of Colonel Blankenship's previous military ties in Europe. Therefore, these opportunities are genuine business prospects that could lead to purchase contracts for Trandect. However, that part is entirely up to Mr. Harvey here."

"What kind of leads are they?" asked Donald, amazed at how all this is put together.

James replied, "It could be a mixed bag of thermoplastic injection-molded products for aircraft or other military uses, and it could also be contracts for the refurbishments of instruments. The latter will require access to Military Specifications of the nations involved. Anyway, it should keep you busy over there to wine and dine Petrowski and grill him for what he knows."

Donald was still trying to figure out how his boss might be an agent of British Secret Intelligence, but he thought he better keep it to himself and not ask questions. This clandestine stuff was tricky. He did ask to no one in particular, "So can I assume that my boss, Colonel Blankenship, will provide me with the SHAPE leads? How is it I will have a hotel already lined up?"

Again James led on this, "I'm glad you're thinking, Don," he said softly, "It means you're paying attention to detail. Our guys at SHAPE have 'generously' offered to pay for your accommodation through their own budgets. I'm not saying it's paid for by the Marshall Plan or anything, but it's all taken care of," he said grinning broadly. He placed a fresh stick of Wrigley's Spearmint in his mouth and sat back to hear any comments.

Richard said, "I think we have covered most of the issues, and I would ask Donald if he has further points that need clarifying and, more importantly, if he still feels game to continue?"

Donald glanced at James Wallace who stared back at him stoically while chewing slowly and deliberately on his gum.

Donald thought to himself, *Well, I don't have a lot of choice do I, but I suppose with some genuine leads for Trandect, plus a trip to Paris, I really can't go wrong, can I?*

He then said aloud, "I think the leads for Trandect are a good trade-off for interviewing your Mr Petrowski, so I'm still in this."

"Good man," said Richard, and James grinned happily, while Freddie got up and moved to the window to take another look.

"Well, she's still there, and she must be getting a cold bum sitting on that balustrade all this time."

"Okay, Freddie," ordered Richard, "Please guide Donald out through the flat, would you?"

They all shook hands, and Freddie led Donald across the hallway at the end of the landing to the door there. This opened into an upstairs room which Freddie explained was an apartment owned by the pub. He closed the door behind him, and guided Donald through the room to the door on the opposite side which, in turn, led to stairs. They both descended the stairs into a nicely furnished living room. From the living room they were able to access the door that fed into an open courtyard. Freddie turned the round knob on the Yale lock and opened the door and, after ensuring all was clear, he gestured for Donald to come outside, and then he released the knob allowing the lock to re-set itself as he closed the door behind them. Freddie then showed Donald the way to a passageway opposite the courtyard and out on to Gilbert Way, which ran behind and parallel with Great Russell Street. No one from the museum entrance would have been able to see them exit the Museum Tavern.

Freddie and Donald walked to the Holborn Tube Station, and Freddie bade Donald goodbye.

Freddie made a parting comment, "I shall be coming to High Wycombe to give you some lessons in surveillance and avoiding surveillance. I will not tell you in advance, but I will simply surprise you in the town one day."

"All right, Freddie. I look forward to that, and I'll buy you a pint or two."

They shook hands and parted company, Freddie returning to MI6, and Donald headed back to Wycombe.

Chapter 12

The Internal Spy

Donald and Paris Itinerary

Donald left a message for Alicja at the Hodgemoor Camp asking her to meet him Saturday night at the Town Hall Dance at 8:00 p.m. He asked for her to bring Ola with her. Donald telephoned Cal Jennings and arranged for him to be at the dance.

'Hey, pal, I'll be there, and do I need to bring some cigarettes?"

"No, I think I'll hold off for now," replied Donald.

It was now Thursday, and he needed to prepare for work the next day at the office.

he next morning Donald was up early and had breakfast. He brewed a pot of tea and made sure there was enough for Mrs. Fenchurch who had not yet woken up. At 8:30 a.m. he entered his office after bidding Jill "Good Morning" at the reception, and sat down to plan his itinerary for Paris. At the same time he looked at his notes from the MI6 meeting in London and began practicing learning the points he was supposed to question Petrowski on.

Jill called through on his extension and told him that the Colonel wanted to see him at 10 o'clock this morning. Donald confirmed he would be there and then got up to go to the tool room to confer with Chalky White. He said hello to a couple of machinists as he entered and said a polite "Good Morning" to Janet Rigby, who turned from her task at the drafting table and returned his greeting with a friendly smile. Donald walked over to Chalky's small office tucked away in the corner, but away from the noise of the precision grinding machines, milling machines, and lathes that were humming away on their respective tasks.

"Morning, Chalky," Donald said as he squeezed into his little office. "I'm afraid I'm not going to be able to get your Lucky Strikes for the time being. Bit of a hold up on the supply line right now, if you know what I mean."

Chalky snorted, "Ah, no problem, mate. I'll carry on rollin' me own now. That four cavity mold for De Haviland is working out quite well, and the first batches are coming out great with just the right amount of sprue and no gassing."

"Excellent," said Donald, "We may have to put on an extra shift in the next couple of months, because I am hoping to get some new business shortly."

Chalky looked up as Janet knocked on the door. "Yes, Janet, what do you need?"

She replied, "I just came for the 421-C blueprint you wanted me to file."

Chalky looked at the pile on his desk saying, "Oh, here it is. Just fold it up and don't forget to log it, Janet."

At the same time, he turned back to Donald who was gazing at Janet's curves and legs, and said to him, "So where are you getting this new business, Donald?"

"In France, Chalky. I'm visiting the Supreme Headquarters Allied Powers Europe. We have some good connections with several of the military members there, and I hope to capitalize on those connections."

Janet meanwhile had folded up the blueprint, and on her way out smiled at Donald who pulled his gaze away from her attractive curves in embarrassment, while acknowledging her with, "Good morning, Janet."

She replied softly, "Good morning, Donald," and went on her way back to her post.

Donald bid Chalky goodbye and headed over to Bill Richardson, and they chatted for while about the the state of the instrument refurbishment business. It was now close to 10 o'clock, and Donald headed to the Colonel's office.

"Hello, Jill," he said, "I'm on time. Is the Colonel ready for me?"

Jill said she would check, got up from her desk, and went into the Colonel's office. Donald heard the big man say something, and Jill returned motioning Donald to enter. Colonel Blakenship leaned back in his chair, and in his deep powerful voice invited Donald to sit down.

"Good morning, Donald. I wanted to follow up with you regarding the Paris trip and meeting with the SHAPE people. I understand a reservation has been made for you at the Hotel Cambon, thanks to the logistics officer for the British contingent. Your daily per diem will be on Trandect's budget, however, so keep it conservative. You don't have to eat bread and water, but you don't need to be eating rack of lamb every day either."

"Yes, sir, I understand," replied Donald smiling broadly. "Here's the list of people you have authority to meet, and these are your letters of introduction." The Colonel leaned over the desk and handed Donald a sheaf of papers. "It's basically a fishing expedition to determine what viable products could be of benefit to each of these SHAPE members."

"Should I take the channel ferry or a plane from London?" asked Donald.

The Colonel responded, "I have asked Jill to book you on the Newhaven to Dieppe Ferry next week, plus booking you on the train from London to Newhaven and on to Paris. The return trip will be configured once you have concluded some business over there. Good luck, Donald, and keep out of trouble."

"Thanks, Colonel. I don't anticipate getting into trouble over there, Paris or no Paris," said Donald grinning again.

In the meantime Janet had been thinking furiously at her drafting table about what she had heard between Donald and Chalky. She needed to find out more. She got up and walked over to Chalky who was conferring with a machinist on a technical point. When he had finished, she asked him if he had seen a particular blueprint that she was trying to locate. When Chalky declined knowing where it might be, she asked him,

"So is Mr. Harvey going to France? I couldn't help overhearing him saying something to you about it."

Chalky laughed, "Yeh, the lucky so and so, and Janet, he can't take you cos he's got a girlfriend already."

They both laughed at Chalky's inept joke, but Janet wanted more information.

"When will he be going, do you know?"

"I'm not sure exactly, Janet, but I expect Jill will have his itinerary anyway." Chalky looked at Janet, puzzled, "Why do you ask?"

"Oh, no reason," she said. "Just curious, that's all." She turned on her heel and went back to her work.

It was getting close to lunchtime as she got up and, picking up a drawing, she walked briskly to the front office. When she arrived there, Jill was not around, so Janet made her way around the back of Jill's desk to the archive room. She had a close look at the desk but could not see anything of interest.

Suddenly the telex machine nearby came to life and began typing out a message. It was a confirmation for a reservation for Mr. Harvey at the Hotel Cambon on Rue Cambon beginning Wednesday evening next week. Janet quickly moved away as she heard Jill returning. There was no time to exit the front office so she quickly popped back into the archive room and made noises like she was busy folding blueprints.

Jill looked in and said, "Hello, Janet, you busy in there again?"

"Yes, but I need to hurry. It's lunch time, and I need to get into town to buy some things at Boots, the Chemist."

Jill sat at her desk and retrieved the telex from the machine, read it, and made some notes for Donald before filing the original.

A little later Janet had quickly made her way to the Red Lion Hotel and found the public telephone booth in the corner of the lobby. She dialed the operator and asked for a collect call to a number in London. This was a special number to the Russian Embassy and was supposed to be secure but could only be accessed by a collect call.

"Привет" (Hello), said a voice in Russian. Здравствуйте, это Наталья Мне нужно поговорить с товарищем Абрамовича", Janet replied,

"(Hello, this is Natalia. I need to speak with Comrade Abramovich)."

"Please wait," said the voice.

After several minutes Victor came on, and Natalia gave him the news, for which he thanked her for her excellent work. He warned her to be extra careful and to maintain her cover. She put down the phone and began walking out of the hotel. As she passed the bar, Bert happened to glance up and spotted her. He quickly gestured to Roger who had come in for one of his regular steak and kidney pies, washed down with a Guiness Ale.

"What's up, Bert?"

"That girl who was with the Russian last week, she just walked through the lobby."

Roger jumped up. "Look after my grub, old chap, while I take a gander."

They both moved quickly to the hotel entrance and looked outside. Janet was just walking into a bakery a little way down the High Street, when Bert pointed her out.

"Thanks, Bert. I need to check her out so you better get back to your bar and my beer."

Roger strolled down the street and waited for Janet to emerge, which she did in a few minutes clutching a paper bag with her lunch.

He discreetly followed her at a suitable distance and stood stunned awhile later as she walked into the Trandect office building.

Oh my God, he thought, *We've got ourselves a Russian spy right in our midst. She is probably after our aircraft industry stuff. But hell, Trandect don't deal very much in real secret stuff. Maybe it's a way of getting to some of the bigger players like De Haviland or Vickers.*

Roger's mind was racing with all kinds of thoughts, but none of them seemed too plausible. He briefly thought of Donald and the deciphered note but could not see the connection to that.

Roger almost ran back to the Red Lion and sank his stale beer. Bert asked him about the girl and Roger said she looked interesting but nothing else. He went to the pay phone and telephoned Trandect, asking for Donald. He told him he had been walking past the firm when he noticed a beautiful young woman entering the building and went on to describe her in some detail.

Donald laughed, saying, "Roger, she's a bit young for you. Anyway you're a confirmed bachelor; at least I thought you were!"

"I'd come out of bachelorhood for that one," retorted Roger.

Donald offered Roger the explanation that she was their new drafting assistant and her name was Janet Rigby. They chatted a little bit longer before hanging up.

Roger thought, *Well I knew her name was Janet Rigby from the Visitor's Book at Hughenden Manor, and maybe she was just a pick-up for the Russian diplomat.* But he knew the Soviets were more careful than that.

Roger decided to put a call through to MI6 and to Richard Bates.

He got through, but before he could tell his story, Richard said, "Oh, Roger, old chap. I wanted to let you know that the business with the special note and the Harvey chap, we have taken care of it, no problem."

"Really?" said Roger. "Let me tell you a story," and he went on to describe the turn of events with the Russian diplomat and the girl now known as Janet Rigby.

When he had finished, Richard was silent for a moment before saying, "I agree with you it may be something simple like a lover's tryst but, on the other hand, we cannot be too careful. I think we need to have her picked up for questioning. She could be looking for some inroads into our aircraft industry or, perhaps, something more invasive. Thanks for your observations, Roger."

"Glad to be of help, old boy. I need to get back to my lunch now."

Embassy Plans for Falcon

Demidov looked over his glasses at Abramovich and Tarasov, "Well, it does seem that our Mr. Harvey has been recruited by MI6 and the CIA to continue the hunt for Kammler on their behalf. I suppose they believe that a non-professional will be a better cover for their assignment."

"Well," Victor offered, "it does seem, according to the report from Natalia, that Harvey is meeting with SHAPE Members to solicit business for his company."

Tarasov broke in saying, "That's true, but we had him followed to a clandestine meeting in London. We firmly believe it was a meeting with secret intelligence sources. We had two people conducting surveillance from the British Museum to the site across the road at the Museum Tavern. Our first man, Oscar, had followed Harvey to the Tavern, and then he had turned into the Museum itself as if to tour. Our second person, Lilly, had remained on station watching with a camera and had monitored who went in and out of the Tavern. After a couple of hours, we had instructed Oscar to leave the Museum and enter the pub, conduct a thorough search inside, and have a beer. He did this, and making sure Harvey was not in the toilet, he reported he was nowhere to be found. As there was no other way out, we have to assume he was in another part of the building and was let out from a different direction. With that subterfuge we have only one conclusion: he has been recruited by the CIA or MI6 or both. There is a faint possibility he came out earlier without our spotters observing him."

The three Russians agreed that the mission now would have to be handed over to their KGB counterparts in the Paris Embassy. Secretary Demidov ordered Tarasov to re-activate the Falcon in Peenunmunde and get him to Paris to receive his orders from there, and track Harvey everywhere.

———

Falcon was getting bored. He was staying at the Pension Am Deich just a block back from the Peenumende harbor. The place was a modest bed and breakfast, but it did have a cafe where Falcon could sit and read his newspaper while also watching the locals. The newspaper, of course, was mostly party propaganda and filled with the glories of the collective efforts of the East German people.

He had toured the V1 and V2 rocket sites and had marveled at the German technology, together with the advances in jet engine fighter planes that were so far ahead of their time. He had also pondered the previous assignment he had been on, in tracking the Polish dissidents who somehow knew about another German super weapon and its Nazi master criminal named Kammler. Falcon's Russian superiors were interested in finding this so-called weapon, and Falcon could care less about Kammler's war crimes. Falcon himself was responsible for the deaths of hundreds, if not thousands of Poles, Ukrainians and Jews. He reflected that he would have liked to have continued that hunt, but was now sidelined in this backwater of history called Peenunmunde.

Falcon's wound had healed, and he was ready for his next assignment when he received word that he must meet his controller the next morning at the cafe. The controller would be drinking coffee but the saucer and a spoon would be placed on top as a form of identification. He would then make conversation and receive his orders.

The following morning he was up early, shaved and dressed. His time off had not found him lacking in maintaining his fitness. His frame remained solid and his stomach flat. His diet in East Germany, of course, had been restricted in relation to what he had been used to in the U.K., but he had maintained an exercise regimen that kept him in shape.

Falcon walked into the cafe and greeted the proprietor who had been his main conversational companion during his exiled sojourn in this town. He ordered a coffee and a piece of bread pudding and strolled over to an empty table against the wall. Sitting down, he looked over the rest of the occupants without making it too obvious. There was one individual in a dark trench coat who, in Falcon's opinion, appeared to be a typical KGB agent. The short cropped hair, the boldness of his posture, the eyes that seemed to be missing nothing. Sure enough, it was just a matter of time when the man placed his saucer on top of the coffee cup and then his teaspoon on the saucer.

Falcon took no notice and carried on sipping his coffee and eating his bread pudding. He knew this agent was technically his controller but, in reality, he was simply a messenger without any seniority over him, so he sadistically let him sweat it out, waiting and wondering if his mark was in the cafe, or was late, or was not coming at all.

Just when the agent was beginning to appear impatient or agitated, Falcon lifted his own saucer and spoon, placing them on top of his cup. The agent's tense face loosened a little and he rose to walk over to Falcon's table, saying in German, "Good morning, sir. I see you like to try and keep your coffee warm like I do. I was wondering if you are familiar with the museum here and if you could help me with directions?"

Falcon responded by moving his tight lips from their usual snarl to a grimace of a smile, "Oh, yes, the coffee. It can get cold quickly, and I usually get the boss over there to top it up with some new brew. The museum? Yes, in fact I am heading that way myself shortly and will gladly show the way."

The agent thanked him for his kindness, and they finished their coffees then moved outside.

It was a brisk morning as they walked along the Haupstrasse.

"Are you wanting to see the Historisch-Technisches-Museum where the V1 and V2 rockets are exhibited, or the Maritime Museum Peenemünde?" asked Falcon speaking in Russian.

"I'm not interested in any of them' I understand there are even more museums here. I'm here to give you your new orders. That's all."

Falcon turned to the agent with his lips curled in a snarl, "You mean you are here to pass on certain instructions, NOT to give me my orders, as you put it."

The killer's glare and menacing voice were sufficient to make the agent falter in his step, and he quickly responded, "Of course, Comrade, I didn't mean to imply you were being directed by me at all. It was a bad choice of words."

Falcon said, "Very well, let's just stop here and admire the harbor entrance on Museum Strasse, while you tell me about my assignment."

There was a park bench nearby and after examining it to determine if it was sufficiently free of seagull bombardments, they sat down.

Falcon said, "What do I call you in the brief time you're here?"

"You can call me Boris for the purpose of this briefing," the other man replied. "I work with the local German Stasi secret police on various counter intelligence operations around East Berlin."

He was somewhat intimidated by Falcon, not just by the way he had just spoken, but also by way of his reputation from the files. He knew Falcon was a cold-blooded assassin and was afraid of no one.

"All right, Boris," Falcon prompted, "Where am I going and what am I to do when I get there?"

Boris then described the situation in England in regard to Donald Harvey, how an agent in his company had obtained evidence that he might be involved in the 'Polish Project.' Falcon could hardly believe his ears, he thought he knew all along Harvey was complicit in this affair, but could not believe the senior officers were going to put him back on the case.

He told Boris, "Please continue."

"Harvey is going to Paris to visit business connections at the Supreme Headquarters Allied Powers Europe," continued Boris. "However, while this may be true, it is suspected it is a cover to track down a Polish dissident living in France who knows more about the so-called 'Polish Project' and a Nazi war criminal. I am to give you this train ticket to East Berlin where you should report to the Soviet Embassy. You will be provided with a West German passport of Gunter Durr, a fatality in the last war who would be about your current age now. Your controller there in Berlin will give a background to study. The passport will have a visa for entry to France. Your cover will be the La Cambe German War Cemetery. After the signing recently of the Franco-German Treaty on War Graves, La Cambe was formally cared for, allowing the remains of 12,000 German soldiers to be moved in from various other locations in the French departments of Calvados and the Orne. You are to be a tourist trying to locate your older brother who died in France. Berlin will give you French money to handle your expenses. You will get more details in Berlin about the mission."

Boris handed over the train ticket to Falcon who placed it in his inside jacket pocket.

Boris said, "I understand your expenses here have been taken care of by the Stasi in Peenunmunde."

"Yes," replied Falcon, "I've been treated well, and the hospital did a good job on my injury which has now healed."

Boris didn't dwell on how Falcon might have received his injury. He would rather not know.

"Right, if that is all, I will be on my way, and I wish you good luck."

"All right, have a good trip back," said Falcon. "I will sit here for a bit longer to gather my thoughts."

Natalia is Detained for Questioning

The Colonel put down the telephone and with a frown on his face called Jill into his office.

"Is Donald in his office?" he asked.

Jill replied that she thought he was out visiting an outside machine shop where they were getting some extra work done.

The Colonel asked Jill if she had managed to get any references on Janet or spoken with anyone where she had worked previously.

Jill was perplexed, "No, I have not been able to establish much at all. I was able to get a call through to one of the numbers she gave me which was a firm in Scarborough. The man had a strong foreign accent, and he gave her very high marks for her drafting experience. I took that as a good reference."

The Colonel then asked Jill what access had Janet had in the front office. Jill mentioned the drawings archive room. He said there was nothing of national importance in those drawings except they would be useful for commercial intelligence. The Fairy Delta II drawings did not show the cockpit configuration.

Jill asked, "Colonel, what is the matter? Is there some problem?"

"There could be, Jill, did Janet have access to your desk or the telex machine, and have you received any Ministry of Defense messages for me lately?"

"No, Colonel, the only message that came in lately without me being there was Don Harvey's hotel reservation."

The Colonel blinked, "Well, Jill, don't say anything to anyone, but the Secret Service are on their way to take Janet Rigby away for questioning. I don't want any publicity or scenes."

Jill looked stunned, "Oh, my God, my antennae were alerted over that young lady for some reason. What do I say to Donald when he returns later this afternoon?"

The Colonel replied, "Leave that to me, Jill."

Late that afternoon when Donald came back to the premises, the Colonel called him into the office and explained what had happened.

"Did Janet, if that's her real name, know you were going to Paris?"

Donald, who was now looking quite pale, thought back on the morning's conversation in Chalky's little office. "Frankly speaking," he muttered, "I had mentioned it to Chalky and, come to think of it, Janet was there scratching around picking up blueprints."

The Colonel then picked up the phone and called Chalky's extension, "Chalky, can you come over to my office for a minute?"

Oh, shit, thought Chalky, *what trouble am I in?*

When Chalky came in, the Colonel quizzed him about Janet. Chalky described how she had asked him about Donald's Paris schedule and when he would be leaving, etc.

Donald sat there thinking, *I'm damn sure she's not after any engineering secrets. She wants me to have a welcome mat in Paris. This quicksand is getting stickier and stickier!*

The Colonel called for Bill Richardson to come to his office, and then asked Jill to step in, as well.

When everyone was assembled he announced, "It appears we have a potential security risk in our company in the form of a female spy by the name Janet Rigby. I am not at liberty to tell you how I came to know of this, but the authorities are heading this way to arrest her and detain her for questioning. Irrespective of whether she is eventually released or charged, she will not be coming back here due to false information she provided as to her credentials. Finally, I want you all to return to your duties and to say nothing about this incident to any of our employees, or to anyone outside of this company. Is that clear?"

A unanimous, "Yes, sir," was the reply from the group.

Bill was about to ask something, but the Colonel cut him off, "I am not in a position to answer any questions. The matter is closed. And one more thing; you're not to give any hint of anything wrong in front of Miss Rigby."

With that, the group dispersed to their respective posts.

At 4:30 p.m. two men entered the Trandect offices and asked for Colonel Blankenship. One was a Police Chief Inspector in uniform and the other was in plain clothes.

Jill asked, "Who shall I say you are?"

The uniformed officer replied, "Chief Inspector Cummings from Scotland Yard and my colleague is a member of the British Secret Service."

Jill showed them into the Colonel's office.

The Colonel had been told by the Secret Service that Janet Rigby had been seen accompanying the Russian Cultural Secretary at Hughenden Manor and had spent the night with him there. The Colonel also knew the implication of SIS concerns over this matter, and he described to the two officers the additional evidence of Miss Rigby's false employment record, the suspicious reference by an alleged employer, and her enquiries about Mr. Harvey's impending visit to SHAPE in Paris. The Colonel also mentioned that Miss Rigby had been in the front office or the Archive Room when Mr. Harvey's reservation for his hotel in Paris had come in via the telex machine.

The SIS agent asked if he could have a copy of the telex, and Jill was instructed to provide this.

The Colonel said, "Look, we don't know if she has seen the telex, but with her curiosity when questioning Chalky, I'm damn sure she would have peeked at the telex machine when it came on. After all you can't miss the noise a teletype machine makes, can you?"

The SIS agent said, "We have enough to be concerned and, to at least take her in for questioning and to check her background. Let's bring her in to the office and we will read her rights before taking her off to London."

Janet was called to come to the Colonel's office, and she had a bad feeling when she told Chalky where she was going.

He simply looked down and said, "Oh, Okay," without further comment.

Janet arrived in the front office, and Jill said, "Go right in, Janet."

She walked in and immediately knew her time in England was over. The SIS agent stepped behind her near the door.

Chief Inspector Cummings enquired, "Miss Janet Rigby?"

"Yes," she replied, "that's me."

He then told her, "I am Chief Inspector Robert Cummings from Scotland Yard and behind you is a member of the British Secret Service. We have reason to believe you may be an agent of a foreign power, and you are to be detained for questioning. You do not have to say anything. But it may harm your defense if you do not mention when questioned something which you later rely on in court. Anything you do say may be given in evidence."

Janet Rigby braced her shoulders and smiled serenely, "I have nothing to say."

The policeman turned to Colonel Blankenship and asked if someone could collect Miss Rigby's personal items and bring them to the office. Jill was sent off to recover Janet's handbag and coat. On her return the officer took the bag, handed Janet her coat and taking her arm, led her outside to the waiting car.

"Well, that's a first for Trandect," said Jill.

"The first we know about," replied the Colonel.

Love And Sadness

On the way home, Donald thought he should stop by his old friend Harold Sloan's house. He was obliged to divert Harold's thoughts away from the note.

"Hello, Donald," Harold exclaimed, as he opened the door to see his old friend standing there.

"Hello, Harold. Haven't seen you in a little while and thought I would pop round for a wee dram o' that honey mead."

"Good idea. I've been going cross-eyed over this side dresser I'm making, and I need a break."

Harold walked over to the cupboard where he kept his precious hoard of honey mead liquor. He poured a couple of shots for them both and they sat down to savor the sweet but alcoholic nectar.

"So what's been happening, Donald? Anything exciting?"

"No," said Donald, "Nothing extraordinary," he lied. "I am going to Paris though next week on company business."

Harold's eyes became wider, "Oh, of course, nothing extraordinary, just a trip to Paris," he said sarcastically with a grin. "How did you wangle that?"

Donald responded, "My boss has been able to get some good business connections with the new military powers in Europe at SHAPE headquarters. So I'm just going where I'm told to go."

He laughed while Harold poured another shot of honey mead.

Harold suddenly remembered, "Hey, what about that funny note thing you found? What did you do with it eventually?"

"Oh, that", said Donald. "I hope you don't mind, but I got in touch with your friend, Roger Hewitt-Benning, and asked him to take it because if it were something sinister, he would be the best person to get it in the right hands."

That's what I should have done in the first place, instead of being up to my eyeballs in espionage., Donald thought to himself.

"I think you did the right thing there," said Harold. After some additional chit-chat, Donald left for home thinking about Janet Rigby and the implications of what this might mean to his Paris assignment.

It was late Saturday afternoon when the telephone rang in the hallway. Mrs. Fenchurch was out grocery shopping, and Donald was getting ready for the Saturday Night Dance at the Wycombe Town Hall. He decided he better answer it and went out to the hall and picked up the phone.

"Hello, the Fenchurch residence," he announced.

"Hi, Donald, that you?" came the familiar slow drawl of James Wallace through the earpiece.

Donald sounded surprised, "I didn't expect to hear from you Major, what's up?"

"Ah, just call me James, Donald. You're not an enlisted man."

"Well, not quite anyway," shot back Donald good-humoredly.

James continued, "Richard has brought me up to date with events this week and as I am going to be running your little caper in Paris, it was felt I should be the one to update you on Janet Rigby."

"Yes, please tell me where the hell did she come from, and how did I come to hire her?"

141

James explained, "Janet broke under intense interrogation after she was unable to give a solid story about her origin. SIS could not verify her story that she came to England as a child from Yugoslavia, but was able to confirm that her name was Natalia Kolkov and born in Russia. She did live abroad for many years and learned her English fluently. She acted as a sleeper agent until a couple of years ago when she was activated for Cold War purposes.

"She was a Russian National?" said Donald incredulously.

James replied, "Yeh, how about that, right on your doorstep, Don? Anyway to continue, the key point that broke her, according to Richard, was a little trick they played on her."

"Gosh, you Brits are a tricky bunch!" he said laughing over the phone.

"She was apparently saying nothing, and the Brits really did not have any way of holding her except a suspicion of her real identity, and the fact she had been seen cavorting with the Russian Cultural Secretary while he was visiting High Wycombe. An amorous tryst is not by itself a criminal offense, nor is it evidence of espionage or a threat to national security.

However, Freddie Simpson produced a little psychological trick by pulling from his pocket the telex message that had come in that afternoon from Paris, confirming your reservation at the Hotel Cambon. Freddie suddenly, and without warning, stuck it in front of her and said, 'We found this in your handbag.'

Miss Kolkov instinctively blurted out, 'You couldn't have, I never took ……' She stopped herself, but it was too late. She had just admitted she knew what the message was. From that point on they applied more pressure by telling her that her little affair with Victor Abramovich was going to look embarrassing to the Soviet Government. The SIS agents told her they knew from witnesses, the dinner she had at The Red Lion, and what time she left in the morning. Richard said it was then she broke down, and also pleaded for asylum. This is totally unlikely to be granted of course."

Donald now spoke up, "This is unbelievable. My cover is broken before I even get to Paris. So what now? Are we going to change hotels now?"

"No," replied James, "Because the Soviets don't know we have picked her up yet, and you will be leaving on Wednesday next week. I will have an agent watching the hotel to see if anyone will be following you. By the way, don't forget on Sunday, Freddie is traveling down to Wycombe to give you a little anti-surveillance training."

"Oh, is he? So my Sunday is shot, too, now? I'll need a bloody holiday when this is over."

James responded, "Donald, let me tell you, if you are able to pull this mission off, or at least enable us to gather some really valuable information, I will personally make sure we get you a trip to the USA."

"Now that would be a really nice reward," replied Donald.

They said goodbye and when Donald put down the phone, his head was pounding. Donald continued getting ready for the dance that evening.

Donald was waiting at the bus stop in Castle Street for Alicja to arrive from Hodgemoore. The bright red Thames Valley Bus came around the corner from Amersham Hill into Castle Street and pulled up at the bus stop. There was quite a crowd getting off, ready for a night on the town. At last, he spotted Alicja stepping off and he caught her with a loving embrace and they kissed warmly.

She hugged him tightly saying, "Oh, Donald, this week has been a nightmare for me and my family."

He led her over to a shop doorway away from the milling crowd and told her, "I cannot imagine the pain you must be suffering, my darling, and I can only offer my deepest and heartfelt sympathy to you and your family."

"Thank you, Donald," she replied with tears in her eyes. "I wanted to see you so much even though the funeral for Uncle Karol was only yesterday. I felt I had to come tonight. But to think he was actually murdered, and by one of our own people, it's just so frightening. Not only that, but in the back of everyone's mind in our community, is the fear that one of Poland's biggest enemies, Russia, is still intent on killing us, even on foreign soil. So we don't know for sure who it was that really killed my uncle."

Donald tried to reassure her, and changed the subject by asking her about Ola because he had told Cal Jennings that she may be coming with Alicja tonight. Alicja said Ola was so slow getting ready that she got impatient. She wanted to see Donald so badly that she told Ola she could catch the very next bus as they ran every 15 minutes.

Soon the next bus arrived, and this one was just as crowded, with standing room only. However, there was Ola, and both Donald and Alicja stepped forward to greet her. Alicja and Ola kissed each other on both cheeks, and Donald offered his hand to Ola.

Alicja smiled and told Donald, "Why don't you learn some European habits and kiss Ola on the cheek in greeting?"

He blushed and reluctantly kissed her cheek quickly.

Alicja said, "Once we are all close friends or family, you don't shake hands, you kiss and embrace each other."

"Well, let's get on down to the Town Hall," Donald said and off they went arm in arm with Donald in the middle of the two girls.

They arrived at the entrance, and Donald paid for both Ola and Alicja. After checking their coats, they stood around the entrance waiting for Cal to turn up. He arrived about five minutes later with several other GIs, and Cal split off from them and casually made his way over to Donald and the girls, leaving his buddies staring with envy and joking among themselves.

Donald said, "Hi, Cal. This is Ola who you remember when you met her at one of the dances here."

Ola blushed as Cal said, "How could I forget such a lovely lady?"

Cal was looking very smart and handsome in his uniform, highly polished shoes, master sergeant stripes on his sleeve, and his war ribbons on his chest, the epitome of a proud American serviceman anxious to impress his English and Polish friends.

They all moved inside with the huge crowd and the 20-piece band had already struck up some of the music of the period — Doris Day, Patti Page, Bill Haley (a new phenomenon with his rock 'n roll hit), and many others. As usual as the night wore on, the crowd called for Tony Corolla to do his Dean Martin imitation, and the band leader did his best to put them off. Eventually he was allowed to do a rendition of "Everybody Loves Somebody Sometime" which, being a nice, slow melody had everyone on the dance floor clinging to each other with stars in their eyes.

Donald felt Alicja was still very sad and understandably so. He thought it might be an idea to cut the evening short and sit in one of the local pubs for a quiet drink and chat. He had other ideas about a romantic walk in the park in the moonlight, but pushed that one out of his head for the time being.

When they came off the dance floor, he asked her, "Alicja, look I know you're feeling pretty upset right now. Would you prefer doing something else besides dancing?"

"What could we do? I don't want to go to the cinema," she replied.

Donald offered the alternative, "Let's go to the Falcon. That's a pretty quiet pub near the Guildhall on the High Street."

"Yes, I would prefer that," she said, "but I should ask Ola first. I don't want her to feel I have left her stranded."

Donald said, "We could ask Ola and Cal to join us if they want. Let's see what she says."

They searched the packed crowd where they found Cal and Ola laughing and cuddling on the other side of the hall. Alicja and Ola spoke for for a couple of minutes, while Donald told Cal the plan. Cal said it was up to Ola, but he could take her home to Hodgemoor after the dance. Alicja and Ola finished their little chat and announced that Ola would stay on at the dance with Cal, as long as she didn't miss the last bus to Hodgemoor. Cal gave the necessary assurances, and with that, Alicja and Donald bade them goodnight.

The two of them retrieved their coats and walked arm in arm around to High Street and into the Falcon pub. On the way they were passed by a jeep carrying US Military Police with white belts and helmets, watching out for any GIs causing mischief or getting into fights. These US Air Force police helped the local constabulary keep the two sides apart whenever an altercation occurred, especially on Saturday nights.

Donald and Alicja settled down in a quiet corner of the pub away from the main crowd. Aljica had a shandy and Donald a pint of Worthington's Best Ale.

"Are you hungry? I can get you a nice pie, if you like," inquired Donald.

"No, thanks," she replied, smiling, "I had a good supper before coming tonight."

The two sat and chatted about their work. She, told stories of both nice and awkward customers whom she had to deal with at the shop where she worked. Donald spoke about his work at Trandect, visiting Farnborough air show, the terrific aircraft he was privileged to see, etc.

"I'm off to Paris next week," he announced proudly. "I have to meet with some high level people in the military at SHAPE."

"SHAPE?" she said, "What's that? And you're going to Paris? You lucky thing, can you take me with you?" she said smiling angelically.

Donald was pleased to see her relaxing and smiling now which was helping to relieve the strain of her uncle's death. He explained the role of the Supreme Headquarters Allied Powers Europe.

"I would really love to take you to Paris. That would be a dream but, sadly, my firm will not allow me to mix business with pleasure." *Well, I don't think so, but I have never really thought about it*, he said to himself.

Alicja looked at him mischievously saying, "I suppose you will have all those French girls chasing you?"

145

"I'll be too busy, but I might just look at one or two as they walk past on the Champs Elysee," he said teasingly. Then came the question he was dreading,

"Donald, you remember that piece of paper that I translated for you? What happened to it and was that anything to do with Uncle Karol?"

"Alicja, I found that note quite accidentally and then after you translated it, I was curious about the strange content. So I showed it to Roger, a friend of mine who is an ex-intelligence officer. He said he would take possession of it, and so I know nothing more about it. Donald hated lying to Alicja. "Obviously, it must have meant something to the intelligence community," he added.

"Did your friend Roger know about my uncle's murder?" asked Alicja.

"Yes, he knew; because his contacts in the Secret Service were aware Roger lived in High Wycombe and asked him get some background information from the local police. The police only know that a Tomasz Bielski was responsible for your uncle's death. The Secret Service, however, now knows that Bielski was someone else, but they do not want the local police to know the identity because it could be diplomatically complicated. Roger was only authorized to give me this information, knowing I had a Polish girlfriend. It would be useful for the Polish community to know that it was not one of their own that killed your uncle."

Alicja was wide-eyed at this time. "So if it was not the real Bielski or even a Polish National Who was it, Donald? Do you know?"

"Apparently, it was a Ukrainian and Russian agent who's nick-named the Falcon. His real name is Igor Martinovich."

As soon as he finished the name, Alicja let out a little cry, and went white as a sheet. Her hands and feet trembled and her eyes started to roll back in her head as she began to faint. Donald reached forward to catch her. Other patrons at the bar came over seeing her plight. One brought over a cold wet cloth, and Donald wiped her forehead while wondering what terrible meaning the name Martinovich meant for Alicja

One of the customers asked how many drinks she had, but Donald responded, "Just one shandy."

"Maybe it is the heat in here or just stuffy," suggested another. Donald thanked them for their help as Alicja sat up, still pale and shaking.

"Shall we get some fresh air, Alicja? Would that feel better? And I'm terribly sorry if I said something awful."

They stood up and Donald put his arm around Alijca's waist, and she held onto him tightly as they walked out onto the street. They walked a little way and stopped at a bench near a bus stop and sat down for Alicja to recover.

"I'm sorry to have embarrassed you," she said.

"Embarrassed me?" he said. "I was scared to death what I had done to you. Was the name Martinovich a bad thing to say?"

"Oh, for the love of Mary," Alicja prayed, giving herself the sign of the cross. "Donald, let me tell you about this evil man."

Donald interjected, "You know this bloke, Alicja? How is that possible?"

Alicja then began to tell him the history of how Martinovich, alias the Falcon, had first helped the Russians deport thousands of Poles to Siberia in the harshest of winter conditions. She described how her own family came face to face with the Falcon that bitter night, how he had beaten her father and then, because Alicja had been slow in moving, he had beaten her, also. She had lain in the snow bleeding from a cut above the eye and her lips swollen. Her father and mother had run to her and had been hit again by this monster. Alicja was only nine years old at the time, and while they had received severe treatment in the labor camp in Siberia and had almost starved to death, her family never forgot the beast, Falcon.

When she had finished, she was sobbing and Donald put his arms around her, holding her tightly while whispering, "Everything is all right now, you're safe here."

She said, "My uncle thought we were safe here, too, and he's dead." Her whole body shook with grief and pain.

Donald resolved right there and then that his mission to Paris took on a whole new meaning. He would like nothing better than to meet up with a Russian agent or a Nazi war criminal, or whoever came first, and right the wrong his lovely Alicja had suffered.

He lifted her up from the bench and said, "Let me get you home. This so- called Falcon, or what I would prefer to call Vulture, has fled the country, according to my friend Roger, but they don't know where. However, you have nothing to fear from him, and you must not let his name become public knowledge outside the Polish community. Be happy to know it was not a Polish person who killed your uncle."

"Thank you, Donald," said Alicja. "I will be thinking of you in Paris instead of this Ukrainian bastard. Sorry, excuse my language. I just learned this word recently. I will tell you the Polish version one day," she tried to smile.

He kissed her gently, and they walked off together to catch her bus to Hodgemoor.

Surveillance Lessons

It was Sunday morning. The weather was bright and mild. Church bells were pealing everywhere as they had for centuries in this land of history and tradition. Donald had jumped off the bus from Micklefield and walked over to the Guild Hall in High Wycombe to meet Freddie Simpson who looked as dapper as ever.

After greeting each other with a handshake, Freddie said, "I'm going to give you a quick crash course on surveillance and counter-surveillance."

"I'm all ears, Freddie," replied Donald.

Freddie asked if he had noticed anyone following him when Donald had travelled to the Museum Tavern last week.

"No, I can't say I noticed anyone in particular following me, but it was really crowded in places."

"Well, you were definitely followed, or at least someone knew you were heading to the Museum or near to the Museum. It was probably more than one person conducting the surveillance. The fact you noticed nothing unusual shows it was very professional, but then the Soviets are masters at this game. Let's take a stroll, Donald."

The two walked over the street toward the Parish Church where the bells were still pealing, calling the parishioners to service.

Freddie said, "Let's assume you notice someone following you. Stopping in the entranceway to a shop where the windows are reflecting the street is one way to see if the person continues walking by, without looking directly at the person. You can take an alternative route immediately, if necessary. Why don't we enter the church here?"

Freddie led the way through the large front door of the church and sat down at the back, and well to the right of the entrance. He pointed out to Donald that a casual glance to the left would provide a view of anyone entering the church. He told Donald to examine all other exits because in the case of a real situation that vantage would offer an alternative escape.

Donald whispered in the quiet that this was the seating area where he had first found the note, but he could not see a red hymn book anywhere.

Freddie gestured to Donald they should make their way out of the side door exit. They nodded to the usher who thanked them for coming, but who wondered to himself why they bothered.

"Please come again," he said. "We would love to have you attend the service."

"I bet he would," muttered Freddie. "Churches are losing congregations in droves these days, but I suppose it's a manifestation of the times in which we live. The war is over, but for many the struggles continue, no matter that they survived the bigger conflict."

After demonstrating some counter-surveillance moves and procedures, Freddie suggested they have some tea somewhere so that he could describe other protective measures. Donald led him to the corner cafe where there were only a few customers. They sat down with their tea at a table near the entrance. Donald listened intently as Freddie told him that in Paris he would have multiple opportunities to slip surveillance.

Freddie said, "Look, if, for example, you think a particular individual has you under surveillance and that person is wearing a dark brown coat, be aware that the next time you glimpse that person, he or she may be carrying the coat over their arm folded with just the lining on the outside disguising the coat color, and the person is now just wearing a blue jacket. You could easily dismiss this person as someone else and just part of the crowd. You want to be as deceptive as possible in your evasion techniques. On the Paris Metro, for example, you will have ample opportunity to, perhaps, study a route map on the wall and head toward a platform, only to suddenly change your mind on reaching the platform and take an exit that puts you on another platform going in another direction. Anyone following you becomes obvious at this point. A street that is relatively empty but with multiple exits to other streets makes it easy to lose a follower. Speeding or slowing down a walking pace can let you know there is surveillance on your tail in a less crowded street or park, but makes it more difficult in a busy or crowded area to spot someone out of place. The main thing Donald, is being aware of your surroundings, and remember — the real professionals at surveillance do not demonstrate much in the way of marked behavior. They will be very ordinary looking with unobtrusive clothing or hair styles. Their shoes may not be highly polished, but slightly scuffed like everyone else on a busy schedule. Hair may be neat but, if garish or styled in an unusual way, will make them stick out like a sore thumb. The follower will blend into the milieu surrounding you. If you are using a car, then take a complex route to your destination, ensuring there are plenty of side streets for you to escape. If, and when you hire a car, pick one that everyone else is riding. In Paris the Citroen 2CV or maybe the Renault 4CV are ideal, but leave the Versailles for the more affluent."

"Obviously, don't go running into dead ends," Feddie added with a grin.

Donald admitted, "After hearing that, I feel a little inadequate and just somewhat green. Having heard what happened during Janet, er, Natalia Volkov's interview, it seems pretty obvious that the other side are going to know I shall be staying at the Hotel Cambon, so aren't I a sitting duck?"

"No," said Freddie, "because they need to know if you are, indeed, visiting SHAPE and, at this time, they do not know if you have any other mission do they?"

"I suppose not," said Donald.

"Just start practicing your counter-surveillance skills," said Freddie. "It will always be a handy skill to have anyway. By the way, did you ever do any boxing or wrestling in the Air Force?"

Donald responded with a quizzical expression, "I am a brown belt in judo, but, hell, that was years ago, must be very rusty now. Why do you ask?"

Freddie answered, "Oh, just gauging your emergency kit, just in case, you understand?"

"Oh, shit, Freddie, where is this thing going?"

"Calm down, Donald, you will be well looked after by Major Wallace's people over there. They are not going to let you out of their sight, so if in the highly unlikely event an incident occurred that necessitated a rescue, a few seconds delay from your brown belt expertise would provide time for Wallace's chaps to move in."

"Freddie, how the bloody hell am I going to know who are good blokes and who are bad following me around?" protested Donald.

"I knew you were going to ask me that, so I saved it for last. Have you ever seen a Yank blowing bubble gum, Donald?"

"Of course, I'm out with these guys so many times. I think it's a disgusting habit, and I often tell them so," pointed out Donald pulling a face.

Freddie was laughing now, "Well, if you see someone with a loud shirt, a camera and blowing bubble gum, that's no Yank tourist; that's your potential bodyguard. Try not to lose him! However, someone that obvious may not always be in the right garb, so it will depend on circumstances or location."

Nobby Clark popped out from the kitchen to collect some dishes from the tables as the cafe seemed to be short-handed. He spotted Donald and sauntered over, "'allo, me old mate. You always busy these days? You don't seem to 'ave time to come an' 'elp out now?"

Donald replied, "Yeh, it's just hectic these days. Oh, Nobby, meet Freddie, he's a friend of mine from London, your home town."

Nobby looked at Freddie who was smiling at this little Cockney, "Freddie, Freddie who, did you say?"

"Oh, just Freddie. All my friends call me Freddie."

"Oh, blimey," said Nobby grinning all over his face. "You must be Freddie No-Name, one o' them secret spies. He's goin' to become invisible in a minute and disappear through that wall, ain't yer mate?"

Freddie roared with laughter, "No, not exactly, but I shall be leaving through that door just now when we've finished our tea."

Donald, in the meantime, was almost choking in disbelief and could not wait to get out of there.

They said goodbye to Nobby and left the corner café, and Donald saw Freddie to his car. Freddie turned to Donald and gave him a piece of paper.

Freddie said, "This a special telephone number at the British Embassy which is for emergencies only. You will only get a response on that line by invoking a code phrase which, in effect, is two words exactly the same, TOC TOC. That's another name for that Death Watch Beetle you told us about in the Wycombe Church. You need to remember it, otherwise the connection will not respond. However, I do not expect you to have any problems, as James Wallace and his men will be behind you. Wallace will be in touch with you at the hotel in due course. Roger and I wish you good luck and look forward to your return at the Tavern. Any questions?"

"Yes," said Donald, "about a thousand of them, but I could not put one coherent question together right now. I can tell you something that may give you confidence that I can finish this job."

Donald then relayed the story of Igor Martinovch and Alicja. Donald felt that even if Martinovich the Falcon was out of the picture, he was sufficiently energized to make every effort to avenge the fate of the Poles and Jews who had suffered under both Russian and Nazi occupation. He felt Kammler was a worthy target as a war criminal, irrespective of any super weapons he may have been responsible for.

Freddie expressed his sympathy and concern for Alicja, but said that bringing Kammler to justice and to answer for the Warsaw Ghetto, the slave labor and design of death camps was, indeed, a high priority mission. However, it was also of the highest priority to determine if he had control of some exotic, almost science fiction weapon technology.

Donald stared at Freddie, as he got the impression that the weapons issue did, in fact, take precedence over the war crimes.

The words "high priority" and "highest priority" in Freddie's statement told Donald that governments knew where their priorities lay.

They bid each other goodbye, and Freddie drove off quickly on the A40 to London.

PART
THREE

Chapter 13

The Gargoyles of Paris

The Journey to Paris

As Donald settled into his seat on the train at London's Victoria Station, he was thinking of two things: Beautiful Alicja and her shining black hair cascading down to her shoulders, looking up at him with her happy, albeit, soulful eyes; and how could the USA and the United Kingdom combine their immense intelligence resources, and then select a lowly engineering manager in the private sector to represent their interests in what is potentially an earth- shattering discovery in the dual areas of science and criminality?

Donald was still pondering the latter as the train pulled out of the station and began rolling through the canyons of South London's smoke-stained railside buildings. It swayed from side to side as it click-clacked over switching points and moved across the wide swathe of rail lines to reach its target line of tracks to the English countryside. Battersea Power Station loomed large as the train slid past. The edifice had now been added to by the building of Phase B, which created the additional two smoke stacks. This second phase was due to produce electricity for the national grid very shortly this year or early next year. Donald had read in the newspaper it was recognized as the largest brick building in the world.

Donald watched out the window as the big factory and warehouse buildings soon made way for the urban semi-detached homes alongside the rail line. The tiny back gardens with the occasional tool shed or greenhouse sped by, occasioned by a woman hanging some laundry on a clothes line. Donald sympathized with her as she must be constantly timing her laundry drying with the passing of smoke belching trains roaring past, depositing layers of soot and grime along the route.

He knew, however, just how resolute those same people were in their little homes which were spic and span inside. Their small collections of crystal nick knacks, and the proud chiming clock on the mantelpiece, which was religiously wound up each week on Sunday, were prized and looked after as diligently as any aristocrat's mansion with its Italian masterpieces and Greek urns. To the average British working class, his pride of workmanship and diligence to any task was as great as that of any Caravaggio, Matisse, or Rodin.

The train was now speeding rapidly through the green countryside with intermittent flocks of sheep and herds of cows grazing in the fields between the hedgerows.

Donald took stock of his four fellow passengers in the compartment and immediately began trying to weigh who might be an adversary. When nothing seemed out of the ordinary which, after all, was what he had been told would be the case, he stopped worrying about it and dozed off in his seat.

The compartment's sliding door opened and a voice saying, "Tickets, please," woke him up. Everyone handed their tickets to the conductor who scanned and punched them authoritatively, before moving on to the next compartment.

Donald asked his fellow passengers if they would mind him opening the window for a short while. They all nodded their agreement, and he pulled on the large leather strap that released the window, allowing it to lower down into the door. The fresh country air came swishing into the compartment, but without any uncomfortable force. Donald stood there for a little while to savor the ambience of the swaying carriage and the passing bucolic scenery before once again closing the window and locking the leather strap into place.

The train began slowing down as it neared its destination and, blowing its whistle, it announced its arrival at the Newhaven Port Rail Station. Passengers began gathering their belongings and suitcases while porters strode outside on the platform ready to offer their services to those who needed them.

Donald picked up his own case and stepped down onto the platform following everyone to the Customs and Immigration Building. There he completed the formalities for embarkation to the cross-Channel ferry, and his passport was stamped.

As Donald climbed aboard the ferry, he thought the name of the vessel, *Brighton*, was amusing, considering it was sailing out of Newhaven and not from the Port of Brighton further along the coast. He was not traveling First Class and, in any event, he wanted a view of the sea, so he made his way to the upper deck. Here he leaned against the ship's rail and drank in the experience and atmosphere of post-World War II international travel. Black smoke was pouring out of the ship's funnel but, fortunately, the wind was sweeping it out into the harbor. Donald could feel and hear the rumbling of the engines through the deck. Then, as the deckhands cast off the ropes and the *Brighton* began slowly moving away from the dock, the engine pitch changed as she started inching forward.

The journey to France had begun.

In the meantime Falcon had received his last minute orders from his handlers in East Berlin. He had travelled from Peeunmunde through East Germany and had been briefed in Berlin on the latest developments on the Kammler case. He was told that Harvey would be doing business in Paris at SHAPE, but it was also possible he was acting as agent for the foreign powers to make contact with Polish dissidents living in Paris. Falcon had then been told to travel with assistance from the Stazi to the small arms manufacturing town of Suhl in the south of East Germany and then travel through the Thuringian Forest to get into West Germany. A guide had then been provided to ensure his safe passage through the forest and over the mountain range to avoid being shot by East German guards, who were ordered to prevent people fleeing to the West during this period of the Cold War.

His identity papers and his passport would show his address in Stuttgart, and the visa for France would allow him to visit La Cambe Cemetery to pay his respects to his older brother. He woke up early and had a solid breakfast of sausages, black bread, and coffee at the small and brand new Geissler Bed & Breakfast on Waiblinger Strasse. After paying his bill and making sure he was using the proper currency he had been issued with in Berlin, he collected his suitcase and took a taxi to the Stuttgart Central Train Station. As this was the city where Mercedes-Benz had their headquarters, he resolved to himself that one day when he retired, he would own one of their automobiles.

The train journey taking him to Frankfurt was uneventful and, upon arrival, he looked for the ticket office where he could purchase a second class sleeper compartment on a train that would take him overnight to Paris. The ticket office sold him the requisite carnet and made a reservation for him. The train would leave at around 22:00 hrs from Platform 15 and would arrive at approximately 6:00 a.m. in Paris.

Falcon searched the 24 mainline platforms until he found Platform Number 15, where he boarded the train at 9:40 p.m., and he walked along the corridor to find his compartment. Once there, he checked the name tag and seat number to ensure his alias was recorded correctly, Gunter Durr. There was one other passenger who he would have to share the compartment with in this second class carriage. He was an elderly man who, when he arrived, greeted Falcon warmly, who responded with a cold stare and a "Guten Abend" (Good Evening) in his best German. Falcon's fellow passenger wisely fell silent and busied himself with settling in for the journey.

At 10:00 p.m. sharp the conductor's whistle blew twice, and the train began to move very slowly as visitors on the platform waved and said good-bye to relatives, friends, and loved ones on the way to Paris. Falcon noted there were one or two American Military Police who had boarded the train. He had been warned that this was standard procedure in West Germany. Many trains were carrying American military mail, foodstuffs, cigarettes, liquor, and other items. These supplies had to be guarded due to the increased level of black market activity in Germany and outright stealing, as the country recovered from the devastation of the war. The cars carrying the goods were coupled to regular passenger trains between Paris and Frankfurt. The MPs were sometimes assigned to look out for children of GI's families stationed in Germany who were being sent to Paris to meet up with a relative. Many in the military thought the MPs had a nice, cushy job shuttling between Paris and Frankfurt as if it were some sort of vacation. Nothing could be further from the truth as they sometimes were required to make three round trips without a break.

Sometimes thieves would drill holes through the floors of the cars and poke pipes up into the interior until they hit bags of sugar or other commodities. This would release the contents down the pipe into waiting containers and hauled away. When the car reached the destination, the military seal on the car would be intact, but much of the contents would be gone! The MPs, therefore, had very little humor, and Falcon resolved to keep out of their way and maintain a low profile.

The train was now under way, and Falcon would know how well his German passport and cover story would hold up when they reached the French border during the night.

After an uneventful crossing, the *Brighton* docked in Dieppe Harbor amidst screeching seagulls whose mistaken instincts guided them to surround the vessel in anticipation of fish to be off-loaded. While the crossing itself had been quite smooth with the English Channel in a quiet mode, one or two First Class passengers had been a little obnoxious by standing on the upper deck boasting about their prior travels. They could have remained down in the First Class Lounge, speaking in more conversational tones, but they obviously relished the idea of promoting their egos to the masses on the upper decks by describing in loud upper class accents for all the world to hear, about the "beautiful Limoges china they had purchased on their last trip to France." They loudly proclaimed that they hoped their reservation for a compartment in First Class on the Dieppe to Paris train had been properly made.

Donald thought to himself, *I'm glad not all the First Class passengers had that kind of attitude, otherwise I think the rest of us would have made them 'walk the plank'.*

As the passengers began disembarking, Donald noticed an American tourist — a very tall, tanned individual who was well dressed and chewing gum. He attempted to see if he was wearing a loud shirt but a smart wind-cheater type jacket covered his upper torso. Donald would take a casual glance toward him every now and then to see if he would blow his gum into a bubble. As nothing happened, Donald felt a little stupid even thinking about it and pushed the matter out of his mind.

He reached the Douane and presented his passport to the immigration official who looked closely at him and the passport.

"Are you here on business or pleasure, Monsieur?" he asked.

Donald replied, "It's business, but I do hope to have the pleasure of some great French food while I am here."

This seemed to please the officer who smiled while stamping his passport.

"Well, if you stayed the full three months that visitors are allowed, Monsieur, you would have plenty of opportunity to acquire the taste of a gourmand."

Donald smiled and moved on to the customs officer who asked if he had anything to declare, to which he said no. The officer placed a chalk mark on his suitcase and waved him through the line.

Donald couldn't help noticing that the two loud First Class ladies were protesting to another customs officer, "What do you mean, my good man, that you have to examine the contents of our suitcases because of possible foot and mouth disease?"

The officer was taking it all in stride and was quite used to such tirades which, of course, only made him look more closely and take more time.

Donald smiled as he went past thinking, *Jolly good show, and I'm sure the French officer must be pleased knowing he is a 'good man'.*

The signs pointed to the railway platform, and he strode toward the train. Declining the help of a porter, he climbed aboard a Second Class carriage and found an empty compartment. Freddie had told him that everyone in France will want a tip, even the usher in the cinema who shows you to your seat. Donald found this incredulous and tried to keep his wits about him. Placing his suitcase and folded coat up on the overhead luggage rack, he settled down on the rather hard seat to take in the sights and sounds of a French railway station.

At last with everyone aboard, he heard the loud hissing of steam from the locomotive, and it began pulling the carriages very slowly out of the station. To Donald's utter amazement, with the whistle blowing, the train was actually moving right through the town itself with vehicle traffic held at a standstill. They cleared Dieppe and rolled out into the French countryside. As the train picked up speed, he was able to see wonderful orchards of fruit and multiple fields of vegetables passing by in the most gorgeous palette of colors. He understood why France had produced such magnificent painters who were able to capture the light and spectrum of these scenes. Donald also reflected, however, these same fields had been drenched in blood over the centuries from wars and invasions by multiple forces of many nations, including in more recent times by Hitler's Germany whose forces had once again fed the earth with the corpses of war, feeding the soil with nutrients that now help camouflage the scars of conflict with abundant produce.

And now Donald mused, *We brace ourselves for the Cold War and pray that a nuclear holocaust will not rip this camouflage from the face of the earth and destroy every nutrient, so that nothing will ever grow there again.*

Donald sat oblivious to his fellow passengers, wondering just what kind of super weapon are we chasing? What could be more devastating to the human race than the atomic bomb? How could God allow a Nazi war criminal to get away with a so-called super weapon when he has been responsible for millions of deaths? But it's not God who makes the choices, our priests tell us; these are our choices. God has allowed us to make these decisions for ourselves. And yet, when a tragedy takes place, the life that's taken is considered God's will. With that conundrum and the clacking of the wheels over the steel rails and the gently swaying of the carriage, Donald fell asleep with his head resting against the window.

———————————

The clanking of carriages and the squealing of brakes as the train from Frankfurt started slowing down woke Falcon from his sleep. They were crossing the border with France as they slowly pulled to a stop just before the station at Metz. Here the immigration and customs officers came aboard and began checking and stamping passports.

The French officer opened the sliding door of Falcon's compartment announcing, "Bonjours, Mesieurs. Vous avez vos passports si'il vous plait?"

Both passengers had already completed their customs declaration forms collected by the conductor earlier. The elderly passenger provided his passport which the officer scanned carefully before finally stamping it, and handed it back to its owner with, "Bienvenue en France, Monsieur."

Turning to Falcon who handed over his passport, the officer looked intently at his face and at the passport. Speaking in French, he asked him about the visa in his passport and the purpose of his visit to France. Falcon was having difficulty understanding the Frenchman but provided him in faltering French with his cover story exactly as described in the visa, concerning his intention to pay his respects at La Cambe Cemetery. The French officer switched to German and re-posed the question, which Falcon understood perfectly. He again answered with his reason for visiting France and was beginning to wonder why the officer was spending more time with him than he did with the old man in the other seat.

The Frenchman eventually stamped Falcon's passport and said in German, "Welcome to France and my condolences for your brother. We have all paid a terrible price in wars."

Falcon muttered a thanks and took his passport back. The officer took one more look at him before moving off down the corridor.

The elderly man was about to offer his sympathy to Falcon over the grilling he received, but the look on Falcon's face suggested he bury his face in his book. He had read that page at least three times already!

The French immigration officer, Francois Ebert, had lived all his life in Metz in the Alsace Lorraine region of France, and spoke fluent German. After reporting back to his office and handing in all the passenger forms and the checked manifest, he asked to see the Superintendent, Georges Ricard.

He was shown into Mr Ricard's office who had also come in early that morning.

"Yes, Mr. Ebert. I am told you needed to see me?"

Francois replied, "Yes, Monsieur. I have just finished checking the Frankfurt/Paris train, and there was a particular German in one compartment by the name of Gunter Durr. He had a visa to visit the La Cambe Cemetery in Normandy. He lost his older brother in France during the war."

"So why are you reporting this to me, Mr. Ebert?" asked the Superintendent.

Ebert hesitated. He didn't want to seem foolish in front of his boss. "Sir, I feel this man is a fraud."

The Superintendent glared at Ebert saying, "Mon Dieu, the war is over. What are you trying to say?"

"What I am saying, sir, is, I don't think he is German at all."

Mr. Ricard sat up straight. He knew Ebert to be an excellent officer, very diligent and not prone to dramatics. "Mr. Ebert," he said, "please explain yourself."

"Well, sir, first of all his appearance did not seem to me to be one who fits the profile of a German from Bavaria or Stuttgart. He looked much more Slavic or from Eastern Europe. But most of all, his German accent did not sound at all like he was from Southern Germany. Again, although he spoke fluent German, his accent hinted at Polish, or Ukrainian, or maybe even Russian. My instincts told me this man looked evil for some reason. I just can't explain it."

The Superintendent stared at his immigration officer whom he trusted the most out of his complete squad.

"All right, Ebert, I'll report this matter exactly how you have described it, and get this to Paris HQ immediately. They can notify DST, Direction de la Surveillance du Territoire (Directorate of Territorial Security). They are responsible for counter-intelligence, and they will be able to handle it. I just hope, Ebert, your instincts are right and that I will not look foolish."

Ebert answered, "I hope not either, Mr. Superintendent."

Being right would give Mr. Ebert the privilege of favorable shift hours, and for the Superintendent, an elevated profile at Paris headquarters.

Bonjour, Paris

As the train pulled into Gare Saint-Lazare, clouds of steam and smoke filled the air. Donald could see the platform now and porters standing around waiting to solicit their services to incoming passengers. They would be eyeing the crowd as they stepped off the train and onto the platform. They would be trying to discern which ones were obvious first-time visitors, looking about and hesitating. The porters would target those people initially, in anticipation of a larger gratuity as they would be more inclined to be grateful or relieved to have their concerns and questions taken care of. After all, these porters knew everything the hapless tourist needed to know; directions to the Thomas Cook office to change currency, directions to the Metro, or hailing a taxi, all the while carrying their luggage to its proper place.

Donald was carrying his own luggage and declined the numerous offers from porters who had no clientele. He made his way through the platform gate and headed for the station exit and to a waiting taxi. The driver wore a traditional French beret, and had a red face with a small thin mustache.

Donald said, "Hotel Cambon, Si il vous plait," to which the driver promptly replied, "Bien, Monsieur."

The journey took about 15 minutes, and Donald was impressed that his hotel was close to the fashion and perfume House of Chanel. He alighted at the entrance to the Hotel Cambon, paying the driver the metered fare plus a decent tip as he had been advised. The hotel was small, having around forty rooms plus some suites. It was a four star property and prided itself on its in-house art collection, which was impressive. At the reception desk he was greeted warmly by a staff member who told him he had been allocated Room 230 on the second floor. It had been pre-booked in the name of Trandect Engineering, Ltd., and Donald Harvey as the guest. He was asked for his passport, as all foreign visitors at this period were required to produce. This information was collected, and the authorities compiled the data to maintain control over who was in the country. This was no different than in England and was of no concern to Donald.

Donald followed the porter across the marble floor and into the tiny lift where a concertina gate was pulled shut, and the lift rose slowly but smoothly up to the second floor. The porter opened the door and he was led into a room which had a double bed with a brightly colored duvet and matching pillows. The whole place was delightfully bright and airy. A separate bathroom with all modern conveniences made him think of the long journey that day, and a relaxing bath would be more than welcome. He remembered to tip the porter and was left to open his case and put away the clothing he would need for his sojourn in Paris.

Once that had been taken care of, Donald strolled over to the French doors and turned the espagnolette rod that allowed the two sections to separate. He stepped out on to the balcony and took in the view of the bustling street below. Further down the street to his right, he was able to see Rue Rivoli and the Tuileries Gardens. The one thing that struck him since arriving in Paris was the wonderful fresh clean air that seemed to make everything look sharp and bright. He went back inside and ordered a light meal to eat in his room in order to have an early night before planning his itinerary for visiting SHAPE the next day.

As he lay in bed, in bed he thought of Alicja and the sadness and tragedy that had dogged her life, and how he wished she were with him here in Paris. He reflected, too, on how this beautiful city had been full of Germans a mere ten years ago, and now was full of promise once more.

––––––––––––

In the meantime, Falcon had arrived in Paris that morning at the Gare de l'Est and, upon exiting the building, he began looking for Hotel Amiot which was supposed to be right in front of the station on Boulevard de Strasbourg. His handler in Berlin had told him it was a two star hotel, but still comfortable and unobtrusive.

Carrying his suitcase he walked across the street and entered Boulevard de Strasbourg and located the Hotel Amiot next to a bar that was on the corner. His enquiry for a room was met with success, and he booked in for seven days. Falcon was unsure just how long this trip might take and would extend his stay if necessary. He was allocated Room 29 and found it spartan but clean. He felt after the years of service he had committed to the Party, the KGB could afford to place him in a four star accommodation.

There was just one thing that was nagging him at this time, and it was the encounter with the immigration officer on the train. His instincts told him that the officer was not fully convinced of his bona fides. Falcon felt he had better make a trip to the La Cambe Cemetery in Normandy as soon as possible to reinforce his cover story.

Jean Fouchet of the French counter-intelligence service, the Direction de la Sureveillance du Territoire, had identified Falcon as he left the station platform. The description provided by the Metz immigration officer had been comprehensive and accurate. Fouchet, who was of average height, deceptively muscular and moved like a shadow, was never in Falcon's line of sight. He watched him enter the hotel and made his report to the office through a nearby public phone.

The French plan was to follow Falcon to determine if he was, in fact, a foreign agent and what was his purpose. They intended to give him free reign on a long leash at this stage.

Donald was up early and went downstairs for his first breakfast in France. He had been warned that he could not expect egg and bacon, or sausage or other similar traditions of an English breakfast, such as kippers and toast. Nevertheless, he thoroughly enjoyed the croissants and coffee. As a tea drinker he only drank coffee on rare occasions and that was usually Camp Coffee, which was a coffee and chicory blend out of a bottle. The Café-au-lait he drank this morning was simply superb. The aroma and the smoothness on the palette were delicious. He was hooked! Donald had experienced American coffee when visiting with his GI friends, but he could not drink it. It was bitter, tasted of tobacco or nicotine and no matter how much milk or "cream" as the Yanks called it, he added, for him it remained unpalatable.

While he was enjoying his petit dejeuner, Donald studied his itinerary and the papers that Colonel Blankenship had given him. His first appointment would be with a Lt. Colonel Patrick O'Sullivan, US Air Force, who was the Logistics Officer at Allied Forces Central Europe in Fontainebleau, south of Paris. Lt. Colonel O'Sullivan would brief Donald on the hierarchy among the military units represented at SHAPE from the various member countries. Most of the officers he would be meeting were based at SHAPE's headquarters in Rocquencourt, about 15 miles east of Paris.

Finishing his coffee he returned to his room to get his coat and map of Paris. If there was time in the day on his return, he would reconnoiter the address of Petrowski to determine the location to familiarize himself with the area. He left the hotel and headed for the Concorde Metro Station.

Falcon, knowing that Donald was staying at the Hotel Cambon from the briefing he had received in Germany, was already up and waiting for him to emerge. As Donald headed for the Metro, Falcon kept a discreet distance behind but on the opposite side of the street. Agent Fouchet, in turn, had been waiting for Falcon to make a move and had followed him to the Corner of Rue Rivoli and Rue Cambon. Puzzled, Fouchet had stayed near a newspaper stand watching to see what Falcon was up to. He noticed that Falcon was observing everyone going in and out of the Hotel Cambon just up the street. And so the procession began, with Donald leading the way to the Metro, and no one aware of each other except the French security agent.

Donald had studied his map and knew he needed to take the Metro in the direction of Chateau de Vincennes in order to reach the Gare de Lyon Train Station. He had taken the precaution of keeping a watchful eye open but had failed to see anyone that looked remotely suspicious.

But then I'm just a bloody amateur at being a spy. Again, why the hell did they pick me for this? He thought to himself.

The train pulled into the station and people streamed out, while the crowd on the platform waited patiently but urgently to board. Donald got on and sat on one of the horizontal benches that faced each other. Falcon, in an effort to keep as anonymous as possible, got on the following carriage and was able to view Donald sitting in the next carriage through the adjoining window. He would wait for Donald to move. Jean Fouchet had decided to keep surveillance on Falcon by getting in the same carriage but at the far end.

As the train rumbled on through the different stations, Donald's thoughts had hardened toward his mission. His conscience had once again been exercised when thinking of the hardships and suffering of Alicja, her family, and millions like her. His resolve now was a duty and an obligation not just for his country but, on a personal level, to bring a tiny level of revenge or recompense to the victims.

The station at Bastille was packed with passengers as the train pulled next to the platform. Donald was still sitting down, but now a large number of people were standing around him as the train began to move. Falcon was having difficulty keeping Donald in sight, so he moved to the nearest doorway and shoved himself in front to be ready to exit if need be. Fouchet, having noticed his move, also shouldered his way to the other door.

The train picked up speed making a loud noise with the steel wheels on the track, as not all trains had yet been converted to the new rubberized wheels that made them run so much quieter.

At last the Gare de Lyon Metro Station came into view as they slowed down and with hissing hydraulics, the doors slowly slid open.

Falcon, who was right in front of his door, stepped down onto the platform. If Donald did not emerge, he could just pop right back in. Fouchet had followed Falcon in the same manner but as Falcon had his back to him, it did not matter.

Donald suddenly appeared from the train with the crowd from his carriage and began heading up the platform to the exit. Almost in a split second, both Falcon and Fouchet turned away because the exit was to their left behind them at the end of the platform. In other words, Donald was heading straight toward them, which was of no consequence to the French agent, but could be disastrous for Falcon if recognized by Donald.

Fouchet quickly blended into the crowd but moved closer to the tiled wall and slowed down his pace. Falcon passed by and was keeping ahead of Donald who he knew would have to continue to the platform exit even if he were to double back through one of the tunnels to another platform. There were four different Metro lines here. Was he going to take another line somewhere or emerge at the railway station?

Falcon stopped to look at the wall map of the Metro as Donald emerged from the platform exit and turned toward the sign pointing to the direction of the railway station. Falcon followed, maintaining the professional covert distance, but failing completely to detect his own follower, Jean Fouchet.

Donald hurried to the bureau de billet, purchased a ticket to Fontainebleau Avon, and strolled over to platform nine to board the train.

Falcon went up to the ticket counter, and pointing to Donald walking away, said to the clerk, "I'm supposed to be traveling with him. Did he buy first class or second class?"

The clerk replied, "You mean to Fontainebleau? He bought second class. You want to show off and buy first class?"

"Just give me the second Class," snarled Falcon, who was in no mood for jokes.

Snatching his ticket he strode off after Donald who he could see was just getting into carriage number four. Again, Falcon decided to get on carriage number five but he was unable to see Donald at all. However, he knew the destination and was not worried about losing him.

In the meantime, Fouchet had kept his distance, and now casually approached the conductor and just as casually showed him his credentials. He told the conductor he could just acknowledge to anyone in earshot he had seen his ticket already. The conductor, like most French citizens, had a healthy respect for their law enforcement and more especially the security services. Fouchet would just wait for Falcon to get off.

Fouchet was by now very curious why Falcon was following this man, and who he might be. He asked the conductor on the platform what time the train was due to leave. He replied in twelve minutes time. Fouchet then quickly walked over to a phone booth and called into his office to report. He asked his colleague there to collect information from the Hotel Cambon on all foreigners staying there. Fouchet was not sure that Donald was a foreigner, but he had no other clues to go on yet.

He made it back to the train in time for its departure. As he was not sure where they were going, he needed to be vigilant at each station. After a forty-five minute ride, they arrived at Fontainebleau Station, and Fouchet scanned the crowd getting off the train. He spotted Donald, and, of course, Falcon departing the platform toward the exit. Fouchet followed quickly and switched his windcheater jacket inside out. It was a jacket that could be worn either way with pockets on both sides. The color of his jacket had now changed from a navy blue to a dark green or taupe color. Nothing about Fouchet stood out or would give Falcon a reason to think he was being followed.

What surprised the Frenchman was when he saw Falcon pull a cloth cap from his pocket and place it on his head. The crowd was thinning out as people went their separate ways.

Fouchet thought, *This man is a professional, knowing he will now look less familiar if had been seen by Donald earlier.*

Following his written instructions, Donald made his way to the Allied Forces Central Europe (AFCE) base offices. Approaching the Military Police guard at the entrance, Donald presented his credentials and his appointment schedule. Another guard escorted him to O'Sullivan's office deep in the complex.

In the meantime, Falcon had seen Donald entering the facility and was suitably convinced he was on a commercial mission for his company as had been described. Falcon felt this was just one day and further observation may be needed. He turned and went back to the railway station with the thought he was going to need some additional assistance in monitoring Donald's movements. More help would allow him to make a one-day trip to Normandy to reinforce his cover story.

Fouchet was now even more puzzled that Falcon had broken off the surveillance and was anxious to find out more.

Company Business and SHAPE

Donald was shown into Lt. Colonel O'Sullivan's office and was met by a slim, pale-faced officer of average height and build. His vice-like handshake belied his mild appearance, and while he smiled warmly at Donald, he felt the officers's eyes boring into his very soul.

He knows everything about me before I even sit down, thought Donald.

"It's a real pleasure to meet you, Donald, and, by the way, please call me Pat. I'm going to be your liaison in Paris, and Jimmy has briefed me on your visit here."

Donald asked, "Jimmy?"

Pat replied, "James Wallace, Major James Wallace."

"Oh, yes," said Donald. "Of course, I was wondering who I would report to over here."

Pat responded, "Well, I wouldn't call it 'reporting to,' but rather it's a matter of liaison for the maintenance of your cover story. That's why I'm a Logistics Officer to help if plans become difficult to implement, or change-ups are needed and so on, you understand?"

Donald nodded agreement.

"Now," said Pat, "you will be visiting the main SHAPE offices at Rocquencourt tomorrow for the first of your meetings with staff officers over there. Which country representatives are you scheduled to meet first?"

Donald replied, "Colonel Didier Marchand, the French Procurement Officer, according to the papers given to me by my boss Blankenship."

Pat responded, "Okay, but don't expect much cooperation in that circle. The French are not too happy with the command structure of SHAPE and feel the USA and the Brits have too much say in the Organization. I think also that the number two in command, General Bernard Montgomery, has pissed off a lot of people with his preparedness and readiness programs, especially the French. General de Gaul is none too happy. Anyway, the fact that you will have spent two days dealing with business at SHAPE may throw off our adversaries and running around between Fontainebleau and Rocquencourt may put them off."

Donald put forward a question, "I was hoping to make a reconnoiter of my main target this afternoon. Not to make actual contact, but just to see the location and to be comfortable with the area for when I do make contact. What do you think, Pat?"

Pat O'Sullivan thought for a minute, "If you were to do that as if you were simply having a stroll and exploring the area, and provided you were not obviously casing a building or an individual residence, I would think anyone tracking you would just believe you were out for a promenade. Our own people will not be tracking you unless there is, what we would consider, a significant threat of some kind. Here is an emergency number for you to call my office twenty-four hours a day. You already have a separate emergency number to call with the Brits and the code name is exactly the same, TOC TOC."

Pat handed Donald a card with the phone number.

Donald took the card and placed it in his wallet. "Pat, if that's all, I would like to get back to the hotel."

Pat invited Donald to stay for lunch, but he declined saying he needed to get his thoughts and plans together. He shook hands with Pat O'Sullivan and proceeded back to the Fontainebleau Avon Station.

Feint and Counter-Feint

Jean Fouchet had quickly gathered official registration papers from Hotel Cambon and Hotal Amiot. After separating Donald Harvey's and Gunter Durr's papers from the stack, he requested the research department investigate the origin of both men.

The information on Donald was relatively straightforward and showed he was a businessman from a company in England, and had authorization to visit the Supreme Headquarters Allied Powers Europe.

Exactly what he was doing yesterday, although we think that particular office in Fontainebleau has a CIA element to it, thought Fouchet.

As far as Gunter Durr is concerned, Fouchet's people had been unable to clearly define this man's background. His visa for France appeared to be genuine. Fouchet pondered to himself. *Obtaining information on a West German who may have originated in East Germany would be difficult enough, but if he rolls back further inside the Iron Curtain, establishing his real identity may be impossible. In any event, why was he following Harvey? He should be looking for his "older brother's grave.*

Fouchet decided to get another team member to conduct surveillance on Durr as he felt if he's a professional, he must try to establish his bona fides by visiting La Cambe Cemetery. In the meantime he instructed his colleagues to call the Memorial Commission in that commune to determine if there was a Durr interred there.

Fouchet himself was determined to keep his eye on Harvey for the time being. As a safeguard, he would co-opt the concierge at Hotel Cambon to notify him immediately if and when Mr Harvey left the hotel.

Donald got back to the hotel and ate a light but delicious lunch of baguette, saucisson, and gruyere with a glass of white wine. He decided a light nap was called for, and he retired to his room. After about an hour he arose fully refreshed and anxious to see the area where Petrowski was living according to the note.

Maybe he's left for somewhere else or maybe he's died. Who knows?

Donald took the tiny lift to the lobby area and handed in his key at the front desk. Before stepping away the concierge called him over.

"Would you like a taxi, Monsieur?" he asked.

"Er, no thank you," replied Donald. "I'm just going for a walk to enjoy the sights and sounds of Paris."

The concierge offered, "Perhaps you would like a map, and I can show you some places of interest?"

Donald smiled replying, "Maybe some other time, thank you," and continued walking out, thinking the concierge needed some additional gratuity. He had not been so attentive before now.

Donald walked leisurely to the Metro station at Tuileries Gardens, carefully stopping at a newspaper stall to scan some headlines while keeping an eye open for anyone following. Satisfied, he continued and took the stairway down to the subway and to the platform that would take him to Franklin D. Roosevelt Station where he would change to another line. However, Fouchet had stationed a car with two of his men just up the street from the hotel, and watched Donald make his way to the Metro. The car had drawn up near the Metro station, and one of the agents had got out and descended in the direction that Donald had taken. This station only had one line so when the DST agent didn't see Donald, he quickly moved through the connecting arch to the other platform. Spotting his target, he moved further away along the platform. The platform was not very crowded. The train could be heard rumbling in the tunnel before it burst into the station with a rush of air, and it came to a stop along the platform. The agent got on the adjoining carriage to Donald's and was able to observe him through the connecting window.

At his destination Donald exited the train and walked briskly to the Pont de Sevres line and waited for the train to Metro Rue de la

Pompe. He was totally unaware of the DST agent reading a newspaper further along the platform. Following the same pattern, Donald was joined by his shadow, who this time sat in the same carriage, but was now reading a Paris Match magazine. At the Rue de la Pompe Station, Donald got to the street and began walking, trying to read the building numbers. When he realized he was going the wrong way, he suddenly changed direction to follow ascending numbers. Fouchet's agent on the other side of the street had to duck into a tailor's shop to avoid Donald seeing him.

Donald had now reached number123, which was a nondescript looking building compared to the other buildings on each side. Being in the swanky16th arrondissement, 123 was a little out of place. On each side of the front entrance were two shops; one empty and for rent and the other a shop for decorator items with lamps, ornaments, and a lot of bric brac.

Above the entranceway was an ornate molding of cast stone in a cornice of flourishing floral design, with casts on each side. The heavy wooden door was open, leading into the small entrance of the building. Donald stood looking up at the five floors, noticing the smaller windows closer to the top of the building. The small balconies of the larger windows lower down were less ornate than the smarter buildings on either side, and they also lacked flowering window boxes like their distinguished neighbors. This was obviously a cheaper rental building than most in the area.

Donald looked around him slowly and as it appeared everyone on the street had their own tasks and agendas, he decided to take a peek into the lobby of the building. There did not seem to be a traditional concierge ensconced as there would be in most 16th arrondissement apartments. The concierge was a well known feature in France at this period, and they guarded their charges diligently, knowing who was coming and going night and day. The place smelt of stale Gauloise and garlic. Donald saw the little intercoms with the names of tenants listed. At #52 was the name he had hoped to see: Petrowski!

He decided to leave a note for Petrowski to come to the hotel, as he felt it would be more secure for him to visit Donald than the other way round. He wrote on his notepad: *Boris Petrowski, please telephone me, Donald Harvey, contact of Zaluski, at Hotel Cambon ***** to arrange meeting Saturday 11:00 a.m. concerning Bell Note.*

Donald took the rickety lift to the fifth floor, found door #52, shoved the note under it, and left.

The DST agent was surprised to have seen Donald studying the building, go inside for a very short time, and re-emerge in a matter of less than five minutes. Donald glanced at the agent as he passed him on the sidewalk, but it was only when he had gone another twenty yards when it struck him the man had a rolled Paris Match in his jacket pocket. Somehow he had seen someone with that magazine today, but then it was probably the most popular publication in France, and so, quite ubiquitous. Donald just brushed it off, while Fouchet would have been angry with his agent for not disposing of the magazine earlier.

On the way back to the hotel, Donald stopped at a tobacconist and purchased a copy of the Paris Match for himself.

On returning to his room, he noticed the concierge watching him and he was greeted with, "Was it a good promenade, Monsieur?"

Donald responded with an enthusiastic, "Paris is just a beautiful city and a joy to walk in."

Later in his room, he relaxed on the balcony, thumbing through the magazine he had purchased. The front page had a blurry picture of a speeding car coming out of a garage or a courtyard onto the street, with the headline, "MOST ADVANCED CAR IN THE WORLD - CITROEN DS." The article went on to describe a hydropneumatic suspension that would enable a driver to raise one wheel off the ground to change a tire without using a jack. The report went on to describe a number of other futuristic features, which were said to be included in the car when it was to be exhibited at the Paris Auto Show later in October.

Donald got up and went inside to begin looking at his program for the next day. He was due to meet Colonel Didier Marchand at SHAPE Headquarters at Rocquencourt, just east of Paris.

Jean Fouchet was disturbed. His agent had made his report that Mr. Harvey had left his hotel, taken the Metro to Rue de la Pompe, inspected the building at 123, entered the building, and then almost immediately had left and returned to his hotel. No meetings and no sight seeing. It seemed inexplicable. Unless of course, if he had gone to meet someone who failed to turn up, then....

Mr. Fouchet ordered his team to have the building's tenants checked for anything out of the ordinary. In the meantime, another report was submitted to him that Gunter Durr had left that afternoon on the train for Normandy. This would fall in line with Durr's story about paying his respects to his lost brother in WWII. However,

Fouchet was still concerned that there was a connection of some sort between Durr and the Englishman. He put a call through to his regional office in Rouen and requested his counterpart monitor Durr's movements and specifically to verify the existence of a brother and to notify the Paris HQ when Durr began the return journey to Paris.

———————

Falcon was frustrated, and frustration was not his friend. It could make him slip up, and he was intent not to let that happen. Having to take this trip to Normandy at this moment in time was making him agitated. However, he was concerned that his cover was in jeopardy and at the risk of losing contact with Harvey; he felt it was imperative to get to La Cambe, even if for a cursory inspection of the cemetery. Thus, he sat and seethed as the train steamed on through the late afternoon toward Normandy.

———————

The phone in Donald's room startled him with its loud clanging. He wondered how the volume could be turned down. He thought this must be Petrowski and felt pleased that his message had been received. He picked up the telephone and said, "Hello."

The voice at the other end replied, "Hello, Donald. It's me, Alicja."

He sat down on the bed in surprise, "Alicja, this is a wonderful surprise. I miss you so much."

"I miss you, too, darling," she said softly. "How would you like me to join you in Paris?"

"What?" he asked partly in shock and partly in horror. He was thinking of the implications of her being here while he was conducting clandestine activities. On the other hand, how could he possibly put her off? What red-blooded man in his right mind is going to refuse having the love of his life join him in Paris? The city of love!

All these thoughts were racing through his mind as he replied, "How soon can you get here? But tell me, how are you able to even think about coming to Paris?"

Alicja explained, "My Dad wanted to know why I was looking so unhappy, so I told him that you were in Paris on business for Trandect and you were going to be away for a couple of weeks or longer. He then told me that we had a cousin living in Paris, and she was an elderly widow by the name of Henryka Lozowski. He telephoned her, and she was delighted to offer me a room for as long as I liked."

The more Donald thought about having her in Paris with him, the more he liked the idea.

"When could you get here?" he asked.

"I have already checked, and I could get the ferry train Dover to Calais tomorrow or the Newhaven to Dieppe on Saturday."

"Why don't you come on Saturday?" said Donald. "Then I could meet you at the station that evening when you get in?"

"Oh, Don, I am so excited. I can't wait to see you." They continued talking for a little while longer before saying and kissing goodbye.

As he replaced the telephone on its cradle, Donald wondered how he was going to handle his mission, his job, and his girlfriend.

Suspicions Mount

The following morning Donald travelled to Rocquencourt about fifteen miles from Paris. He took the Metro to Gare St. Lazare and switched to the train that took him to Versailles and just a short distance from Rocquencourt. This time, Donald made a distinct effort to be alert, and he was suspicious of an individual that he thought had been on both the Metro and the regular train.

Coincidence? Possibly, but just as Donald presented himself to the guard at the entrance to SHAPE and proffered his credentials, he glanced back and the same man wearing a brown suit was on the other side of the street, pausing to light a cigarette. Donald knew then the game was on, and he was under surveillance.

I hope my back-up is out there somewhere.

The meeting with Colonel Marchand was cordial but restrained. The Colonel, a thin aristocratic-looking man with a mustache, was not inclined to think there could be much in the way of business between French military requirements and a British manufacturer. However, he was interested to receive further communication about some intricately engineered parts for the proposed Mirage fighter plane currently on the drawing boards. These would require some high impact-resistant material, such as nylon with metal inserts for some electronic components.

Donald provided credentials demonstrating Trandect's capability in that specialized field and promised he would follow up at the proper time. The Colonel arranged for the secure transmission of preliminary drawings to Trandect to conduct their due diligence. The polite and cordial meeting came to a close, and Donald thanked the Colonel for his time. He came out of the facility and returned to the Hotel Cambon in order to prepare his report for Trandect. There was no sign of the man in the brown suit and Donald assumed he had been satisfied he was on a business mission. Donald obviously thought he was being sought out by Russian agents and did not give a thought about French agents.

Jean Fouchet was trying to make sense of what appeared to be a series of nebulous events that were defying clarification. We have a *suspected* Russian agent following an English businessman, while seemingly trying to maintain his cover story, and the Englishman validating his journey to Paris by bona-fide visits to SHAPE. However, the building Harvey visited at Rue de la Pompe had one or two interesting people living there. One was a Jewish holocaust survivor from Poland, Josef Korczak, who had been freed from Auschwitz by the Americans. The other foreigner living in that building was Boris Petrowski who had escaped Russian-controlled Poland more recently. Both men had been vetted by the French secret service; Korczak after the war and Petrowski about a year ago. The file on Petrowski indicated he had been a member of the Polish underground movement and had come under intense scrutiny for reasons never fully established. However, it was known that a relative had been interrogated and beaten by the Komite do Spraw Bezpieczenstwa Puubliczego or Kds.BP, or Committee for Public Security, again for reasons unknown. It was on the basis of his relative's death at the hands of the secret police in Poland that Petrowski as a Polish dissident had been given asylum in France. Since then he had kept to himself and had a job on the assembly line at the Quai André-Citroën automobile plant.

Fouchet was now seriously concerned that the strange triangle between Gunter Durr, Donald Harvey, and 123 Rue de la Pompe had a connection for which he must get to the bottom of.

The telephone rang, and Donald picked it up saying "Hello?"

It was Pat O'Sullivan. "I would like you to telephone me from a pay phone when you get the next opportunity."

Donald replied with a concerned voice, "Is there something wrong, Pat?"

"Nothing of a major urgency, no, but just something you need to be aware of."

Donald followed up with the comment, "I will find a pay phone in the next fifteen minutes or so, goodbye."

He left the hotel and walked up Rue Cambon and soon found what he was looking for. He made sure no one had followed him. He dialed the number given to him by Pat earlier who answered immediately.

"That was quick, Donald. You could always become a fireman," he joked.

"Bloody funny!" said Donald. "I'm sure you didn't get me out my comfortable hotel room to practice your jokes for your own future employment as a comedian at the London Palladium."

"Touche, Monsieur Don," replied Pat laughing. "Listen, I wanted to give you a warning that the French Secret Service has been following you around, but they must be totally confused because you have behaved exactly as the business person you are supposed to be. Now the only reason they could have been tailing you was because there was a non-French person on your tail, but he has now vanished and I don't think he has been picked up. Whoever it might have been was probably one of our Russian friends who gave up after your genuine visit to SHAPE. I guess the French wondered why he was following you."

Donald understood now why he had spotted the brown-suited man at Rocquencourt, and he told Pat about him.

"Yeh, we know that," replied Pat. "What are your plans for meeting Petrowski?"

Donald told him what happened and how he had arranged for him to come to the hotel on Saturday morning. Donald thought he had better come clean about having his girlfriend come to Paris Saturday night and stay for the duration. He explained who she was and how she had been a victim during the war. He also described the incident with Falcon with her as a child and the latest with Zaluski.

Pat went quiet.

Donald spoke up, "Pat, are you still there?"

Pat replied, "Yep, Don, I'm thinking of the complications here, but, frankly, you may have just done yourself a big favor."

"Oh, how's that, Pat?" Donald sighed in relief. Pat then described what he thought might transpire next.

"If the DST are tracking you, they are going to want to know why you are talking to this guy Petrowski. I'll bet you a bottle of Canadian VO they have got your hotel concierge in their pocket. He will be informing them of your movements and who your visitors are."

"Oh, bloody hell, yeh," interrupted Donald. "I thought he seemed over friendly. Anyway, sorry I interrupted you. Why may it be a good thing I'm bringing Alicja over here?"

Pat continued, "Alicja is Polish. You told me she will be staying with her relative, some cousin of Alijca's dad. Petrowski is Polish. If the French do happen to question you, which I am pretty sure will happen when the concierge tells them you have a visitor in your room, they will have an agent take a picture, they will identify him and, voila, come knocking on your door. In that case I suggest you get yourself over to the rail station to meet Aljica, and take steps to lose anyone following you. We may have someone help out if necessary by getting in the way, if you know what I mean? Just keep out of the way until you meet Alicja and tell her everything, and that you need her help by telling her that Petrowski 'is an old friend of her family,' and then try to set up a dinner for everyone to get together. I am sure she will go along with that because of her history and the cause you are on. You need to advise Petrowski of the plan, too. I'll update Jimmy Wallace, and he will keep Brit SIS informed. Give me a ring Sunday morning with an update, but don't call from the hotel."

Donald whistled, "My God, Pat, you make it sound so convincing, even I am believing your story. I'm going to have to ring off just now because I'm running out of francs."

"Okay, I'll let you go, Don. Don't be too concerned. No one has a clue what your real motives are here," assured Pat.

Donald bade him goodbye and put down the phone. He took a leisurely stroll back to the hotel. He was looking forward to meeting Boris Petrowski at last discover what direction matters would take him.

On the way, Donald was feeling hungry and passing a little street to his left, he spotted a quaint looking restaurant called Le Soufflé. He made a quick left turn and found himself in a delightful eatery where the maitre d' made him very welcome despite Donald's decidedly poor French.

There were a couple of options: Le Menu Tous Soufflé (a menu made up of different types of soufflé), or Le Menu Tradition (Traditional Menu). Not wishing to experiment, Donald went with the Traditional. He was not sorry. For the first course (Entre au Choix) he chose Soufflé au fromage (emmental et comté), a cheese souffle with Emmental and Comte cheese. The souffle that the waiter brought to the table was a towering, quivering edifice that when Donald touched it with his fork, a spurt of steam emanated from its interior that brought forth the aroma of the two classic cheeses. The taste and texture was of such a delight that Donald could hardly believe that food of this calibre was available to him. He had truly never tasted anything so heavenly. He looked at the waiter who was watching him intently, and Donald smiled at him and made a gesture of gratitude for serving this gift of the gods. The waiter clasped his hands together in acknowledgement. Donald sipped a glass of Chateau Neuf Du Pape that sank him further into the realms of the gourmet at large.

His next choice for the main dish, or Plat, was Filets de Bar au Poivron Rouge (Fillets of Sea Bass with Red Peppers). The waiter, who was by now very pleased with his foreign guest who so obviously appreciated good French cuisine, placed his next dish in front of Donald with a flourish, "Voila Monsieur, et Bon Appetit."

Donald responded, "Merci, er.. que'est que votre Nom?"

"Je suis Henri, Monsieur."

"Merci, Henri."

The sea bass was done to perfection, and Donald, who really loved his fish and chips in England, had just never tasted anything like this in his life. The fish simply flaked gently onto his fork, and it virtually melted in his mouth with the flavor of the freshest fish he could imagine. Accompanied by the red peppers and sauce that matched the softness of the fish with opposing flavor for balance, he was well satisfied, indeed.

To finish off this outstanding experience, Donald ordered a chocolate soufflé, followed by a cafe-au-lait. He vowed he would return to this little gastronomic piece of heaven with Alicja. This was the kind of meal that should be shared. He paid his bill while adding a hefty tip for Henri who thanked him and hoped he would come again. Of course, Donald assured him he would.

G T Z

Finally - The Petrowski Story

Falcon spent the day roaming around La Cambe Cemetery in a futile and misleading attempt at finding his "brother" who had been killed in France during WWII. His attempts to locate this relative could be neither proven nor dis-proven, as there were still many un-marked German war graves that had yet to be re-interred at La Cambe.

His efforts, however, had not been lost on Fouchet's agent from Rouen. Felix Geroud of the DST Western division had received a detailed description of Gunter Durr. His scowling face, thick neck, and general posture were not hard to pick out. His cursory examination of the war grave monument and the brief scanning of the records were enough to convince Felix Geroud this man was an uninterested party. Stationed in Normandy, he was used to seeing a great deal of emotion, even reverence, on the part of visitors to the war graves and battlegrounds of this area of France. Falcon gave no indication of real interest, empathy, or dedication to his supposed mission.

Falcon was looking at his watch and was determined to get back to Paris on the first train he could find. Once Felix was able to see Falcon board the Paris- bound train, he immediately telephoned his colleague Jean Fouchet to notify him.

He said, "Ce mec est-il semblant à coup sûr (This guy is faking it for sure). I don't know if he's a German, a Russian, a Frenchman or a Chinese. He has no interest in that Cemetery at all, I am convinced."

"You think he's a Russian agent, Jean?"

Jean replied, "Oui, bien sûr. Yes, most definitely. But I have no idea why he is monitoring an Englishman here in Paris. Maybe it's simply industrial or commercial espionage. I am just not sure or convinced."

"So where is he now, Felix?"

"He just boarded the Paris-bound train, and he is definitely being cautious. I had to be very careful, as he was reviewing everyone and everything around him," reported Felix.

Fouchet signed off with the comment, "Thanks for the good work, Felix. I owe you a good lunch. We will be waiting for Herr Durr at the station. Goodbye for now."

Fouchet got up from his desk and moved to the archives office. He requested one of the records clerks locate the file on Boris Petrowski, Asylum Refugee, Polish National. He was handed a slim manila folder and returned to his desk. There, he opened the file and began reading. There was not a large volume of information but the more he read, the more interested he became.

Fouchet thought Petrowski was not simply a refugee because of his underground activities or because he was being targeted by the UB or Polish Ministry of Public Security. In his briefing he mentioned that a cousin of his had been arrested and died in detention. The cause of death had not been officially determined, but was recorded as the result of old war wounds from a Nazi weapons site where had been a slave laborer. He had not named his cousin since he was worried about other relatives not engaged in underground activities.

The next part of the report struck Fouchet like a bolt of lightening!

Petrowski had mentioned in his plea for asylum that the reason for his hasty escape from Poland was he had received word the Russian KGB were pressing UB State Security to have him arrested. When the French officer asked Petrowski why the KGB was involved instead of leaving matters to the Polish Ministry, Petrowski had answered that the Russians were worried about the Polish underground movement among the unions, particularly in the machine and ship building industries, and wanted to make some examples of people like Petrowski.

The French officer interviewing Petrowski at the time was satisfied with what seemed a plausible explanation. Fouchet was now making a far different interpretation. The key was the cousin who had been a slave laborer in a Nazi weapons facility. Then the KGB was suddenly involved and wanted Petrowski for some reason, which Fouchet now surmised was because his cousin had passed on some secret to him.

Was this the reason Mr. Harvey had been researching Petrowski's residence? And to put this into perspective, could this be the reason Herr Durr, aka an unknown Russian, agent was following Harvey?

Damn! Thought Fouchet. *This is all conjecture, but after all, what else is there? It's a nebulous theory but it's making a little bit of sense now!*

He closed the Petrowski file and wondered if Harvey was working for the CIA or MI6. He had not blown his cover and seemed to be following his business plan with SHAPE. If there were some plans to secure secret weapon technology, then France had the right to share in this. He knew the French Government was getting restless with the structure of SHAPE and the dominant role the Americans and British were exercising as the NATO forces were being set up. He also had wind from the powers of government that it would be just a matter of time until France would pull out of NATO, and SHAPE would have to move their HQ elsewhere. France also had a problem with their former colony, Algeria, whose native Algerians wanted their independence while hundreds of thousands of 'pied noir' or French Nationals living in that country did not want to hand over power. The Americans were putting pressure on Britain and France to give up their colonies. The age of empires was over. However, on the technological front, even though France was lagging behind the USA and Britain in the field of nuclear physics, it was intent on becoming a nuclear power. Therefore, every effort was being made through the intelligence services to secure nuclear and other powerful weapon technologies wherever possible. Fouchet was mindful of this as he surmised the possibility of Petrowski as a potential link to something very important.

All this was going through his mind as he devised his plan for confronting the protagonists in this little drama. He decided, however, that he would monitor all concerned, and do nothing until something broke out.

He set up his team for monitoring Petrowski, Harvey, and Durr over the next few days.

———————————

Falcon arrived back in Paris and went straight to his hotel to reflect on his situation. He would have to make a report in the morning to his controller in France. He would have to report his misgivings about his cover in France and whether he should continue.

———————————

It was Saturday morning, and Donald was sitting on his hotel room balcony enjoying the fresh Parisian air. Even the breezy atmosphere in the Chiltern Hills around High Wycombe could not compare to that of Paris. The fuliginous smog of London seemed so far away. Proprietors of shops in the street below were busy watering the sidewalks and sweeping any detritus of yesterday's foot traffic into the gutter where the water was carrying it away. The city's workers would complete the job of sweeping and cleaning the gutters, giving Paris a refreshing and clean look to the new day. After ten years, the sense of relief for the inhabitants from the miseries of war was palpable as it revived its cultural pre-war prominence. The new Citroen car came bursting on the scene with amazing technological advances previously unimagined in an automobile, together with its fashion and elegance, demonstrated, once again, the re-emerging Parisian cultural pre-eminance.

As Donald ate the sharp but creamy yogurt with a small sprinkling of sugar on top, he could see people beginning to enter the Jardins des Tuileries. There were ladies with their prams comparing babies, and men walking with dogs, straining at leashes in their effort to break free to enjoy the ambiance of this pocket of nature within the city.

As Donald sipped the coffee which, he thought, God himself must have bequeathed to the French exclusively, he reviewed in his mind the discussion he would have with Petrowski this very morning. He reflected on how far he had travelled on this journey — not in geographical distance but, rather, through the vortex of bouncing and spinning from one contact or event to another. The spiral of all of these events would this morning culminate in what he hoped would be some answers everyone was seeking. Or, would it simply become an eddy with further varying streams of intrigue and mystery?

The night before, he had called Alijca's relative who had the telephone and obtained her travel schedule for Saturday. If the cross-Channel ferry and the train were on schedule, she would arrive at Gare St Lazare at 5:30 p.m. He should have plenty of time after his Petrowski meeting to lose any potential trackers and wait for Alicja.

Petrowski entered the hotel lobby at precisely 11:00 a.m. and asked the front desk to let Mr. Harvey know he had arrived. The front desk clerk asked who should he say was waiting for him and he replied, "Mr. Petrowski."

Donald came down and met him at the front desk, "Mr Petrowski?"

They shook hands.

"I'm Donald Harvey and my fiancé, Alicja Kozlowski, has told me all about you. Let's go up to my room."

He took Petrowski's arm before he could react and gave it a squeeze.

Petrowski understood immediately and said, "Oh, Alicja, she's a wonderful girl."

They got in the lift which had just enough room for two people and ascended to Donald's floor.

The concierge who had not missed anything down in the lobby had quickly reported to Fouchet, "Mr Harvey has a visitor — a Mr. Petrowski. They have gone to Mr. Harvey's room."

Fouchet thanked the concierge for his help. He checked that his men had the hotel covered to ensure both Harvey and Petrowski would be monitored whenever they left.

In the meantime in Donald's room, he invited Petrowski to sit down in one of the comfortable chairs, and Donald sat in the other with a small table between them.

"May I call you Borys?" asked Donald.

"Yes, of course," the other man replied.

"And please call me Don for short."

Borys nodded in agreement.

Borys was of medium height, around 5'8" or so, and approximately 165 pounds, with thick gray, almost white hair swept back with no parting. He had a full round face with a high forehead. The face was gray with heavy lines and gray/green eyes that were sunken that gave him a tired appearance. His hands, though, were broad of palm, and obviously used to hard physical work with strong veins on the back stretching upward until they disappeared under his jacket sleeve.

Donald opened the conversation by saying, "Borys, before we begin, apart from your Polish accent, how do I know who you really are?"

"I was thinking the same thing, Don. We both need some reassurance and, therefore, we must both assume that we each know something about a coded message, correct? After all, you invited me here by mentioning Zaluski and the word 'Bell.'"

"Correct," said Donald, and he proceeded to ask Borys in what language was the message written.

Borys responded with, "Polish, and what would one of the other key words be, Don?" he asked.

Donald thought for a moment and mentioned "death." Donald then asked Borys for one confirming word from him, and he replied with "Natal."

Donald began by saying, "Borys, before we start discussing the important matters, I need to set up a cover scenario for us as I suspect the French DST are looking at me because of a suspected Russian agent had followed me, but has since vanished. I am officially here on business with Supreme Headquarters Allied Powers Europe. But, just in case they have any other kind of suspicion after knowing you, a Polish refugee who had been meeting with me, I have a plan to allay their suspicions."

Borys smiled, "I'd rather have the French on my tail than the Polish security Ministry or the KGB any day. What is your cover plan?"

Donald explained, "My fiance, actually she's my girlfriend, but fiance sounds better, is arriving in France this evening. I will be leaving here immediately to go to Gare St Lazare to meet her when the 5.30 p.m. Channel ferry train gets in. Her name is Alicja Kozlowski, and she is Polish. She is going to stay with her cousin, Henryka Lozowski, who is a relative of her father, Dymtri Kozlowski. I want you to be the other token 'distant cousin' to give me the reason for looking you up. We are all going to get together for dinner one night and have a good time."

Borys thought this sounded like a good plan.

Donald, however, had one small caveat, "There is one little kink in our story and that is you, Borys, do not know where Henryka lives! And, frankly, neither do I. But as soon as I meet Alicja, she and I will go immediately to her cousin and get her to acknowledge your existence also as a 'distant cousin' and unaware you had been living in Paris."

Borys again nodded in agreement, "If I were to be questioned this afternoon or this evening, I know you as my cousin's Alijca's fiancé, and you and I had a nice family chat."

"Exactly, that's splendid," said Donald. "Now, let's get down to brass tacks," Donald suggested.

"Brass tacks?" repeated Borys, looking puzzled.
"Sorry, English expression. I have to watch myself sometimes when talking with Alicja. Let's get down to business. I will be writing notes, so forgive me if I ask you to repeat something."

Borys had a question of his own, "Just who am I dealing with, the British or the Americans? The reason I ask is because my communication through the Polish underground was to be the Brits."

Donald replied, "It's actually both, Borys. It's a joint effort on the basis of prior technology transfer by the Americans after the war, code named Paperclip, as well as the Alsos Project, and the British who will share in any discovery of this current project through their intelligence network, including you."

Borys nodded his understanding.

"First of all, Borys, what is your status here in France?"

"Well, I was engaged in underground activity in Poland, and the KGB was pressing the Ministry to have me arrested, ostensibly for seditious activities with the shipping unions. But the real reason was because they suspected my cousin had passed on to me vital information about German advanced weapons technology, or rather, the location of where it might have gone. With some help I escaped Poland and was granted refugee status in France."

"What was the name of your cousin, and how was he involved?" asked Donald.

Borys replied, "His name was Czeslaw Cieminski, pronounced Cheslor Chiminski, and he was a cousin of mine that I knew well from my own home town. Prior to the Nazi invasion, he was a structural and civil engineer. He was fortunate that he did not get caught up in the Russian annexation and subsequent transfer to Siberia in 1939. He took his chances by moving prior to the invasion, to western Poland. However, when the Germans invaded he was subsequently arrested and placed in a slave labor camp. He was interrogated by the Germans, and they discovered that he had engineering skills. He was transferred from one labor camp to another over the next couple years and was practically starving to death. He had managed to live because his engineering skills had been useful. A high level Nazi SS officer by the name of Obergruppenfuehrer Hans Kammler, who was known as the architect of slave camps, and Czeslaw later learned, had been responsible for the sealing of the Warsaw Ghetto and its leveling, claimed Czeslaw as a slave laborer for his weapons engineering laboratory in Poland near the Czech border. There were thousands of slave workers at this site. It was an old, disused coal mine, and the workers were engaged in expanding the workings and developing infrastructure deep inside. Czeslaw saw no minerals or mine-working machinery, such as ball crushers or stamp mills used in normal mining. My cousin was used for his skills in structural engineering and, because of his status, he was reasonably well fed. Others were not, and many fellow prisoners died of starvation or ill health. They were quickly replaced. There appeared to be an extreme urgency in what they were doing, which to us now is obvious. The war was pressing the Germans back to their homeland, and the Russians were closing in from the East."

Borys paused, and Donald asked, "Where exactly was this site?"

Borys said it was on the Polish side of the Czech border near Widnica in lower Silesia, close to the Owl Mountains. The place was called Wencezlaus

"Czeslaw told me what he worked on was just a very small part of a truly massive project. There were numerous slave camps in the surrounding region, filled with emaciated workers of all nationalities, as well as Jews. The camp he was assigned to was Gross Rosen Camp and was filled with all kinds of inmates: Poles, Russians and East European nationalities. Many had little or no clothes, and many froze to death. He had heard the name of the complete project was code-named Riese, or Giant in German. The area where Czeslaw worked was highly secure. It was a separate area from the Riese workings. It had previously been an old abandoned mine and then was taken over by the SS. The Germans put up a sign in the Czech language which read 'Slezská T žební Spole nost' (Silesian Mining Company). It was connected to the rest of the subterranean workings through two separate tunnels. However, he told me the access to those connecting tunnels was sealed with massive steel doors, and he only saw them open on one or two occasions when machinery was being brought in or out."

Donald interrupted him by asking, "How many rooms were in this facility at Wencezlaus, and what did they contain?"

Borys answered, "Unfortunately, I don't know. Czeslaw told me he was forbidden to enter certain areas, so he never did see the whole complex. However, he did see many many scientists and engineers at various times, in a number of different caverns, or rooms. Some scientists were German, and some were Czech Nationals. My cousin was fortunate that he could speak Czech, Polish, and very good German. This was the reason that Hans Kammler, who had an office in the sub-terranean facility, had selected Czeslaw almost as his personal slave. In addition to conducting some structural engineering design of some foundations for certain equipment or machinery, Czeslaw was told by Kammler to keep his office clean on a daily basis. He was given extra rations, which meant he would receive sufficient food that would pre-vent him from dying sooner than his fellow slaves."

"So how did his duties allow him to see some of the technology or research being conducted?" asked Donald.

Borys nodded, "He was responsible for assisting in the building of reinforced foundations for certain types of testing machinery or equip-ment. They were heavily engaged in testing an advanced method of using certain high-powered radio beams for navigation and targeting for weapons. He understood that an earlier device of this sort had been used on the bombing of London to a high degree of accuracy late in 1941. Now, late in 1945 they were preparing to advance this system further in some way, in which the bombs themselves would be guided to the target."

Donald broke in at this point by enquiring, "How could your cousin know this? Was he able to physically see the details of these research projects or hear about them directly?"

Borys replied, "It's like the days of old, when the masters and mis-tresses of the upper classes would hold conversations among them-selves, but were completely oblivious to the servants bustling about their duties. The servants probably knew more about the happenings in the house than some of the family members within it! It's as if the servants were not meant to be listening, therefore, they didn't hear a word! It's like the psychology of a child who puts his hands over his eyes and declares, 'You can't see me. I'm hiding.' It was the same with the Nazi scientists and engineers. To them, Czeslaw was a piece of equipment or a tool that happened to be in the same room. However, he was anything but an inanimate object. He understood Czech and German, and he knew that the work here was to build Kriegswichtig, or secret devices or weapons that were important to the war effort. There was, however, a project that Czeslaw discovered was classified as Kriegsentscheidend, or decisive to the war effort. It was called the 'Death Bell'."

Donald declared, "Now this is what we are most interested in. Firstly, why was it called the Death Bell? Secondly, did it work as planned, and was it a successful device? Thirdly, exactly what did it do?"

Boris answered carefully, "Czeslaw thought it was called 'Death Bell,' for two reasons. First, a number of people working on it had died inexplicably as well as a number of animals used in experiments or testing of the device, and, second, it was to be one of the world's ultimate weapons and would be a deciding factor of the war.

Remember, Don, he said 'one of the scientists in their internal discussions had referred to other Bells in different locations. It seemed to Czeslaw that the device at Wenczeslaus was the most important of all the Bell devices, and an extreme urgency was imposed on everyone to bring it to completion. But my cousin later discovered something else, which I will describe later."

Donald asked Borys to pause, as he was writing furiously and finding it difficult to keep up.

Borys went on, "Thirdly, there was no way one could tell exactly what the device could do. It seemed to have multiple functions. It most definitely was some kind of cyclotron, and it also gave off radiation. The amount of electricity to operate it was staggering and, in Czeslaw's estimation, was in the millions of volts.

Donald asked Borys, "Let's come back to its operation later. What materials were being used for the Death Bell project?"

"Czeslaw told me that Thorium was being used in significant quantities and may have come from a nearby mine, but towards the end, sometime after June or July, a very large shipment came in via the narrow gauge rail line that linked the facility to a nearby airfield. Someone mentioned, 'Here's the Thorium from France.' Raw materials included beryllium metal oxide and mercury in large quantities. There was a material or compound where red mercury was mixed with a jelly-like substance containing beryllium oxide and Thorium. It was marked as X- something. I don't remember exactly what he said. The device when activated gave off a strong vibratory noise like a generator, and the pulse could be felt in one's chest. A violet glow or hue surrounded the bell which was about eleven to twelve feet in height and approximately eight to nine feet in diameter."

Borys produced a sketch from his pocket, which he handed to Donald.

"Czeslaw told me that the device was producing nuclear weapon-grade Uranium 233 by spinning the mercury compound in vaporized form with the beryllium oxide combining it with Thorium which produced an x-ray plasma."

Borys said, "Don, when I was acting in my underground ring in Poland, we had a mole in the State Security Ministry who we linked up with the British SIS. Anyway, this mole told us that there were other Bells that had been operating in Germany and Czechoslovakia, and that the Russians were very upset the Americans had captured them in their sector and in the French sector of Germany. The Russians were bitterly disappointed when they arrived in Poland and found the Wenczeslau Bell was gone. The Americans had not reached there; only the Russians. The Russians did, however, secure the services of some German scientists."

"But getting back to the main story, however, it was understood that Hans Kammler, who was in charge of all secret weapons development and of jet engine aircraft manufacture, was given full authority to maximize the output of the Wenczeslau Bell. It apparently was their most superior device compared to any of their other Bells. Furthermore, it had a dual purpose for some kind of biological capability, and horrendous experiments had been carried out at nearby hospitals and inmate camps."

Donald broke in at this point to say, "So did the Bell leave with Kammler or are there other explanations as to where it went? Additionally, if the Americans already have Bells, why would they want to pursue this one?"

After all, he thought, *what's the point, unless this thing had some exceptional capability?*

This is where Borys dropped his bombshell!

"Don, I don't know why they would want the Bell from Wenczeslau, although I'm sure the Russians would like to have got their hands on it. No, I believe the Americans knew about something else, but they are just not sure. Well, I am about to tell you something that will make your jaw drop."

"Go on, Borys," said Donald, "I'm all ears."

"I told you that my cousin was only allowed access to certain areas. In fact, even some of the scientists and engineers were restricted to certain locations within the facility. In some of the very last few weeks deep within that facility, Czeslaw was taken to a large room or cavern where he was told he would be building a framework for some high voltage apparatus. On entering, he stopped in his tracks, he said, because before him was a Bell device that looked like an upside down cup on an inverted saucer-like platform. The platform was convex on top and flat on the bottom. But it was standing motionless in mid-air, two feet off the ground with a slight shuddering back and forth. There was no sound except for a faint humming, but the air smelt like ozone and a violet halo seemed to surround the Bell part. It was approximately fifteen feet across and eight feet high. Czeslaw could see no wires or any means by which this device could sustain itself in mid-air. He said he must have been standing open mouthed because he was told to stop staring and get on with the job of building an instrument panel.

He looked over at the people surrounding the device, and Hans Kammler was there himself together with several other high ranking SS officers, as well as senior scientists. There were no foreign or 'guest' scientists or engineers. Kammler looked directly at my cousin and had a slight smile on his face.

My cousin knew then he would never leave that place alive. As the Russians drew closer, a mad rush began with truck loads of materials, documents, and equipment being shipped out. Czeslaw was tasked with transporting items from Kammler's office. It was there he spotted in Kammler's own hand, a written list which had names and places in the Czech language: Afrika Herenigde Nasionale strana, rodný, Pine m sto, Walfischbucht, U234, 2 390 nákladních automobil , Bell Vortex Stroj.

It was in this moment of haste and turmoil that the highly detailed and efficient Hans Kammler had inadvertently left this 'to do list' on his desk. The only person who was allowed in there was Czeslaw to retrieve the items he had been instructed to get and take them to the rail truck waiting to leave. Kammler came marching in to the office, saw his list, snatched it up and, turning to Czeslaw, stared at him intently. My cousin said he was entirely frozen in place while holding a box of documents and looked at this stone cold face with the penetrating gaze that ate into his very soul. The lips in that face were thin and tight, but they gradually turned slightly upward at the corners, especially on the right side into what could be called a cynical smile or smirk.

Kammler said, 'Cieminski, come with me. You are going to be part of a loading crew at the airfield.' My cousin said he had stammered, 'Yes, Sir.' But he was sure that Kammler knew he had seen the list on the desk. He also knew then that was his death sentence.

The rail cars that carried the Death Bell and the odd looking 'Vortex' device from Wencezlau also transported a great number of documents, several people including Kammler, all of whom were guarded by a large squad of SS Stormtroopers. They arrived at the airfield where my cousin was astonished even further, because there sat two aircraft, the likes of which he had never seen or even dreamt of. They were massive in all respects, and each plane had six engines. The fuselage ended with twin tails and a rear machine gun position. The rear end of the plane remained off the ground, but there it did have a large rubber-tired wheel that must have taken the shock of landing this giant aircraft before the full landing gear under the wings touched down. A large loading ramp dropped from the belly of the craft which operated with hydraulics. The two planes were painted differently. One had a light blue color, while the other one was a dirty gray. He could not remember seeing any identification markings of any kind, although the blue one might have had a couple of dark blue circles with three yellow roses or crowns. He couldn't quite tell, as it was getting dusk.

Both the Bell and Vortex disassembled into sections before being loaded on the dirty gray plane. There were a large number of people milling around, and Czeslaw noticed a couple of those who he recognized as senior scientists. One of them was a woman who Czeslaw thought looked like Elizabeth Borman, a mathematician who had been seconded to the Bell project by the Reich Research Council and a key assistant to some of the top members of the scientific team. She had previously been an assistant to Professor Walther Gerlach who was head of the Research Council. Professor Gerlach and Otto Stern discovered spin quantization in a magnetic field, known as the Stern -Gerlach effect."

Donald interrupted Borys with the question, "How could Czeslaw know the history of what you are telling me?"

Borys replied, "You will recall that Czeslaw had a little time after the war until quite recently to research the history of those few people he knew."

"I see," said Donald, "So what happened after the planes were loaded? Did he see them take off?"

"No, he did not. He only heard them or maybe just one of them. He was not clear on that point. However, the talk that he overheard at the airfield was the word 'Argentinien' in German. However, Czeslaw's later analysis was Kammler escaped to Africa and that Argentina was just a decoy for spies and listeners. My cousin reminded me that Southwest Africa was once a German colony and also that South Africa's ruling Afrikaans or Boers had large factions of Nazis or Grayshirts as they called themselves."

"So what happened next when your cousin returned to Wenczeslau?" asked Donald.

Petrowski looked at Donald with a pained expression saying, "That's when matters became very serious, indeed. On the way back the slave workers, including Czeslaw, were escorted by the SS guards, and they heard massive explosions taking place at the facility. They were sabotaging the workings and collapsing as many of the tunnels and rooms as they could.

The men were led over to an area near to the tree line. What astounded Czeslaw was they were joined by a significant number of scientists and engineers. There were a few Germans among them, but most were so-called guest researchers and they, too, were ordered at gunpoint to stand in line. They were told they would be transported to a new facility in Germany, as this plant and lab were being closed. With that, everyone relaxed and began talking softly among themselves. Czeslaw said he was very worried as he knew Hans Kammler would never let him live knowing he must have seen the 'to do' list. He said he moved closer to the very back of the group.

It was almost dark when, suddenly, the SS at the bark of an order raised their weapons and began pouring rapid fire into the mass of bodies. The terrible screaming was something he lived with every night of his life thereafter. Two bodies crashed into him just as a bullet hit him in the shoulder and another in his upper thigh. Fortunately, the thigh injury missed an artery, but the bullet that went through his shoulder shattered the bone. He lay in agony with one body over his legs and another one over his upper torso. He found superhuman strength as one sometimes can in such a situation and while watching where the SS men were, he pulled himself out and rolled away in the dark. The SS were busy bringing drums of gasoline to the area, but if any one of the bodies raised a wounded cry he was shot in the head. They began checking for more who may have been still alive, but the Oberführer ordered them to get the fuel distributed over the bodies.

Meanwhile, my cousin had found a thick twig while he was rolling away out of sight, and had clamped his teeth onto the piece of wood to prevent himself from crying out in agony. Almost at the tree line to the forest he came across a drainage block in the ground, which was some sort of French drain. It had a concrete cover in sections of about three feet in length. He forced the cover up with his good arm and wormed his way underneath. The ditch underneath was just deep enough to take his body lying down horizontally. The bottom of the ditch was covered in coarse sand which, in turn, was covering a pipe perforated with holes. He thanked God for German engineering and drainage expertise in, of all things, French Drains! Suddenly, he heard more screams as the fuel was lit as the wounded that, by hoping to keep quiet, would save their lives, were now incinerated alive. This being about seventy-five yards away made the heat and the stench almost as unbearable as his own wounds. Czeslaw told me, Don, that he kept repeating over and over in the hell hole he was lying in, 'bastards, bastards, bastards!'"

Donald was listening to this account in horror as Borys, who now had tears in his eyes, said, "You can understand, Donald, why we Poles cannot stand the yoke of oppressive rule, and why we now work diligently underground to have that Russian Bear off of our backs. As far as we are concerned, they are no better than the Nazis we had before. This is why I gladly joined the State Underground."

Don nodded in agreement, "I have my own personal reasons to agree with you wholeheartedly."

"So tell me, Borys, how did Czeslaw escape from the area?"

Borys responded, "He lay in that ditch for two days just sipping the drainage water as best he could. He was in a state of shock through the injuries and loss of blood. After two days the whole place was quiet. All he could hear were the forest noises of the wind in the trees, the birds chirping and singing, happy that springtime was around the corner. However, that was not the only thing around the corner. In the distance he could hear very faint rumbling, and he was not sure if this was thunder although no cloud was in sight. He realized soon enough, this was the sound of Russians advancing in to Poland and Czechoslovakia."

Borys went on to describe his cousin's ordeal of crawling out from his refuge and making his way deeper into the woods.

"The Germans fled the villages from this part of Poland and escaped into Germany. It was a party of Free Poles who had begun the re-occupation of this area of their country who found Czeslaw and helped him. He told them he was like them coming to return to his homeland but had met up with fleeing Germans who had shot him. This was the story they told the incoming Russians who provided him with medical treatment.

Eventually, he returned home and told his story to me. By 1952, Poland was solidly in the grip of Soviet domination. However, we in the underground movement were determined to undermine this Polish puppet State, and unions were penetrated far and wide, especially in the shipping industry where dissidents grew like mushrooms in the forest. The Polish secret police had been doing routine examinations of German wartime files around the country, including those discovered at the slave workers camps around the Reise Project. It was at the Gross Rosen Camp they found Czeslaw's name and where he had been assigned.

You should know, Don, that Germans keep meticulous and detailed records of everything they do, even prisoners and sometimes of those they kill. The police discovered my cousin had worked at Wenczeslau and the Russian NKVD was anxious to interview anyone who had worked there, slave or not. I later learnt that the Russians had visited the place but found nothing there. However, a Swiss scientist, Dr. Walter Dallenbach, who had before the war applied for patents of what is termed the Wirbel-Rohr, or Vortex Tube, had reportedly by some sources worked with the Soviets to copy the Nazi Bell. I understand from anonymous sources the Russians called it the Tokamak. Maybe it had not been too successful in developing fissile material, because the KKVD pressured the Polish Ministry to intensify their investigation.

Czeslaw had been observed talking with me, and I was under observation as a suspected dissident. Czeslaw was in a pretty bad way due to his wartime injuries when he was suddenly arrested. He died in custody, and the family has never received a cause of death. Our mole tipped us off that I would be next to be brought in for 'questioning.' It was then I escaped to France as a refugee and England Free Poles notified. You know the rest of the story."

"My God, Borys," exclaimed Donald, "this is on the one hand, a horrifying story, and on the other, a story of courage. The courage not just of a man with individual fortitude, but of a whole nation bent on shedding the yoke of historic deprivation and persecution. For me personally, your story reinforces the belief I have that I should remain steadfast in my role of uncovering the trail of Obergruppenfuhrer Kammler."

Donald did his best to tidy up the scribbled notes he had made as he thought it was imperative to get this information to his controllers at the earliest opportunity. His mind was racing right now. He and Borys discussed the plan for creating the family reunion dinner and agreed they should get together on Sunday evening at 7:30 p.m. at the Le Soufflé. In the event an authority wanted to query their current rendezvous, it was for the purpose of everyone meeting Alicja on her arrival from England.

Borys and Donald parted company in the lobby of the hotel, with Borys striding off toward the Metro and Donald hailing a taxi to take him to the rail station of Gare St. Lazare.

Chapter 14

Springtime In Paris

The Hand Off

As Borys and Donald parted company in the hotel, Falcon, who had been patiently sitting and sipping coffee in the small cafe adjacent to the lobby, got up and followed Petrowski at a comfortable distance. He was curious who this might be and what relationship he had with Harvey. Falcon was getting used to the idea that maybe Harvey was, after all, just here on commercial business and had nothing to do with the all important note in the church. His training and instinct, however, told him he must explore all possibilities and this man was simply another unknown that needed to be qualified and assessed.

Fouchet's agents were also doing their job and keeping observation on Falcon and Harvey. After all, they knew Petrowski and his background and where to find him, if necessary. Meantime, Donald had hopped out of the taxi at the Arc de Triomphe after having paid the driver an agreed fare in advance. Thus, the occupants of the car whom he knew were following his taxi had no chance to organize their chase. He sprinted down the steps of the Charles de Gaulle Etoile Metro Station. One person, a DST agent under orders from Fouchet, had managed to exit the car and made it to the platform where Donald was just boarding the train. The agent leapt on the carriage nearest to him before the doors closed!

Donald wasn't sure if he had been followed, but he thought it would have reduced their numbers and their chances of tracking him to his destination. The next stop on this train was George V and here he stepped off and onto the platform and walked slowly forward, gauging the short distance to the next open door of the train. Just as the hiss of hydraulics noisily indicated the train's impending departure, he leapt sharply back on with the doors closing on one arm which he managed to pull in before the automatic opener was activated. The train, like all Paris Metro trains, began pulling away instantly the doors thudded closed. Sure enough, to Donald's great satisfaction, he a saw a man frantically was running alongside looking at him with the worried face of someone who was going to be facing his boss later.

The final elusive maneuver came when Donald descended at the next stop, Franklin D. Roosevelt, changed direction and caught the Metro to Gare Saint-Lazare Railway Station. He relaxed a little now that he had lost his pursuer, and concentrated on his next move. He had sufficient time before Alicja's Ferry train got in at 5.30 p.m. to call Pat O'sullivan.

At the rail station he looked for a public telephone which he hated because the French telephone system was not easy to use. He got through to a woman who answered the phone number that Cololnel O'Sullivan had given him. Donald gave her the code word "TOC TOC" and asked for the Colonel. She told him to please wait a moment, some clicking took place, and then Pat O'Sullivan was on the line.

"Don is something up?" he asked. "We have not seen any problem activity to cause us any alarm. I'm referring to the Soviet menace, not the French."

Donald replied, "I had to shake off someone and did so successfully, I might add."

Pat said, "Good for you. We'll turn you into a professional operator pretty soon."

Donald ignored the quip saying, "I have interviewed Petrowski, and I have written notes that I need for you to retrieve. Can you come to the Gare Saint-Lazare right now, this afternoon?"

Pat replied earnestly, "You sound pretty serious, Don. I can be there in about an hour. What's the size of your notes or how many pages?"

Donald told him it was around fifteen pages of foolscap and was a very hurried scribble as he was not skilled in shorthand, obviously. Pat told him to buy a La Figaro newspaper and place the notes in the middle of the paper.

Pat said, "There's a cafe or croissant place just in front of the station in the Havre-Les Passages à Paris. Grab a table and a coffee, place the folded newspaper right in the middle of the table, and sit back and watch the world go by. I'll be there as I said, in about an hour, okay?"

"Okay," repeated Donald, "I shall look forward to seeing you."

Falcon had successfully tracked Petrowski back to his apartment building at 123 Rue de la Pompe. He held back examining the knick knacks in one of the interior decorator shop windows until he saw his man enter the building. He approached the entrance cautiously so that he could hear any footsteps or noise of a lift that would tell him an approximate destination. He heard the lift making its creaking noise of a concertina gate opening and closing. The sound came from quite high up in the building as Falcon began scanning the names on the buzzer pads in the lobby entrance. He was glad there was no concierge in attendance to poke his or her noise into his investigation. Looking at the names might tell him something, and there were only two names that caught his attention. One was Korczak and the other was Petrowski. He decided he would run these names through his Paris controller and wait for any identification that may shed light on why Harvey would be talking to one or both of them. Falcon left immediately for his hotel. Fouchet's agents also made their reports to their 'patron.'

Donald sat sipping the coffee and enjoying a delightful croissant at the little cafe La Croissanterie. Dipping the end of the croissant in the coffee and eating the soaked morsel tasted so wonderful, he almost forgot why he was there, until a voice said, "Hi, Don, you look like you're really enjoying that."

"Oh, hi, Pat. You know something? One always hears about the French and their cuisine, but in reality you just don't fully understand what that means until one experiences it first hand. I never knew the taste buds could be so stimulated by even the most simple of foods. Just take bread, for example. Your American bread that I've tasted from the PX is so artificial it's nothing more than bland, soft, tasteless dough. English bread is better, has more resilience, and at least has some flavor. French bread, on the hand is like an art form, hand-made by artisans in all these little bakeries around Paris. Each one having their own characteristic flavor or crust and baked in different ways. It's just incredible."

"Yeh," replied Pat, "At least I can keep my bread for a week, but here in France I have to buy a loaf every day."

Donald sighed, "At least you get the exercise here to have to buy a loaf a day."

"So you met Petrowski, and it sounds like you got the scoop. I can't wait to read your hieroglyphics, so I hope your writing is not that bad. We may need you to come to my office to discuss the contents and get clarification. We certainly don't want to have Petrowski in contact with us. Were you able to set up the relationship between you, your girlfriend, and Petrowski?"

"Yes," said Donald, "I have to give an explanation to Alicja this afternoon when she gets off that train, and I hope she will accept the story. We have arranged to have dinner Sunday evening all together."

"Well, Don", said Pat as he leaned forward to pick up the newspaper, "I had better get going. I will be calling in to Jim, and I expect he will be in touch with the Brits to give them a briefing, as well. I will be in touch after that, okay?"

"Okay, Pat, call me if you can't read my writing."

He watched Pat walk out of the cafe and on through the passage toward the street.

Donald sat drinking coffee for a while and eventually decided he would take a look around the station and locate the platform where Alicja would arrive. After scanning the overhead giant information boards, he found that the Dieppe to Paris train was on time and was due to arrive Platform 7 at 5.30 p.m. He walked from where he was stand-ing near Platform 18 to where he needed to be. Once there, he settled down on a wooden bench nearest to the exit gate and prepared to wait. It was now 4:15 p.m.

He felt like dozing off, but the cacophony of sound from incoming and outgoing steam engines, train whistles, guard whistles, people streaming past, and, of course, the excitement of seeing Alicja kept him on edge. After all, this station was the busiest in the whole of Europe, and it contained the bustling hordes of as many as the population of some small cities on any given day.

At last, the information board near to Donald began clicking as the mechanical letters and numbers tumbled over each other until they came to rest in the desired combination. For Donald this meant in the column, Paris Dieppe, "Now Arriving" 17:30. He walked quickly over to the exit barrier just as the steaming, hissing locomotive came into view, slowly making its way to the buffer stops and came to a halt with a large discharge of hydraulic air released from its braking system.

Porters were standing in place with their barrows and trolleys in anticipation of some luggage handling. Doors began swinging open with loud clunking noises as the mechanisms were worked to release the catches that held these solid barriers in place. Passengers followed the opening doors and stepped down onto the platform some looked wonderingly at the huge cavern of a roof above them. Others, expertly dodged the hesitant newcomers to Paris, and quickly contracted with a porter, before marching to the exit.

There among the throng stood Alicja, tall, beautiful, shimmering black hair cascading to her shoulder, her handbag over one arm and carrying her suitcase in the other. Donald was waving, and at last she spotted him, then with a flashing smile, quickened her pace from a slow walk to almost a run. As she burst through the exit, she dropped her case at his feet and fell into his arms. They kissed and hugged passionately for almost a minute before she pulled away gasping for breath.

Alijica laughed, "Oh, Donald I missed you so much. I know it's stupid, but it just seemed so long ago when I saw you last."

"I know," he replied, "I, too, didn't know what it meant to be away from you, but I realize now that we have a bond between us that can only be described as love."

There, he thought, *that's hard for an Englishman to say, but I said it.* Donald thought he needed to give Alicja an explanation of what he had planned but felt he should wait until he had her settled in with her cousin, Henryka Lozowski.

"So what is the address of Mrs. Lozowski, Alicja?" said Donald as he picked up her suitcase.

She opened her handbag and pulled out a paper with the address and handed it to him. It read: 82 Avenue Daumesnil, Paris, 75012.

Alicja said, "Aunt Henryka lives in a flat above the Cafe Le Remontaloo. My Dad said it's not far from Le Gare de Lyon."

He said, "Let's get out of the station and take a taxi. That's way over the other side of Paris, and we don't want to be traipsing through the Metro underground with your suitcase. So your father didn't mind about you coming to Paris by yourself?"

"Well, he was worried, but my mother thought you were such a nice young man, and she felt comfortable about it. If she was happy, then my father said it must be okay."

"Well, I'm glad I'm in your Mom's good books!" exclaimed Donald, seemingly pleased with himself.

Donald secured a taxi and gave the driver the address.

As his French was not all that proficient, he asked the driver if he spoke English and was given an affirmative, "Oui, a leetle, you need somzing?"

Donald asked him to take a route that would take them along the Quais by the River Seine. This would give both he and Alicja some nice views of Paris.

The taxi took off and entered the Rue du Havre for a short distance before turning into Rue Tronchet and passing around the church of La Madeleine with Donald and Alicja admiring the beautiful architecture. Donald said he had read that the Madeleine Church was designed as a temple to the glory of Napoleon's Army.

Passing the church and entering Rue Royale, they could see the magnificent vista of the largest square in Paris, la Place de la Concorde, in front of them.

Again Donald quoting from his guide book and showing off his knowledge said, "Here was where they chopped off heads with the guillotine during the French Revolution."

The driver piped up, "Ten years ago, Monsieur, I wish we 'ad ze guillotine for les Nazis around 'ere. You see zat Hotel Crillon," he said pointing to one of Paris' most luxurious hotels. "Zat was ze 'eadquarters of ze Boche 'igh Command."

Alicja said, "Glad they are not there now. What a beautiful square. Look at the fountains and the Obelisk. It's all just so gorgeous."

They drove around the square and coming back left onto the Quai des Tuileries, the road that runs along the side of the Seine, the taxi drove toward the Ile de la Cité, the island in the middle of the river. There on the island sat the most famous cathedral in the whole of France, Notre Dame. Both Donald and Alicja holding hands in the back of the taxi were enthralled with the spectacle of the spires and gargoyles. The grotesque gargoyles built to dispel rainwater from the parapets as well as ward off evil spirits were a fascinating contrast from the overall beauty of the edifice itself.

The taxi continued along the Quai's and, at last, turned toward the Gare de Lyon and Avene Daumesnil. At number 82 the taxi pulled up to the curb. Donald paid off the driver and gave him a handsome tip, thanking him for taking a scenic route.

Donald and Alicja entered the apartment building through the double doors and squeezed into the small lift which Alicja said was to take them to the 5th floor. They took advantage of the small space with a tight embrace and kiss on the way up. At her Aunt's door a brief knock and the door flew open to reveal a small elderly lady with thick gray hair pulled back in a tight bun. Aunt Henryka had a kindly face with a huge smile.

"I was listening for that lift and just waiting for it to stop on my floor and, now, here you are," she said. She was speaking Polish and Donald was, of course, unable to understand a word.

Henryka beckoned them inside, and Alicja introduced Donald, who shook her hand politely. Speaking French in a very heavy Polish accent, she asked Donald if he would like a glass of wine, and he looked at Alicja who, of course, knew very little French, so he declined and suggested a Perrier. Between bouts of Polish and fractured French among the three of them and lots of laughter, it was decided that Alicja and Donald would go downstairs for an aperitif while Henryka would prepare a little light supper. Donald was happy with this arrangement as he needed to make a presentation to Alicja concerning the plans ahead. He quickly swallowed the remaining Perrier in his glass and suggested they pop downstairs.

The Cafe Le Remontaloo was quite busy, but they found an empty table outside and ordered two Dubonnet's. Alicja said her aunt had been so surprised when her father had telephoned from England asking if Alicja could stay with her for a week. Of course, she was delighted. She remembered seeing Alicja when she was no more than two years old before the war. Henryka's husband had died during the Siberian win-ter after they were taken to the gulag to work in terrible conditions with very little food.

Donald put his hand out to hold Alijca's hand and said, "Alicja, my love. I have something to tell you, and I have something to ask of you. I need your help and, at the same time, it may be something that could bring some honor to you and your people."

"Donald? What are you saying? What do you mean?"

He then began to tell her about the note he had accidentally found, his knowledge of her uncle Zaluski, his subsequent meetings with MI6 and the US 8th Army Air Force Major Wallace. After the murder of her uncle and his gaining more knowledge of the war crimes perpetrated by the Nazis and the cruelty of the Russians during this period, he had resolved to do all he could to find Hans Kammler and bring him to justice. Maybe he was being naive, but surely the superpowers would not be pursuing this objective so rigorously unless there was a glimmer of something more valuable to them than a Nazi war criminal. He explained to her the importance of keeping his cover of representing his company in Paris and also of protecting Petrowski. He was concerned about the French Sureté or DST who would also love to obtain weapons secrets. The French were heavily invested in nuclear research at this time. Alicja was concerned about the Russian aspect and whether Donald could be in any danger from them. He said although a suspected agent had been tracing his movements, his controllers said the man had since vanished. The conclusion was they had been satisfied with his cover story and his ensuing business activities which had probably convinced them of Donald's ignorance of the affair.

Finally Donald presented his plan to have a special dinner at Le Soufflé near his hotel on Sunday evening, with Petrowski and Henryka. He suggested Henryka and Petrowski could be distantly related from back in Poland.

At last he finished and looked at Alicja and asked her, "I know I have kept all this from you, but I had been sworn to secrecy. Only now I have been given the approval to reveal this matter to you as your help is critical at this time."

Alicja was stunned by the revelation, but she remained composed and thoughtful. She eventually replied, "Donald, I know you are a good person, and I love you."

He wanted to take her in his arms right there and then, but he held back his emotions as she still wanted to say something more.

She continued, "For the sake of protecting you more than anything, I will help you, and if it is something that brings satisfaction to our people, then so much the better. However, I feel apprehensive about safety."

Donald assured her that he was being protected although, in all honesty, he didn't know how; he just had to trust his controllers.

She said, "I'm starving. Let's see what Aunt Henryka has cooked up for us. I will make sure, of course, if she is willing to be our guest for dinner on Sunday night."

Donald responded with, "She doesn't need to know everything, but simply to help my business activities, yes?"

"Yes," agreed Alicja. "Salut."

They touched glasses and finished their Dubonnet aperitif.

The Brush Off

It was late when Donald got off the Metro at Tuileries and began a slow walk to his hotel. As he entered the lobby, he was greeted by a man neatly dressed in a dark suit.

"Monsieur Harvey?"

Donald responded in French, "Oui, je suis Harvey, ou est vous?" (Yes, I am Harvey, who are you?)

"My name is Jean Fouchet, and I am with the Direction de la Sureveillance du Territoire or DST. This is the French security service. I think it may be better I speak English. Here are my credentials."

Fouchet presented his Government ID, and Donald nodded with the comment, "But what could you possibly want with me, Mr. Fouchet?"

"We have one or two puzzling questions, and we would like you to help us by answering them. Perhaps we could sit down over there which is more private and would demonstrate that you are under no obligation at all." Fouchet pointed to another, more discreet part of the lobby area where they could talk.

"Certainly," said Donald, and moved to the suggested area and sat down.

Donald looked closely at this French security officer, confident his cover was safe and the only reason there might be a question was his relationship with Petrowski. Fouchet was of medium height, slim build, black hair slicked back, clean shaven, piercing dark brown eyes almost black, thin lips and a constant worried look because of small furrows in his forehead between the eyes. Although Donald towered over this man, he could tell that his physical appearance belied his keen intelligence by how he observed Donald with those dark eyes.

Fouchet began, "Monsieur, we have been tracking a foreign national whom we felt was not who he purported to be. This was a routine role for us until we suspected he may be a Russian agent. It was at this point we noticed he had been following you. Is there any reason why you think he would do this?"

Donald pretended to look shocked that someone was keeping track of his movements. "I really have no idea," he replied. "Perhaps it's because I have business with a number of military agencies within SHAPE. We are, after all, discussing my company's know-how in certain types of manufacturing processes in unique materials, as well as other business to do with aircraft maintenance support."

Fouchet nodded, "Yes, I think that must have been the angle they were after. I understand you had a meeting with Colonel Didier Marchand, the Procurement Officer at Rocquencourt?"

It was more of a statement than a question.

Donald said, "Yes, Colonel Marchand is in the process of transmitting by courier preliminary drawings to my company in England so they can begin calculating an estimate of work." He was surprised the DST had delved that deeply to check his credentials.

"Mr. Harvey, I have one other important question. In our surveillance, which I trust you understand was necessary for your own security because of a possible Russian agent; you had a meeting with a Mr. Petrowski. Who was this man?"

Donald thought, *I'm bloody sure you already know he was a Polish refugee because the French bureaucracy must have vetted him to give him asylum.*

However he said aloud, "Oh Borys? He's a cousin of my girlfriend, and we were having a chat at my hotel before she arrived from England today."

Fouchet's dark eyes narrowed, and then his face seemed to relax as his permanent frown smoothed out, his thin lips broke into a smile.

"Is that where you were going when you rushed off in a taxi today?"

Donald thought carefully before replying, "Yes, as a matter of fact it was, although I had forgotten something, a card for Alicja, and decided to return on the Metro to retrieve it. I then discovered it in my other pocket, changed to another Metro line, and went to Saint Lazare to wait for her."

Mr. Fouchet smiled some more, "The mind can get confused when you're in love, especially in Paris, Monsieur. You have had a long day, and I expect you are tired. I mustn't keep you up any longer. I wish you and your girlfriend a memorable stay in Paris. Just keep your eye open for the Russian in case he shows up again."

Donald asked, "So what does he look like?"

As Fouchet described the Falcon, Donald's blood ran cold as the description sounded like Igor Martinovich. He shook it off. Maybe many Russians look similar.

"Are you all right, Mr. Harvey? You seem a little surprised."

Donald reassured him, "No, no, Mr. Fouchet, it's been a very long day and, as you suggested, I am very tired."

They shook hands, and Donald set off to the hotel lift to take him to his room, while Jean Fouchet left the building, feeling reasonably satisfied Harvey was telling the truth.

Sunday Promenade

It was Sunday morning, and Donald telephoned Alicja, using her aunt's number, and arranged to pick her up at around 10:00 a.m. They would walk and explore Paris.

In the back of his mind he was concerned about the Russian whose description sounded very much like Martinovich. He was careful to maintain a vigilant outlook as he travelled to Alicja's lodgings. Alicja met him at the door and invited him inside to say hello to Henryka, who promptly kissed him on both cheeks, as is the French fashion. He thought Alicja looked totally stunning in a gray skirt, white cotton blouse, and navy blue single breasted jacket. The whole ensemble accentuated her perfect curves and form.

He said, "We are going to be doing some walking during the day, so what shoes will you be wearing?"

She pointed to some smart flat shoes on the floor. Alicja added, however, "When we go to dinner tonight, I would like to wear these high heels," and she pointed to another pair of elegant black patent shoes.

Donald said, "No problem. I can carry those in my small backpack, and later you can change and freshen up at my hotel."

They chatted with Henryka before saying goodbye and descended the lift to the street. Hand in hand, the couple took the Metro Gare de Lyon to Charles de Gaulle Étoile where they gazed in awe at the Arc de Triomphe and Tomb of the Unknown Soldier. Climbing to the top of the Arc gave them a panoramic view of Paris that was breathtaking. To Donald, just having Alicja next to him, holding her around her slim waist and gazing at her was, to him, as breathtaking as any geographic view of this great city.

They took a walk down the beautiful Champs Elysée, admiring the expensive shops, the boutiques of high fashion, and other displays of Parisian elegance. Donald marveled at how Paris had come back into its own after the Nazi occupation. He was impressed too, how this great avenue had not succumbed to the crass trinket and souvenir shopping mess of other great cities of the world, trying to re-establish themselves in changed times. There were no cheap cafes springing up or burger joints imported from more modern climes.

The couple was just about to pass a group of men standing outside one of the luxury hotels when Donald paused, "Look, Alicja, isn't that Tony Curtis there? You remember him from the film we saw, called *Houdini*."

"Oh, yes," she exclaimed, "That's him. He is so handsome. Ask him for his autograph."

Donald timidly walked up to the man, saying, "Er, excuse me, are you Tony Curtis?"

Tony turned to Donald with a smile, "That's me."

Donald stammered, "Er, well, er, could I have your autograph, please?"

"Sure," the star replied. Donald felt in his pocket, but had nothing to write on or write with, and had to ask a nearby waiter from the hotel for some pencil and paper. After successfully obtaining the autograph, Donald and Alicja continued their stroll with the memento stowed carefully in Donald's wallet. It was later the next day when they read that a film crew from the USA was in Paris to make a film called *Trapeze* with Burt Lancaster, Tony Curtis, and a new star by the name of Gina Lollobrigida.

They explored as much as they could of this grand city, including the Eiffel Tower, Montmartre, and the Sacré Cœur Basilica, which Alicja found to be the most beautiful Catholic church she had known. Here she lit a candle and prayed, while covering her head with a white handkerchief as she had no scarf with her.

They drank crème de menthe at a sidewalk brasserie and watched the crowds passing by, simply enjoying the ambience of the occasion and the closeness of their friendship. They talked of their upbringing and Donald, whose parents were of typical British middle class status, had made sure he studied hard at school which enabled him to obtain a good education.

Soon, it was time to get back to Donald's hotel, and the Metro train rumbled through the Paris tunnels to bring them to their destination at Tuileries. Arriving at the Hotel Cambon, the concierge was surprised to see Alicja with Donald but gave him a knowing smile as they passed by on the way to his room.

Donald showed her the balcony and the view to the Tuileries Gardens. They were due to meet her cousins at Le Soufflé in about an hour and a half so he asked if she would like to freshen up and change shoes while he waited on the balcony.

In the meantime, he made a point of calling the concierge downstairs to ask him to make a dinner reservation for four people at Le Soufflé for 7:30 p.m. He knew this would make it to Mr. Fouchet, thus reinforcing his story. He was still concerned about the Russian but, hopefully, Pat had his people watching out for him. He was pondering these thoughts when Alicja came to him and kissed him.

"Thank you for such a lovely day. To be in Paris is such a thrill and to have you with me is beyond words."

He pulled her to him, and their embrace became increasingly passionate. He was kissing her while caressing her body and her curves were pressing into his, but as his hormones, multiplied she pushed away saying, "This is not what we should be doing, you know."

As she spoke, the phone rang. It was the concierge confirming the reservation.

They were a few minutes early arriving at the Le Soufflé and Henri, the waiter, recognized Donald immediately, and arranged with the Maitre d' to have him placed at his best table. Borys arrived promptly at 7:30 p.m., and Henryka a few minutes after that. General introductions followed, although Donald requested they act very familial, just in case observations were being made.

Alicja played her part very well with the greeting, "Witaj kuzyni tak dobrze ci widzie . (Hello cousins, so good to see you)

After settling in their chairs around the table, Donald asked Borys his opinion about ordering an aperitif. Borys suggested a Pernod Anise, as this would sharpen the appetite for everyone.

Henri took the order as he presented the menu for the first course. Henryka and Borys talked in Polish and reminisced about their old lives in Poland before the war. Henryka also chatted to Donald either in broken French or in Polish translated by Alicja. For the first course everyone had the Symphonie Gourmande de Saumon, except Donald, who had the Autour du Fois Gras.

Everyone was delighted with their first course, and Donald was immensely pleased that his little gem of a discovery on 36 rue Mont Thabor had not only the best food he had ever tasted, but a consistency of quality that some restaurants found hard to achieve. Henri had also recommended a superb Bordeaux wine that complemented virtually all the dishes the party ordered. By the time they were halfway through the main course, the conversation was happy and animated. This was much to the amusement of the other patrons who were fascinated by the diverse languages and accents they could hear.

Alicja was in heaven with her dish of cod and mashed potatoes. She thought nothing could be more basic than a traditional Polish dish of cod and potato. However, this restaurant was special. She found the cod to be so meltingly tender with not even a hint of bone anywhere. The squeeze of lemon brought out the freshness of this Atlantic offering. Her mashed potatoes were of the finest French Ratte potatoes and pureed with butter and a little milk. The velvety texture was something she had never seen or tasted before. The small Ratte potato was only now coming back in France after the war, when it was virtually unobtainable — except, of course, to only the most senior German officer staff.

After a great deal of laughter and good conversation, there was a general consensus on ordering a chocolate soufflé for dessert. When these were placed on the table, the four of them gasped at the height of each of these towers of soufflé perfection. The aroma of chocolate wafted out from the creation as their forks penetrated the delicate shells. To finish off this wonderful repast, Henryka suggested they have a small cheese plate in the French tradition with their coffee.

Donald thought this a great idea and asked Henri for his advice. Henri brought a selection, a chevre or goat cheese from the Pyrenees, Brie from Mieux in Seine et Marne, a portion of Comté, and a Swiss Gruyere. After more good- natured conversation in which Donald felt he had become more Polish than English and being outnumbered by those around him, he asked Henri for the bill.

This was one expense the CIA and MI6 should be happy to bear, thought Donald. *We have succeeded in gaining the potential whereabouts of Kammler, together with the fact he had something more than a uranium enrichment device— something that seemed to silently defy gravity. Plus, we have succeeded in providing cover for ourselves in the face of the French Secret Service suspicions.*

He paid the bill while leaving Henri a handsome tip, who again thanked Donald for bringing his guests to the restaurant. They all turned out from the little street onto Rue Cambon and walked toward the Metro at Tuileries. Borys shook hands with Donald and kissed Alicja and Henryka. He said he would keep in touch with Henryka and walked off to the platform for the train to take him to the Rue de la Pompe.

Donald and the two women went in the opposite direction for the platform to take them home to Avenue Daumsnil. Everyone was tired, and Alicja rested her head on Donald's shoulder as the train rumbled through Paris. The rhythmic swaying of the carriage was soothing and relaxing. They arrived at Gare de Lyon, and Donald gently woke Alicja All three made their way to the apartment where Henryka kissed Donald good night and diplomatically went inside allowing Alicja to say good night to him alone.

They hugged and kissed for awhile and, again, Alicja thought passions were getting a little heated, resisting but not rejecting him. He made a joke, and they both laughed. He arranged to pick her up again tomorrow night when they would take a river cruise on the Bateaux Mouches.

Falcon Foiled and Felled

Falcon, in the meantime, had received his briefing from his controller.

"They confirmed that the Russian NKVD agents in Poland or KGB, as they were now named, and who were closely aligned to the Polish State Security, had found the name Petrowski was linked to his cousin Cieminski. Czeslaw Cieminski was in the detail of workers at the secret weapons site and must have passed information to Petrowski who fled to France. Russia gained a scientist from that facility who built a Bell-like device for uranium enrichment called the Tokamak. However, they believe Cieminski may have seen something even more significant than the Bell because he and numerous other workers had been targeted for execution at the time of evacuation by German forces. He had survived and been found in the forest nearby with severe wounds. He told Russian soldiers who treated his injuries that fleeing Germans had shot him. The Polish State Security later found his name among Nazi records concerning the camp he was placed in, and the work he had been assigned at Kammler's orders. We concluded his wounds had been from the execution squad. He was taken in for questioning but later died in custody without yielding any information except acknowledgement about the Bell. Our interrogation may have been a little too severe for his weakened condition.

We were convinced that, from documents retrieved from the facility, a mention was made of a different kind of Vortex-Principled device marked ***Kriegsentscheidend.*** Russian intelligence interpreted this as decisive for the war. If Kammler did get away, he may have this device or the capability to build it. We do not believe the Americans, the British, or the French have him but are trying very hard to locate him. One of our British agents inside MI6, who you know as nom-de-plume "Homer," had given Deutsch, his controller in London, information about Project Epsilon. The British in 1945 immediately at war's end had detained ten scientists who had worked on the Nazi nuclear program. Homer was able to provide Deutsch enough information for us to know that no mention was made of a secondary device to the Bell. We also understand the Americans had already recovered at least four other Bells in and around Germany. General Patton made an attempt to rush to Czechoslovakia and Poland, but our forces were already close to Wenczeslaus, so we know he did not get there. Therefore, wherever Kammler disappeared, we need to find him, if he's not dead. Petrowski is the key if he has not already passed on the information to MI6 or the CIA. We don't believe from Homer that MI6 has any agent working this case, but we are certain that the CIA must have."

Falcon was told it was now up to him to get the necessary data from Petrowski or eliminate him or both.

Armed with this information, Falcon was ready to get to work, but he was frustrated by the French surveillance as there appeared to be an increase in activity. He decided he would pay for his hotel one week in advance and then leave without taking his belongings. He would then endeavor to lose his trackers before finding alternative accommodation where he would not have to register his passport.

Fouchet meantime believed he has identified Gunter Durr for who he really is. The police in England had notified Interpol that a Ukrainian Russian agent by the name of Igor Martinovich was wanted there for suspicion of murder. There was no photograph but a very detailed description of the man closely resembled that of Fouchet's quarry. Jean Fouchet could still not fathom why the Russian was after Harvey. However, Harvey's story remained solid by his actions with SHAPE. What made Harvey's story even stronger was the revelation by MI6, with whom Mr. Fouchet had conferred, about the Interpol report. They had told him that Harvey's company, Trandect Engineering Ltd., had been infiltrated and a female Russian agent had been arrested on charges of spying for classified information.

So, Jean Fouchet was now satisfied that this was nothing more than spying for classified aircraft industry secrets. As there was no need for counter- intelligence work here or threats to the State, he handed the matter over to the Paris Police. They would now have the responsibility for finding and arresting Mr. "Gunter Durr." He provided his counterparts with the name of the Hotel Amiot where he was registered and last seen. His men had seen him leave the hotel that morning and spend some time at a nearby cafe, before taking a leisurely stroll near the Gare de l'Est. The agent used the telephone nearby to check in and was told if Durr had not checked out of the hotel, then he could leave his post. He was told that the police were taking over the case and would pick him up on his arrival back at the hotel. Meantime, Falcon in his brown sport shirt continued ambling until he melted into the milieu.

It was a very pleasant day at Rocquencourt as Donald was able to meet with Logistics and Procurement Officers of Norway, Denmark, and Belgium. These three prospects alone were enough to provide him with sufficient homework to prepare for transmission back home. His company would have to modify some existing designs to meet the regulatory approval of the various governments involved, but Donald had assured them it was well within the scope and capability of Trandect Engineering, Ltd.

He got back to the hotel and set to work on preparing requests for proposals and arranging the courier service to get them back to the UK on the next flight. Then he relaxed, and settled his mind on the evening he would have with Alicja. He was excited thinking of the romantic excursion they would have on the River Seine that night. He had given Alicja directions on how to use the Metro so she could meet him outside the Tuileries Metro Station at 7:30 p.m.

Pat O'Sullivan telephoned him and asked what he had planned for the night to which Donald told him he was having a nice private evening with his girlfriend who he hoped would soon be his fiancé.

Pat chuckled saying, "You may be having a private evening, but remember you're still under our protection."

"Oh, come on, Pat. Give me a break, mate."

"Look, Donald. Don't worry. We are very discreet and unobtrusive to the point of being risky. You never saw a soul near or around Le Soufflé the other night, did you?"

Donald exclaimed, "Bloody hell, no, Pat. What did I have to eat?" he asked sarcastically.

"I told you we are not that obtrusive," replied Pat. "Anyway, have a good time. London and Washington are pleased with the way things have gone and are looking forward to seeing you soon."

"Well, je t'aime Paree. I love Paris right now so they can wait," responded Donald.

Donald took a slow walk down Rue Cambon, turned left along the Rue de Rivoli to the Tuileries Metro Station. Alicja turned up twenty minutes late. She was laughing partly because of the worried look on Donald's face and partly because as she explained, she had taken a train in the wrong direction. However, once she realized what was happening, she was delighted that navigating the Paris Metro was so easy. She jumped off at the next stop, walked quickly through the connecting tunnel to take the right train going in the direction of Tuileries.

"Et voila," she said.

"Oh, right," Donald replied. "So we are a now a fully fledged Parisienne, oui?"

They embraced lovingly and kissed, while passersby looked on approvingly.

Donald indicated they had better get going, so they descended to the Metro together and headed for the boat dock at Pont L'Alma to board the Bateaux Mouches. They were just in time to embark for their reservation that Donald had made earlier. A maitre 'd' led them to a table with a magnificent view, and an all- around vista of Paris which was lit up in all her splendor. Alicja herself was lit up with a face that simply glowed in the romantic light of the scene. Her beautiful skin, deep blue green eyes, and shimmering dark hair simply captivated Donald. He could not help but notice the form fitting emerald green dress with a v-neck that accentuated her sensual bust-line, without it being too provocative. He held her hand as the boat began to move out into the flowing Seine River.

After consulting with Alicja about the menu, they both agreed it was time to have a French tradition. They ordered "Steak Frittes," or as Nobby Clark would say Steak and Chips, or his American friends, Steak and Fries. Either way, no one can cook chips or fries like the French. Like everything else they do in cuisine, it's an art by itself. The potatoes are first fried in a pan of medium hot oil to cook properly. Once done, they are drained and transferred immediately into a second pan of very hot oil where they are fried until brown and crispy. By this method, the chips/fries are fluffy on the inside and just perfect on the outside. To keep the quality consistent, the oil is changed frequently.

The sights of Paris landmarks passed by in a dreamy world of historic battlements, palaces, and churches, bathed in hundreds of subtlely placed floodlights. As the Cathedral de Notre Dame loomed out of the night on Ile de La Cité, its grandeur and majesty stirred the soul, just as it must have done for Victor Hugo. Again, the sight of the great Cathedral almost had Alicja in tears as her deep-seated Catholic upbringing brought memories pouring forth of the harshness of those not so far off days in Poland and Siberia — when praying to the Virgin Mary was the only hope they had of survival, and praying for her parents to survive, for without them, she and her siblings would surely die. As the boat glided slowly past with its engine gently humming, Alicja made the sign of the cross.

"It's so beautiful Donald, thank you so much. If I never do anything else in life, this moment with you will always be treasured by me forever."

Donald responded, "I could not imagine being with anyone else here on this cruise or anywhere else for that matter."

They leaned forward together and kissed just as the waiter brought the sizzling steaks to the table.

They whispered to each other because the hushed conversation of the other diners was a stark contrast to some noisy restaurants. Maybe the reverence of the sights this evening was so captivating that conversation seemed just too intrusive for the ambience of the moment.

At last, the journey was over as the vessel settled alongside the dock and the passengers disembarked. Donald and Alicja strolled back to the Metro and their destination of the Tuileries. He wanted to experience a walk on the Pont d'Arts, the Bridge of Arts. He told Alicja this pedestrian bridge was built in 1802 and had a wonderful view of the   le de la Cité. It was getting very late as they began their stroll to the center of the bridge. Looking back, they could see lights in the Tuleries Gardens and, on the other side, stood the great edifice of the Institute of France. Facing them was the Île de la Cité with the great towers of Notre Dame rising above the buildings. They stood there arm in arm, engrossed in their own world.

It was now well past midnight and closer to one o'clock in the morning, and they began their walk back toward the bridge entrance. It was such a beautiful night, and together they decided they wanted to walk on the Quai below the bridge. They descended the steps to the Quai de Louvre and began a slow promenade, admiring the reflections of the lighted buildings in the water. Donald and Alicja exchanged some passionate kisses and sensual embraces.

They were turning back toward the steps that would take them back up to the Tuileries access and had just passed under the Pont d'Arts when a vehicle's headlights from across the other side of the Seine cast their beam very briefly into the recesses of the concrete and steel structural base of the bridge. A figure that had been standing there hidden in the shadows was suddenly exposed for a second or two.

Alicja screamed, "Martinovich!"

Falcon was stunned at first. He had simply been keeping out of sight because he had not yet found suitable covert accommodation after buying a new jacket, and he wondered who this hysterical female was. In the split second of processing the image, he then was able to recognize Harvey and this chance meeting came into focus.

 He leapt forward as he was not about to allow himself to be exposed for subsequent capture, but Donald stepped in between him and Alicja. Falcon felled him with a blow to the side of the head and grabbed at Alicja who was screaming bloody murder!

Donald, now in a rage of anger realizing who this man was, spun Falcon around, and employed a little technique he had learnt years ago and always showed off at parties. He was able to open the four fingers of his right hand into a V — the forefinger and second finger together as one side of the V and the third and pinky fingers as the other side. With this rigid tool of stiff fingers, he rammed them straight into the eyes of Falcon who immediately screamed in agony. Virtually blinded, the man's animal instinct drove his muscled bulk into Donald who, drawing on his modest past judo experience, allowed Falcon to use his full force to subdue Donald's resistance and just as he was giving way he swiftly grabbed Falcon around the waist with his right arm, took hold of Falcon's jacket with his left hand, and lowering his body while turning to the left, he stepped his right leg low across Falcon's legs below the knee. Falcon's own force allowed Donald to throw him completely across his hip and smashed Falcon to the concrete where his skull cracked with full force. It was then that Donald came down with his fist and a protruding middle knuckle to smash viscously into his assailant's Adam's apple.

With his windpipe crushed and his eyes bleeding profusely, Falcon gasping and croaking, rolled and jerked in agony, falling over the Quai toward the river below. Somehow, self preservation allowed him to gain two hands on the edge of the Quai, but Alicja in those seconds that Donald had gained began stamping her heels into the fingers of the man who had caused her and her family so much suffering.

The blood was flowing from those fingers as he desperately gasped for breath while also trying to maintain his hold.

She screamed at him, "Ty draniu, teraz twoja kolej na   mier i   do piekła (You bastard, now it's your turn to die, go to hell). To jest dla Załuski" (This is for Zaluski).

With the last utterance she jammed her heel right into his temple almost falling into the water herself. With a strangled half scream, the KGB killer fell into the river and sank below the surface. Alicja took off her shoes which were covered in blood and threw them into the Seine. Donald took her in his arms, and she lay against him sobbing and shaking in terror. He looked toward the river but there was no sign of Martinovich.

The whole episode had taken no more that minute or two from start to finish, although to Donald and Alicja it seemed hours.

Right at this moment, a man ran up and, speaking with an American accent, said, "Sorry, 'ol buddy. I was giving you some privacy with your lady there and didn't expect any trouble, so it took me a minute or so to get to those steps and get down here. I saw the guy slip into the water. Man, what did you do to him?"

Donald responded in anger, "I don't know your name yet, mister, but bloody hell, you're late getting here. We could've been killed by this KGB son of a bitch."

The American replied, "I'm Sam CIA at your service. Look, I need to get you two away from here ASAP, so follow me. I have a car nearby. We will get you cleaned up and get you back to your hotel."

A small group of people who had gathered at the sound of screaming on the road above the Quai were looking down on the scene. Donald and Alicja followed Sam to Rue de L'Amiral de Coligny, where they jumped into a large black Ford Versailles car which had diplomatic plates and a waiting driver.

Sam instructed, "Straight to the Embassy Brandon, quickly!"

Sam looked at Alicja who was still shaking and said to Donald, "We need to get her something to calm her down."

Donald had his arm around her to comfort her as best he could, although he felt inadequate. They sped along Rue Rivoli, around Place de la Concorde, and into Avenue Gabriel and up to the gates of the United States Embassy where, upon inspection of Sam's credentials, they were allowed in.

Sam said, "Follow me."

They were shown into a small, well-furnished room. A few min-utes passed, and Sam returned with a lady who gave Alicja a sedative and some water. She then helped her to another room to clean up her feet.

She soon came back looking refreshed and with some white plim-solls. Sam asked Donald if he would like a drink, and he replied he wanted a stiff Scotch, which rapidly appeared together with some ice. He then asked Donald, "Tell me, just what did you do to the Russian? I couldn't believe you dealt a KGB guy a fatal blow."

"Well," Donald began, "I think I got lucky with a jab in the eyes, but more than anything, it was the judo move. In all the years when I used to do judo, I never fully mastered the Taoi Toshi, so when this opportunity presented itself from the way this bloke was all over me, I just concentrated on making sure I stayed very low and kept my right leg tight up against his leg below the knee. The pull by my left hand on his lapel and his own kinetic force spun him over, and when he hit the ground, I knew it was a perfect throw. I could just hear my old Sansei shouting 'Ippon!'"

"I think the crack of his head hitting the concrete and me hitting him in the throat was enough to disable him or even kill him maybe, but my heroine here made sure his fingers and hands were made incapable of normal use to save himself. If he's dead, then he got what he deserved, believe me. You should know how he disposed of one of his victims in England. You can look it up in the files. Plus his cruel history with the Ukrainian Nationalists goes way back to the beginning of the war."

Sam said, "Again, I'm sorry I was not able to get to you in time, but who knows, maybe this ended better than we could have hoped for in a way?"

At this moment, Pat O'Sullivan strode into the room and was given a briefing.

He listened intently and finally turned to Donald saying, "Look, tomorrow I think it's best we wind this thing up here in Paris. I need you to get back to London for a briefing. I propose you speak with Petrowski and ask if he would like to move to another apartment or, if he wishes, he can come to the States.

He turned to Alicja and took her two hands in his, "Alicja, my name is Lt. Colonel Pat O'Sullivan, and I want to thank you for helping us and Donald, together with my sincere apologies for what happened tonight."

Alicja replied, "I am feeling a bit better right now. You can never know how I feel inside about that awful man, but I just hope he has gone. It will be a justice well served. He should have been hanged after the war, but better late than never."

Still holding her two hands in his, Pat said, "Alicja, we need to get Don back to England on a flight tomorrow. Would you like to join him on the plane?"

She looked at Donald, "I want to be with him, yes. Paris would not be the same on my own."

"Okay, in the meantime let's get you to wherever you have to go tonight, and we'll make all the arrangements tomorrow."

She thanked him, and he squeezed her hands saying, "What a lucky guy."

Turning to Donald he said, "Don, you better look after this gal. I'll call you at 9:00 a.m. tomorrow to confirm travel. I'm suggesting you get organized for pick- up at your hotel later tomorrow afternoon."

They got back in the car and drove to Donald's hotel, where Donald suggested to Alicja she spend the night with him. She agreed, and called Henryka to tell her. She understood and was not objecting. After all, Alicja was a grown woman.

Alicja knew from that evening they were bonded together not just in love, but by a synergy of circumstance by which they had survived an ordeal that would live with them forever. They expressed their love for each other that night in which each released their passions both in expressions of tenderness, and of the deepest intensity. The Parisian night passed at last in peaceful serenity for the two lovers.

Dawn broke the shadows of the night, and the flapping wings of pigeons on the roof tops and their tiny burbling calls began to break the stillness. The high pitched teet teet of swifts starting their aerial ascent and swooping flight to begin the day's meal could be heard. The traffic noise increased in volume as the morning light broke through the curtains.

Donald slowly rose from the bed while looking down on the beautiful body of Alicja. He gently covered her while got up to make some coffee with the in-room percolator. As this was working away, he opened the door to the balcony and went outside to breathe in the fresh morning air of Paris that he found so unique.

Later, after they were both dressed and were ready for breakfast, the telephone rang. It was Pat, who told Donald to have himself and Alicja ready to leave at 3:00 p.m. from the hotel. Sam would pick them up in a car and take them to Le Bourget Airport for a 4:30 p.m. flight to London. He told Donald that Freddie Simpson would meet them in London on arrival and take them home. Pat thanked Donald and said he would try to meet up with him for a more secure conversation and appreciation. Pat told Donald that there would not now be an opportunity to make any enquiries with the French about Nazi hunting. There was no time now since last night's incident, and, in any case, one of Paris Police's top officers, Maurice Papon, had been a Nazi collaborator, and an unlikely ally in the hunt.

Donald told Alicja there would be no time to go and see Borys so, "I will write him a note and make sure Sam or someone gets it to him. We owe him everything so far."

Alicja agreed and suggested, "Why don't we get Henryka to take your note to him. That way it's a regular Polish person interacting with him."

"Great idea," replied Donald. "Let's get to your aunt's place, and I will write the note while you get yourself packed."

The next few hours flew past rapidly with Alicja explaining to Henryka that they needed to get back to England. Henryka agreed to take a note to Borys on behalf of Donald, and said she thought he was a nice man, plus it would be good Polish company for them both. Alicja and Donald smiled to each other.

At last they said their good-byes with lots of kisses and hugs and went downstairs to meet the taxi.

Promptly at 3:00 p.m. Sam rang from the lobby that he was ready for them, and Donald and Alicja came down. Sam took the luggage and Alicja to the car while Donald checked out at the lobby. The concierge said goodbye with a grin.

At last on the tarmac and inside the Vickers 610 Viking aircraft of British European Airways, Donald and Alicja, who were sitting on the left side, waved to Sam standing at the terminal. The plane revved up the big turbo jet engines, and they taxied off toward the runway.

The plane took off smoothly and climbed steadily while turning over the city of Paris. The lovers held hands and looked down at the symmetrical avenues bathed in the late afternoon sunlight, with both nostalgia and regret, over the hurt and danger they had suffered together.

U J I Z L E

Chapter 15

Home, De-Briefing and Assignment

Home Sweet Home

The plane touched down and taxied to the terminal in London. Donald and Alicja were the last off the plane, and they descended the steps to the tarmac. Picking up their luggage, they passed through customs, and one officer smiled as he asked to see Donald's suitcase. Upon opening it, there sat facing him the ugliest gargoyle ashtray imaginable, with its insolent tongue sticking out. This was Donald's souvenir gift for Bill Richardson. The officer closed the suitcase and remarked jokingly, "Don't let that thing loose out there."

Donald replied, "Oh, we'll keep it under control."

They moved on through Immigration and Passport Control to meet Freddie who was waiting patiently at the International Exit. Donald introduced Freddie to Alicja telling her that Freddie was a work colleague. He wanted to reduce the emphasis of MI6 in their relationship in order to keep Alicja from feeling so nervous. With the introductions and salutations finished, they followed him to his car. It was decided they would drop off Alicja in Amersham and then Donald at Micklefield.

Donald and Alicja had decided to keep the death of Martinovich and the manner of his demise away from her parents at this point in time. It would give Alicja time to adjust to the events before placing more strain on her and her parents.

The one happy announcement she would be making, however, was the fact that she and Donald had decided to get engaged! Donald had wondered how her parents would accept him as a future son-in-law.

Freddie kept up a friendly conversation with them as they flashed through the towns on the way to High Wycombe and Amersham. The car eventually pulled into the High Street and then barreled up Amersham Hill to Hodgemoor Camp where Freddie diplomatically said he would wait while Donald helped Alicja with her suitcase to her front door. Donald said he would call her as soon as he knew his upcoming schedule. They engaged in a long, lingering kiss before saying goodbye.

The ride to Micklefield was uneventful except Freddie said that a meeting was scheduled at the Museum Tavern for Tuesday at 10:00 a.m. James Wallace would be there, as well as Richard and Freddie. It would enable Donald to provide a complete de-briefing of events in Paris. There would be one other person present, who would be nameless at this time.

Freddie dropped Donald off and made a last comment, "Donald, we are all terribly sorry, old chap, about your confrontation with the KGB fellow, but we are also extremely pleased with the way you have handled things. By accepting Pat O'Sullivan's plan in Paris and bringing Alicja into the scheme with Petrowski, it completely fooled the French Secret Service. Excellent job, my friend!"

Donald nodded, "For me, Freddie, there's more to this agenda than just super weapons — due justice for Alicja and her people. The Poles have for centuries been caught between their powerful neighbors, and have suffered the consequences. Today in 1955, they are still under the yoke of a totalitarian power."

He waved goodbye and, carrying his case, he went inside for a nice cup of tea with Mrs. Fenchurch.

———————

The next day Donald was back in his office, taking up his duties as Engineering Manager, and fending off jabs about his Paris "jaunt" or "fling." Bill Richardson thoroughly enjoyed receiving his gargoyle ashtray, which he said would cope with his American cigars quite handily. Chalky White was anxious to know if he was going to get another assistant and one that could pass a background check. Donald was able to spend time on the specifications for the various Requests for Quotations (RFQ's) for his SHAPE clients and getting these into the work flow process.

At the front office Jill told Donald to be ready for a meeting with Colonel Blankenship at 3:00 p.m. Donald was on time when Jill welcomed him back and asked if had enjoyed Paris.

"It was wonderful," said Donald, not wishing to bring up his engagement plans or to complicate matters relating to his real mission there. Jill showed him in to the Colonel's office who boomed a big greeting at him.

"Helleva job, Donald! Those SHAPE RFQs could bring us some pretty nice business. Well done."

"Thank you, Colonel. I thought the connections worked out very well."

Donald looked at the Colonel quizzically, wondering just how much this man really knew about what had transpired in France.

"Well, Donald, being the great ambassador that you are as well a great salesman; I'm giving you another overseas assignment."

The Colonel was beaming at Donald, who was apprehensive as to what was coming next.

"You have me intrigued, sir. Where may I ask are you sending me next?"

"You're going on safari, m'boy," he replied and then continued, "The South African Air Force is modernizing, and they are in the process of ordering a significant number of new Viscount Turboprop aircraft. They are programming these for delivery beginning in 1958. I have a very good connection there with a fellow who flew Spitfires for us in North Africa as a Squadron Leader. A really damn fine fellow you know. Now apart from the electrical terminals, I am sure we can bid on the subcontract for some of the other components."

Donald asked, "What position does your man hold in the Force?"

The Colonel replied, "His name is Colonel Gerald Forest, responsible for the acquisition process and contract administration. He reports directly to Major General Wynand van Niekirk, the Number Three in the South African Air Force Command structure."

"When are you expecting me to embark on this 'safari,' Colonel? I mean, I have barely got used to drinking tea again. What's more, I haven't tasted a decent beer since I left England, and I'm off to correct that tonight."

The Colonel said, "I think it will be about a week or more before we have everything set up for you to go, but I'll let you know in due course, Donald."

Y T X R N T U S D

A Double Engagement

Alicja met Donald at the Red Lion where they shared a light supper. He indulged in a draught ale and she with a small glass of Bristol Dry Sherry. They had made their commitment to one another during that night together in Paris. Donald visited Ratner's Jewelers on the High Street before meeting Alicja at the Red Lion, and now he produced the small gift box that contained his symbol of undying love and devotion.

He said, "Alicja, you told me you didn't need a ring to know we are engaged, but for me it's more than just a symbol. This ring is part of me, and every time you see or touch it, you will be touching my heart."

She opened the box, and there lay a gorgeous white solitaire diamond set in platinum and white gold on an 18ct gold ring. She gasped in astonishment at the flashing piece of jewelry, and her eyes misted over as she leaned toward him. They kissed and held hands while talking for the next couple of hours, oblivious to all the other patrons and the noise.

He asked what her parents thought about their engagement. She said her mother was very happy, but her father was a little unhappy as he had wanted her to marry a nice Polish boy.

"He will get over it as he gets to know you more," she said.

Donald replied, "I can understand how he feels losing a beautiful daughter to whomever it might be, but I will certainly try to be the perfect son-in-law."

"Now, Alicja, I need to tell you about another engagement I have," Donald said with a smile on his face.

She looked at him in shock, "What do you mean, another engagement?" she said, horrified.

"It's a work engagement," he said grinning at her.

She punched him on the arm, "Don't give me frights like that. So what's this engagement for your work mean, then?"

"I am being sent to Africa on an assignment for my company, so I will be leaving for a short period. I'm not sure for how long or exactly when."

"Well, don't get eaten by lions then, and bring me back a souvenir."

Donald suggested they go to the Town Hall Dance on Saturday night and catch up with their friends. Ola and Cal would be invited, as well as Tony Carolla and his girlfriend. Donald saw Alicja to her bus for Amersham and Hodgemoor before he went home to prepare for his trip to London in the morning.

Assignment Africa

Donald walked from Paddington Station to the Museum Tavern in time for the scheduled meeting at 10:00 a.m. This time he was doubly sure he had no followers but, just in case, he did a reverse transit by walking right past the Tavern, turned down Bury Lane, doubling back on Gilbert Place then up toward Great Russell Street to the Tavern entrance. He entered the premises, and Freddie was sitting at a small table waiting for him. He asked Donald if he wanted a beer, but Donald declined as it was too early in the day for him. Maybe lunchtime, he suggested. Freddie led the way through to the back and up the stairs to the meeting room they had used previously.

The room seemed full of people and full of cigarette smoke that hung over the green baize cloth that now covered the mahogany table.

Richard Bates appeared from the throng and greeted Donald enthusiastically with, "Really well done, Donald. You have made a big impression on everyone, I can tell you."

"Thanks, Richard, I'm not going to say, 'Oh, it was nothing,' because, frankly, I was scared out of my wits half the time. I must give thanks though to Pat O'Sullivan. If it wasn't for him, I would not have been able to pull it off so easily. The French DST was hot on my heels."

Richard said, "You can thank him yourself. He's over there in the corner talking with James Wallace."

Donald checked and, sure enough, there was Pat who, looking up, saw Donald and came right over, as did Major Wallace.

"Hi, Don," said Pat. "Great job, man, and I must apologize again that my guy Sam was not able to assist with the Russian bear."

Wallace also interjected, "I never meant for you to get so entangled, but I thought you were a perfect cover for the Paris operation."

Richard interrupted them by asking Donald to meet Colonel Blignaut, Head of Special Section MI6, as well as his assistant, Bill Osbourne. Donald shook hands with both while wondering why this massive show of top brass.

Lastly he was introduced to Janet, Colonel Blignaut's secretary. Richard called the meeting to order, and the group began seating around the table. To Richard's left sat Major James Wallace, then Pat O'Sullivan; to Richard's right was Colonel Blignaut, then Bill Osbourne, followed by Freddie Simpson, and next to Freddie was an empty chair. Donald was invited to sit next to Pat O'Sullivan, and, finally, Janet.

Richard opened the proceedings by saying, "I would like to introduce Donald to some new faces here before we get down to business."

He explained the role of Colonel Blignaut who was in charge of the British side of the Bell project and reported directly to the British Minister of Defense and shared information and tactics with Major Wallace.

"Of course, Donald," Richard went on, "you already know Major Wallace's function. He reports to CIA headquarters in Washington, D.C. with assistance from the Military Attaché at the US Embassy here in London. Lt. Colonel Pat O'Sullivan, who you met in Paris, is our key person in Europe for this project. Then there is Bill Osbourne, one of Colonel Blignaut's special agents and, of course, Freddie Simpson and myself, who have been seconded to Colonel Blignaut from another section at MI6. We have an empty chair at the moment because we are awaiting another agent of ours from South Africa. He should have landed this morning and is expected at any moment. Finally, we have Janet here who will try to keep track of our deliberations as we go along."

Donald acknowledged the introductions noting to himself, this is a really big deal. The meeting then got started in earnest.

The Colonel said, "Donald, both Major Wallace and I have read the internal report here about your exploits in Paris, together with your notes on Petrowski. I want to personally thank you for such a great effort and to offer my department's personal apologies for the difficult incident you and Miss Kozlowski had to endure. I don't think you or anyone else need worry about that individual anymore."

The Colonel picked up the Daily Telegraph newspaper from the table in front of him, and pointed to an item on the front page in the bottom right hand corner. He handed it to Donald. The heading read, "Interpol Suspect's Body Found."

Donald went on reading, "*A body found trapped against a caisson of the Pont Neuf Bridge in Paris on Sunday has been identified as Igor Martinovich. He had been sought as a suspect in England for the murder of a Polish man. Cause of death was by blunt force trauma and drowning. He was suspected of being a Russian or Ukrainian agent. Neither the Russian Embassy in Paris or London has commented on the report.*"

Donald thanked the Colonel for the newspaper saying, "I'm ambivalent about the outcome, because part of me is delighted he cannot harm anyone again, and part of me is sad that I had to take someone's life. I'm just an engineer, not an assassin."

The Colonel responded gently, "We all understand your dilemma, Donald. None of us were expecting anything like this to happen and, again, we apologize. Now, let's move on to the important part of this meeting."

Colonel Blignaut said the information provided by Petrowski clearly demonstrated that a significant variation of the Bell had been or was being developed. Based on the description provided by Petowski's cousin Cieminski, a new kind of aeronautical system had evolved out of the Bell device.

He turned to Wallace, "Jimmy, maybe you could take it up from there."

James, chewing on his usual wad of gum said, "Yeh, sure. Look, we did, in fact, pick up some other Bell devices in Germany and elsewhere. This remains classified. However, all of them were related to enriching uranium in some form or another. The method, although extremely complex, we can say for simplicity purposes involved the rotation of two opposing cylinders at very high rates of speed. We believe that the Nazis had somehow found a correlation between the cyclotron-type action of the Bell with its physical and chemical reactions, and with the Shauberger Repulsin engines or discoid motors. Let me explain.

Viktor Schauberger is an Austrian who had been a hydrologist or water engineer of some kind with some very unique ideas in using water and air in a form of turbine power. He was co-opted by the SS when Austria was annexed by Germany in 1938. He patented a device known as the Repulsin discoid motor in March 1940. It was known as the Repulsin A. I won't get into the physics or details of this device, but it entails creating a Coanda effect by forcing a differential aerodynamic pressure between the outer layer and inner surface of the primary hull. The vortex chamber at very high speed creates hydrostatic particles, and the machine begins to glow, due to ionization of the air. In the Repulsin B machine, the vortex turbine was improved for increasing the implosion effect and, therefore, the lifting force. Due to the design of the turbine blades and other enhancements, it was able to generate much stronger thrust than the Repulsin A. It was capable of generating a type of force that creates tornadoes or cyclones through the effect of implosion.

In the meantime, another secret machine of a flying disc known as the Flugkreisel was being designed by a Rudolf Schriever, but it proved unstable. The SS brought in a Dr. Richard Miethe who thought the Schaumberger-type turbine could create a spinning lift of massive force and could be adapted to this newer device.

I'm giving you a simple description here. We believe Miethe's design worked and was a type of manned Repulsin-type aircraft. Now, we understand that a Flugkreisel or Flight Gyro, as it was called, actually flew at 1,300 mph and to a height of 33,000 feet. These are unsubstantiated reports and the Germans supposedly destroyed all matters relating to the disc or saucer type aircraft before the Russians got to Prague or Poland. However, it has been reported that a Dr. Habermohl, yet another scientist engaged in the Flugkreisel Project, was captured by the Russians and probably forced to work on secret designs in the USSR. We, the Americans, were able to secure Schaumberger and Miethe, as well as some of the discoid motors designed by Schaumberger. Dr. Miethe is helping us on a classified project at AVRO Aircraft in Canada, but Dr. Schaumberger has declined to work with us and wishes to remain a research scientist for water development. He was never a willing player in the Nazi war effort."

Wallace paused to allow his presentation to sink in and then continued; "Now we have always suspected that a more highly sophisticated craft had been developed and that other scientists besides Dr. Miethe had worked on something similar to the Repulsin model but was some-how connected to the Bell. Don Harvey's report certainly lends cre-dence to this theory, and we must try to get to the bottom of it. In some way the Germans were defying the laws of the conservation of energy and, thus, the Law of Gravity. It's bizarre, but apparently it may be fea-sible."

There was a silence around the table with everyone's eyes on Wallace. Each had a look of incredulity that seemed to say, "You've got to be kidding!"

"Gentlemen and Janet, for the classified record," continued the Major, "I can assure you that Dr. Miethe continues to work on disc-type aeronautical machines for us in the United States. However, the type of hovering device described in Don Harvey's report from Paris is clearly something completely different. We do know that the SS conducted their secret development schemes in a very compartmentalized manner. It is very possible that another scientist may have come up with a modified design that incorporated certain aspects of the Bell attributes into the Flugkreisel. It is also feasible that this was the final

Kriegsentscheidend or final decisive war machine of the Nazi regime. I will let Richard continue from here as to the speculation of what might have happened to that device."

Richard said, "Thank you, James," and then addressing everyone around the table, he went on, "Before we continue, I have received a note from downstairs that our visitor has arrived. Freddie, would you escort our guest up here, please?"

Freddie got up and left the room. He returned very shortly with a young sun tanned-looking man with an athletic build, blond wavy hair, and an engaging smile. Richard introduced him as Mike du Toit, an MI6 operative based in Durban, South Africa.

He shook hands all round and apologized for being late, ". . . but a thirty hour flight from South Africa was no fun," he said.

Richard said, "Mike will be invaluable in helping us gauge the South African scene. Please, Mike, take a seat."

Richard picked up where he had left off earlier. "I would like to bring to your attention the so-called "to do list" that Janet has reproduced in your notes in front of you. The list has been copied for you as it was given by Petrowski who said it was in the Czech language. We understand Donald got Petrowski to verify the dictation. Afrika Herenigde Nasionale strana, rodný, Pine m sto, Walfischbucht, U234, 2 390 nákladních automobil , Bell Vortex Stroj. The English translation of this is: Africa Herenigde Party, Pine City, Natal, Walvis Bay, U234, 2,390 trucks, Bell Vortex Machine.

Richard said, "The Africa Herenigde party was the Nazi Party of South Africa or Grayshirts, as they were known. Pine City, Natal we believe is a place called Pinetown in the Province of Natal. Walvis Bay is as you probably know from your geography, the main port in South West Africa."

Richard continued, "U234, we are not sure if this represents an isotope of Uranium or possibly a German U-Boat submarine Number 234. There have been reports among different intelligence circles that approximately 100 of these U-boats had gone missing at the war's end."

"The next item is 2,390 lorries. Based on captured documents, Albert Speer had requested Hans Kammler to release a Junkers lorry. Kammler had refused on the basis that on direct orders from Hitler, he was responsible for the highest priority of the war effort of jet aircraft production and, therefore, he could not release the Junkers lorry. *We are saying lorry here as this is the British term for what Americans would call a truck.* The 390, in fact, was the massive Junkers 390 six-engined aircraft, and the list refers to two of them. That ties in with the report from Petrowski. The British had bombed an airfield in Norway where these planes were being prepared for introduction into the Nazi war effort."

Richard paused, allowing the information to be absorbed before saying, "The Bell Vortex Stroj. Simply the Bell Vortex Machine. We don't know if this was a Bell, plus one other device, or a combination of the two. The way it was described by Petrowski, it seemed to be a hybrid of some sort."

Richard turned to James Wallace and asked if he had anything to add, to which James declined. Richard then asked Bill Osbourne if he would give his opinion on how the next phase of the investigation should proceed.

Bill began by saying, "The JU-390 plane was a monster aircraft, and intelligence sources indicated that it had been designed to carry an atomic weapon directly to the United States of America."

He looked over to Wallace who nodded in agreement.

"The Petrowski Report described some markings on one of the two planes, which seems to describe the decal for the Swedish Air Force. However, that is not entirely clear. Additionally, post-war unconfirmed intelligence described just such a plane landing in a remote area of Argentina and subsequently being dismantled. Now, where else could the second plane have gone for safe haven? Only one or two places seem likely. Based on the so- called 'to-do list,' we must assume it was South Africa or South West Africa. I'll let Mike here bring us up to date on that part of the presentation."

Mike sat up, fighting a time zone change, "I received Don Harvey's encrypted report via telex before leaving South Africa. I have been trying to get my head around it since. Here's my opinion.

South Africa took control of German South West Africa in 1915 upon the German surrender there and as part of the British Empire. It has always retained a strong German influence, however, and, of course, politically since 1948, the Boer or Afrikaans presence has been even stronger. In South Africa itself the popularity and sympathy for the Nazi ideology has always been quite strong. We should remember the Afrikaaner has fought England in two wars where England became the ultimate victor. The Boer Republics were annexed by Britain and were incorporated in the Union of South Africa. While today there is cooperative detente between the English-speaking population and the Afrikaans-speaking peoples, an underlying current of animosity to a degree on the part of the Afrikaans remains. Today, of course, the Afrikaaner is on the ascendancy, having gained control of the government through their

National Party and have begun to implement a policy of apartheid or separation of the races. The common opinion is that this policy had its infancy in German South West Africa and the Afrikaans has made it a cornerstone of their rule. While the Afrikaaner has gained the political power in South Africa, the English retain the bulk of all economic activity in industry, mining, and commercial interests.

You can see, therefore, that a Nazi fleeing from the Allies might have found a sympathetic partner with certain elements of the South African underground. That underground may not be so deep unless the upper layers of the political spectrum feel there could be a military advantage. For example, I am aware of at least two ex-World War II Germans who own a couple of engineering firms there. Both individuals have contracts with the South African Government, and one of them is well protected by an element of the South African Police Force. The chief of that force, we believe, is trying to set up a counter-intelligence agency they intend to call BOSS or the South African Bureau of State Security.

Neither of those two Germans is Hans Kammler, and they are not on any war crimes list that we know of."

Mike du Toit paused to drink some water.

Pat O'Sullivan asked, "Could a U-Boat access the port of Walvis Bay?"

"It could," Mike replied, "but the whole world would know about it. There are some more remote spots where a sub could lay off-shore and receive service from an on-shore tender or smaller vessel. Re-fueling would be difficult, though."

Pat enquired further, "Where in South Africa or South West Africa could a really massive aircraft land undetected, Mike?"

Du Toit thought for a moment, "I would say that it would be unlikely to arrive completely undetected. In the Namibia desert regions, however, the only people who would detect such a thing are the Bushmen — the native aboriginal tribes in the desert. They would consider it a sort of official phenomenon, and they would not report the fact to any authority. They would consider it part of the South African government anyway, with whom they have no positive relationship."

Colonel Blignaut spoke next, "Mike, where are the two German immigrants in South Africa? Where are their businesses and what exactly do they do?"

Mike replied, "Wilhelm Koch runs a machine tools engineering shop in Durban, and Johann Schultz owns an engineering manufacturing firm making mining machinery and equipment in Pinetown."

Richard interjected, "Durban is a major port in South Africa, but where exactly is Pinetown?"

Mike replied, "It's about twenty miles inland from Durban, and both that city and Pinetown are in the Province of Natal."

Everyone around the table was now fully aware of the implications of du Toit's last statement.

Major Wallace summed up, "It appears South West Africa may have been Kammler's entry point, either by U-Boat or a Junkers 390, or possibly both. A connection may exist with influential Afrikaaner Nazi sympathizers, with existing or previously set up engineering/manufacturing machine shops in the Pine City/Pinetown area of South Africa. The only question marks are, the huge distance between South West Africa and Natal province in South Africa, plus the mystery of the U234."

Mike du Toit went on to say, "Because both Germans were emigrés from WWII, while we needed to ensure they were not suspected war criminals, it was necessary for us to monitor their movements for a short while. During this process I did report that Schultz, in particular, had made several trips to the Colenso and Dundee areas of Natal. There was nothing untoward in that travel, as there are many mines in the area and Schultz is engaged in mining machinery. But strangely, he also visited Tsumeb in South West Africa a few times, which has one of the most highly enriched mineralized geological areas in the world. I say strangely because we have been discussing the possibility of Kammler in both Natal and South West Africa. We stopped monitoring him and Koch in 1952, so we have no current data."

Major Wallace spoke next, "I believe there have been some strange UFO-type sightings in South Africa, Mike. Do you have any reports of these in your files?"

"Only copies of reports from the news media," Mike replied. "There was a report of one in Durban, February 1951, Johannesburg 1953, and just a few months ago in December 1954 in Cape Province."

Colonel Blignaut turned to Donald, "Do you think we could get your boss to allow you to make a trip to South Africa on matters of State interest?"

Donald was once again, having a hard time not choking on hearing a proposal of such coincidence before he replied, "Colonel, my boss has, in fact, set up a meeting for me with a very senior officer in the South African Air Force to begin negotiations for sub-contracting projects. The SAAF are purchasing a number of Viscount aircraft from the UK for future delivery in 1958. I am to have two objectives: one, to determine what components could Trandect manufacture or source through a sub-contract, and two, what investment could Trandect engage in South Africa that would enhance our position as a vendor to the South African military."

Wallace deferred to Colonel Blignaut who posed the next question to Donald, "If Colonel Blankenship knew that it was an important national security issue for you to help gather information while in South Africa, would you personally be willing to devote a short amount of time in continuing to find Herr Kammler and whatever technology he may or may not have fled Germany with?"

Donald replied immediately and without hesitation, "In the context of the lives with whom I am associated with, and to the extent to which Kammler and the Nazi regime has inflicted such untold horrors, how could I not now be willing to pursue this to the bitter end? I could never live with myself to have refused your request."

"Well said," intoned the Colonel, "I commend you for your diligence and conscience."

Major Wallace broke in with his slow deliberate drawl, "Donald, you are to be congratulated, and we are very grateful for you to have brought us this far in our quest without drawing attention to yourself by other nations. Your cover has been perfect for us and will be for South Africa, too. However, I would respectfully caution you," and here Wallace sounded serious and deliberate, "don't let your emotional involvement override your practical requirement in finding the technology, device, machine or whatever it is that Kammler has fled with. Yes, we need to bring him to justice but first, let us determine what he has."

Donald responded, "Yes, of course, I understand what you're saying," and to himself Donald thought, *I think I know exactly what you mean*, and he added, "And being practical, I can understand why this very high level Nazi war criminal was never tried in absentia at Nuremberg like many others were. It does provide for some leverage, no doubt."

"A good observation, Donald," replied Wallace his face impassive, "You've done your homework, I see."

"Well, I'm sort of invested in this," said Donald smiling and breaking the tension, "You must 'know your enemy,' to quote the Chinese warrior Sun Tzu."

Richard broke in at this point and declared that lunch was being sent up from the Tavern and the general logistics of the mission to South Africa was discussed over a meal of shepherd's pie, sticky toffee pudding, beer, tea and coffee. It was agreed that Donald would liaise with Mike du Toit on the finer details of the plan. Pat O'Sullivan and Major Wallace wanted to ensure Donald was well protected on this venture. Mike indicated he had just the right person in the form of a Zulu native who was well educated and had been fully vetted by him. The man's name was Mandla Dube. It was tabled that the group would continue the planning after lunch.

PART
FOUR

Chapter 16

Into Africa

The Embarassed Embassy

Comrade Demidov picked up his phone and told his secretary to tell Comrade Tarasov he must come to his office immediately. Soon after, the Military Attache and KGB officer, Leonid Tarasov, entered his office.

The 2nd Secretary of the Russian Embassy in London was in a bad mood. Scowling, he threw the newspaper across the desk and told Tarasov, "Read that, Comrade, and tell me if we have a problem with Moscow."

Tarasov looked at the news item in the Telegraph and shook his head in disbelief.

"I can't believe it. Falcon is murdered? It does not appear to be a CIA job, but who else could it have been? Those kinds of wounds must have been from a street fight with thugs of some sort. I just can't imagine Martinovich getting involved with thugs; he was a professional."

Mr. Demidov interrupted Tarasov's musings, "Live by the sword, die by the sword. Look at the emblem of the KGB, Tarasov. What does it have as its main image running through every version of your badge? A damn sword!"

Demidov then spat out, "Comrade. And I say that in all sincerity because you are going to need every comrade you can muster. What does it mean when one of our operatives does not report in within a certain period?"

Tarasov replied, "It means they have been picked up by the other side. I think I know why you ask. Natalia Kolkov has not reported in for more that a week."

"Exactly, Comrade," whispered Demidov menacingly, "I suggest you as the Military Attache and political officer of this embassy should have a talk with Comrade Abramovich. Someone is going to have to pay for this mess, so make sure that his little cultural exercise in researching Disraeli implicates him, one way or the other. Just make sure he is the one that returns to the Kremlin, not us."

"Yes, Comrade Demidov. We know from past history he had an affair with Kolkov, and it would not be difficult to make the case that there has been a repeat offense."

"Exactly!" growled the 2nd Secretary.

Victor Abramovich was enjoying his lunch at the Claridges with Sir Thomas Downing Kendrick, the current Director of the British Museum. Victor was having a distinct conflict of conscience with himself. The more he interacted with British society at whatever level; he could not help himself to comparing the apparent well being of the population as a whole, to that of his own country. The propaganda of people's rights, the collective distribution of produce and wealth, the pretense of equality when, in fact, some were more equal than others, the despair of the less equal who had no hope of rising above their station, the punishments metered out by the more equal to the less equal — all of these elements were now beginning to challenge his own moral judgement.

His train of thought was broken by Sir Thomas who asked him, "So, Victor, when do you think Nikita Krushchev will help thaw relations by allowing a Hermitage collection to be exhibited here at the British Museum?"

Victor gathered his thoughts for the right diplomatic answer, "With Comrade Stalin no longer with us, it's possible that First Secretary Krushchev may consider some form of cultural exchange."

It was at this point that the maitre 'd' came to the table, "I must apologize for the interruption Mr. Abramovich, but, there is someone who says she is your personal secretary, and she has an urgent message for you."

Victor rose saying, "Sir Thomas, would you please excuse me for a moment? I am sorry for the interruption."

Sir Thomas responded courteously, "Oh, please, Victor, absolutely no problem."

Victor had gone pale, as this circumstance was unprecedented. The secretary said that she was told to go to wherever his diary specified his next appointment would be, and to inform him that he must report back to the embassy immediately. A very urgent matter needed to be addressed. He asked the secretary who had issued the order and did she know why?

She replied, "It was on the orders of Comrade Demidov," and looking at him sympathetically, she added, "Maybe it's because Comrade Kolkov has not reported in."

"Thank you, I will be on my way immediately."

He walked slowly back to the table thinking furiously, *this is looking very serious. They want me back at the embassy to lay the blame at my feet if Natalia has been picked up, or defected. I need to make a decision right now.*

Sir Thomas said, "Victor, you look like you've seen a ghost. Nothing serious going on, I hope?"

Victor looked at Sir Thomas and stated, "I think the ghost I have seen is my own. You have some contacts in the higher levels of government, Sir Thomas. Do you think that this afternoon, in fact, right at this moment, you could ....?"

Safari Africa

It was decided that Donald would use Durban in South Africa as his base while in that country. Durban was to the east and south of Pretoria, the judicial capital, and it was east and north of Cape Town, the legislative capital, thus making it a convenient midway point for travel to those centers.

It was two weeks after the Tavern meeting, and Donald looked at his British Overseas Airways ticket which listed all the stops the plane would be making along the way. It seemed like a re-enactment of Livingston's travels in Africa. As he sat on the plane waiting to take off, he reflected on his last evening with Alicja and how she had held him tightly to her. She was anxious that his journey would be a safe and happy one, to which he reassured her that it would be a straightforward business project with some information gathering on the side.

They had gone over his flight schedule and marveled at the distances that would be covered. His BOAC flight would take him over the Alps to Italy where they would touch down in Rome for a light supper. Taking off again, they would head for Benghazi in Libya where the plane would be re-fueled and the passengers refreshed with coffee. Flying through the night, they would touch down at Wadi Halfa in Eygpt, but if the following winds were satisfactory, the captain would make the decision on whether to continue straight on to Khartoum in The Sudan.

Alicja had laughed after noting that the itinerary called for the passengers to have breakfast at the Khartoum Airport, saying Donald was going to be overfed all the way to his destination. Further stops would be made at Entebbe, Uganda for lunch and then onto Ndola in Northern Rhodesia. Further stops in Salisbury, Southern Rhodesia and, finally, Durban, South Africa. All told, it was a journey of well over thirty-six hours!

Donald smiled to himself as he thought of Alicja asking about his hotel in Durban. He told her it was the Edward Hotel on Durban's beachfront and supposedly a first class establishment that his boss had selected for him. He had kissed Alicja and held her warm body close to his, and she had responded in memory of their intimacy and deepest love for each other.

He was still smiling to himself when the stewardess approached him to ensure he was properly strapped in as they were preparing to take off. Ironically, they were flying in a Viscount Turboprop, and Donald was thinking of all the electrical components that he was personally responsible for in that aircraft.

The props revved up, and the pitch of the motors changed to a powerful roar as the plane began its roll down the runway, picking up speed and finally lifting off toward the gray clouds over London, then climbing and turning east toward Rome.

Donald sat back in his seat and admired the view from the Viscount's unique large oval window and contemplated his upcoming mission. On arrival in Salisbury, he was to telephone Mike du Toit who would have an assistant meet him at the airport in Durban to take him to his hotel. Mike ran a surfboard shop in Durban which was the cover for his MI6 activities. The shop itself was self supporting as the surfing scene in Durban was highly active, particularly when an international competition was being held there. Mike's role in South Africa was keeping abreast of and making reports on the political climate, as well as monitoring the state of the English community in relation to the rise of the Afrikaaner and the burgeoning separate race policies, or apartheid. Donald thought, no wonder Mike looked so fit and tanned with a cushy job in the world of surfing.

The meal in Rome was quite palatable, but the coffee in Benghazi was even worse than any American coffee he had ever drunk. It made him think of Paris. The breakfast in Khartoum was a typical English one with sausage, egg, and bacon and a good old English cup of tea. Before arrival in Entebbe, the captain flew them around Lake Victoria where the passengers got a wonderful view of raw Africa and the lush fauna. Here they enjoyed a light lunch in the airport restaurant under cooling electric fans that tempered the tropical heat all the passengers were now feeling.

Taking off again, the plane headed to Ndola in Northern Rhodesia and then on to Salisbury in Southern Rhodesia, penultimate stop before Durban. At Salisbury the passengers who were scheduled to continue onto South Africa were led to the international lounge where Donald found a pay phone. He was able to obtain some change in local currency and after figuring out how to make a call to South Africa, dialed the operator who told him how much to place in the coin slot.

Mike du Toit answered, "Hello, du Toit here."

Donald spoke up, "Hello, Mike, it's Donald here in Salisbury, and I'm looking forward to getting my six foot two frame into a decent bed."

Mike laughed, "Great to hear from you, Don. I know it's a damned long trip. I much prefer to travel on one of the Castle liners. It's so much more relaxing and better way to travel."

"Yes," replied Donald, "but this is quicker."

Mike said, "I'll have Diana Marlow, my shop manager, pick you up at the airport and bring you into town. She will know what time your plane will arrive. So see you soon, okay?"

"Okay, Mike, thanks. I look forward to seeing you again."

Donald replaced the receiver. He thought he heard two clicks before he put it down, but believed that may be typical for Africa.

––––––––––––––

The flight from Salisbury to Durban was uneventful, although the seaside tropical climate provided a bit of a buffeting on landing. After receiving some close scrutiny by South African Customs and Immigration, Donald made his way out to the International Arrivals Hall. Diana Marlow was scrutinizing the passengers as they came into view. She recognized Donald from the briefing by du Toit and began holding up her arm to gain his attention. Diana was pretty stunning to look at, and it would have been difficult for Donald to have missed her as she gestured for his attention.

Donald grinned at her and put out his hand, "Diana?"

She shook his outstretched hand, and he was shocked at the strength of her grip as she said, "Hello, Mr. Harvey. Welcome to South Africa."

"Thank you," he replied, "but, please call me Don or Donald. We don't need to be too formal here."

"No problem, Donald. Let me show to the car. I'll just warn you the humidity here is pretty stifling for those not used to it," she said in her clipped South African accent.

On the drive into Durban, he asked her how she had got into the surfing business. Diana told him that most white kids in Durban grew up with the Indian Ocean as their playground, and the Durban beaches drew hundreds of youths to the abundant surf every day. Diana had surfed as a teenager, as well as during her university studies to the point where she had become a champion in her own right, winning many national and international titles.

Diana drove along the Esplanade past the shipping docks taking South African sugar to world markets, as well as shiploads of minerals and raw materials. Donald marveled at the wide road, little traffic, modern buildings, and graceful palm trees, so unlike the Africa he had pictured in his mind. They turned onto the Marine Parade, and Donald got a view of the magnificent blue Indian Ocean with its white-tipped waves rolling and crashing into the beach. Lifeguards sat up on their wooden towers, keeping an eye open for anyone getting caught in the many rip tides that frequent this coast.

He turned to Diana saying, "I can see why you got caught up in the surfing business."

She laughed replying, "You cannot know just how exhilarating it is until you have ridden one of those big waves. You just get hooked."

They pulled into the driveway of the Edward Hotel, a hotel of established Victorian Elegance and of a bygone era. A hotel porter strode over to the car as Donald was getting out, "Welcome to the Edward Hotel, Baas," he said with a big smile. "Let me get your bags, sir."

Donald said, "Thank you," and turning to Diana, he remarked, "What was the funny expression he used, sounded like boss?"

Diana smiled, "You're going to have to get used to some strange expressions. Baas means boss or master, and it's the typical greeting by the blacks toward the whites."

They went inside, and Donald checked in with the registration desk and identified himself. After receiving his room designation and key, he thanked Diana for the delightful ride to the hotel.

Diana said, "Mike told me to ask you if you would pop into the Surf's Up shop near Addington Beach, and he will have a chat with you then, okay?"

The "okay" came across with Diana's South African accent in a sort of sing song way, and Donald thought it sounded cute.

"Sure," he said. "How do I get there?"

She replied, "You just walk out the front doors of the hotel, turn right and keep walking down the Marine Parade past West Street, and you will see the shop on your right. It's quite gaudy, and you really can't miss it."

As Diana finished giving Donald the directions, a man came out of the public lounge and walked past them. He was around six feet one and very solidly built with a thick neck and black hair cut short. What struck Donald was that he seemed to look at Diana rather intensely, which by itself didn't surprise him, considering the attractiveness of this young lady, but it was Diana herself Donald noted, who had gone a little pale and acted nervously.

"Are you okay, Diana?" he asked.

"Yes, I'm fine," she responded, quickly recovering herself. "It's just that guy is someone you don't want to meet in any kind of official capacity. His name is Johannes Joubert, one of South Africa's top police officers. Mike can fill you in while you're here about Joubert, but with the business trip you are engaged in, you should never have any problem with authorities."

Donald thanked Diana for the ride to the hotel, while wondering about her concern over the police officer. He told her he would see Mike tomorrow morning, and right now was looking for a good night's rest.

Donald went to his room and having asked specifically for a sea facing room, he was pleasantly surprised with the magnificent view of the Durban beachfront and the Indian Ocean. After unpacking he returned downstairs to the Terrace overlooking the Marine Parade. He ordered a light supper and took in the sights and sounds of local life. He marveled at the Zulu rickshaw owners plying their trade up and down the street in costumes so ornate and colorful. He laughed at one tourist couple being conveyed in a rickshaw when suddenly, the Zulu operator would allow the weight of his passengers to overpower his own leverage on the handles, allowing him to soar into the air, while his charges sank almost to the ground. He would at the right moment kick his legs and, moving his arms to just the correct place on the handles, bring the vehicle level again. If the passengers squealed in terror, he would just do that once, but if they squealed in enjoyment he would do that several times on his way down the Marine Parade. This would ensure a handsome tip at the end.

Finishing his meal, Donald was now dog tired and retired for the night.

Mike's Briefing

Donald awoke refreshed and as the time difference between London and Durban was only two hours, he was unaffected by such a small change in the circadian rhythm. He had slept well with the sound of the surf from the open window creating what the Greek goddess Panacea would call "a soothing remedy for everything."

After eating a hearty breakfast, he exited the hotel onto the Marine Parade and commenced walking to the Surf's Up shop. Although it was still early in the morning, the humidity of this tropical paradise soon began showing its presence on Donald's shirt, as the perspiration began accumulating. As he passed the swimming pool and beyond that to the crashing waves on the beautiful sandy beach, he thought he, too, could easily take to the water at that moment.

As Diana had mentioned, there was no mistaking the surfing shop. Two outsized brightly colored surf boards stood upright like sentinels outside the entrance — one each side to guide the visitor through the portal and into the world of fiberglass, epoxy resin, psychedelic colors, and a language exclusive to the surfing crowd.

Mike du Toit was there waiting for him as Donald strolled in, bathed in sweat. The air conditioning in the shop now made it very chilly so Mike turned it off, saying, "You need to get acclimatized, Don, and get yourself dry. Let's have a couple of Fantas. You must be thirsty."

Donald thanked him and drank the orange soda which went down quickly and smoothly.

"Phew," he remarked, "that's better. You have quite a set up here. Do you make money in this business?"

"Absolutely," was the reply. "This pays for our upkeep and some extraneous expenses that crop up from time to time. Let's move to the back room where we can talk some more."

He called to a young man who was treating a surf board with resin. "Clyde, just watch the shop for awhile. I'm going to be in my office, okay?"

Just like Diana, he finished his request with that little lilt or sing song "okay". Clyde responded in the affirmative, and Donald followed Mike to his office at the back of the shop.

His office was a stark contrast to the shop. It was bare of posters, just a few papers on the lone desk against the wall and three chairs and a stool, with a single window that looked out onto an alleyway. The window had open blinds and was treated with a sun filter. A double-bolted and barred doorway also led onto the alley. The walls were bare except for a picture of Buckingham Palace, which surprised Donald.

Mike spoke up, "Have a seat, Don. That's a picture I keep on the wall to remind me this is a little bit of England in here. Having a portrait of Queen Elizabeth would be a trifle brazen or provocative, so the Palace is a little less 'in your face'."

There was one other item in the office that struck Donald as odd and that was a massive safe in the one corner.

Mike saw Donald looking curiously at it and then explained, "I am also a registered diamond dealer, and I have the credentials of a DeBeers sightholder, which in essence means I can attend the regular sales of the DeBeers Trading Company when they offer diamonds to the market. We sightholders, or buyers, will then re-distribute the diamonds through our own channels where we operate."

Donald looked at Mike in amazement, "But aren't you a member of MI6?"

"Yes, I am," Mike replied, "but look at this way. It's a double cover for me — the Surf Shop in a casual carefree kind of environment, and my diamond business that allows me to travel internationally and to my customers throughout South Africa. It's the best of both worlds, plus there is minimal cost to Her Majesty's government, and MI6 feels it's perfect."

"Are we able to talk freely in here?" Donald asked.

Mike replied, "This place is bug free. I have it swept for surveillance and monitoring systems on a regular basis. Let's discuss your mission. Don. Firstly, I want to give you some background on the South African police and how you need to be careful. Diana told me she saw Johannes Joubert yesterday at the hotel. He, in turn, reports to Hendrik Johan van den Bergh in Pretoria. What's important about that, you may ask? Van de Berg is a giant of a man whose history is rather tainted from our perspective.

He is an Afrikaaner and a strong nationalist who was against South Africa participating in the Second World War. He and the current MP for Nigel in the Transvaal province, John Vorster, had been members of the Ossewabrandwag or 'Oxwagon Sentinel,' a paramilitary organization modeled along the lines of the Nazi SA in Germany. The organization involved themselves in numerous acts of sabotage against the South African Government to undermine the war effort. The two of them, Bergh and Vorster, were detained under wartime emergency powers.

After the war both men were released, van den Bergh to become a high ranking police officer and Vorster a Nationalist MP. We believe that Bergh has a secret intelligence agency within the police force which has not been formally recognized by the government but secretly sanctions its activities."

Donald asked, "And what are those activities?"

Mike replied, "Its aim is to crush any and all resistance to opponents of apartheid. Now what has all that to do with you, Don? While we have no proof, we, that is MI6, believe the strong support of the Nazi regime and the anti British feeling among the ruling nationalists in South Africa may have welcomed numerous Germans fleeing prosecution for war crimes undetected, and possibly established new identities here as well as businesses that benefit the country in processes and technology. It's ironic that the gas and oil from coal, the Fischer-Tropsch process, was adopted here in 1950 and came on stream in 1952. South African Synthetic Oil, Ltd. (Sasol) began producing synthetic fuels this year. I say ironic, Donald, because the Germans were using this process extensively during the war and relied heavily on it. Coincidently, the USA took seven of Germany's synthetic fuel experts, and they helped build a plant in Louisiana."

Donald queried Mike with the question, "Have you been able to verify or establish any Nazi connections at all with any South African projects?"

Mike responded carefully, "None, definitively, but suspected, yes. There are several around the country. Look, when your report surfaced about Petrowski and Natal, I began thinking beyond Mr. Schultz and Mr. Koch and who they were associated with. My gut feeling comes down to an individual by the name of Hani Coetze. He owns a company in Pinetown; north of Durban and not far from Mr. Schultz's engineering facility.

Now Coetze is an Afrikaans name, but my understanding is his Afrikaans language is not perfect, and he may be operating as an alias.

The name of his company is Glovortx. The company manufactures specialized arms for the South African Government. He spends a great deal of time in Colenso, Natal, where his company has a large ranch of around 10,000 acres. Interestingly, there is an old mine on the property, and it has its own railhead with links to the main line in Dundee. The town of Colenso has a decent sized power plant that supplies the area with electricity. The townsfolk there often complain of power shortages, and a couple of new generators are to be installed. Glovortx uses the land to test its weapons, and the perimeter is guarded by South Africa military."

Mike paused in his narration, "So, Don, you can see the coincidences to which I am drawn to, by the Petrowski story?"

Donald broke his silence, "Yes, Mike, I can see a pattern including an underground facility, a weapons program, gobs of electricity being consumed, a rail link to a main line. Do you or anyone else have a photo of Mr. Coetze?"

Mike shook his head, "That's another thing. He's a very secretive chap. He has rarely been seen, and certainly not photographed. However, there is a Zulu native here who works for me as a driver, whose name is Mandla Dube. He has seen him two or three times and describes him as of medium height, roundish face, thinnish blonde hair slightly reddish, and one of his eyes, the right one is a little droopy. He looks around 60 years old so. If this was Kammler, he would be about 53 years old right now. That's about all we have."

Donald said, "Doesn't sound like Kammler. From his wartime Party affiliation records in the MI6 files, Freddie Simpson showed me a photo that indicated his hair was slicked back and it was black, not blonde."

There was a knock on the door, and Mike got up to see who was there.

Enter Mandla Dube

Mike walked over and opened the door to the shop and called out a greeting, "Sabona Mandla Sikona?"

A large Zulu man strode into the room, "Sikona auchena wena, Mr. Mike," he boomed in a deep baritone voice.

Mike introduced Don to Mandla who stuck out a huge hand as big as a plate, "Nice to meet you baas."

"Nice to meet you, too, Mandla," replied Donald who turning to Mike said, "What's this 'baas' thing?"

Mike grinned, "This is an Afrikaans word meaning boss or master, and is used by the blacks when addressing a white man. Don, you're here for only a short amount of time, therefore a couple of centuries of tradition, and now with the Nationalists in power, things will not change any time soon. They will only get worse, and there's nothing you can do about it."

"Yes, I see," said Donald. "I'm beginning to understand how some Germans might have felt under Hitler and how a democratic process can be used to weaken democracy itself."

"Well, Don, let's keep our eye on the ball. I am going to provide Mandla to you as your driver and assistant while you are here. You probably won't need him when flying to Pretoria or Cape Town on official business, but you will need him here locally in Natal as you begin to investigate our German friends."

"Well, I'm off to Pretoria this afternoon for a meeting tomorrow with Colonel Gerald Forest to discuss requirements for the South African Air Force, so maybe Mandla can take me to the airport today?"

Mandla replied for Mike, "Yes, baas, what time should I pick you up?"

Donald said, "Look, Mandla, everyone calls me Don or Donald. Why don't you do the same?"

"Ah," Mandla exclaimed, "I can't do that, baas. I can maybe call you Mr. Don, but never Don, otherwise if the wrong person hears me, I could be verbally abused or even beaten, and maybe you could be accused of being a kaffir lover."

Donald had heard that the word "kaffir" was a derogatory term for black people in the country, nevertheless, he was shocked that he must be called baas by the black population. He later learned from Mandla and Mike that the higher the social or educational level of the native, the less rigid was this unspoken protocol.

Donald addressed Mandla, "Can you take me to the airport at 2:30 this afternoon?"

"Yes, and just telephone Mike here when you want me to pick you up on your return," replied Mandla.

Chapter 17

New Business

South African Air Force

As Donald flew into the Pretoria airport, his mind was more focused on how he was going to track down Kammler. Not just how, but whether he really was in South Africa. Could Hans Coetze really be Kammler? He sounded older than his real age, and he had blonde hair or a little reddish. Nothing added up. An interesting fact that Mandla had brought up while driving Donald to the Durban airport was that Africans in the Colenso area were scared stiff of the actual mine on the Glovortx property. They believed it was haunted by a tocoloshe or ghost and would not venture into that mine shaft. Glovortx employed a large number of Zulus, but none inside the mine, and no one knew what was being produced there.

The workers were all employed in areas surrounding the mine. Periodically, large wooden crates would be brought to the surface of the inclined shaft at the mine-head, and these would be loaded onto rail cars. These cars would eventually be picked up by an engine and subsequently joined together with a goods train at Dundee.

Donald had wondered what he would do or say if confronted directly with Kammler. He had decided that if the opportunity ever arose, and if Kammler was captured in Donald's presence, he would say to him, **"Hans Kammler, the Jews want your rotting body in hell!"** but, he would say it in German, **"Hans Kammler, wollen die Juden Ihre verrottenden Körper in der Hölle!"** He then took it upon himself to learn and repeat this phrase over and over, until it was almost second nature.

Donald was pondering all of this as the plane touched down. Taking a taxi to the Colosseum Hotel on Schoeman Street, he checked in for the night and to prepare for his meeting with Colonel Gerald Forest the next day.

He would use the meeting as an opportunity to not simply act as a potential vendor to bid on open contracts, but also to help sweeten the negotiation by offering a potential capital investment from Trandect Ltd. If accepted, this would provide Trandect an opportunity to expand its capability overseas, and it would help Donald justify investigating potential "partnerships" and direct start up opportunities. He would then be in a position to talk with the two Germans in Natal, with the hope he could get into Glovortx for a look around.

The following morning Donald had an early breakfast. He was happy that the South Africans knew how to make tea the proper way. Leaving the hotel he took a taxi to the Union Buildings, the government's main ministry and official buildings in Pretoria. He had already called ahead to ensure he was expected, and the appointment with Colonel Forest was still on. The sandstone building, designed by Sir Herbert Baker, was started in 1910 to commemorate South Africa's Union status in the British Commonwealth.

Donald was directed to Colonel Forest's office and was greeted by his secretary, Miss Stein, "Goeie môre mnr Harvey, die kolonel is verwag dat jy."

Donald, with a puzzled frown on his face, said, "Er, sorry.. I er…"

Miss Stein then exclaimed, "Oh, my apologies, Mr. Harvey. Most people walking through that door are speaking Afrikaans. I was saying, Good Morning, Mr. Harvey, the Colonel is expecting you."

Donald smiled, "I hope the Colonel speaks English."

"Yes, of course," she replied, "He is English-speaking, but anyone who works for the government must be bilingual."

Miss Stein entered the Colonel's office to announce Donald's arrival, and he was invited to step inside. The Colonel shook Donald's hand enthusiastically and was very affable from the beginning. Gerald Forest was forty-five years old and had served in North Africa during the war and displayed his ribbons proudly on his uniform.

"Please, Mr. Harvey, have a seat here," he gestured for Donald to sit near the window overlooking the immaculate gardens below them.

The two got down to business to discuss the various aspects of the Viscount deal with the British company and what parts the SAAF needed to be supplied under their own specifications. As Trandect was an accredited vendor and supplier to Vickers, the plane's manufacturer,

Donald had full authority to bid on certain component layers in an OEM or Original Equipment Manufacturing capacity.

After about an hour of back and forth, an agreement was reached on how Donald's company could provide components for the cockpit and for the electrical terminals of the plane, in accordance with SAAF's particular configurations. At this point Donald thought he should broach the subject of inward investment possibilities.

"Colonel, my company, Trandect Engineering Ltd., has an interest in investing in South Africa, so would that translate into better odds of securing a contract with the SAAF?"

Colonel Forest responded immediately, "It's no guarantee, of course, but South Africa is intent on sourcing locally as much as possible. It still comes down to price and quality, of course. What kind of investment were you thinking of?"

Donald said carefully, "We have expertise in two or three areas of the aircraft industry: Specialized plastics manufacturing, prototype engineering, and aircraft instrument refurbishment and calibration. I would need to look at suitable sites or maybe look for South African partners initially."

The Colonel thought for a minute and then as if an idea had come to him said, "Mr. Harvey, it might pay you to meet a very important official while you are here in Pretoria. His name is Hendrik van den Bergh, and he is a senior police official who pays special attention to security issues that may help South Africa become self sufficient in military hardware and less dependent on overseas purchases. He would be a strong ally to have when starting a company that's going to be supporting the South African Air Force or Army."

Donald had been a little surprised on the mention of van den Bergh's name, considering what Mike du Toit had told him. Nevertheless, he was happy to get such a powerful lead that could help him in his quest.

He addressed Colonel Forest, "That sounds like a very promising way of getting important introductions instead of through Chambers of Commerce contacts. I would very much like to meet Mr. van den Bergh. Is he available to talk with while I am in Pretoria?"

The Colonel replied, "I will ask my secretary to telephone his office and check his schedule. I will speak with him about our discussion and get back to you this afternoon. When are you returning to Durban?"

"I had intended to return this evening, but I could delay that until tomorrow, if necessary," responded Donald.

Colonel Forest had his secretary draw up an official RFQ document for Donald to take back for future action and after shaking hands, Donald bade him goodbye and returned to the hotel to wait for a possible meeting with the senior police official.

Just before lunch, he telephoned the Surf Shop and Diana answered. He told her he wanted to speak with Mike. She said she would call him to the phone.

Donald said to her, "Diana, you remember telling me about Mr. Joubert and then about Mr. van den Bergh?"

"Yes, I remember."

"Well," Donald continued, "I may be meeting Mr. van den Bergh."

"What?" cried Diana, "Oh, my God, are you in trouble, Donald?"

"No, No, Diana it's official business, don't worry. Let me explain to Mike."

Diana brought Mike to the phone who said, "Hello, Don. Diana tells me you're meeting van den Bergh, heh?" Donald then explained the situation and how this may help his cause indirectly.

Mike replied by saying, "Look, Don, that could be helpful I agree, but listen, you need to be bloody careful. This guy was and is really anti-British and a powerful Afrikaaner Nationalist very much intent on ensuring the policies of apartheid are carried out to the fullest extent. He will be testing you, Donald, so when he casually calls the blacks, these bloody kaffirs or savages, or boys, he will be watching your reactions. If you in any way come across as a liberal 'kaffir lover' with ideas of treating the natives as equals, you will be sent packing."

"So how do you suggest I handle the conversation if it smacks of rabid racism," asked Donald?

"Just act neutral, Donald, as well as expressing a sufficient amount of sympathy for the Afrikaaner position in the history of the continent, of which you know so little about. That way he will have to acknowledge that you are not intent on undermining the government's policies, but your company through an investment of capital, could provide jobs for a number of South Africans, both black and white."

Donald thanked Mike for the advice and said he would act accordingly. He had a nice lunch and then sat by the hotel pool to wait for further developments. He did not have to wait for long.

Mr. van den Bergh

The hot South African sun shone down brightly as Donald lounged under a large umbrella next to the swimming pool. The pool was surrounded by a green manicured lawn, interspersed with various tropical flowering bushes, including pink frangipane. Jacaranda trees were also prevalent along the perimeter wall of the pool area.

Donald was in a contented state of relaxation when he was addressed by a member of the hotel staff who said he was wanted on the telephone in the lobby. Donald quickly walked over there and, picking up the telephone receiver, announced, "Donald Harvey here."

The voice on the other end sounded deep and resonant, "Goeie middag Mnr Harvey, dit is van den Bergh. Oh, excuse me, you have only just arrived in South Africa, so you obviously don't speak Afrikaans. So many English speakers who have lived here for generations also don't speak my language either."

A huge laugh erupted at the other end of the phone. Donald thought, *Yes, he was laughing good-naturedly, but he could tell it was a sore point for him.*

Donald answered, "Well, Mr. van den Bergh, I'm a quick learner so maybe it won't take a generation for me."

Another laugh erupted, "I'm pleased to hear that, Mr. Harvey. Anyway, Colonel Forest has updated me on your visit with him today, and any time we can entertain the possibility of a foreign investment in our military or aircraft industry, it is worth checking out. I will be in the vicinity of the Colosseum Hotel later this afternoon at around 4:00 p.m. Would you be available for a chat then?"

"Yes, sir," replied Donald. "I would like that opportunity to meet with you."

"Good, I will ask for you at the reception desk, Mr. Harvey."

Donald took to his room to rest a little before his meeting with the police chief. It was 4:04 p.m. when the phone rang. Donald acknowledged he was ready, and he went down to the lobby. He walked over to the reception desk where one of the biggest men he had ever seen stood. Hendrik van den Bergh was 6' 5" and looked approximately 300 pounds. He was weathered like a farmer and, as Donald later found out, he was nicknamed "Lang Hendrik" in Afrikaans or "Tall Hendrik."

Donald stuck out his hand saying, "I'm Donald Harvey, Mr. van den Bergh?"

The big man swallowed Donald's hand in his, but, surprisingly, shook it in a polite and gentle manner. Donald felt the man could easily have crushed his hand to a pulp.

"I'm Pleased to meet you Mineer Harvey. Why don't we find a suitable spot to sit and have a chat for while?"

They decided to have a coffee in the restaurant where some privacy was possible. Some of the staff who knew who he was looked on in apprehension as this giant of the apartheid system moved through the hotel with Mr. Harvey.

"So, Mr. Harvey, I understand that your company, Trandect Engineering, has some special capabilities. Tell me, what do you think you could do for us in South Africa?" Van den Bergh spoke with the sharp Afrikaans accent that emphasized some consonants and rolling r's.

Donald explained at length where he could see advantages for both his company and South Africa with the expertise and manufacturing Trandect could bring to the country. It may be necessary initially to find a South African partner who has similar but not competing skills where they could both benefit. He asked van den Bergh if he was aware of any companies that might fit that profile, specifically in Natal.

"Why Natal?" van den Bergh asked. Donald explained because it was a midway point logistically between Cape Town and Pretoria or Johannesburg.

Van den Bergh thought for a little while and then asked Donald, "Do you have anything against Germans?"

"No," replied Donald. "The war's been over for ten years."

"There's a company in Durban by the name of Umgeni Toolworks Ltd. It's run by a Wilhelm Koch, and I will notify him that I have recommended you to visit him. He has mentioned in the past he would like to expand his business, so this may be just the opportunity for both of you."

"Thank you, Mr. van den Bergh. I shall look forward to getting in touch with him."

"Just call me Hendrik, which is nicer that what some people call me. The kaffirs call me a lot worse names."

"Kaffirs?" asked Donald. "Yes, kaffirs or Africans as you people call them. Just remember Donald, if I may remind you, that you are very welcome here in South Africa, but do not attempt to bring ideas of false freedom or to undermine our system of government."

Donald answered, "I know when I am a guest in someone's house, Hendrik."

Hendrik guffawed, "That was a good answer, Donald, my man. I think we can do business together, heh?"

"Yes, sir, I think we can," responded Donald with a smile.

With that, Hendrik gave Donald his personal telephone number and his official card, which he was free to use as a recommendation to gain access to certain officials that he may need. Donald gave him his own credentials and where he was staying in Durban. They parted company with another handshake from "Lang Hendrik."

Donald thought to himself, *Talk about doing a deal with the devil, and here if I was a resident of South Africa, I'm emulating the actions of many Germans who found themselves supporting Hitler and the Nazi regime. Ironically, this is really not much different.*

Closing In On The Quarry

Donald returned to Durban the following morning where Mandla was waiting to pick him up at the Louis Botha Airport. Colonel Forest had asked him to visit with the SAAF Commander at the airport during the week in order to look at aircraft instrument refurbishment; not just for the squadron that was based there, but for other squadrons around the country. He made a mental note to follow up on that later in the week. In the meantime Donald was anxious to make contact with Wilhelm Koch at Umgeni Toolworks Ltd. Mandla dropped Donald off at the Edward Hotel where he remained checked in as guest.

It was still around mid-morning when he telephoned Umgemi Toolworks and asked for Mr. Koch. The secretary said he was unavailable and asked for Donald's name and reason for his call. As soon as Donald mentioned van den Bergh, the secretary's demeanor changed completely on the mention of the police chief's name.

The secretary said, "Oh, please hold Mr. Harvey. I will see when he will be available to speak with you."

Donald waited until he heard a voice on the other end say, "Ya, can I help you?"

Donald then explained the reason for his call and the referral by "Lang Hendrik." Mr. Koch thought it would be a good idea to meet at his machine shop on Umgeni Road in the industrial area and a time was set for 3:00 p.m. that afternoon.

Donald had time for lunch on the veranda overlooking Marine Parade where he enjoyed watching the Zulu rickshas gliding up and down the street. He had time to telephone Mike du Toit and give him the latest news. Mike was impressed on the progress Donald had made but suggested that he keep Mandla nearby to him at all times. He said that Mandla would be able to casually question any Zulu employees wherever Donald went, not just at Umgeni Toolworks, but with any other company.

He said Mandla Dube was a descendant of a prominent Zulu family, and he acted and was received by other Zulus with authority and respect. He was often able to come up with information about a company or organization that a white person would not be able to secure. There was almost an unwritten code among the black population that information among themselves was something that was their own, and could be used for their own advantage, if necessary.

Donald enquired how Mike came to hire Mandla. He had employed him in the Surf Shop because he was very literate having gone to school, plus he was big and strong. However, because every African who worked in the city had to have a special pass, Mandla had somehow run afoul of the law and was put in jail for failing to have his pass.

Mike had rescued him from jail and made sure he always had the proper papers or 'Dompass,' as it was called. Mandla became a loyal employee and a good source of information from within the black community.

It was almost 2:30 p.m. when Mandla pulled up at the Edward Hotel where Donald was waiting. After a fifteen minute drive, they arrived early at Umgeni Toolworks Ltd., and Donald decided to wait a few more minutes in the parking area and get a good look at the machine shop in front of him. It was a nondescript building next to a Bandag Tyre Retreading company. It was painted a dirty white with the company's name painted in red on one side of the large metal door. There were a couple of small windows that had not been cleaned in years, and it was doubtful anything could be seen through them. A smaller door to the right of the large metal door appeared to be the main entrance and had three solid locks.

Donald got out of the car and, telling Mandla to wait for him, he strolled up to the smaller entrance door and knocked.

Some shuffling occurred inside, and the door opened to reveal a smartly dressed black woman who smiled a greeting, "Mr. Harvey I assume? Mr. Koch is expecting you. Please come in."

Donald stepped inside and was quite shocked with what he saw. The property inside was expansive and much larger than the appearance given outside. It was also spotlessly clean, with up-to-date machinery humming away operated by white men in immaculate dark green overalls. He could see Cincinnati milling machines, Monarch and

Colchester lathes, and numerous other excellent equipment; all in the brief walk to Mr. Koch's office, which was on the second floor that looked down on the workshop floor below.

They shook hands, and Mr. Koch asked Donald, "You leaving your boy outside?"

Donald looked at him, "Boy?"

"Ya man, your kaffir driver. You left him out in the parking lot."

Donald was irritated at the man's racist remarks, but also with the fact he knew Mandla was waiting in the car. How would he have known that? The windows were caked in dirt.

He replied to Koch, "The public transport here is non–existent, so I have to have a hired driver and a car."

"Yes, I can understand that," responded Mr. Koch.

"Well, Mr Harvey, I understand that you are interested to find a partner in an engineering venture in South Africa?"

Donald said, "Yes, either as a stand alone investment or in a joint venture with a suitable partner that can offer some value to the project."

Both Donald and Wilhelm Koch exchanged ideas on how such a partnership could work. After listening to Donald's explanation of the kinds of specialties Trandect was engaged in, Koch offered another alternative that might appeal to both parties. He proposed that Trandect set up a separate and independent company, but with a contract to supply Umgeni Toolworks with a negotiated variety of specialized products. The contract would be underwritten by the South African Government and endorsed by Frederik van den Bergh because of the nature of the products involved being essential to national security.

Koch said, "My own company has similar agreements and contractual obligations with other companies. As you have been recommended by 'Lang Frederik,' I can tell you about Springbok Mining Machinery Co. Ltd., known as SMCO, and another company by the name of Glovortx Ltd."

Donald put forward, "Are these other two companies similar to your own and just what kinds of products are being produced? Hopefully, we would not be duplicating the specialties of either yours or the others."

Mr. Koch said, "Mr. Harvey, from what you have told me, Trandect could complement the areas of what we and the others are engaged in. I cannot speak too much about Glovortx because that is a top secret government protected site and the complete range of what they do is unknown to me or anyone else. Now, my company produces precision components for armaments, self loading breech blocks, recoil systems, gun sights, cannon loading systems, etc. We supply these products under contract to SMCO which, in turn, manufactures larger components, such as the base blocks for the heavy weapons, long range cannons, howitzers, machine guns, etc. They also produce some highly sophisticated components in specialized alloys that I am not privileged to know about. All of SMCO's output is supplied to Glovortx in Colenso. There, all of SMCO's and Umgeni Toolworks products are assembled and tested on the Glovortx ranch property. Some of the specialized items are removed to an underground facility for further processing and manufacturing."

Donald put another question to Mr. Koch, "As a non-South African, even with Frederik supporting us, how could we be awarded a contract to provide services to these armaments projects?"

Koch replied, "Well, frankly speaking, there is already talk of certain countries wanting to implement sanctions against South Africa and although nothing has come of it as yet, the government wants to become self sufficient in as many areas as possible. Armaments are a priority. I can't speak for them but van den Bergh has opened the door for you, hasn't he?"

"Yes, I would say he has opened the door for Trandect, and it's an interesting opportunity. I need to do a lot more due diligence; however, it would certainly be helpful if I could meet with the owners of SMCO and Glovortx."

Wilhelm Koch looked pleased, "I can arrange for you to meet Johann Schultz of SMCO, but I will not be able to get you an introduction to Mr. Hani Coetze, the owner of Glovortx. You would have to get permission from Hendrik for that."

"That sounds like a good plan, Mr. Koch," said Donald.

"Call me Wilhelm. It's a little less formal," the German replied.

He seemed a little more relaxed now and comfortable with Donald who also offered, "Okay, Wilhelm, please call me Donald or Don. I hope we can work out an arrangement eventually for our mutual benefit."

They went downstairs, and Wilhelm gave Donald a tour of the premises and the operations. He was very impressed with the extreme thoroughness and quality of the finished products. African workers in clean and neat uniforms were hovering around the white tradesmen operating the milling machines, lathes etc., and keeping the metal swarf or waste from accumulating around the machines.

Donald congratulated Wilhelm on the efficient and tidy machining process he had in the shop, and he joked it did not give that impression in the front of the building outside.

Wilhelm laughed for the first time saying, "That's done on purpose, Don. It attracts very little attention, and that's just the way we want it."

Donald nodded in understanding before enquiring, "Will you telephone me with the details, when you have set me up with an appointment to meet Mr. Schultz?"

Wilhelm Koch replied, "Yes, I will get a message to you at the Edward Hotel by this afternoon or this evening."

Donald thanked him and left the premises feeling well satisfied with events that day. He got back in the car, and Mandla drove off down Ungeni Road back to the beachfront and the hotel. He explained to Mandla his plan of action and intentions to meet with SMCO and hopefully Glovortx.

Mandla said, "Baas, if you have trouble getting into Glovortx, I have a way to get in, but it might be dangerous."

"Mandla," exclaimed Donald, "how would you know how to get in? I thought the place was well guarded?"

"Baas, the Boers or Afrikaaners have been here for centuries, but the Africans, the Zulus in Natal have been part of the ground itself since 1000 years. We know how to make use of special skills. Local tribes' people in the Colenso area know about certain abandoned ancient mine shafts, some of which lead into the Glovortx property. If you are unable to get in, Mr. Don, I will help you get in some other way."

"Well, thank you, Mandla," said Donald looking surprised at his Zulu driver, "but why would you want to risk getting caught in such a place on my behalf? I know you are loyal to Mr du Toit, but you don't owe me anything."

"I know, Baas Donald, but I think you are an important person for Mr. Mike so I must help you, and I think I can."

They had reached the driveway and entrance to the Edward Hotel, but Donald was curious to talk more with Mandla. He told him to pull forward a little more on the driveway so they were not right in front of the main entrance, or blocking the through traffic.

He questioned the big Zulu some more, "What did you mean when you said you think you can help me?"

Mandla thought for a moment, "When we say goodbye to someone and to wish them well, we say 'hamba kahle' which is pronounced 'hamba gashle' and means, go slowly. This is the Zulu name for the chameleon which is slow, but deliberate, and camouflages itself according to its surroundings. Mr. Don, I can help you get into Glovortx by showing you how to 'hamba kahle'."

"Well, thank you Mandla, I really appreciate your kind offer and I will more than likely take you up on it if I cannot get in through normal means. What do you think is going on there?"

"Mr. Donald, the tribes' people around the area of Colenso are worried about the strange sights they see there. They think there is an 'umthakathi,' a 'tagati,' or wizard operating there, or even a 'tokoloshe' or evil spirit of some kind. They know about the armaments that are tested on a special firing range which include massive field artillery, machine guns, and mortars. The noise scares the cattle even several miles away and reduces milk production. They are more concerned about the big mine shaft where they are scared of 'tagati.' They talk among themselves, Mr. Donald, about peculiar lights in the sky at night that float but suddenly shoot off at a rapid speed. They say sometimes they have seen these things come from the shaft and return."

Donald was looking at Mandla in amazement, "Are you sure they are really seeing these objects or do you think they are just caught up in the local superstitions? Just how big is the mine shaft and what kind of headgear is operating the lift?"

Mandla answered, "There is no headgear. This is what you call an inclined shaft. You should talk to Mike because he would know more about actual mining in this area of Natal."

Donald enquired a little more, "You said there were other hidden shafts. Are they also inclined workings or are they vertical?"

Mandla said, "They are mostly incline and hidden because they start up in the kopjes or hills, as you call them, and are covered in heavy bush and rock formations. They are inhabited by baboons and leopards. In addition to the danger from wild animals, the locals told me the shafts are full of death because they hear the Toc Toc beetle. In Zulu legend, if you hear a Toc Toc beetle knocking at night, you will soon die. Now the mine shafts are very very old, and they are supported by timbers, so they are probably infested with the Toc Toc beetle."

Donald thought to himself, how utterly ironic, *I started out on this adventure because of the death watch beetle and now here we are, dealing with the same little pest with the nickname Toc Toc.*

"Mandla, you talk about this like you have no fear at all of these Zulu legends. Why is that?"

"I respect all of them, Mr. Donald, but I have no fear of any. I am not immune, but have learnt to live in the modern world while respecting my ancestral world."

There was knocking on the car window, and a white member of the hotel staff began remonstrating with Mandla.

"Hey, boy," he shouted. "You can't park here all day."
Donald opened his window, "He's my driver, and I told him to park here while I give him his orders for tomorrow. I'm staying at this hotel and paying through the nose for it."

The man replied, "Oh, sorry, sir. I didn't realize that, but, in any case, these kaffirs still take liberties. He knows he shouldn't park here, but they just like to be cheeky."

Donald said, "Listen, my man, I don't know who the fuck you are, but I am paying this man to be my driver while I am in Durban, so who do you think he should listen to, his baas who's paying him, or some arse-hole who's calling him a kaffir boy?"

The man turned deep red and, muttering under his breath, strode off.

Mandla grinned from ear to ear and said, "Baas, thank you, but you should not do that for me. You might get into trouble. I am used to it, no problem."

Donald also grinned, "Mandla, what's he going to do, have me thrown out of the hotel? Anyway, he doesn't know it, but my friend Hendrik van den Bergh could put him straight, couldn't he?"

They both laughed out loud and Mandla said to himself, *I need to look after this white baas. He is a good man and I don't want him getting into trouble.*

Chapter 18

Out Of Africa

Meeting Mr. Schultz

Donald rose early the next day and took his breakfast on the hotel veranda once more. The sea air coming off of South Beach and the sound of crashing surf was to Donald an exotic experience and one that he would wax nostalgic about in later years. Donald had picked up a message from the front desk the previous evening from Wilhelm Koch giving him directions to Pinetown Mining Machinery Co., Ltd., and an appointment to meet with Johann Schultz at 3:00 p.m. in the afternoon.

Mandla was waiting with the car as Donald left the hotel, and they drove down the Marine Parade to the Surf Shop. Donald's driver parked the car, and they both entered the Surf Shop together. Clyde, Mike's shop assistant, and Diana Marlow were busy with a bunch of young surfers who were discussing the merits of various boards. Diana called out to Mike du Toit in his office to come out and see Donald.

Both Mike and Donald retreated to Mike's office, and Donald said he wanted to discuss the Glovortx company and some aspects of the geology of the area that Mandla had brought up.

Mike turned to Mandla who was still in the shop, "Come in the office, Mandla."

Donald described his meeting with the South African Air Force in Pretoria, his introduction to "Lang Frederik," and finally his meeting with Wilhelm Koch at Umgeni Toolworks.

Mike said, "That was a busy couple of days. I'll make sure to get a report back to the UK. Are you hopeful that you are on the right track here?"

Donald said, "I'm not sure at all. It's just the only logical lead we have right now. Tell me, Mike, Mandla says you have some knowledge about the mining history of Colenso area. He says the mine on the Glovortx property is an inclined shaft. Is that typical because it cannot go that deep, right?"

Mike answered, "Yes, the mines in Northern Natal were mostly open pit or inclined shafts. My father, in fact, was a geologist and mining engineer for one of the big mining companies, and he told me the coal mines in this province could not go below a certain depth because of penetration of methane. There was sufficient coal in the seams down to a moderate depth and, therefore, it was unnecessary to drive vertical shafts anyway, thereby minimizing the risk of methane explosions."

Donald asked further, "Mike, have you heard the stories about the Africans in the area talking about strange objects or lights coming in or out of the mine at that location?"

"Yeh, Mandla has mentioned it, but I have always discounted these stories as Zulu superstitions. I mean they have a multitude of superstitions, ghosts, tagati magic, not so, Mandla?"

"Yes, Baas Mike, if you are a Zulu, they are very real."

Mike remarked, "It lends credence to the fact that it supports your story, Don, from Petrowski, so maybe I should be less skeptical."

Mike continued with his description of the geological formations in the area consisting of granitic and metamorphic rocks with plateaus of sedimentary rocks and basalts.

He said, "Some of the hidden shafts described by Mandla, if starting out from the surrounding kopjes, or hills, may have been cut from granite or basalt. These may lead to the coal seams lower down. Some of the ancient workings may also have been gold mines centuries ago."

Donald announced, "I have an appointment to meet Mr. Schultz at SMCO this afternoon at 3:00 p.m. Mike, do you want to know the address and how bizarre this really is?"

Mike responded, "Well, I know where the company is, but the address had no real significance for me when I was checking it out, but you're going to tell me anyway," he grinned.

Donald also smiled, a little wanly however, "SMCO is in Eyrie Place in the FALCON Industrial Park, New Germany, which is part of the Pinetown area. Falcon was Igor Martinovich's Code name, and here we are dealing with a suburb called New Germany, isn't that ironic?"

Mike said, "Agh man, that is really ironic, I agree. So what's your plan Don? How are you going to play the Schultz card to get into Glovortx?"

"I'm not sure yet, Mike," responded Donald, "I may have to use my van den Bergh trump card in some way or another. I shall make a routine visit with SMCO this afternoon and formulate my moves after that."

Mike wished Donald luck on his mission and asked him, "Don, I am supposed to remind you that London gave you a special camera for your use in South Africa. Do you have it in case you get an opportunity to use it?"

"Yeh, Mike, it's a Minox A III. I've played with it in my hotel room, trying to practice holding it at a specific distance from printed matter to ensure a document can be readable when reproduced. It has a special chain in the back so you can use it as tool to measure objective distance from the lens. I'm just a bloody amateur at this game, so London can't blame me if stuff doesn't come out right."

Mike reassured him, "For a bloody amateur, you're not doing too badly so far, my friend."

As Mandla fed the Mercedes 280 through the afternoon Durban traffic up Berea Road out of the city and toward the suburb of Westville, he asked Donald, "Do you want me to talk to the black workers there at SMCO?"

Donald replied, "Absolutely, Mandla, if you can obtain any useful information, it might turn out to be invaluable. You just never know. However, you must be careful in case they suspect you of spying on their boss."

Mandla let out a huge guffaw, "Baas, as long as they know I'm not with the police and you are just a business visitor, they will tell me a lot of things you could never obtain from Mr. Schultz. The political system has built a barrier between the races, and no matter how well or how badly the whites treat the black races, it's them and us!"

Donald said, "I must say I did, in fact, notice a very distinct difference in the general attitude of the African in Southern Rhodesia toward the whites compared to how I perceived the Africans here. They were genuinely affable up there, and there was little or no tension, but here I do see a sort of surliness or rigidity when interacting with them at the hotel. They are courteous enough, but as you say there, is a definite barrier between us."

"That," said Mandla "is because of apartheid. We don't trust the white person because we can never tell when he or she may start calling us, 'you bloody kaffir', or 'boy.' Imagine yourself as a Zulu, a descendent of the greatest warrior nation ever seen in Africa, and some-one calls you 'boy.' It builds resentment, and ultimately, Mr. Don, their system will not last."

Donald said he understood, and again felt he was witnessing a mirror of recent history. This system was not the replica of the Nazi holocaust, but was, in effect, the holocaust of the African mind and spirit.

As the car climbed higher up the escarpment, Donald looked back at Durban bathed in bright African sunlight with the shimmering blue of the Indian Ocean of Durban bay in the background. It was a gorgeous sight for the eyes.

Arriving in Pinetown they drove to the industrial area of New Germany and Eyrie Place. The car pulled up to SMCO's large brick building, and Mandla parked to the far left of the front of the building so he had a view of both the front entrance and of the side where some workers were having their tea break. Donald got out and was grateful the temperature was a few degrees cooler than in Durban and less humid. He left Mandla with the vehicle and entered the main office.

He addressed the receptionist, telling her his name. She said he had been expected and would inform Mr. Schultz of Donald's arrival. The receptionist came back a short time later and invited Donald to follow her to Johann Schultz's office.

Mr. Schultz rose from his desk and greeted Donald warmly and shook his hand vigorously. "Mr van den Bergh told me you would be coming, and my friend Wilhelm has also told me about you. Welcome to Springbok Mining Machinery Co. Ltd." He spoke with a heavy German accent and made no attempt to disguise it.

Donald replied, "Thank you, Mr. Schultz for your warm welcome. I've been looking forward to this visit."

The German beckoned him to sit down, and Donald had a look at his office. Donald had a good grasp of assessing a person's personality by the state of the office. In this case, it was fairly spartan and devoid of unnecessary posters or pictures. It did carry a picture of the Prime Minister, Johannes Strijdom, and the South African flag. He noted that there was no picture of Queen Elizabeth as there might have been in some offices at this time. The furniture was from solid teak, but of a utilitarian or functional design, and the floor was of a practical black rubber covering. Mr. Schultz was around 40 to 43 years old, 5'11" tall, weighing around 185 pounds, the bulk of which must have been quite muscular as he had quite a flat stomach. There was grey CA-13 Facit hand-cranked mechanical calculating machine on the desk, which Donald recognized because he owned one himself. He felt it was an invaluable tool in the engineering field.

He pointed to it saying, "I see you have the same Facit that I have in my office. It certainly saves a lot of time fiddling with log tables when doing mathematical calculations."

Schultz was immediately impressed that Donald had similar equipment.

"We have some very fine tolerances we work to, so calculations are important," he said.

"So tell me, Mr. Harvey, just what do you have in mind here in South Africa as far investments in engineering and manufacturing are concerned?"

Donald began a similar discussion that he'd had with Wilhelm Koch and how his company might be able to form a synergistic partnership that could complement the product lines of both companies. Donald stressed he was keen to bring British aircraft engineering specialities to South Africa.

From a personal level he was now re-thinking his position on this as he felt uncomfortable in supporting an apartheid regime. At the moment, however, he was able to justify his personal conscience in terms of achieving something more immediate. Plus, he was representing Trandect, not himself.

As Donald continued his talk with Mr. Schultz, Mandla meanwhile had strolled around the side of the building and began chatting to the Zulu workers who were having a tea break.

"Sanibonani nijani, hello how are you?"

"We are well," they said in unison.

"Why are you here, and who is that white guy you bringing here?"

Mandla assured them, "his baas was a good person coming from overseas, maybe to start a company and employ some workers."

That got their interest and asked if he would pay better than their current boss. Mandla asked them if they were not paid well and said they got the absolute minimum. They said the boss was okay and treated them quite well, and he never shouted at them or called them 'kaffirs.' Mandla talked to them some more and asked in the Zulu tradition how were their families and if they had good cattle at home. Most Africans lived in the designated rural areas where they had some cattle and their wives and children. Mandla asked what kind of things they were making at this factory, and they told him all different kinds of parts for guns or artillery. Some parts would come from another company in Durban, and they would assemble them. There were other pieces of machinery that they had no idea what they were. These pieces came from a foundry in Pinetown and were large round wheels with spirals inside. They were not made of steel, the metal looked like copper but was much harder than copper.

One man said to Mandla, "We think these big wheels are tagati or magic. There is something we don't like about them. The white men inside put extra pieces of metal all around the wheel until it looks like the inside of a snail."

Mandla was puzzled by this and asked, "What happens to these?" He was told by the men they are crated up and shipped to Colenso. Mandla asked, "How do you know it's going to Colenso?"

One of the men who called himself Mdala Sithole or Old Man Sithole said, "I have been with the big truck several times myself to help with loading and offloading."

Mdala was, in fact, quite elderly looking, with gray hair on his head and gray stubble on his chin. Both of his ear lobes were pierced in the traditional Zulu fashion and hung down the side of his neck like a beagle's ears.

Mandla spoke softly to him so that the others could not hear and asked him where he lived. Mdala told him he lived in the African township of Kwa Mashu, not far from Pinetown. Mandla asked if he could meet him and buy him some African beer, to which he readily agreed.

At this point the bell rang, indicating the end of the tea break and the men said to Mandla, "Hamba kahle," to which Mandle replied, "Hambani kahle."

He returned to the car to wait for Donald.

Donald in the meanwhile had been given a tour of the plant and once again was impressed by the factory floor and its organization. Among the various components produced by SMCO, including long precision made gun barrels for field artillery pieces, he noticed some of the Umgeni Toolworks products being integrated with SMCO's equipment. He was also shown some actual mining machinery in the form of some pumping equipment and rock drills and other conveyor-type devices.

As they continued the walk through, Donald asked Schultz how he had come to South Africa as he had an obvious foreign accent.

Schultz hesitated for a moment and then relaxed saying, "I was desperate to get away from Germany. I got trapped in East Germany as we retreated out of Poland, but I managed to make my way to the American Zone, and they cleared me to remain in West Germany. I was lucky enough to meet a South African who told me there were opportunities in this country."

Donald posed a question, "But you could not have had money to build this business, surely?"

"No, of course not, I worked for someone else for a while and then was able to get a loan to start a small workshop, and I built it from there."

Donald probed further, albeit it gently, "So what area of Poland were you posted to in the war?"

Schultz was visibly uncomfortable answering this question and said, "Why do you ask? Do you know much about Poland at that time?"

"No, no," Donald replied, "I just know it was a tough time when the Ruskies came through Poland and into Germany."

Donald thought he was rather defensive about having been in Poland, but thought he should not push it.

As they walked though the factory, he noticed a separate room where some large wheel shapes were being worked on. Some were being burnished with power sanders removing foundry sprue and rough edges; others were being machined, while still others were being fitted with numerous curved blades. The castings had a sort of spiral cavity that led to the center of the disc.

Donald asked Schultz what these were, and he simply guided Donald on through the plant, saying, "That's just another type of turbine contract we have."

Donald was thinking it was an odd looking turbine. Donald was amazed at some of the armaments being assembled in other parts of the plant. There were smaller arms similar to the old British Bren Gun but with lighter steel alloys and a larger magazine. He watched while components of a field artillery gun were assembled on a massive jig to ensure a perfect fit to very fine tolerances.

As he finished the tour, Schultz asked him the same question Koch had asked; would Trandect be more interested in a joint venture or a stand-alone investment with individual contracts? Donald said they were more inclined to be private investments but nothing would be decided while he was in South Africa, and it would be up to his boss in England.

Donald asked if Mr. Schultz could get him an introduction to Mr. Coetze of Glovortx, but as was the case with Mr. Koch, Schultz declined.

He said, "You have a good relationship with Mr. van den Bergh, and only he can get you in to see Glovortx."

Donald asked, "Why is it so secret, after all I have seen nothing more that standard military hardware, I don't think I have seen anything significantly proprietary?"

Schultz turned to Donald as they got to the front door, "Mr. Harvey, it's just that if, for example, you saw those turbine discs in the workshop, and if you were to see them in a complete assembly, you might come away with the wrong impression. You know, sometimes people can add two and two and come up with five or six."

Yes, that's true, thought Donald to himself, *but what if they come up with four?*

They shook hands at the door and Donald said, "Thank you, Mr. Schultz, you have a very well run engineering business here, and I feel privileged that you have allowed me to tour your facility. I hope we will be able to do business together."

Schultz looked pleased with Donald's comments and reciprocated by saying, "Well, thank you, Mr. Harvey. It's been a pleasure dealing with a fellow engineer. It's sometimes frustrating dealing with the bureaucrats I get visiting here from Pretoria."

"But not 'Lang Frederik,' though, I assume," shot back Donald with a laugh.

"Oh, no, definitely not with him," replied Schultz. "You never want to cross that man."

Donald went down the steps outside, and Mandla opened the car door for him.

"Sorry to keep you waiting in this hot sun, Mandla."

With his usual deep laugh, Mandla said, "I'm a Zulu, and I'm used to the sun, and I am used to waiting for the white man."

Donald grinned at him, acknowledging the man's sense of humor.

Mandla told Donald about his conversation with the workers and particularly with Mdala. "I am going to meet him tonight baas, and buy him some beer and sadzsa. The old man is skinny and looks like he could eat a good meal."

"What's sadzsa, Mandla?"

"It's cooked maize flour, and you eat it with some meat and gravy. I will not be going in Mike's car as it is too dangerous to drive in Kwa Mashu."

"Do you think this Mdala Sithole could be helpful to us?"

"Yes, baas, because he has been to Colenso several times in the truck delivering stuff from SMCO."

"And why would he want to help you Mandla? What can you offer him?" enquired Donald.

"He will help me because I respected him as a Zulu elder, and this is something that is being lost in our culture."

"Baas Don, if you cannot get into Glovortx through the front door, I am sure I can get you in there through the 'back door.' I have allies in the area like I told you before, and by this evening, I will have another ally in Mdala, I am sure of it."

"Mandla, you cunning bugger, I can see you expect me to do some trespassing. I am hoping I can get an official welcome mat at the front door. If I can't, I will take you up on your offer. In the meantime, I will telephone 'Lang Frederik' to get me an interview with Mr. Coetze."

"Let's arrange to meet at Mike's place tomorrow and plan accordingly. I have a feeling that Mr. Koch and Mr. Schultz are just the buffers on the engine that helps Hans Coetze avoid contact that would reveal his true identity."

On arrival back at the Edward Hotel, Donald went immediately to his room and telephoned Mr. van den Bergh. He got through straight away and thanked the police chief for the introductions to Koch and Schultz. He told him the meetings were productive but he would, of course, not be in a position to make a decision about investment strategy until he returned to England. Van den Bergh understood and asked Donald how else he may be able help him.

He said, "You know, Donald, we are very keen to bring foreign investment in, and our Department of Commerce has a number of incentives to make that happen. I will give them your information. In fact, I will be in touch with the Deputy Minister of Commerce later today, and will ensure Trandect is given priority and fast track processing if you decide to form a new South African subsidiary."

Donald thanked him again for his invaluable assistance, and the pressed him with a new request. "I would like to visit Glovortx, as I understand that any sub-contracting work I conduct with Umgeni Tool Works or with Springbok Mining Machinery Co. might require final integration in systems at Glovortx. I thought I should try to meet with Mr. Hani Coetze as a way of completing my business analysis."

There was a moment of silence at the other end as van den Bergh digested this request.

He replied, "Mr. Harvey, my role is to protect the Afrikaaner nation, which requires that I make sure we encourage the right kind of people to help us. Nothing you have seen at Koch's plant or at Schultz's factory contains any serious security risk for South Africa. However, at Glovortx, that is another matter. This is a top security site, and no foreign entities are allowed. However, there is one part of the property where certain certain sub-assemblies are integrated like you say, into complete systems for testing on the range. I can arrange for you to meet

Mr. Coetze at his field office within the grounds of Glovortx, but you will not be allowed to visit the underground area which is a highly restricted area."

"I would be happy with that, Mr. van den Bergh," said Donald. "I'm not here to spy on South Africa's secrets. I'm here to see if we can bring our expertise to the country for our mutual benefit."

That seemed to appeal to van den Bergh because he said he would make arrangements for Donald to visit Glovortx the next afternoon. "I will leave a message at your hotel, Mr. Harvey, with details. Oh, one more thing Mr Harvey. Colonel Forest said he had given you an introduction to Lt. Colonel van de Merwe, the SAAF Commander at Louis Botha Airport in Durban?"

Donald acknowledged that was correct but he had not yet had time to make the connection. The Police Chief said it would be a good time to meet van de Merwe, as he was responsible for the instrument workshops for the whole of the SAAF. He said refurbishment and repair of aircraft instruments to within Military Specifications was an important skill needed by South Africa. Donald said meeting van de Merwe was high on his list of priorities.

They bid each other good evening, and Donald was well satisfied with events so far. Later in the fading light of the afternoon, he took a walk along the beach to let the Indian Ocean's breaking waves slide over the sand and cover his bare feet, before rushing back to the depths. The water felt so warm and inviting he thought he should get Mike to teach him how to surf. Better still, he thought of beautiful Alicja and wished she were with him now, enjoying this tropical ambience.

Glovortx in Colenso

The Surf Shop was busy with a large contingent of Durban's young surfers who were checking out the latest boards that had just arrived.The throng of enthusiasts was joined by a number of foreign visitors who were in town for an international surfing contest that was to be held next week.

As Donald moved past the bronzed and muscled bodies of both sexes, he waved hello to Diana and Clyde before entering Mike's office at the back of the shop. Mandla followed him a few moments later, after parking the car.

They got down to business, and Donald related to Mike the prior day's activity with Schultz and his conversation with van den Bergh.

Mike was a little apprehensive as to why the Police Chief was taking so much interest in matters relating to military and State issues.

Mike said, "We think, that is MI6 thinks, he is intent on setting up South Africa's own State Intelligence unit, in which case, this stuff would be monitored by such a department. Anyway, Don, did you get a meeting with Coetze confirmed?"

Donald replied, "Yes, I received confirmation this morning that I could see Mr. Coetze at 2:00 p.m. today."

"You will have to leave here fairly soon because that's about a 2 1/2 hour drive to get there," said Mike looking at his watch. "I suggest you keep your Minox camera handy in case there is an opportunity to a get a shot or two. Basically Donald, I have been told to tell you, you are not to get yourself in any danger. If you are able to observe any interesting stuff, that's fine, but your main task is to identify Kammler, if you can. That's all. If you are convinced Coetze is the man we want, our professionals will take over and formulate plans in line with British and American joint actions. Is that clear?"

Donald was surprised at Mike's tone. "I'll make sure I follow the line that's needed," he agreed.

Mike pointed out that the Edinburgh Castle liner was due to dock in Durban harbor shortly and would be sailing in three days time for Southampton, England. He wanted to know if Donald would like a leisurely cruise back to England on that ship. Donald agreed, knowing he would be finishing up soon after negotiations with the Air Force officer at Durban Airport tomorrow. Mike said, just as a precaution, he would also have a reservation for Donald on BOAC's flight from Johannesburg on the same day.

With the details of his mission to Colenso established, Donald and Mandla left the Surf Shop to return to the hotel. On the way, Donald said out loud, "I've come this far, and I'm not leaving until I know what this guy Coetze is up to. Did you learn anything from that guy Mdala you said you were going to see last night, Mandla?"

Mandla smiled and replied, "We had some African beer, meat and sadzsa. We had a good talk about many things, such as what is happening to our tribal culture, our history, and then we talked about Glovortx. Mdala has relatives in the umuzi's or villages in the area. Some of them I have already met, like I told you. Baas Don, we can help you get inside that place. There are many old tunnels leading a long way underground. These people can lead you to the entrances, but many will not go in, as I mentioned before."

Donald was curious as to why Mandla was being so helpful, "Mandla why do you want me to go inside and underground?"

"Mr. Don, we know whatever is being made in this place is going to be bad for Africans. We know that 'Lang Federik' goes there, and he wants to get all Africans out of white areas and move them away from their traditional homes. They are making special guns and vehicles at Glovortx to help suppress us. Coetze is supported by a secret group of Afikaaners called Gryshemde or Greyshirts. I know that you and Mr. Mike think that Coetze is maybe an ex-Nazi war criminal, so anything we Zulu's can do to have him removed, we will do it. Glovortx is a bad place, Mr. Don, I am sure of it."

Donald thanked him for his information. "Mandla, I will know after I meet Mr. Coetze if he is who we think he is. If he is Hans Kammler, I will take you up on your offer, but what more do I need to know? I can just report back to Mike, and the powers overseas will act accordingly."

Mandla looked at Donald seriously, "You must get to see some mysterious objects that Mdala and his people say are tested at night."

Donald was now convinced that maybe he should take the risk to follow this thing through to the end. He had better make sure he had the Minox camera with him at all times.

"Mandla," muttered Donald, "you had better make sure I come away from this in one piece. I don't want to end up in a South African jail. What do we need to get in there later tonight?"

Mandla said, "None of us want to end up in jail, and I will make sure you will just see what you have to see, and get out of there. For you, Mr. Don, it's just one big mission to right a wrong in WWII. For us Africans, it might be a lifelong mission to spend underground, before we see the light of freedom."

Donald understood his meaning, "I am not a politician, neither am I a Mahatma Ghandi, but I have seen enough evidence so far of man's inhumanity to man to know that the forced separation of peoples because of race, or for any reason than a contagious plague, will inevitably fail. Unfortunately, its failure may come at great cost to the suppressed victims. If you're helping me is in some way helping you, then so be it."

Donald held out his hand which the big Zulu took in his, and they shook hands in solemn understanding. Mandla told him to wear strong shoes and trousers as they would be walking in the bush that night.

"We will bring water and flashlights," he said.

Donald asked, "Who will be venturing down any tunnels if Africans there are so scared of the place?"

"Me, Mr. Don, I will be the one. The others will be guides for the outside and in support."

The car pulled into the hotel driveway, and Donald told Mandla to come back in one hour when he would be ready to leave for the official Colenso trip. The plan would be to conduct the official visit and afterward to move to a safe area in the bush and await nightfall.

Donald had time to get changed into suitable clothing that still provided a business appearance, while being practical for the African climate. For this he wore a traditional tan colored safari suit that comprised of lightweight trousers, over which was a jacket of the same color. The safari suit jacket is typically a long tunic with buttons up the front and is open-necked. The jacket extends below the waist and had two buttoned down breast pockets and two side pockets. He placed the Minox camera in one of the breast pockets and buttoned it up.

He thought about telephoning Alicja, but as it would be in the middle of the night in England, he decided against it. As he busied himself in the hotel room, he looked out of the window and saw a large liner easing its way past the Durban Bluff and into the harbor entrance. Donald thought that must be the Edinburgh Castle that Mike mentioned this morning. He briefly imagined himself lounging in a deck chair on board the ship while it steamed along the azure blue waters of the Indian Ocean on its way to Cape Town and Southampton. Snapping out of his reverie, Donald went downstairs to the waiting Mercedes.

They drove out of Durban through Pinetown toward the city of Pietermaritzburg, passing through the emerald green and rolling 'Valley of a Thousand Hills'. Donald sat watching the vistas of Zulu kraals scattered across the landscape and pondered the future of these proud people as the Afrikaaner Nationalists reinforced their policy of forced separation.

The Afrikaaners were a tough and independent people. In a bid to escape the control of the Cape by the British, they had undertaken the Great Trek in ox wagons, one of the most incredible epic journeys in world history. After incurring untold hardships while moving into the unknown African interior, and crossing the formidable Drakensburg Mountains, the Voortrekkers or pioneers set up new republics of the Orange Free State, Natalia, and the Transvaal.

Donald wondered if the inevitable wars and conflicts between the Voortrekkers and the native tribes of the interior could have been resolved over time to yield a synergistic partnership. Sadly, neither the times nor the circumstances had been favorable to such a philosophical utopia. In Natal in particular, the clash between the Boers and the greatest warrior nation in the whole of Africa, the Zulus, was severe, and the Zulus took a harsh beating. Of particular note was the 'Battle of Blood River', or as the Afrikaaners call it, 'Dingaans Day.' Dingan was the Zulu ruler at that time, and three thousand of his warriors were killed when they attacked 470 Voortrekkers and their servants. The Voortrekkers made a vow before the battle, that should God allow them to win, they would build a church on the spot and forever remember the day they would name, 'The Day of the Vow' or the Covenant.

As the car continued northward toward the town of Escourt, with the massive dolerite rock of the Drakensburg Mountains towering upward in the distance on their left, Donald spoke to Mandla who had been deep in his own thoughts.

"Do you know anything about American history, Mandla?" he asked.

Mandla replied, "At school we learnt about the founding of America and the Constitution and about the Civil War and so on."

Donald pressed a little further, "What about the pioneers who opened up the West of the United States and Indian wars? Do you see any parallels with what has been happening in Africa?"

Mandla could see what Donald was getting at, "Yes, it is very strange that America has forced their native populations into reservations and the same thing is happening here."

Donald added, "But time has a habit of reducing the history of subjugation of peoples into a plausible acceptance of inevitable fate. It becomes an attitude of, 'Well, that was then and this is now!' Let us hope Mandla that no such fate will prevail on your people."

Mandla suggested to Donald, "But you British have contributed your share of subjugation of many countries across the globe."

"Indeed we have, Mandla, albeit in self defense I have to say, we implemented a parliamentary system of civil rule and justice for all."

The discourse on colonialism ended abruptly as they took the turn off the main highway to the smaller road leading to the town of Colenso. The little town nestled in a bend of the Tugela River, and as they approached they could see the two large cooling towers of the power station with the steam rising into the sky and the half-built new one under construction.

On Sir George's Street they stopped to fill up with petrol so they would not need to later that night. A white man who had just finished filling his truck spoke to Donald, "Youse must be an important man to be 'aving a kaffir driver jong?"

"Not really," said Donald, "I'm just here from overseas on business to visit Glovortx, and my driver knows the way and the roads. I would probably get lost."

The man said, "You're lucky. It's bloody 'ard to find good boys these days. They are all so lazy and cheeky." Donald thought to himself, *I'm not surprised if you keep calling them boys and kaffirs. I wouldn't work for you either.*

The man continued, "Hey, man, when you talk to them at Glovortx, ask them to give us a break. We're always getting power cuts, but that bloody power station never seems to cut off power to them."

"Aren't they supposed to be putting in new generators and boilers?" asked Donald.

"Well, they are building a new cooling tower, but we haven't seen the new generators yet," said the man. He rattled on with his complaint,

"The management told the Town Council that the 'C' extension was completed and the fifteenth boiler was taken into service in April 1954 last year, but we 'aven't seen much improvement for us folks in town."

Donald suggested he or the Town Council could go and talk to the owner of Glovortx.

The man laughed, "Are you kidding? The place is crawling with army personnel. You can't get near the place, let alone talk to the owner, Meneer (Mr) Hani Coetze. I 'ope youse 'ave a special pass to get in?"

"Yes," said Donald, "they are expecting me, so I had better be on my way. Goodbye."

The man responded with, "Totseins" in Afrikaans.

The road followed the bend in the river until they were on the other side of town. Here, nearby to the power station, they crossed the river using the bridge. The road then followed the rail line north east for approximately five miles when the Glovortx property came into view. A road sign directed the visitors down a smaller side road where they were waved down by two soldiers at a guard post with a boom pole barrier across the road.

Mandla stopped the car, and a sergeant approached Donald on his side of the vehicle greeting him with, "Goeie middag meneer, wat is jou besigheid hier vandag? (Good afternoon, sir, what is your business here today?)

Donald apologized, "I'm sorry I don't speak Afrikaans, and I'm here to see Mr. Coetze."

The sergeant looked at him and remarked sarcastically, "If you're living in this country, you had better start learning Afrikaans because there are two languages here."

Donald was actually enjoying the exchange because he knew he had a trump card, but Mandla was getting worried.

"Well, sergeant," Donald said matter of factly, "I don't live in South Africa, so I have no need to learn the language and, anyway, I believe there are dozens of different languages here."

The sergeant was about to explode in indignation but attempted to remain calm, "Sir, on what authority are you coming here to try meet with Mr. Coetze?"

"On the authority of Mr. Frederik van den Bergh," said Donald and flashed "Lang Frederik's" card at the sergeant who, upon reviewing it, practically fainted.

"I'm very sorry sir, but the main gate which is further up the road about half a mile did not tell us a visitor was coming today. I did not mean to be disrespectful, sir," he almost begged Donald.

"No harm done, sergeant," said Donald magnanimously. "I'm not going to make a report, but you should tell your people up ahead they need to maintain proper communication with you so you don't get embarrassed like this."

The sergeant was practically groveling when he said, "Thank you, sir. I will be radioing them as soon as you leave sir, and thank you, again."

With that, Donald nodded to Mandla, and they took off toward the main gate. Mandla was grinning from ear to ear as he looked in the rear view mirror at the sergeant ranting and raving into his radio system.

Donald said, "Mandla, you know, he didn't even ask me my name."

They could see the main gate up ahead and an eight foot security fence stretched on either side for as far as the eye could see. It was topped with barbed wire at least two feet high tilted outward. Donald noticed the tell-tale signs of little white insulators indicating an alarm system was wired into the fence.

The car drew up to the gatehouse, and two security guards came out to inspect the visitors.

One guard carried the insignia rank of lieutenant, and it was he who addressed Donald, "Good afternoon, sir. Do you have official business here today and please identify yourself?"

"My name is Donald Harvey, and I have a meeting scheduled with Mr. Coetze at 2:30 p.m. on authority of Frederik van den Bergh in Pretoria." Again the name of Bergh made a solid impression, but the officer was still intent in carrying out his duties with due diligence, and asked Donald for his identity. Donald showed him his passport and van den Bergh's card.

The officer brought himself to attention and saluted Donald saying, "We have been expecting you, sir." He signaled to another guard at the massive entrance gates who pressed a button on a control panel to allow them to swing slowly open.

The other guard nearest to Mandla told him to drive through and continue for about one mile when he would see a large building on the right where they would be met by other personnel. The road was a typical African bush road but well maintained with proper drainage culverts to take care of heavy rains and run off. Off in the left distance, they could see some rail trucks on what must be a spur off of the main line. This spur was obviously transporting heavy machinery either in or out of this large property. There were large towers evenly spaced carrying heavy transmission lines, and these were traversing back from the property toward the direction of Colenso.

The large building came into view, which was a two story brick office, and behind it was a very large warehouse or workshop of some kind under a metal roof. A few hundred yards away beyond this cluster of buildings, Donald was able to see the rail spur ended in a siding and platform adjacent to the base of a kopje or rocky hill. He could just make out a very large opening at the base where there appeared to be much activity with people and vehicles coming in and out of the opening.

Donald was met by Miss Elize Kruger, a voluptuous blonde of around 30 years old, who introduced herself as the Personal Assistant to Meneer Coetze. She told Donald that Mandla could go around the back of the office where there was a non-white compound where one of their "boys" would show him toilets and water, if needed. She asked Donald to accompany her to Mr. Coetze's office, and he followed behind as she gracefully made her way along the corridor, with Donald trying hard not to gaze at her tight skirt and backside. He gave up try-ing.

Reaching her destination at the end of the office building, she knocked on the door marked Managing Director.

A guttural voice inside said, "Kom in," and Miss Kruger ushered Donald inside announcing his name, "Meneer Donald Harvey from Trandect Engineering in England."

Hani Coetze stood up holding out his hand, "Pleased to meet you, Mr. Harvey. I am Hani Coetze."

Donald said, "Likewise Mr. Coetze. I am pleased to make your acquantence."

He was looking hard at Coetze; his hair had receded from the front as is normal for some men, and would match the Kammler profile. It was obviously dyed a blond color, which typically can yield a slight orange hue when using the wrong shade. The key to the original color lay in the roots, which according to Donald's observation, was definitely a much darker color than blonde. Coetze's face was egg shaped, although the jaw line was quite square. The convincing factor for Donald was the man's right eyebrow and eyelid that drooped lower than the left one. His mouth tilted slightly upward on the right side, giving him an unintentional sneer. All of these observations took no more than a few seconds while Donald was performing his salutations.

Coetze gestured to Donald to take a seat, and he did so somewhat shakily as he realized he was now face to face with one of the world's most wanted men. He could hardly believe that here in front of him was the facilitator of the holocaust, the mad engineering design and construction genius of the concentration camps, the architect of the sealing and destruction of the Warsaw ghetto, and, last but not least, Hitler's protegé for the Reich's last desperate hope in charge of jet aircraft production and unknown super weapons.

Donald sat down and found himself saying almost mechanically, "I have met with both Mr. Koch and Mr. Schultz, and I am continuing my investigation as to the viability for my company to make an investment in South Africa. Although there are many factors that go toward making a firm decision, one very key area is trying to determine if we would be allowed to bid on important South African government contracts. We would like to sub-contract as an independent company similar to SMCO and Umgeni Toolworks and work with them to manufacture components that could integrate with their systems and yours, Mr. Coetze."

Coetze looked at Donald with those tight lips with one side slightly upturned giving the appearance of a smirk, but one could not tell. "Mr van den Bergh said you might have some interesting capabilities to offer, Mr. Harvey. What I suggest is, let's go to my workshops and also go to see some field testing."

Donald asked him what areas of military armaments Glovortx was involved in. Coetze said he was not at liberty to divulge the complete range of equipment, but it included specialized armored vehicles, a modified version of the British 25 pounder howitzer.

"We have increased the range of that gun by as much as fiftenn percent," he said. "We are working on some other advanced howitzer-type guns, which we hope to put on the export market to earn foreign currency. Why don't we go take a look?"

Coetze led Donald out of the back of the office building and through a windowless corridor to a solid metal door. The door must have been soundproof because as it was opened, the noise of a highly engaged engineering plant blasted at the two men as they entered.

Donald was intrigued by a vehicle that was parked just inside some double doors on his right. Coetze noticed him looking at it and motioned Donald over for a closer examination.

Coetze explained, "This is a normal four wheel drive armored small platoon carrier, but carrying a .50 Browning-type machine gun. What's unique about this is we have designed the cradle and the swivel anchoring mechanism so that if the vehicle and its occupants found themselves becoming surrounded at an ever closer range by hostile forces, the gunner can tip this weapon down around the vehicle at almost ninety degrees. This virtually eliminates (pardon the pun) an enemy fighter getting to the vehicle under the level of fire of a regular Browning machine gun."

Donald said, "Handy and effective in hostile crowd control or riots, no doubt?"

"Devastatingly effective," responded the German.

In another part of the building, Coetze showed him a different vehicle that he said was almost mine-proof. The underbody was angled and rounded so it gave the appearance of almost being a tube. With special alloys being used, the armored underbelly of the vehicle would disperse the initial blast of a mine.

"What kind of steel are you using for that protection?" asked Donald. "That's classified," replied Coetze.

Continuing the tour, Donald was impressed with much of the manufacturing processes and machinery. He noticed a door at one end of the building that had the international sign for radioactive material. On enquiring, Coetze simply dismissed that as an area where they conduct metal hardening and treatments. Donald wondered how he might use his Minox camera, but so far there had been no opportunity. To get a picture of Kammler would be an earth-shaking moment in world history. He wondered how he might palm the camera and get a surreptitious shot as they continued to tour the massive complex.

Donald caught sight of a heavy duty fork lift truck carting what appeared to be a massive pie-shaped piece of metal that looked like a section of what could only be described as a portion of a turbine. This was followed by another fork lift carrying a similar piece of equal size.

At the sight of this, Coetze nearly exploded in rage, and in Afrikaans he shouted, "Wat doen jy hier jou fokken idioot? Daardie artikels is beperk tot area nommer vier." (What are you doing in here you fucking idiot. Those sections are restricted to area number four)

The poor driver stammered, "Ek weet meneer, maar Louis het gesê wat hulle nodig het 'n paar brame verwyder en die enigste toerusting wat die metaal werk, is Joubert se spesiale freesmasjien." (I know, sir, but Louis said they needed some burrs removed and the only equipment that can work this metal is Joubert's special milling machine.)

Coetze blasted back at him, "Louis moet weet dat kan slegs gedoen word op die nag skof, dammit!" (Louis should know that can only be done on the night shift dammit!) He added, "Jy is nou hier, so kry dit na sy werk gebied." (You're here now, so get it to his work area.)

During this furious exchange, Donald had palmed his camera and held it near his leg away from any eyes. He had taken the precaution of pre-cocking the camera and setting the exposure to low light. He had managed to take two shots of what he hoped were the two pieces of machinery. The second shot was difficult because he had to re-cock the camera without being seen. To Donald it looked if three or four of those sections were joined, they would form a complete circle — the insides of which would look like a deep spiral groove toward the center and the outer edges containing numerous curved or banana shaped blades.

Coetze turned to Donald, saying let us continue and I want to show you something outside.

Donald asked what happened just now, and Coetze just dismissed it by saying, "Oh, it's not important, Mr. Harvey. One idiot employee was bringing the wrong components to the shop floor."

Donald remarked, "They were nicely machined components, Mr. Coetze. Was that for a special turbine?"

Coetze looked at Donald in a way that sent a chill down his spine, "Mr. Harvey, yes, you could say that, but I'm not at liberty to tell you what kind of turbine and it is not your position to ask. However, one day if and when we have a solid business relationship and if you are part of the South African security system, we may be able to discuss the matter further."

Donald quickly changed the subject, "No problem, Mr. Coetze, what else can we discuss?"

Coetze led Donald outside, and walking to a clearing about a hundred yards away and pointing to the ground said, "This piece of land here is where we want to build a new facility for aircraft component manufacture and jet engine assembly, maintenance, and modification. We also want to maintain and refurbish all of our aircraft electronics, instruments, and avionics. This center will be away from any airport where prying eyes can report to foreign governments and help to keep South Africa independent. This then, Mr. Harvey, with Trandect's expertise in the British aircraft industry could be the opportunity you need to justify an investment."

Donald made an observation, "If we were to operate a facility from here, would we be free to seek commercial contracts in addition to government sub-contracts with Glovortx and the others?"

"I don't see why not," stated Coetze. "Anyway, Mr. van den Bergh said you were going to visit the SAAF Commander at Louis Botha Airport in Durban, so I expect you still have some work to do in your deliberations."

They walked back to the office, and Miss Kruger approached saying, "Die spoor aflewering het aangebreek met die torium en die voorrade van berillium koper." (The rail delivery has arrived with the Thorium and the supplies of Beryllium Copper.) She presented some paperwork to Coetze, who scanned it and signed the document.

Donald thought he heard the words Thorium and Beryllium and, maybe, Copper. An African worker was sent to fetch Mandla, and after shaking hands Donald said goodbye to Hani Coetze, and they agreed to arrange a telex communication between themselves and van den Bergh.

As they passed the second gate, the sergeant there leapt to his feet and saluted vigorously. Donald said he felt he needed to wash his hands after shaking with Hans Kammler. He was still in a bit of a shock, actually coming face to face with the ex-SS General.

"So Mandla, where to now?" said Donald.

"Mr. Don, when we get to the main road, we are going to travel north for a short way and then turn off into the bush where you will visit a typical Zulu kraal, just like a tourist. We will have some beer, meat, and sadzsa, and then we will check on the night shift at Glovortx."

"Sounds good to me," said Donald.

The Death Watch Beetle

They returned to the main highway and drove north for a while before, once again, turning off to the east on a dirt road. After traveling a couple of miles, Mandla pulled off the dirt road onto a track leading to a small kraal. They were greeted by a crowd of small children and a few adults who shouted greetings at Mandla. The old man, Mdala, who Donald had seen at SMCO's plant, came out of the crowd to greet the visitors. Mandla made the introductions, and Donald shook hands all round.

The men sat in a circle, and Donald took his place next to Mandla. Some African beer was brought out, but just in case it was not to Donald's liking, some Castle Laager had been purchased. This had been pre-arranged between Mandla and Mdala.

Donald tried to taste some of the African beer and bravely swallowed some. It was a milky watery substance and had a small kick to it, but it was not something he would want in his bar at home. Still, he did finish it to show his appreciation of their hospitality, and they all laughed and clapped as his face made an involuntary grimace as the last drop went down. Some African music was playing on a radio, and a couple of men began a traditional Zulu war dance, while another couple beat a rhythmic tattoo on primitive drums. The dancers hopped around athletically and then, lifting one leg very high in the air brought it down to the ground with force. This would be done with each leg alternately, and Donald could feel the vibration through the ground as they stomped. In between the stomping, the men would beat a shield of cow leather in a rhythmic motion, using a wooden club called a knobkerrie. The hand that held the shield would also hold the Ikiwa or short stabbing spear. Donald could only imagine the effect the sight and sounds of thousands of these warriors must have had on the Afrikaaner Voortrekkers and later the British who fought these people on their homeland.

The bare breasted women brought out the cooked meat and maize meal. Mandla showed Donald how to take some meat and sadzsa together in his fingers and eat. The meat they were eating was a small duiker or antelope, and it was grainy, but deliciously tender. This was a contrast to Le Souflé in Paris, but no less memorable.

Discussion began regarding the impending covert mission to Glovortx later that evening. Mdala said the mine complex on the Glovortz property had been abandoned about fifty years ago because the coal seams started dipping below the 200 meter level. It was found when incline shafts went below that level, methane gas would enter the workings from below and create hazardous conditions. He said that Glovortx had built a huge complex of rooms or caverns at around the 100 meter level. After they began operations, local Africans refused to work underground because they felt it had tagati or magic, or it was cursed.

Donald asked Mdala, "What did your people say the rock is made of underground?"

He replied, "The coal seams are approximately one meter to three meters thick, and the rest is like the kopje over there," and he pointed to a rocky hill with large boulders.

Mdala pointed to another wizened old man in the group sitting around Donald.

"He knows the way into the underground workings. He is like the headman in this kraal and we call him Induna. He is very old and remembers much about the old days."

Mdala asked Induna about the tunnel into the Glovortx property. The old wrinkled face and small watery eyes turned to Donald and started talking in Zulu. Both Mandla and Mdala interpreted to give Donald a picture of what he was up against.

The small incline shaft was originally an ancient gold mine. It started out on about halfway up a kopje not far from the Glovortx boundary fence. There were several ancient workings, but most had collapsed in the ensuing centuries, but the one they would use tonight had been reinforced with wooden beams cut from local hardwood trees like yellowwood with some acacia. The people who had built these had come from the east. The shaft had initially been cut through gold-bearing quartzite and had continued following the vein in an incline plane. Further down into the bedrock, the ancients had managed to remove the dolerite rock as it formed in volcanic layers much like slate. It was this slate-like structure that had destroyed and probably killed ancient miners when unsupported or broken supports allowed over-head dolerite to split, fracture, and collapse. As there was no rock formation able to support itself, the pressure of the whole area above it would cause everything to fall in on any workings. This particular shaft had been been built with more experienced workers with skills in placing vertical and overhead wooden supports.

Donald then asked the critical question, "This is all very well, Mandla, but we're not trying to find King Solomon's Mines here. What I want to know is how will it bring me in to the Glovortx workings?"

Mandla turned to Induna and posed Donald's question. The old sage grinned, showing a mouthful of gums and just a solitary tooth rising from the center of the lower jaw. Mandla interpreted his response.

"Mr. Donald, the shaft ends on the roof of the main cavern underground. As it ends, our shaft turns slightly to the right, and is then enlarged into a small room. On the floor of that room you will see a large rock that appears to be half buried in the floor. By lifting that rock it will reveal the working area about five meters or sixteen feet below. It would be difficult to spot the opening from below because the whole roof would be a range of uneven rock formations.

Donald asked, "What caused the locals to fear the "tagati" as you call it and also how did the 'spyhole' in the ancient workings appear?"

Mandla asked the Induna, who responded with his explanation, "It was during the Glovortx operations and the enlarging of the old mine to make underground workshops. Some of our men got sick from moving some of the equipment or machinery. Their hair fell out, and they vomited a lot. Especially when the magic wheel is floating! Some had burns on their skin, but there had been no fire. Some were taken to King Edward VIII Hospital, Durban. The elders of our area decided to use the ancient shaft to see if they could discover anything. When they reached the end of the shaft, they realized they were directly over the workings below. They found the loose rock and the opening by accident. But soon after that, they heard the Toc Toc beetle. They knew this was a warning of death and from then on, no one would go underground for Glovortx. The company had to hire Indians in Durban and some Coloureds to do the work. Many workers wear special clothing to keep the magic away."

Donald smiled to himself; *they must be using anti-radiation suits of some kind. It's no good telling them that the Death Watch Beetle or Toc Toc is simply looking for a mate. It is ironic though; how we have come full circle from High Wycombe Parish Church to this ancient African site each, with its own problems of the Xestobium rufovillosum.*

"Mandla, what did he mean by the floating magic wheel?"

Mandla replied, "I don't know, Mr. Don, Induna said one of the burn victims said it was like a big wheel, and it had a blue light all over." Donald said, "How soon can we get in there to take a look?" He felt in his top pocket to make sure his little camera was there.

Mdala told Mandla we can get going as the light is fading fast now, and guards around the fence border at night are very few anyway.

The plan would be to get in position, make some observations, and take photographs, if possible. Donald felt it would be necessary to get back to the kraal and then make the journey back to Durban some time after midnight. He was hoping to meet the SAAF officer in Durban the next day. The time was now 6:30 p.m., and light was fading fast. Mdala had said it would take about one hour steady walking in the bush to reach the shaft entrance. Based on that assumption, Donald calculated it would take one hour for observation or less, and one hour to get back to the kraal by around 9:30 p.m.

Gathering their flashlights and water, Donald and Mandla set off following Mdala and two other Zulu natives who offered their protection. Most Africans do not venture out at night because wild animals own the night on that continent. However, it was relatively safe in this area of South Africa as it contained few wild animals except for leopards, and their main lunch menu, baboons!

They made a steady pace through the bush, although Donald was jabbed a couple of times when the low acaccia wag-'n-bietjie or wait-a-bit thorns caught his clothing or sometimes gouged his arm or leg, causing him to "wait a bit" while he freed himself from the vicious crooked barbs.

The group ahead halted and held up their arms for everyone to stop. Induna whispered for them to be quiet and listen. There was a cough, cough, up in the rocks above them, and then all hell broke loose as baboons began barking and scampering before a squeal erupted, followed by a silence that signaled a mission had ended successfully. Mandla explained to Donald quietly that the cough was a typical leopard sound and baboons have a bark similar to dogs. The leopard had simply gone out to dine on, "Baboon on the Rocks"!

"Very funny", said Donald, as he sweated from exertion and nervousness over the leopard incident.

They continued their journey until at last Mdala motioned them to stop once more. At about two hundred yards ahead, they could make out the white ceramic insulators of the Glovortx fence. There, a shadowy figure of a guard on the inside moved slowly along the perimeter. To the right was a rocky kopje rising to a height of about two hundred feet. There were boulders of varying size from footballs to several thousand tons. There were even car-size boulders balancing on top of other car size boulders. The whole landscape, for what little Donald could see in the blackness of the night, was very surreal for him.

Mdala told everyone to follow him up the kopje, and they picked their way up slowly to avoid kicking loose stones or rocks. The hillside was covered in bushes and scrub, and they also had to be careful of snakes. Most snakes would hear them coming and move off, but the dreaded puff adder was one of the most feared. It habitually lies on a path or is hidden by undergrowth and does not slither away when threatened. The people who get bitten are often the ones who tread on the reptile accidentally. The bite can be exceedingly painful, and limbs can become infected or gangrenous. If not treated quickly, the bite can be fatal.

The party had reached about halfway up the hill when Mdala stopped and beckoned to Donald. He showed Donald and Mandla a large granite boulder that was wedged up against another rock face. Behind the boulder was an opening in the rock face that was approximately ten feet high and three feet wide. Donald went up to the opening and shone his flashlight into the interior. Mandla stepped up and threw some small rocks inside.

He said, "We want to make sure a leopard is not using this for his residence. I don't see any bone fragments from meals or any other evidence."

Mdala said, "I and the others will wait while you two investigate, but please be careful, nkosi."

He said that to Donald, a Zulu word of respect.

With Donald and Mandla entered the cave, which soon narrowed down to a shaft-like tunnel of about five feet high and three half feet wide. The sides and ceiling were supported by what appeared to be yellowwood timbers in some places and acacia timber in others. The wood was badly aged and in some places was just a shell because of termite damage. In certain places along the shaft, there were no timbers as it appeared no supports had been needed due to large solid rock formations that had been sufficient. The slope began to get much steeper the further they went and became ever more uncomfortable as both men were tall and needed to bend extensively in order to make progress.

The air was becoming more oppressive the further they went. Donald was fighting off claustrophobia and only by thinking of Alicja was he able to keep going. He and Mandla were sweating profusely as they inched further and further down this ancient mine shaft. Every now and again Donald swore he could hear a creaking noise but when he stopped Mandla to listen, they could hear nothing.

At last they came to the end of the tunnel, sure enough just to the right was a small opening, and they scrambled through to find themselves in a room about ten feet square. The floor was uneven and consisted of solid dolerite rock, but the wall on one side was dolerite and above it another type of granite. In between was a thick seam or vein of quartzite. There was a trace of coal seam below the dolerite but was not obviously part of the main coal deposit of the old mine. What little Donald knew of geology told him this must have been a highly mineralized area of volcanic activity in the past. It more than likely yielded gold to the ancient miners before petering out.

They could hear a faint humming sound coming from below, so they began looking in the corner for the rock that the old man had told them to find. There were numerous rocks they tested until at last one in particular seemed to budge a little when pushed. Mandla began testing its weight. Getting a firm grip on the uneven sides, he inched it upward and Donald helped with the final lift from underneath. The rock weighed about forty pounds, and they laid it down next to the hole. Brilliant light from below flooded the little room they were in. The hole was approximately eight inches in diameter and gave a wide angle view of everything below. As a safeguard, Donald reached out and ran his hand over the black coal seam and other rock dust. He smeared this on his face to blacken it, and Mandla grinned seeing Donald with a black face.

Donald peered down into the room below. What surprised him was the thickness of the floor he was sitting on, which was, in effect, the ceiling of the room below. It could not have been more than six to seven inches thick. He could not see what support had been built for the ceiling below him, but the walls appeared to be well engineered with steel uprights and strong mesh holding back the rock face. The sight that caught his attention with startling clarity was the large wheel-like device with a dome or bell shaped housing on top. The bottom part, as far as he could tell, looked like the pie-shaped sections he had seen earlier. The circumference of the disk had what appeared to be tiny apertures or vents all the way around. The whole device was levitating and had a violet or bluish haze pulsing from it. Men in protective suits surrounded it as it began to move.

Donald quickly took the camera from his pocket and took several shots as it moved away from his line of site toward the mouth of an immense tunnel. There were two other rooms on one side of the main room below him. One of those had an open entrance, but the other was secured with two massive steel doors marked 'DANGER' and 'GEVAAR.' Donald could feel the pulsing high voltage electrical energy rising from below. He placed his head closer to the hole in the floor in order to get a wider view. Men without protective clothing had now entered the area, and it was then Donald spotted the pie-shaped pieces of metal being assembled into a large wheel shape of approximately twenty-five feet in diameter. The spiral channels were now very

285

evident, and it reminded Donald of the Schaumberger-type turbine and Repulsin B devices the Nazis had been developing.

There were three of these large devices being worked on, but he could only see two of them clearly with the third one half hidden from his view. It was the third one, frustratingly, that needed his attention, because the workers were lowering an upper section and carefully aligning it with the lower one. It had a large opening in the center, but he was unable to see the size of the opening.

Donald was concerned about the time, as he did not want to be out very late at night after visiting this secret facility. He took the measuring chain on the Minox camera and wrapped it around his wrist. He did not want to drop the camera accidentally through the hole. He was able to get one or two decent shots. The men continued working, and then a dome-shaped structure was brought from another area and fitted on the opening. There appeared to be little or no electrical systems that Donald could identify.

As he was withdrawing the Minox, he caught a glimpse of the opposite side of the room where one of the big steel doors was slowly opening. Two men in silver protective suits and head covers came out, but it was what was behind them that caused Donald to begin frantically trying to photograph the object of his attention. It was the Bell as described by Czeslaw Cieminski, only this one appeared a little bigger.

Using a specially designed lifting cradle, the men in protective suits carried a circular container from the Bell area to the partially assembled wheel device. Without being able to see exactly how they were installing the container or its contents into the interior of the device, Donald could only assume it was positioned in the center of the device.

Donald suddenly thought how all this might fit together. The Bell is a sophisticated cyclotron providing nuclear fuel that is somehow utilized by the disk shaped object for propulsion. If, by using nuclear energy, it were able to achieve extremely high revolutions in a Repulsin B type vortex, the cycloidal spiral of the inner flow channels would create immense implosion forces sufficient to create an anti-gravitational effect. Is this the flying saucer phenomenon? Was this the ultimate **Kriegsentscheidend** of the dying Nazi regime? He took more photos and then shoved the camera into his top pocket again.

Mandla tapped Donald on the arm, startling him. Mandla put his fingers to his lips and told Donald to listen. Donald strained to hear but could only detect a faint humming and the occasional voice from below. Mandla pointed to the roof of their little hiding place. There it was: toc toc toc.

Donald whispered to his Zulu friend, "That's just the beetle calling for a mate, Mandla, with all this timber, the place must be infested with it."

"No, no, Mr. Don, listen again; not the Toc Toc beetle, something else."

Donald listened, and then he heard or rather felt it — a rumble or vibration that brought dust down from the ceiling.

Mandla said, "We must go, the toc toc is telling us, baas. I must listen to my ancestors. We must leave now."

Donald said, "Okay, I think you're right. We should leave now."

He turned to make for the exit and had one last look below.

Donald stopped. Right there in the far corner of the big room below was Kammler directing his team of engineers. Donald gestured to Mandla to wait. A cracking sound was heard from further along the passage and more short vibrations.

Donald turned toward the hole and putting on his deepest voice and with a strong and heavy accent, shouted in German, **"Hans Kammler, wollen die Juden Ihre verrottenden Körper in der Hölle"** (*Hans Kammler, the Jews want your rotting body in hell*)

Donald saw Kammler spin around with fear in his eyes and face. He began screaming in Afrikaans and in German at those in the room, wanting to know who said that. He ran to one man and tore off the protective helmet who denied saying anything. Mandla grabbed Donald, pulled him away and shoved him into the passage. Supporting timbers were beginning to crumble in the tunnel as they went forward.

The Death Watch Beetle had completed its destructive progress through the mine timbers over eons of time. Nature was reclaiming its territory with Donald and Mandla scrambling to avoid the inevitable collapsing rock formations.

The small cavern that enabled them to see the Glovortx operation below was almost centrally located over that facility. This meant that as the two scrambled up the tunnel, doubled over because of the limited height, they were still located above the ceiling of the workshop. A loud, terrifying roar erupted from where they had just been, as thousands of tons of rock had broken under enormous compression through the tunnel ceiling behind them. A cloud of choking dust began billowing toward them as Donald and Mandla struggled to reach the exit. The support beams, weakened by years of beetle larvae, began bursting under the increasing pressure causing a domino effect along and above the whole structure.

The immense burden of rock falling on the ceiling of the Glovortx operation caused it to collapse, simply crushing and burying everything below in its path. The realignment of the rock formation created fissures in many directions, including further underground where deadly methane gas began permeating upward. The high voltage cables carrying the enormous loads of electricity used by Glovortx were already sparking from the collision of giant rocks. Almost immediately, a massive explosion took place, sending shockwaves in every direction of the underground facility.

The force of the shock wave blew Mandla off of his feet as he had pulled Donald along after Donald had been hit by a falling rock. Mandla managed to stand up and drag Donald under his arms toward the exit.

Donald opened his eyes and looked up at the night sky that was full of stars. He thought for a moment he was in heaven, but the pain on the side of his head told him otherwise. Mdala, Induna, and the the other two Zulus helped Mandla and Donald away from the tunnel entrance which had now filled completely with debris of broken timbers and rock.

After regaining some strength, they made their way slowly back to the kraal where water was made available and they were able to clean up. Donald didn't want to return to Durban in the clothing he had on, so he arranged with a few of the locals to buy a shirt from one, trousers from another, and Mandla did the same.

His wallet was intact, and he was able to reimburse his guests plus extra for the trouble he had caused them. It was then the awful realization hit him when he picked up his dirty and torn safari jacket to retrieve his Minox camera.

It was gone! In the scramble to get out he had not done up the button to the top pocket of the jacket. It must have fallen out in the tunnel and was now buried under tons of rocks. Donald was devastated. This would have been the proof the world needed to know, or at least for his colleagues at the CIA and MI6.

Pushing it from his mind, his thoughts came back to Alicja whose image he had seen in the collapsing tunnel. He now wanted to get home and regain his life. It was important that he and Mandla return to Durban quickly, so they could not be linked to the mine disaster he knew would be reported.

Mdala said a large red ball of fire shot up into the sky over the Glovortx property. After hearing what Mandla told them about the weakened timbers by the Toc Toc beetle, Mdala and Induna agreed that Zulu tradition had not failed them.

Donald and Mandla bade goodbye to their Zulu friends and left for Durban. Donald asked Mandla to drive faster to make up for lost time, but Mandla said the cops are always looking out for cars breaking the speed limit so he maintained a steady speed.

Arriving at the Edward Hotel at 12:48 p.m., Donald thanked Mandla for everything he had done and especially, "For saving my life."

Mandla replied, "I had to save you, because who knows, you may have saved the Zulu nation, Baas Donald. Hamba Kahle Nkosi."

"It wasn't me Mandla it was the Death Watch Beetle! Hamba Kahle futhi impolintle. (*Good-bye and Good Health*).

They shook hands, and Donald got out of the car and entered the hotel.

Epilogue

As the big ship glided almost noiselessly along the channel from the harbor, Donald could see the hordes of sightseers and fishermen on North Key waving to the Edinburgh Castle. Mike du Toit had seen him off, and Donald had waved farewell from railings on the boat deck. Diana and Clyde had been there, as well. Mike told him that Mandla was going to try and catch his attention on the North Key as he was not allowed at dockside.

Sure enough, just as the big liner increased her speed at North Point, he spotted Mandla waving a knobkerrie and a Zulu shield. Donald lifted his leg high in the air and brought it down hard, then the other leg while lifting his arms. Mandla saw him and did the same.

Other passengers looked at Donald as if he was mad, but another man said, "Is that kaffir dancing for you?"

Donald replied, "Yes, he is, and that kaffir, as you call him, is one hell of a great warrior, and I'm proud to call him my great friend."

Later as they sailed south to Cape Town and on to Southampton, he reflected on the last forty-eight hours. The Durban newspaper, the Natal Mercury, had a report of a mysterious explosion on a government-controlled property near Colenso, Natal. They believed it may have been caused by a cave-in in an underground facility. The government had made no comment, and as it was recognized as a proving ground for weapons, shelling or explosions were common. This larger than usual incident, had raised no eyebrows.

Donald had received a telephone call from Mr. van de Bergh. He had enquired if Donald had conducted his meeting with Mr. Coetze, and he had replied in the affirmative. He declared it had gone well, and he was hoping to receive more information about putting an aircraft component and refurbishment facility at the Glovortx property. He also mentioned his visit to Louis Botha Airport in Durban to confer with Lt. Colonel van de Merwe regarding a central location for instrument refurbishment and re-calibration.

This seemed to satisfy 'Lang Frederik,' although Donald felt he sounded subdued and unnaturally quiet.

After a thorough de-briefing with Mike, Donald checked out of the hotel and was now watching the fading evening light on the Indian Ocean and the twinkling lights of Durban fading in the distance. His thoughts, of course, lingered back to his lost camera and the questions of the Glovortx connections to South West Africa.

Did everything get destroyed in the underground facility? Was there radiation exposure to local people? Was there a nuclear powered antigravity device now buried at that spot. ? There were still many unanswered questions.

However, he was satisfied that Kammler's rotting body was in hell, and for that, he was happy for the Jews of the world as well as for the Polish people.

He was thinking now of his Polish fiancé, Alicja, and how he was eagerly looking forward to walking with her again on the lush green grass of Wycombe Rye, and feeding the white swans on the Dyke.

THE EN..........?

HONORING THE WWII VETERANS

This book is dedicated to the Americans and British who together with their Allies took part in the Normandy Invasion in World War II, and went on to other battles and campaigns in Europe. Without them this author may not have survived the bombing of London, and my wife might have remained under German occupation in France. Our four children and six grandchildren would not now being enjoying the fruits of liberty were it not for the great sacrifice of those brave souls.

As a small token of our thanks, this author is listing below, some surviving veterans of World War II whom he is proud to have met or interviewed. Sadly, some have passed on since our first printing.

Allan Pixton: was a 24 year old Lt Colonel 5th Engineer Special Brigade (Big Red One) Ist Infantry Division June 6th 1944 Normandy Invasion. Retired as Brigadier General. Was 94 at time of original publication.

James D. Hammet: based in Mayberry and Ramsberry UK. Flew as co-pilot of glider for 436 troop carrier over Omaha Beach Normandy June 6 1944. Pilot was E.J. O'Donnel. They picked up 4 German prisoners on the way back to the beach.

Joseph J. Turecky: was a lieutenant pilot in the 440th Troop Carrier Group. Participated in the Normandy Invasion by delivering supplies to Omaha Beach. Also participated in airborne invasions in Southern France, Holland and the Rhine Crossing towing gliders, and dropping paratroopers. Retired as a Lt. Colonel and was 91 years old at time publication

Printis Sibley: 2nd Infantry Division U.S.Army. Was a medic and a 1st responder to Normandy Invasion injured soldiers. Also involved in Battle of The Bulge, Brest, Crossing the Rhine and battles in Ger-many, Retired T5. Aged 92 at time publication.

Jeff Watkins: Was a British bomber pilot who had joined the Royal Air Force in 1940. He saw action in Africa and Europe eventually flying Lancaster and Halifax four engine bombers. He was part of the mission that sunk the German battleship Tirpitz. Jeff was awarded the Distinguished Flying Cross. He left the RAF as a Flight lieutenant and went on to make a fine career in aviation engineering. At 94 years old Jeff is enjoying retirement in San Diego California.

Robert Blatnik: U.S. Army 26th Regiment - 1st Infantry Division. Was part of Omaha Beach Red Fox day 1 Normandy Invasion. He also fought in Nigerian French Morocco, Tunisian & Sicilian Campaigns. He went on to fight in Belgium & Germany being wounded and returning to the USA to recover.

His medals include Purple Heart, Silver Star, Bronze Star with 5 Oak Leaf Clusters, Good Conduct Medal, French Citation Medal, Belgium Citation Medal, Expert Rifleman & Expert Pistol, French Fourragere, Belgian Fourragere, American Campaign Medal, American Defense Service Medal, Presidential Unit Citation, European-African-Middle Eastern Campaign Medal with one Bronze Service Star with one Silver Service Star with arrowhead, WWII Victory Medal Combat infantryman bade 1st Award and Honorable Service Lapel Button WWII Retired Sergeant Major. Was 94 at time publication.

Ralph C. Jenkins: Was a 25 year old Flight Commander flying Thunderbolt fighters in the 510th Squadron, 405th Group 9th Air Force. Became Squadron Commander and flew 129 combat missions beginning on D-Day Normandy. An airfield was established in Picauville near St Mere Eglise by demolishing an apple orchard, laying down tar paper on the grass. He was happy when Germans left Cherbourg airfield so the Thunderbolt squadrons could land on a concrete runway.

Flew combat missions into Holland, Arnhem, and Market Garden campaigns. Received Silver Star, 3 Distinguished Flying Crosses, 24 Air Medals with Oak Leaf Cluster, and Croix de Guerre Etoile de Vermeil. Retired as Lt Colonel. 97 years old at time of 2016 re-print

James L. Miller: US Army 1st Division, 16th Regiment, E Company. Normandy Invasion Omaha Beach on D-Day.

Medals include Bronze Star, Purple Heart and in 2010 was awarded the Legion of Honor by decree from French President Nicholas Sarkozy.

Charles D. Morhle: Was a 2nd Lt Thunderbolt pilot in the 510th Fighter Squadron, 405th Group, 9th Air Force. Charlie flew 97 missions beginning on D-Day over Normandy. The Thunderbolt was certified to operate from 5000' all concrete runways, but, reality of war he flew from 4500' wire mesh in the UK, Christchurch and in Picauville France from 3800' Tar Paper. Was told once he flew so low he got grass stains on his plane, but really it was a wheat field and it stained his propeller tips! Sadly, Charlie passed away a few weeks before this book became published.

He flew missions into Holland and Germany from his base air-field in St Dizier South of Paris. Awarded the Distinguished Flying Cross, Air Medal, and 16 oak Leaf Clusters, as well as the Presidential Unit Citation. He retired from Service as a Captain. He volunteers his time to the Frontiers of Flight Museum in Dallas. Go hear his stories! Charlie is now 92. Postscript; Sadly Charlie passed away just before publication. Sadly, Charlie passed away at 92 soon after this was first published.

Leon C. Sparkman: Was a 21 year old Lieutenant flying Thunderbolt fighters in the 510th Squadron, 405th Group 9th Air Force. He flew air cover over all the Normandy D-Day Beaches. Was hit 3 times but was never shot down. Like his fellow Thunderbolt comrades in the 510th Squadron he had to land and take off in a French field on Tar Paper runways until they were able to capture the airfield at St Dizier where they could utilize concrete runways. Went on to fly missions in Holland, Luxembourg & Germany. Awarded the Air Medal with 16 Clusters, a Distinguished Flying Cross, and Campaign Medals with 4 Stars. Retired as a Lt Colonel. Was aged 90 PLUS! at time of publication.

Sergio A. Moirano: Army Serial Number l # 42015454 He was involved in the Day+2 landings on Utah Beach. Originally he joined 357/F as a replacement. Then was transferred to Co G on June 23, 1944. Wounded on June 27 and sent to hospital. Returned from hospital December 26, 1944. Promoted to Private First Class January 3, 1945. Was re-hospitalized January 24, 1945. Currently living in Belgium at time of publication.

William (Bill) Singer: Navy Amphibious Assault Beach Battalion 3rd Class Electrician. Normandy Invasion-Omaha Beach. Also served at Iwo Jima, Okinawa & Osaka. Medals include IWO, Silver Star, Oak Leaf Cluster, Normandy Medal. Was 88 years old at time of first publication.

Raul Trevino: Joined Army March 23, 1942 aged 17. 45th Infantry Div, 180 Infantry Regiment, 2nd Battalion, "G" Company. Rank at D-Day Sergeant. Landed Casablanca Oct 1943. Campaigned in Anzio & Rome, Italy. Campaigned at St. Maxime, Southern France. Aug 1944. Made amphibious landing at Epinal & on to Vosges (Rambervillers sector) POW: Captured in Rambervilles-Fremifontaine Oct 1944; Trans-fered by Germans to St Die & Strassburg, Lienberg, & finally to Stalag 3C in Krustruin, Germany. Liberated by Russians ..

..in February 1945. MEDALS: Silver Star, Bronze Star, Purple Heart, POW as well as 5 additional Campaign medals including another four Bronze Stars and numerous Bronze loops.INAL RANK: Discharged Oct 1945 as Sergeant; Re-enlisted in Air Force & retired Sr Master Sergeant Sep 1965. Aged 88 at time of first publication.

Jack Bennett: 18 years old when drafted & after training was assigned to the 1st Infantry Division (The Big Red One). At age 20 he landed on Omaha Beach in the Normandy Invasion. His platoon fought their way through the fortifications, and advanced through dairy farms & apple orchards while liberating a series of small villages in NW of France as well as Belgium.They were the first to enter Germany at AAchen where he was wounded Oct. 13 1944 near there, and spent 6 months in an army hospital in England before being returned to the USA..

Jack was awarded the bronze Star, Purple Heart w/Oak cluster, Good conduct, Atlantic Theatre, North Africa-Eurp w/arrow Head and 4 battle stars, CIB, French Saint Maurice.

On Friday May 10, 2013, the Vice-Consul General of France from Houston came to Jack's house & on behalf of the French Government awarded him the Knight of the French Legion of Honor. Was 89 at time of first publication and lives with his wife of 54 years Dorothy.

Conrad L. Lohoefer: Drafted into the Army at 19 before being transferred to 8th USAAF & trained as a Gunner. Was switched to Flight Engineering before being assigned to a B17 crew in Bassingbourn AFB in England 1943. Conrad flew 35 bombing missions, including 3 over Berlin. He Received the Air Medal with 5 Oak Leaf Clusters. He ended the war as a Technical Sergeant. 89 years old at first publication but has since passed away.

Robert N. Bray: Joined the Navy after college and trained as a Navy pilot. During the war he served for 2 years on anti-submarine duty in the Atlantic while based at NAS in Bermuda. German U-boats were creating havoc on Allied convoys to Britain and Russia. Robert played his part in helping to chase & destroy enemy submarines. Robert served additional time on Kaneohe Marine base on Oahu Hawaii. He helped rescue and pick up Air Force pilots in the Pacific Ocean from their downed planes.

Richard Overton: Believed to be the oldest living American WWII veteran. Richard served in the Army and fought in the South Pacific campaigns from 1942 to 1945. He served in Hawaii, Guam, Palau and Iwo Jima among others. He has a number of medals to his name. At time of re-print of this publication Richard lives in Austin Texas and is **110 years old**!

Arlie Blood: USAAF 510th Fighter Squadron 405th Fighter Group. As a Captain he flew as C Flight Commander on the Normandy Invasion missions from England. He then flew from airfields in Normandy on missions against German targets, His Thunderbolt was hit by enemy artillery which set his plane on fire. With 500 gallons of 100 octane fuel right behind his head, he had no choice but to bail out. Soon after leaving the aircraft it blew up. The Germans captured Arlie and put him on a Germany bound prison train. He cut a hole in the end of the box car and jumped off in the night. Arlie then joined the French Resistance.

He ran into a German roadblock and was captured again. Escaped at night while guards slept. Re-joined the French Underground. He located the new French base of his old squadron and re-joined them. Arlie was sent back to an Escape & Evasion School to teach new pilots how to evade the enemy and if captured, how to escape.

Arlie received the Air Medal-Distinguished Flying Cross as well as the Campaign ribbons. He retired as Col., USAF with 23 years of service. He was still active at age 97 until he passed away in 2015 and is survived by his wife Lucille.

Arthur A. Kirscht: Was drafted out of college at age 17 and trained as an infantryman in the 100th Infantry in the 7th Army. Partic-ipated in the invasion of Southern France through the port of Mar-seilles. He fought through the France up into the Rhone area where the 7th Army met up with the 3rd Army and the Free French Army.

At Strasbourg during a battle at St Blais where they fought for the possession of Hill 578 Arthur was wounded by a German 88 that ripped through his left leg. He ended the war with a Purple Heart, Bronze Star and a Combat Badge.

Robert Lee Swofford: Was a 21 year old B24 pilot in the 445th USAAF Bomb Group and in the 700 Squadron when sent to England. He and his crew flew 30 missions beginning with the Normandy invasion bombing the bridges of Cairns. Robert received 2 DFC's & 5 Air

Medals, The Freedom of Normandy & his Unit received the Croix de Guerre. Robert retired as Captain and then flew for United Airlines. Sadly Robert passed away 2015 after our 2nd printing.

Roy A. Elsner: Entered USMC 1943 in San Diego. Made Corporal March 1944. 27th MarReg, 4th MarDiv. Attacked IWO JIMA , D Day, H Hour. Helped carry body of comrade John Basilone, CMH for burial on Day 2.

A mile from volcano & attacking main airfield when famous flag raising made on IWO JIMA. Wounded in action 11th March 1945, lost tricep, left arm. Also head wound. Awarded Purple Heart with Star, Presidential Unit Citation, Asiatic-Pacific Medal, WWII Victory Medal. Dischargd as Cpl, 23 Feb 1946 Current age 89. Often invited as a guest speaker on IWO JIMA. Sadly Roy passed away in 2015 after our 2nd printing.

Joesph W. Geary: Captain, US Army Air Corps. Navigator - B-24's 15th Air Force, 450th Bomb Group, & 21st Bomb Squadron -Manduria, Italy.

Flew over 50 missions, including Ploesti,Vienna,Munich & Budapest. Awarded Air Medal & 3 Oak Leaf Clusters, Good Conduct Medal, America Campaign Medal.

European-African-Middle Eastern Campaign Medal with one silver (in lieu of 5 bronze) Service Star for participation in Normandy, North Apennines, Southern France, Northern France & Air Combat, EAME Theater Campaigns. WWII Victory Medal, Distinguished Flying Cross, French Legion of Honor.

James Megellas: Retired United States Army officer who commanded a platoon in Company "H" of the 3rd Battalion, 504th Parachute Infantry Regiment, 82nd Airborne Division during World War II.

Wikipedia states; He is "the most-decorated officer in the history of the 82nd Airborne Division"

Born: March 11, 1917 (age 98), Fond du Lac, WI
Education: Ripon College
Rank: Lieutenant colonel
Service/branch: United States Army
Allegiance: United States of America
Books: All the Way to Berlin: A Paratrooper at War in Europe
Awards: Distinguished Service Cross, Silver Star among numerous others.

Albert E. Huntley. Author's father

Albert E. Huntley. Author's father
British Army. The Buffs Regiment. He fought in World War One in France and again in World War Two. Wounded and evacuated from Dunkirk. He retired as Sergeant Major. Was awarded several medals WWI & WWII. Acted as Fire Warden each night of the London blitz outside our house in Clapham, London

298

DON'T EVER FORGET
THE GREATEST GENERATION OF THEIR TIME!

If you are, or you have, a WWII veteran living relative today, and would like them to be honored on my web site, please email details to admin [at] deathwatchbeetle [dot] net. I will also publish their names in any re-printing of the book. Author - David E. Huntley.

CPSIA information can be obtained
at www.ICGtesting.com
Printed in the USA
FFHW020134190119
50240733-55229FF